How is the trip?
R u there yet? lmk xx mum

Not Delivered

 VOLUME
ONE

NOM

VOLUME ONE

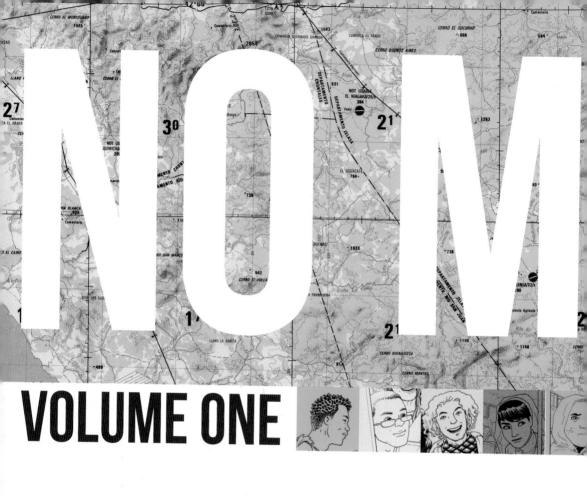

NO MERCY, VOL 1. FIrst Printing. September 2015. Published by Image Comics, Inc. Office of publication: 2001 Center Street, 6th Floor, Berkeley, CA 94704. Copyright © 2015 Alex de Campi and Carla Speed McNeil. All rights reserved. Originally published in single magazine form as NO MERCY #1-4. NO MERCY™ (including all prominent characters featured herein), its logo and all character likenesses are trademarks of Alex de Campi and Carla Speed McNeil, unless otherwise noted. Image Comics® and its logos are registered trademarks of Image Comics, Inc. No part of this publication may be reproduced or transmitted, in any form or by any means (except for short excerpts for review purposes) without the express written permission of Image Comics, Inc. All names, characters, events and locales in this publication are entirely fictional. Any resemblance to actual persons (living or dead), events or places, without satiric intent, is coincidental. PRINTED IN THE U.S.A. For information regarding the CPSIA on this printed material call: 203-595-3636 and provide reference # RICH – 644568. For international rights, contact: foreignlicensing@imagecomics.com
ISBN: 978-1-63215-442-9

IMAGE COMICS, INC.

Robert Kirkman – Chief Operating Officer
Erik Larsen – Chief Financial Officer
Todd McFarlane – President
Marc Silvestri – Chief Executive Officer
Jim Valentino – Vice-President

Eric Stephenson – Publisher
Corey Murphy – Director of Sales
Jeremy Sullivan – Director of Digital Sales
Kat Salazar – Director of PR & Marketing
Emily Miller – Director of Operations
Branwyn Bigglestone – Senior Accounts Manager
Sarah Mello – Accounts Manager
Drew Gill – Art Director
Jonathan Chan – Production Manager
Meredith Wallace – Print Manager
Randy Okamura – Marketing Production Designer
David Brothers – Branding Manager
Ally Power – Content Manager
Addison Duke – Production Artist
Vincent Kukua – Production Artist
Sasha Head – Production Artist
Tricia Ramos – Production Artist
Emilio Bautista – Sales Assistant

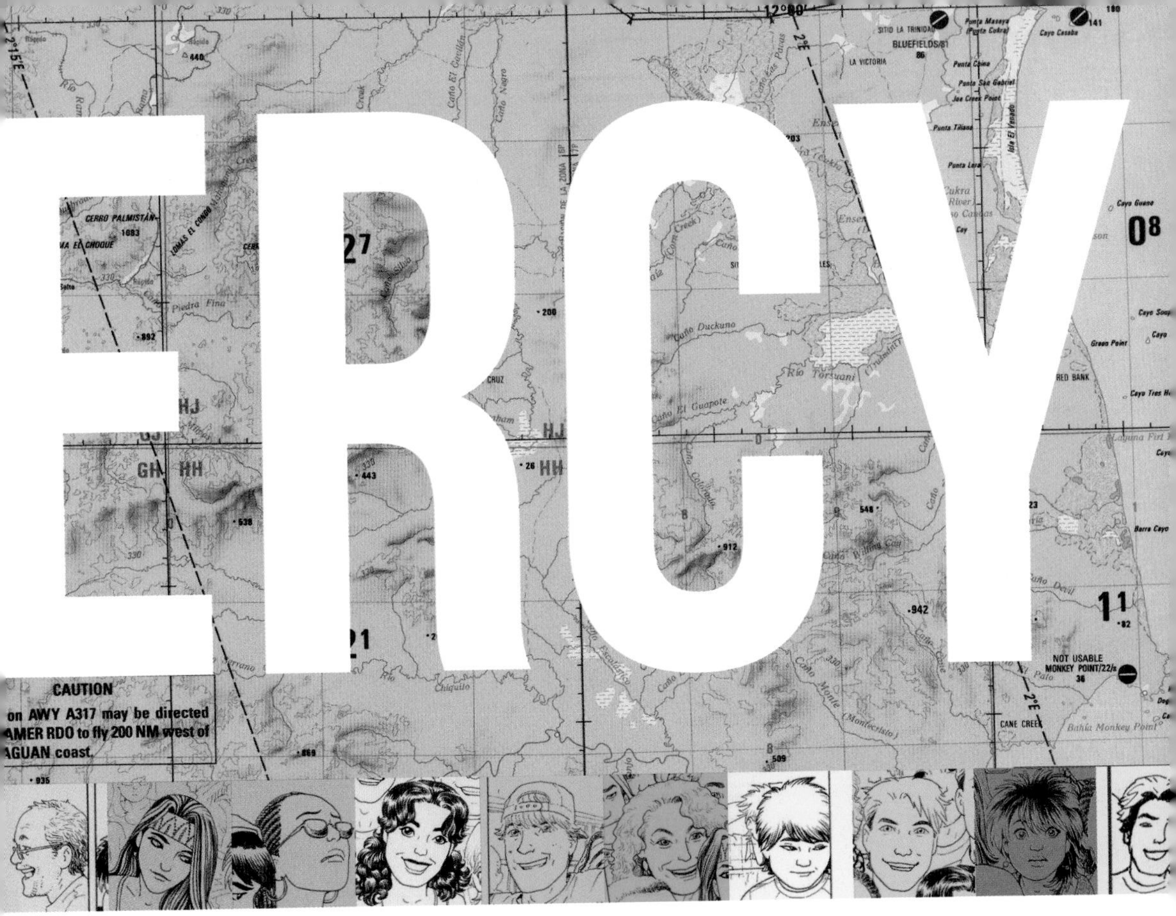
ERCY
CAUTION
on AWY A317 may be directed
AMER RDO to fly 200 NM west of
AGUAN coast.
BLUEFIELDS
LA VICTORIA
CERRO PALMISTAN
Piedra Fina
Caño Duckuno
Río Torsuani
Caño El Guapote
Chiquito
RED BANK
Green Point
NOT USABLE
MONKEY POINT/22/s
CANE CREEK
Bahía Monkey Point

ALEX DE CAMPI
CARLA SPEED MCNEIL
JENN MANLEY LEE
AND FELIPE SOBREIRO

WITH SUPPLEMENTAL DESIGN BY SASHA HEAD

CHAPTER ONE

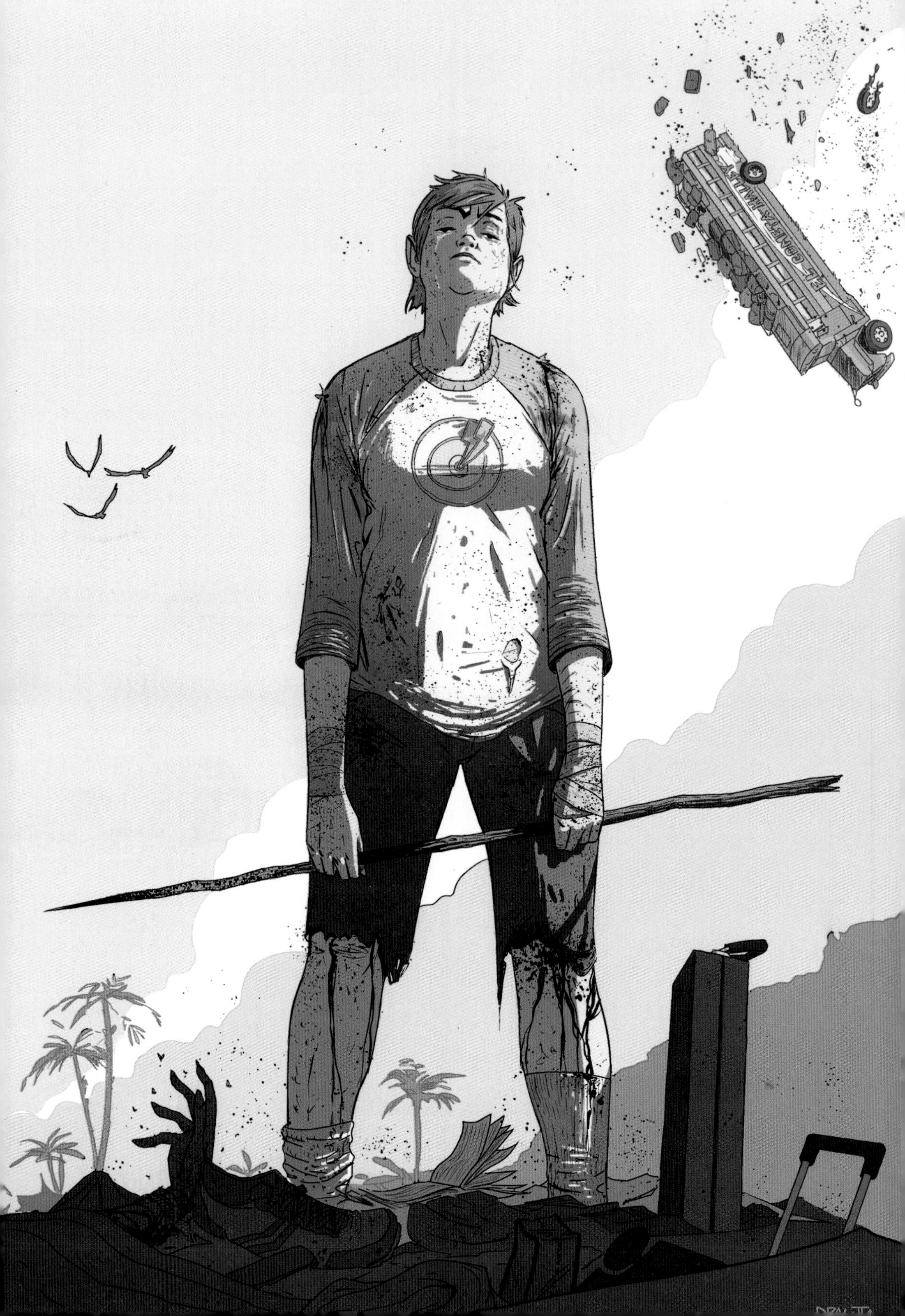

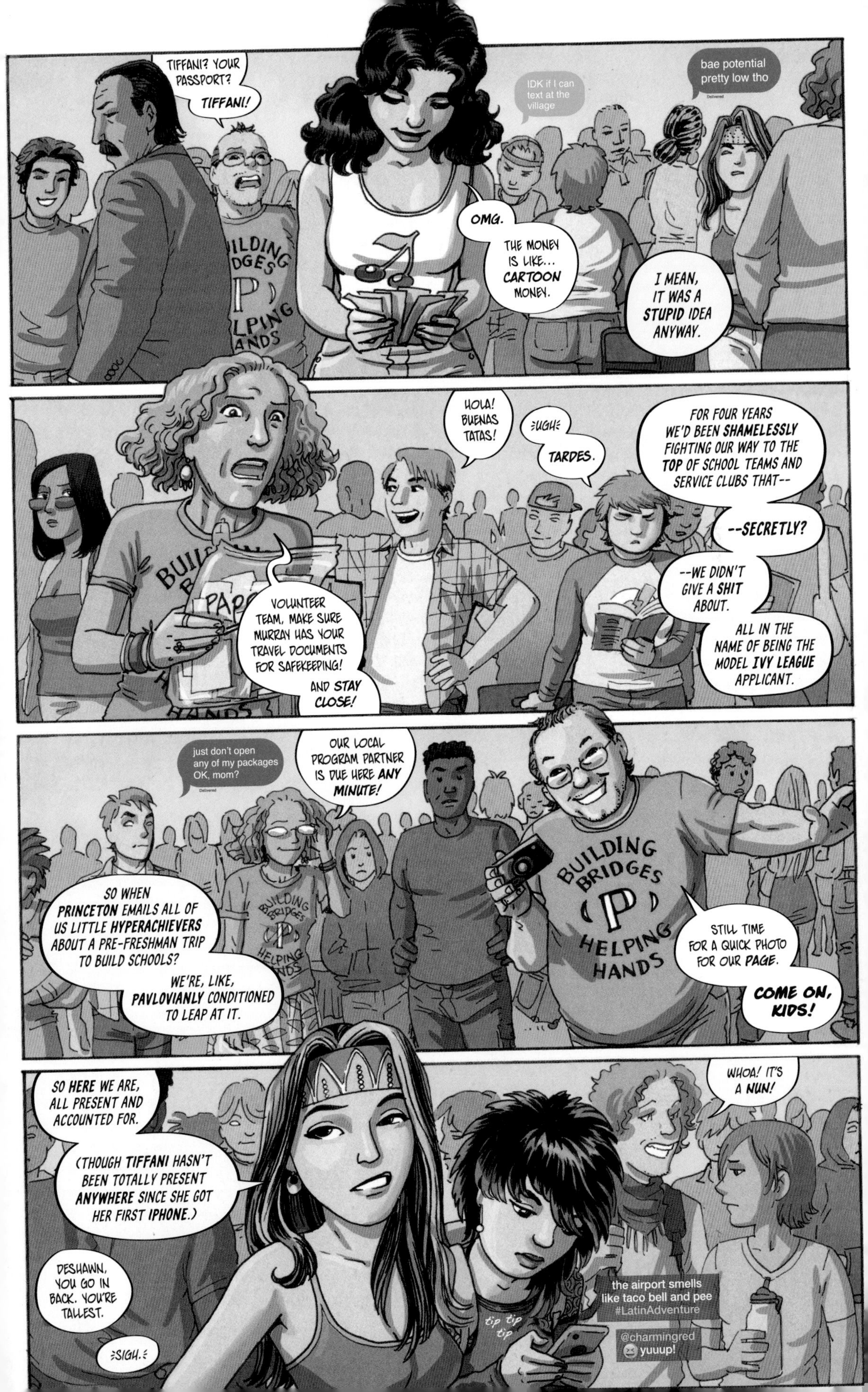

TIFFANI? YOUR PASSPORT?
TIFFANI!
IDK if I can text at the village
bae potential pretty low tho
Delivered
OMG.
THE MONEY IS LIKE... CARTOON MONEY.
I MEAN, IT WAS A STUPID IDEA ANYWAY.
HOLA! BUENAS TATAS!
UGH
TARDES.
FOR FOUR YEARS WE'D BEEN SHAMELESSLY FIGHTING OUR WAY TO THE TOP OF SCHOOL TEAMS AND SERVICE CLUBS THAT--
--SECRETLY?
--WE DIDN'T GIVE A SHIT ABOUT.
ALL IN THE NAME OF BEING THE MODEL IVY LEAGUE APPLICANT.
VOLUNTEER TEAM, MAKE SURE MURRAY HAS YOUR TRAVEL DOCUMENTS FOR SAFEKEEPING!
AND STAY CLOSE!
just don't open any of my packages OK, mom?
Delivered
OUR LOCAL PROGRAM PARTNER IS DUE HERE ANY MINUTE!
SO WHEN PRINCETON EMAILS ALL OF US LITTLE HYPERACHIEVERS ABOUT A PRE-FRESHMAN TRIP TO BUILD SCHOOLS?
WE'RE, LIKE, PAVLOVIANLY CONDITIONED TO LEAP AT IT.
BUILDING BRIDGES P HELPING HANDS
STILL TIME FOR A QUICK PHOTO FOR OUR PAGE.
COME ON, KIDS!
SO HERE WE ARE, ALL PRESENT AND ACCOUNTED FOR.
(THOUGH TIFFANI HASN'T BEEN TOTALLY PRESENT ANYWHERE SINCE SHE GOT HER FIRST IPHONE.)
WHOA! IT'S A NUN!
DESHAWN, YOU GO IN BACK. YOU'RE TALLEST.
SIGH.
tip tip tip
the airport smells like taco bell and pee #LatinAdventure
@charmingred yuuup!

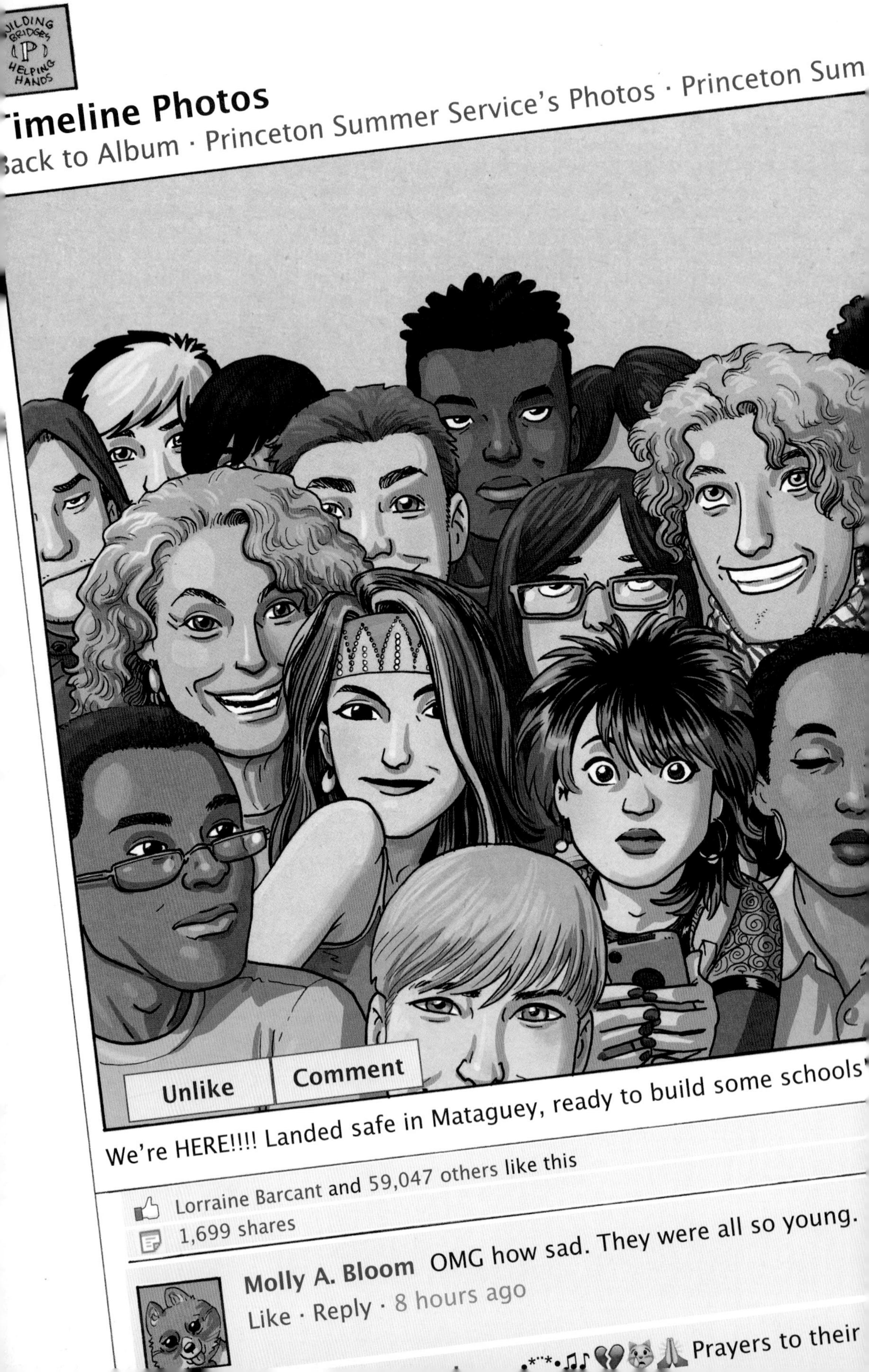
ILDING BRIDGES P HELPING HANDS
imeline Photos
ack to Album · Princeton Summer Service's Photos · Princeton Sum
Unlike
Comment
We're HERE!!!! Landed safe in Mataguey, ready to build some schools
Lorraine Barcant and 59,047 others like this
1,699 shares
Molly A. Bloom OMG how sad. They were all so young.
Like · Reply · 8 hours ago
Prayers to their

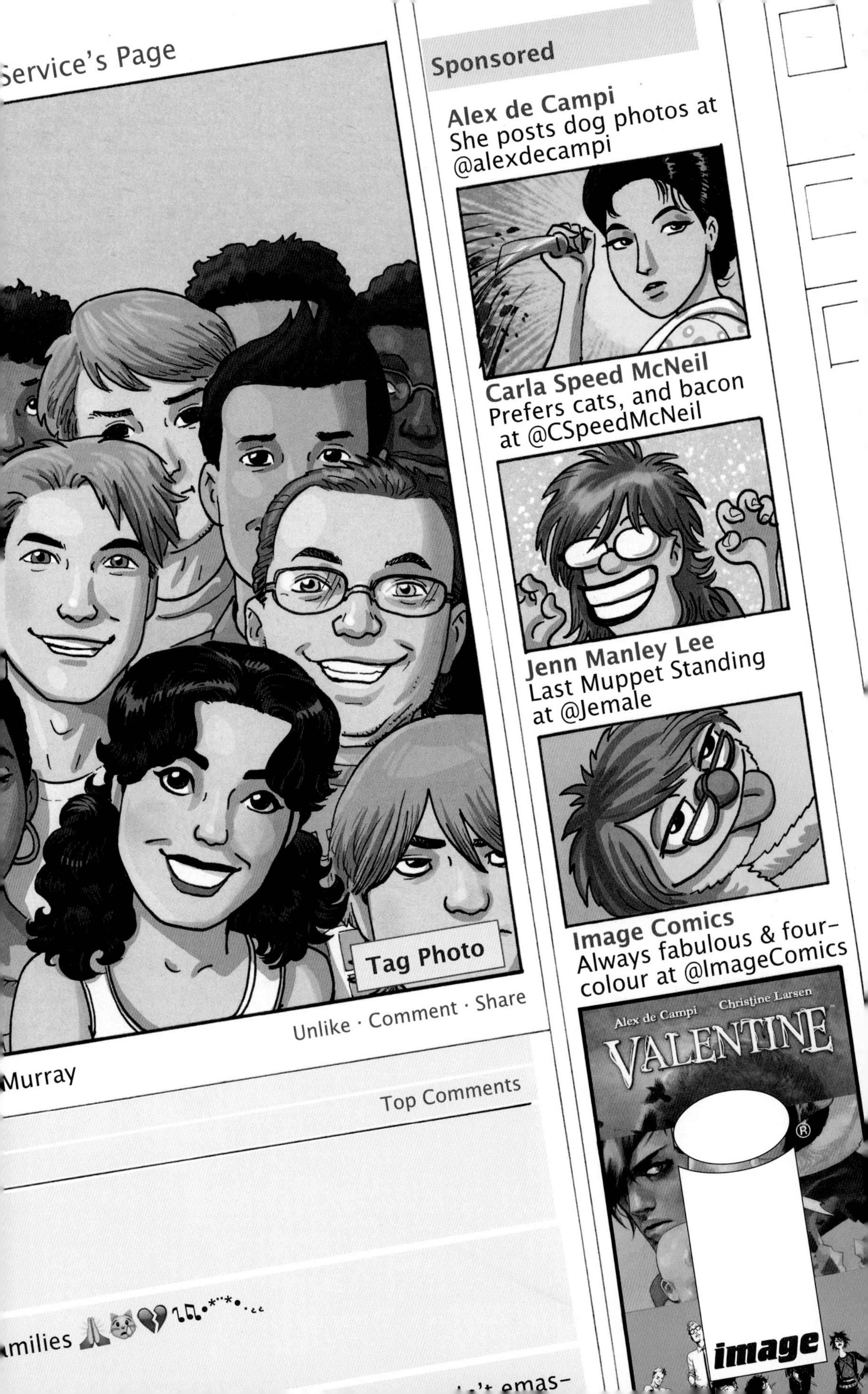
Service’s Page
Sponsored
Alex de Campi
She posts dog photos at @alexdecampi
Carla Speed McNeil
Prefers cats, and bacon at @CSpeedMcNeil
Jenn Manley Lee
Last Muppet Standing at @Jemale
Image Comics
Always fabulous & four-colour at @ImageComics
Alex de Campi
Christine Larsen
VALENTINE
image
Tag Photo
Unlike · Comment · Share
Murray
Top Comments
milies
emas-

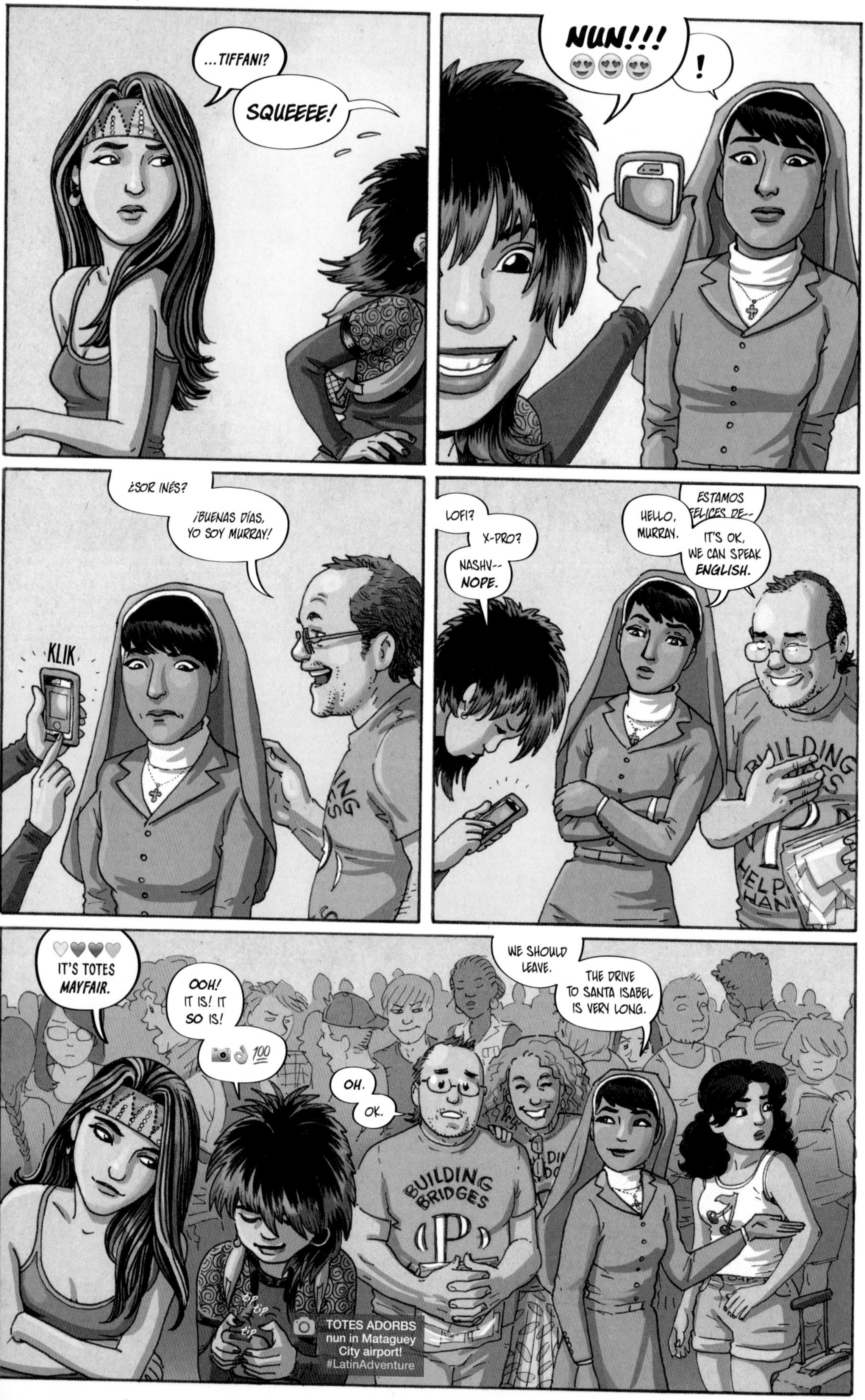

...TIFFANI?
SQUEEEE!
NUN!!! 😍😍😍
!
¿SOR INÉS?
¡BUENAS DÍAS, YO SOY MURRAY!
KLIK
LOFI?
X-PRO?
NASHV-- NOPE.
HELLO, MURRAY.
ESTAMOS FELICES DE--
IT'S OK, WE CAN SPEAK ENGLISH.
🤍🖤🖤🤍 IT'S TOTES MAYFAIR.
OOH! IT IS! IT SO IS!
📷👌💯
OH.
OK.
WE SHOULD LEAVE.
THE DRIVE TO SANTA ISABEL IS VERY LONG.
BUILDING BRIDGES
tip tip tip
TOTES ADORBS nun in Mataguey City airport! #LatinAdventure

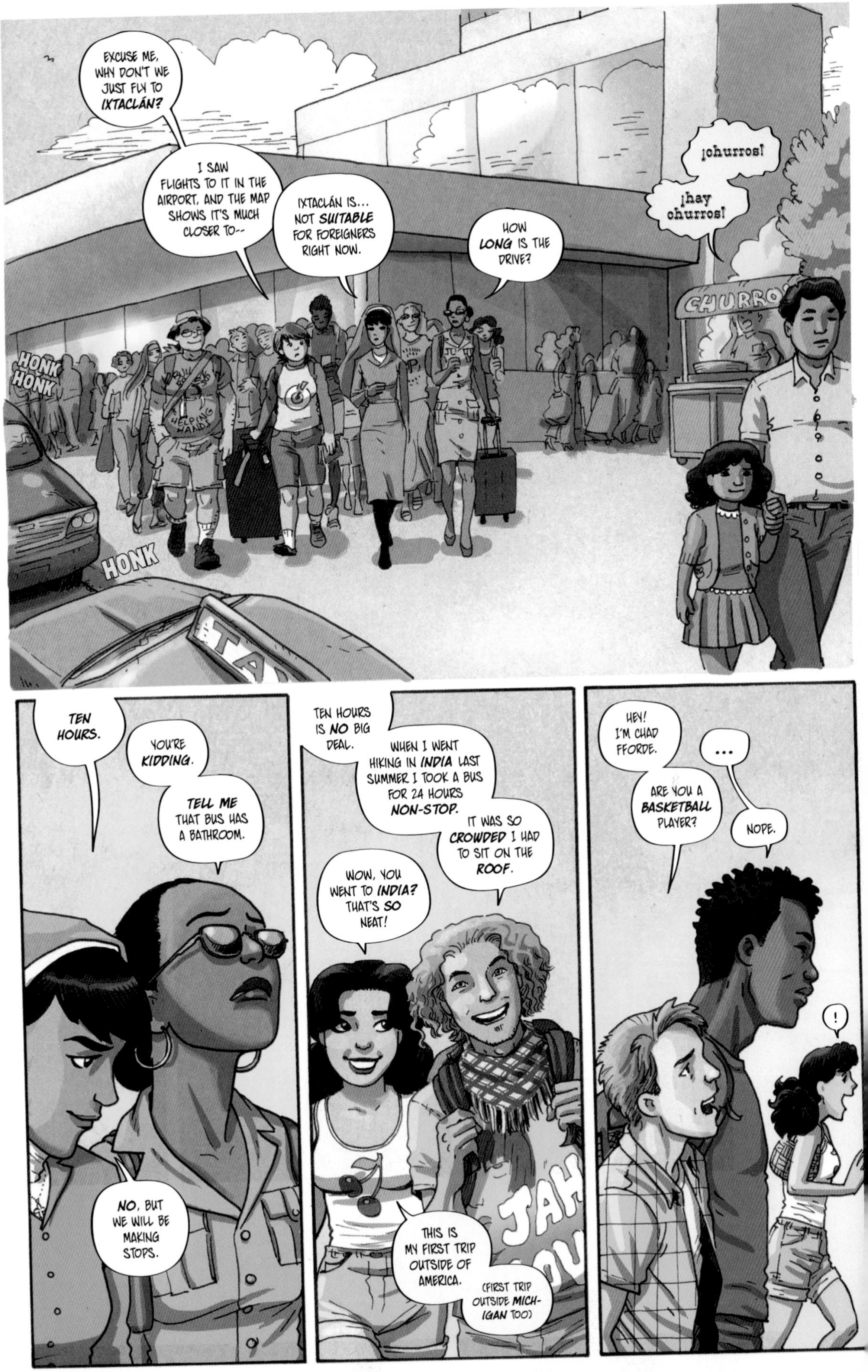
EXCUSE ME, WHY DON'T WE JUST FLY TO **IXTACLÁN?**
I SAW FLIGHTS TO IT IN THE AIRPORT, AND THE MAP SHOWS IT'S MUCH CLOSER TO--
IXTACLÁN IS... NOT **SUITABLE** FOR FOREIGNERS RIGHT NOW.
HOW **LONG** IS THE DRIVE?
¡churros!
¡hay churros!
CHURROS
HONK HONK
HONK
TAXI
TEN HOURS.
YOU'RE **KIDDING**.
TELL ME THAT BUS HAS A BATHROOM.
NO, BUT WE WILL BE MAKING STOPS.
TEN HOURS IS **NO** BIG DEAL.
WHEN I WENT HIKING IN **INDIA** LAST SUMMER I TOOK A BUS FOR 24 HOURS **NON-STOP.**
IT WAS SO **CROWDED** I HAD TO SIT ON THE **ROOF**.
WOW, YOU WENT TO **INDIA?** THAT'S **SO** NEAT!
THIS IS MY FIRST TRIP OUTSIDE OF AMERICA.
(FIRST TRIP OUTSIDE **MICH-IGAN** TOO)
HEY! I'M CHAD FFORDE.
ARE YOU A **BASKETBALL** PLAYER?
...
NOPE.
!

OH, FOOTBALL, RIGHT? YOU'RE OUR NEXT STAR LINEBACKER, RIGHT?

HELLO BUS!

YAY!

...DON'T PLAY SPORTS.

#smdh

MISS, *NO!*

GINA--!

ESTE AUTO-BÚS NO ES PARA USTEDES.

YOU GO BACK WITH OTHER TURISTAS.

OOPSIE!

I AM *SOOOO* SORRY!

DE NADA.

HAHA, GINA, YOU ARE SOOO *FIRST WORLD!*

WELCOME TO THE BEST AND THE BRIGHTEST.

OUR BUS IS OVER *THERE.*

the drinking age here is like 15 for real!!!

Ǝpptнpt/ᴇ

I'D *LIKE* TO SAY THIS IS THE *DUMBEST* THING THEY'VE EVER DONE?

BUT *LOOK AT THEM.*

Silencio

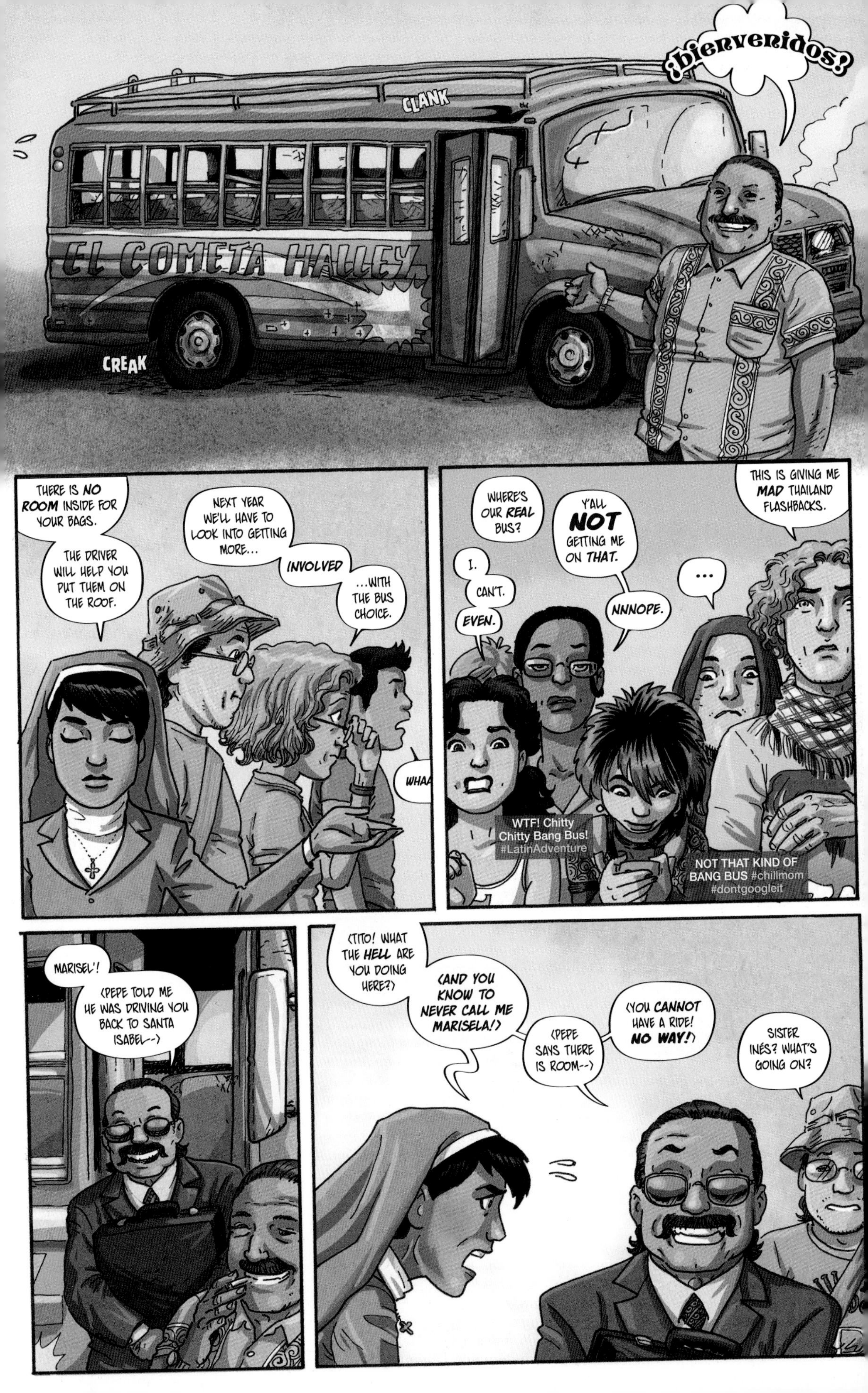
¡bienvenidos!
CLANK
EL COMETA HALLEY
CREAK
THERE IS NO ROOM INSIDE FOR YOUR BAGS.
THE DRIVER WILL HELP YOU PUT THEM ON THE ROOF.
NEXT YEAR WE'LL HAVE TO LOOK INTO GETTING MORE...
INVOLVED
...WITH THE BUS CHOICE.
WHAA
WHERE'S OUR REAL BUS?
Y'ALL NOT GETTING ME ON THAT.
NNNOPE.
I.
CAN'T.
EVEN.
...
THIS IS GIVING ME MAD THAILAND FLASHBACKS.
WTF! Chitty Chitty Bang Bus! #LatinAdventure
NOT THAT KIND OF BANG BUS #chillmom #dontgoogleit
MARISEL'!
<PEPE TOLD ME HE WAS DRIVING YOU BACK TO SANTA ISABEL-->
<TITO! WHAT THE HELL ARE YOU DOING HERE?>
<AND YOU KNOW TO NEVER CALL ME MARISELA!>
<PEPE SAYS THERE IS ROOM-->
<YOU CANNOT HAVE A RIDE! NO WAY!>
SISTER INÉS? WHAT'S GOING ON?

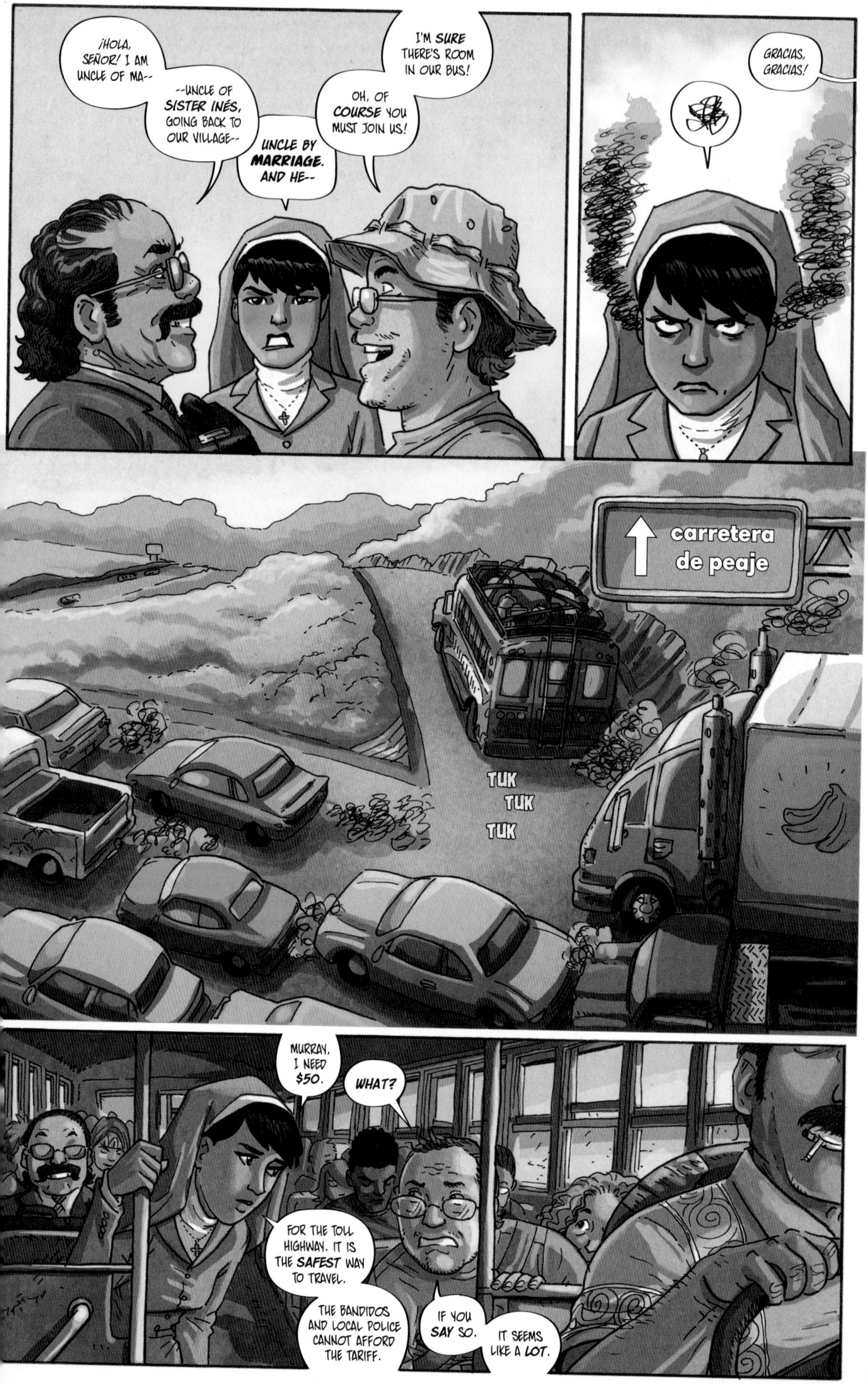
¡HOLA, SEÑOR! I AM UNCLE OF MA--
--UNCLE OF SISTER INÉS, GOING BACK TO OUR VILLAGE--
UNCLE BY MARRIAGE. AND HE--
OH, OF COURSE YOU MUST JOIN US!
I'M SURE THERE'S ROOM IN OUR BUS!
GRACIAS, GRACIAS!
carretera de peaje
TUK
TUK
TUK
MURRAY, I NEED $50.
WHAT?
FOR THE TOLL HIGHWAY. IT IS THE SAFEST WAY TO TRAVEL.
THE BANDIDOS AND LOCAL POLICE CANNOT AFFORD THE TARIFF.
IF YOU SAY SO.
IT SEEMS LIKE A LOT.

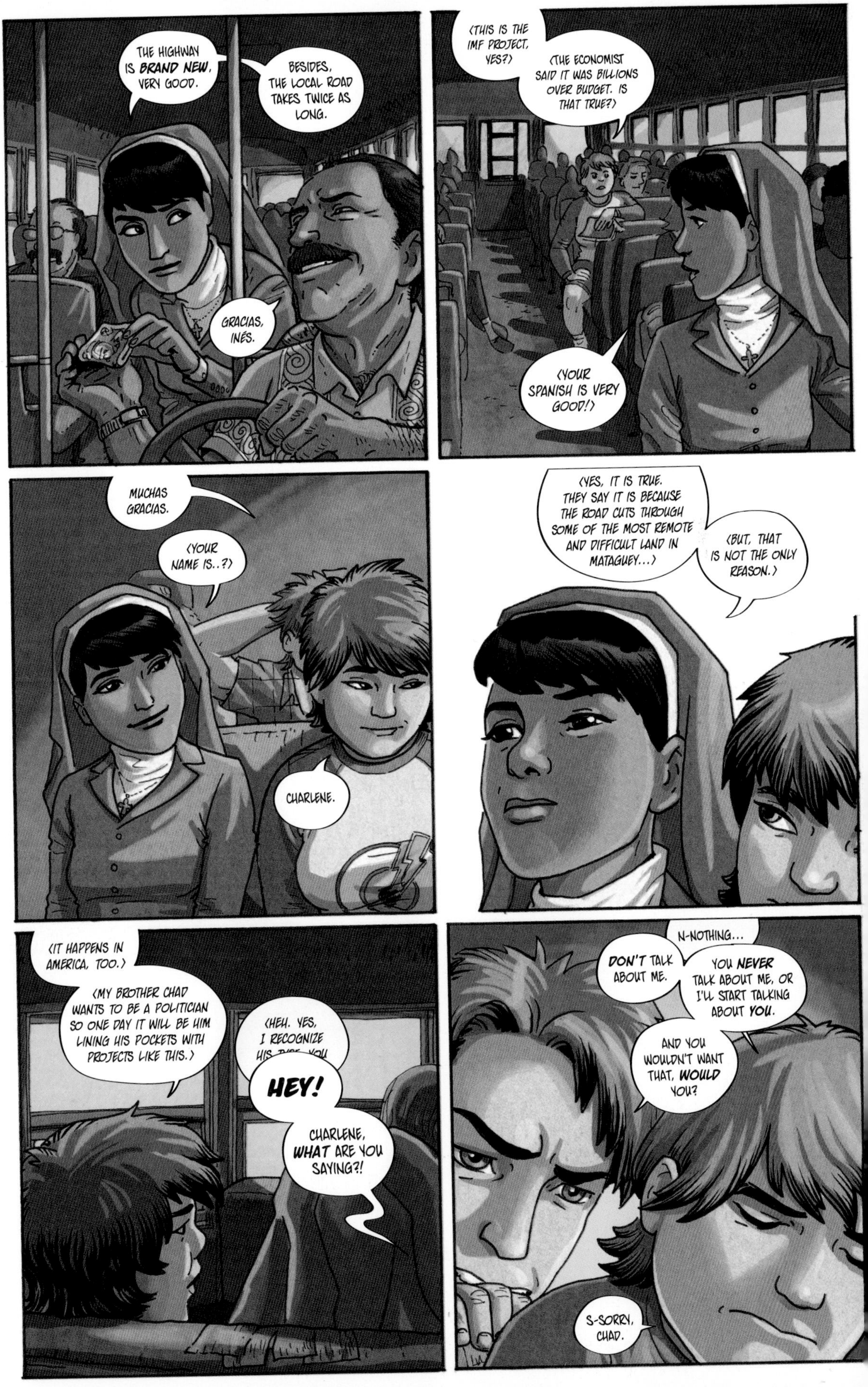

THE HIGHWAY IS **BRAND NEW**, VERY GOOD.
BESIDES, THE LOCAL ROAD TAKES TWICE AS LONG.
GRACIAS, INÉS.
‹THIS IS THE IMF PROJECT, YES?›
‹THE ECONOMIST SAID IT WAS BILLIONS OVER BUDGET. IS THAT TRUE?›
‹YOUR SPANISH IS VERY GOOD!›
MUCHAS GRACIAS.
‹YOUR NAME IS..?›
CHARLENE.
‹YES, IT IS TRUE. THEY SAY IT IS BECAUSE THE ROAD CUTS THROUGH SOME OF THE MOST REMOTE AND DIFFICULT LAND IN MATAGUEY...›
‹BUT, THAT IS NOT THE ONLY REASON.›
‹IT HAPPENS IN AMERICA, TOO.›
‹MY BROTHER CHAD WANTS TO BE A POLITICIAN SO ONE DAY IT WILL BE HIM LINING HIS POCKETS WITH PROJECTS LIKE THIS.›
‹HEH. YES, I RECOGNIZE
HEY!
CHARLENE, **WHAT** ARE YOU SAYING?!
N-NOTHING...
DON'T TALK ABOUT ME.
YOU **NEVER** TALK ABOUT ME, OR I'LL START TALKING ABOUT **YOU**.
AND YOU WOULDN'T WANT THAT, **WOULD** YOU?
S-SORRY, CHAD.

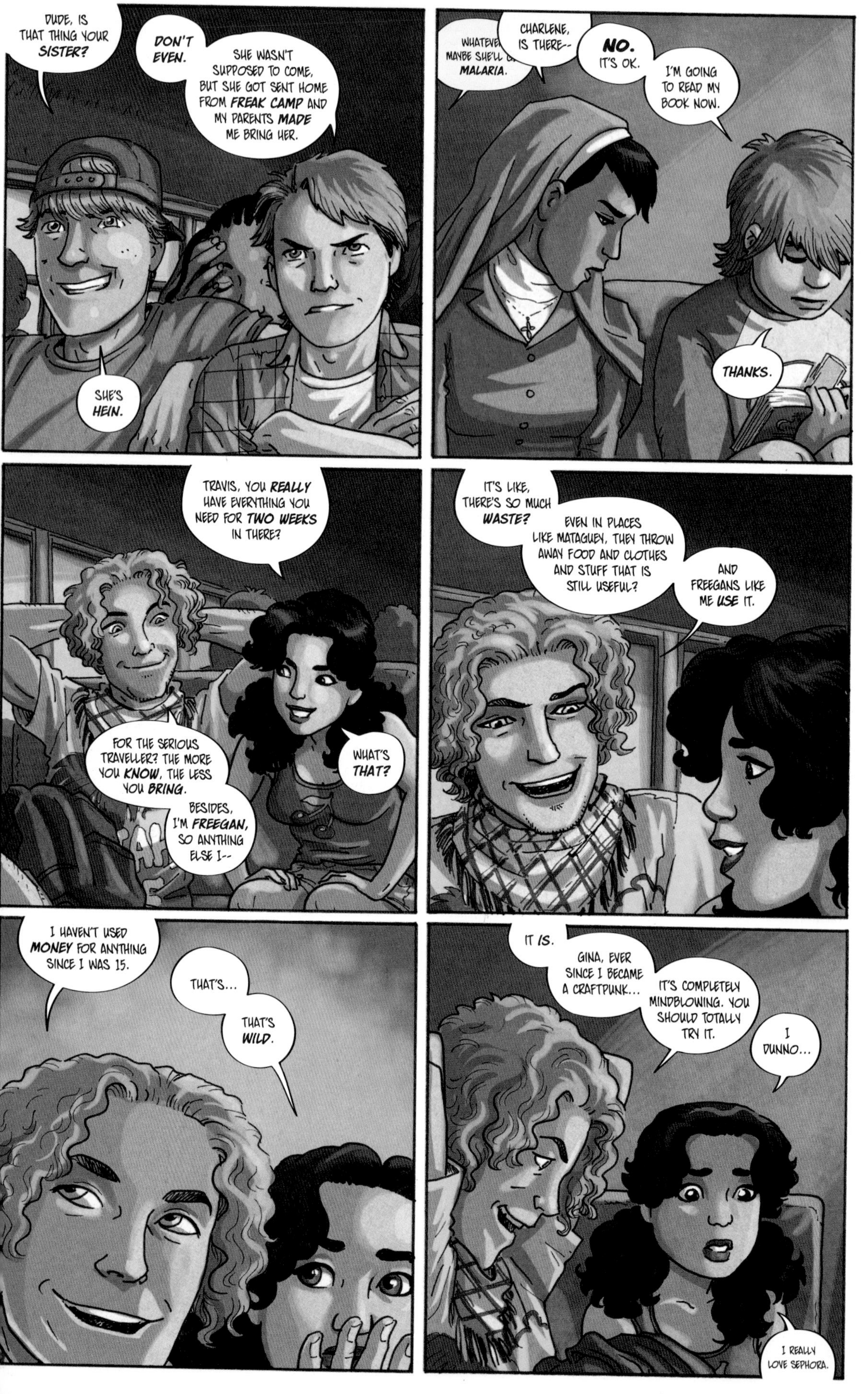
DUDE, IS THAT THING YOUR SISTER?
DON'T EVEN.
SHE WASN'T SUPPOSED TO COME, BUT SHE GOT SENT HOME FROM FREAK CAMP AND MY PARENTS MADE ME BRING HER.
SHE'S HEIN.
WHATEVE
MAYBE SHE'LL C
MALARIA.
CHARLENE, IS THERE--
NO. IT'S OK.
I'M GOING TO READ MY BOOK NOW.
THANKS.
TRAVIS, YOU REALLY HAVE EVERYTHING YOU NEED FOR TWO WEEKS IN THERE?
FOR THE SERIOUS TRAVELLER? THE MORE YOU KNOW, THE LESS YOU BRING.
BESIDES, I'M FREEGAN, SO ANYTHING ELSE I--
WHAT'S THAT?
IT'S LIKE, THERE'S SO MUCH WASTE?
EVEN IN PLACES LIKE MATAGUEY, THEY THROW AWAY FOOD AND CLOTHES AND STUFF THAT IS STILL USEFUL?
AND FREEGANS LIKE ME USE IT.
I HAVEN'T USED MONEY FOR ANYTHING SINCE I WAS 15.
THAT'S...
THAT'S WILD.
IT IS.
GINA, EVER SINCE I BECAME A CRAFTPUNK...
IT'S COMPLETELY MINDBLOWING. YOU SHOULD TOTALLY TRY IT.
I DUNNO...
I REALLY LOVE SEPHORA.

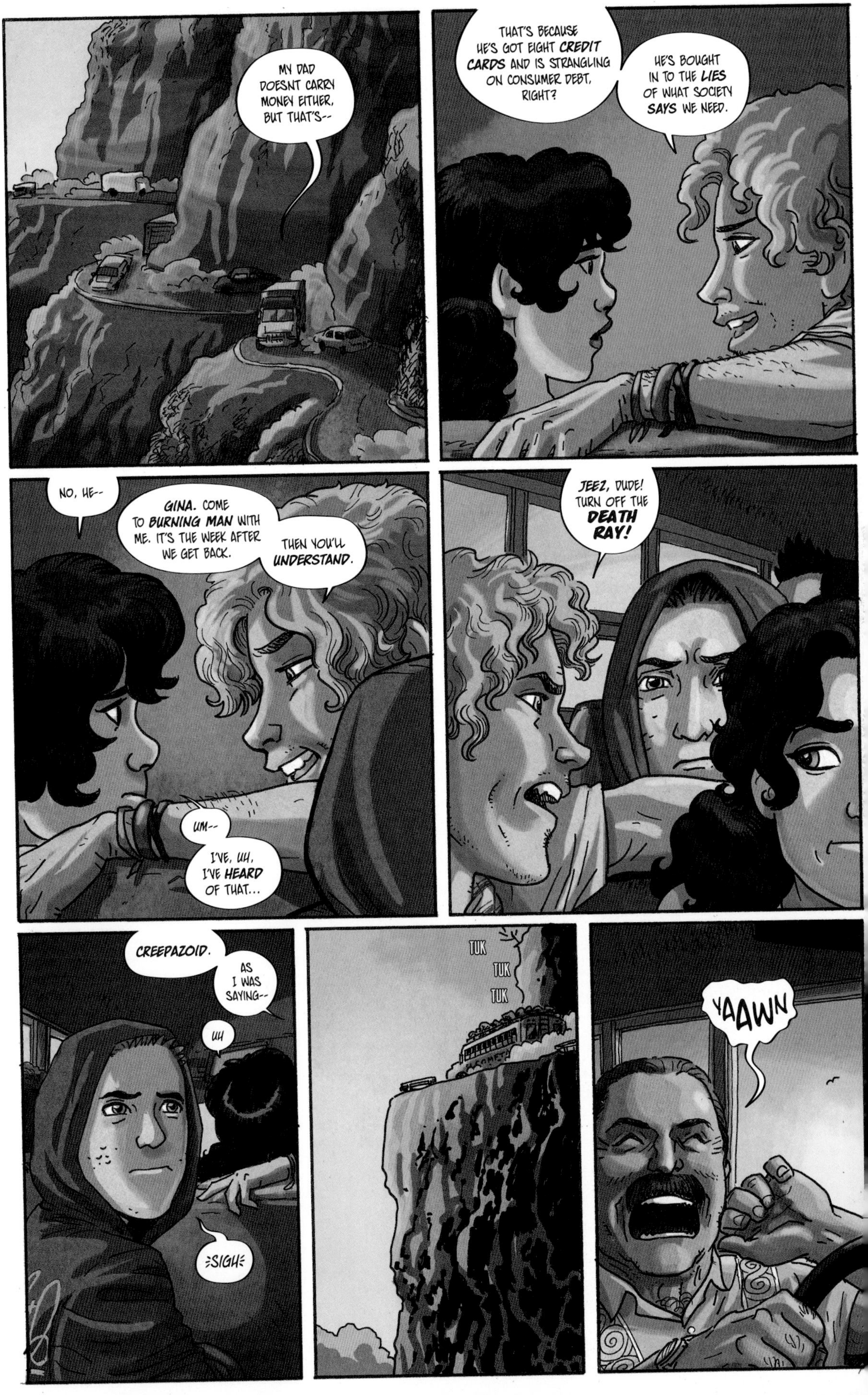
MY DAD DOESNT CARRY MONEY EITHER, BUT THAT'S--
THAT'S BECAUSE HE'S GOT EIGHT CREDIT CARDS AND IS STRANGLING ON CONSUMER DEBT, RIGHT?
HE'S BOUGHT IN TO THE LIES OF WHAT SOCIETY SAYS WE NEED.
NO, HE--
GINA. COME TO BURNING MAN WITH ME. IT'S THE WEEK AFTER WE GET BACK.
THEN YOU'LL UNDERSTAND.
UM--
I'VE, UH, I'VE HEARD OF THAT...
JEEZ, DUDE! TURN OFF THE DEATH RAY!
CREEPAZOID.
AS I WAS SAYING--
UH
SIGH
TUK
TUK
TUK
YAAWN

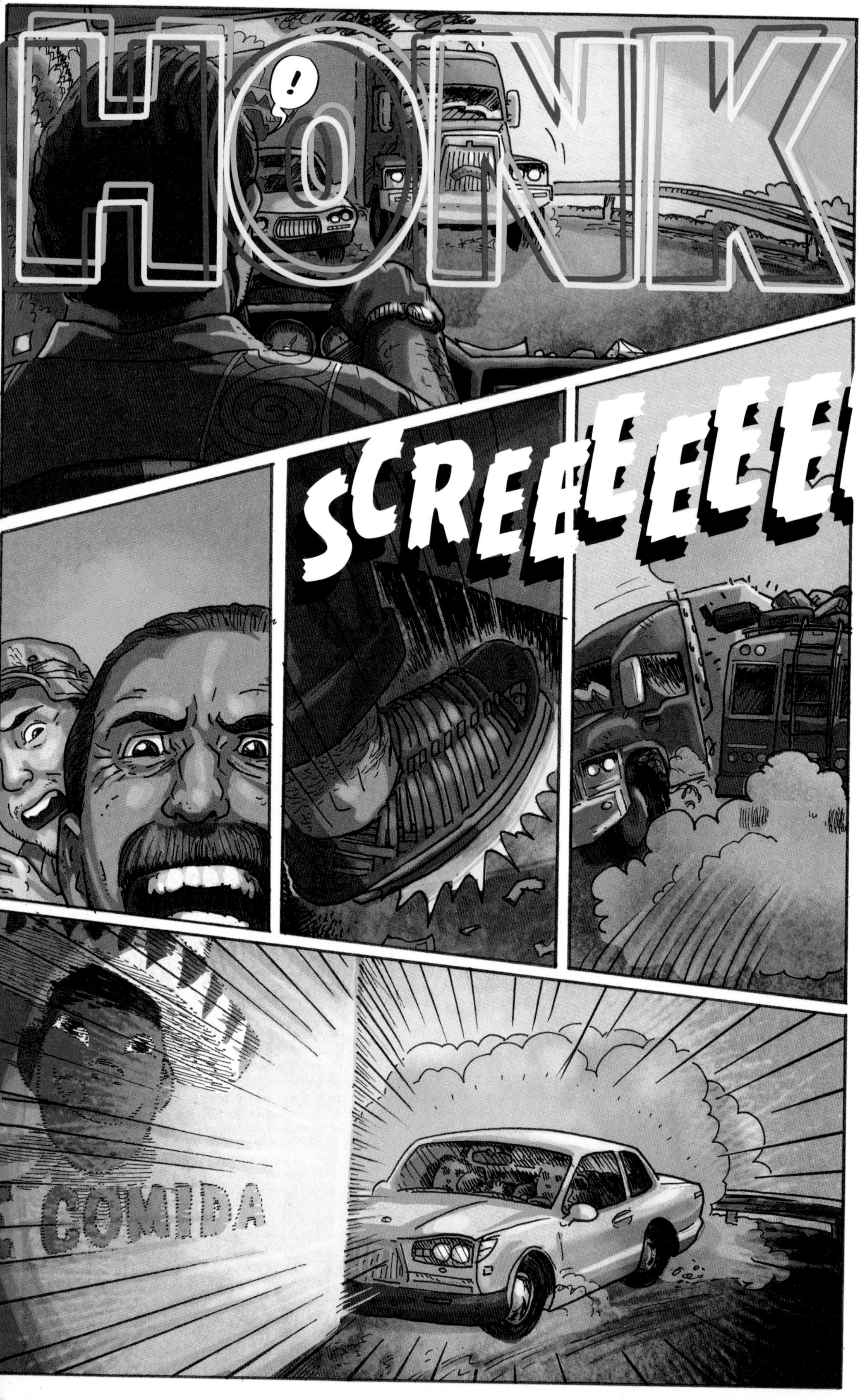
HONK
!
SCREEEEEEE
COMIDA

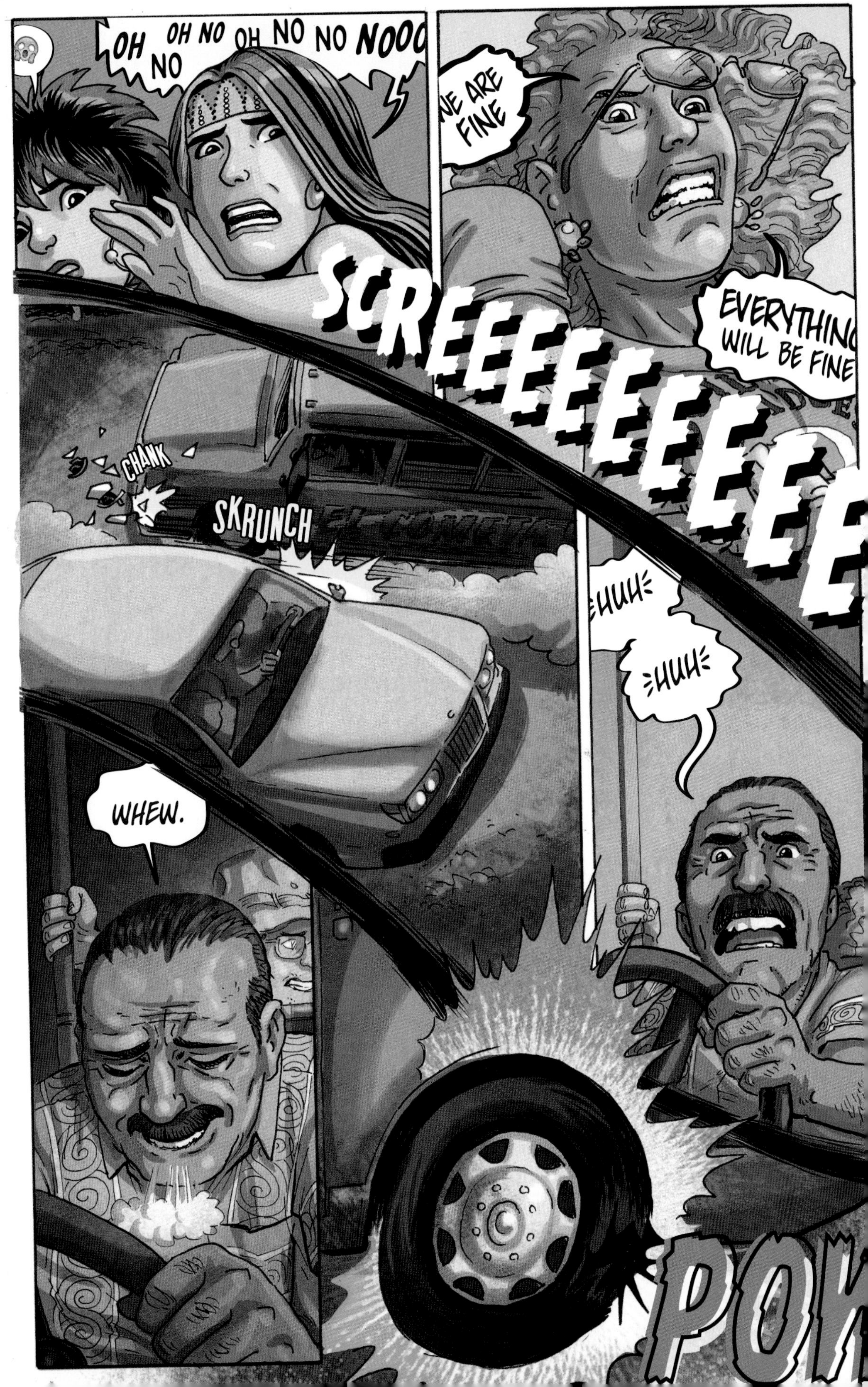
OH NO OH NO OH NO NO NO NOOO
WE ARE FINE
SCREEEEEEEEEEEE
EVERYTHING WILL BE FINE
CHANK
SKRUNCH
HUH
HUH
WHEW.
POK

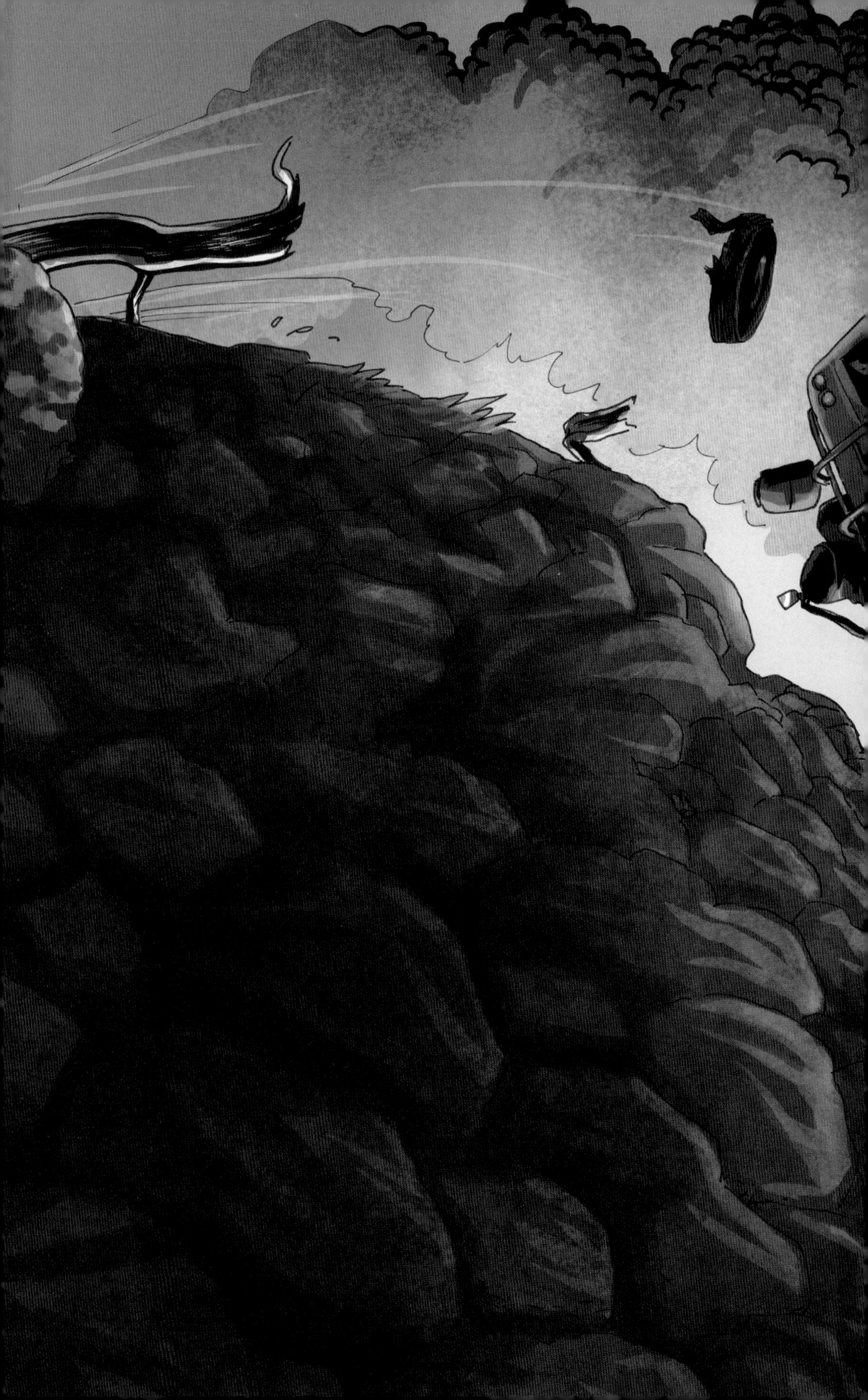

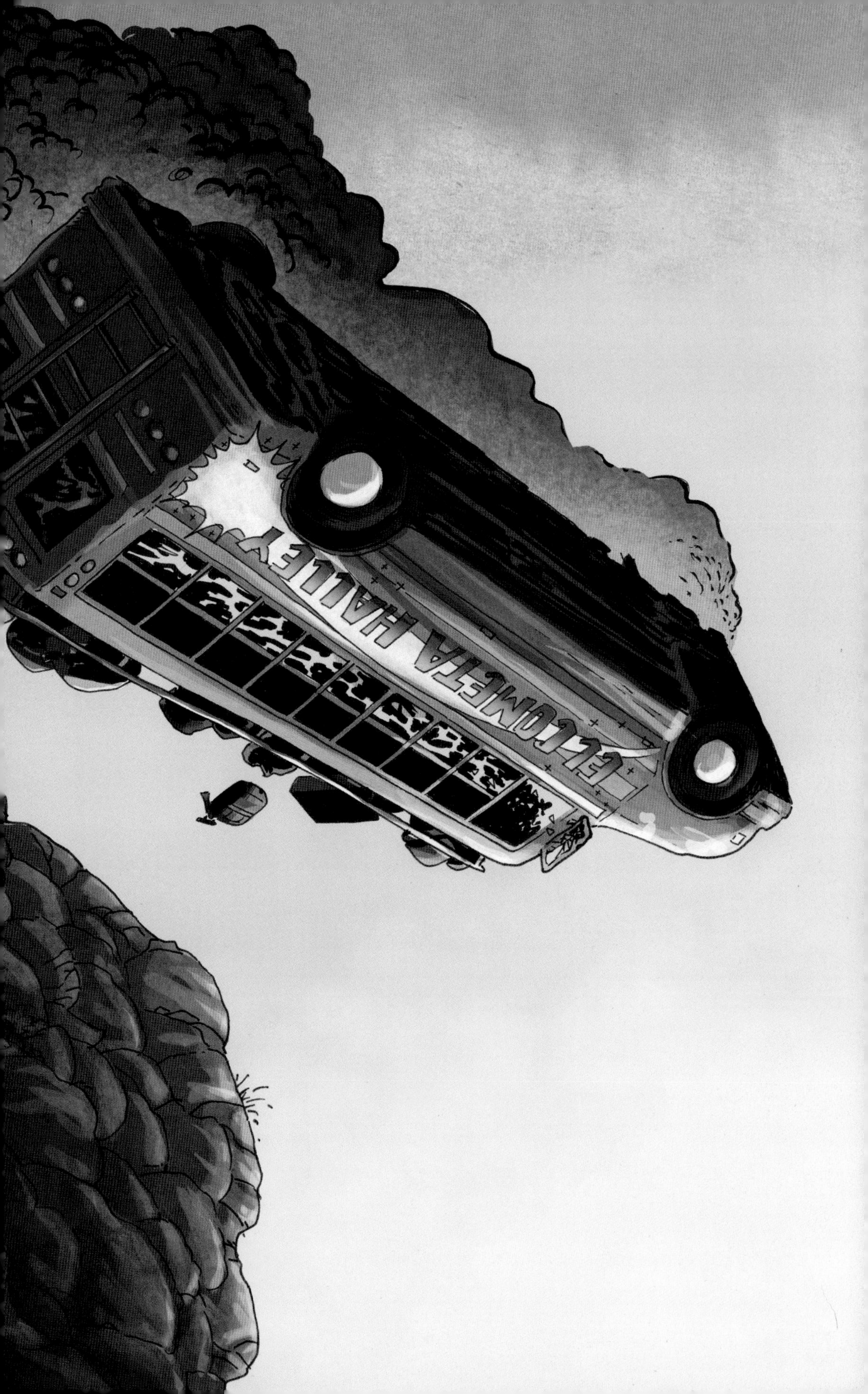
EL COMETA HALLEY

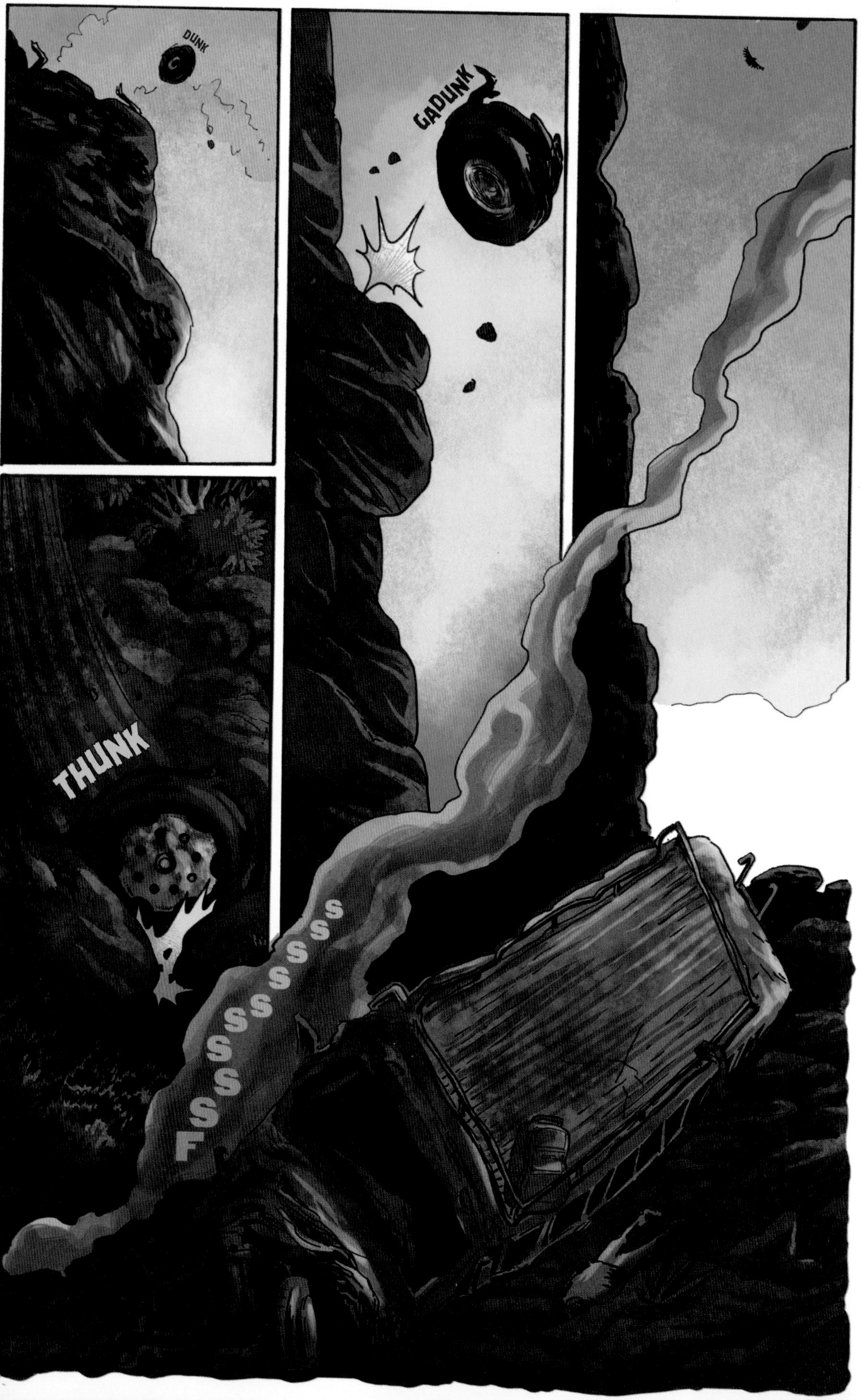
DUNK
GADUNK
THUNK
FSSSSSSSSS

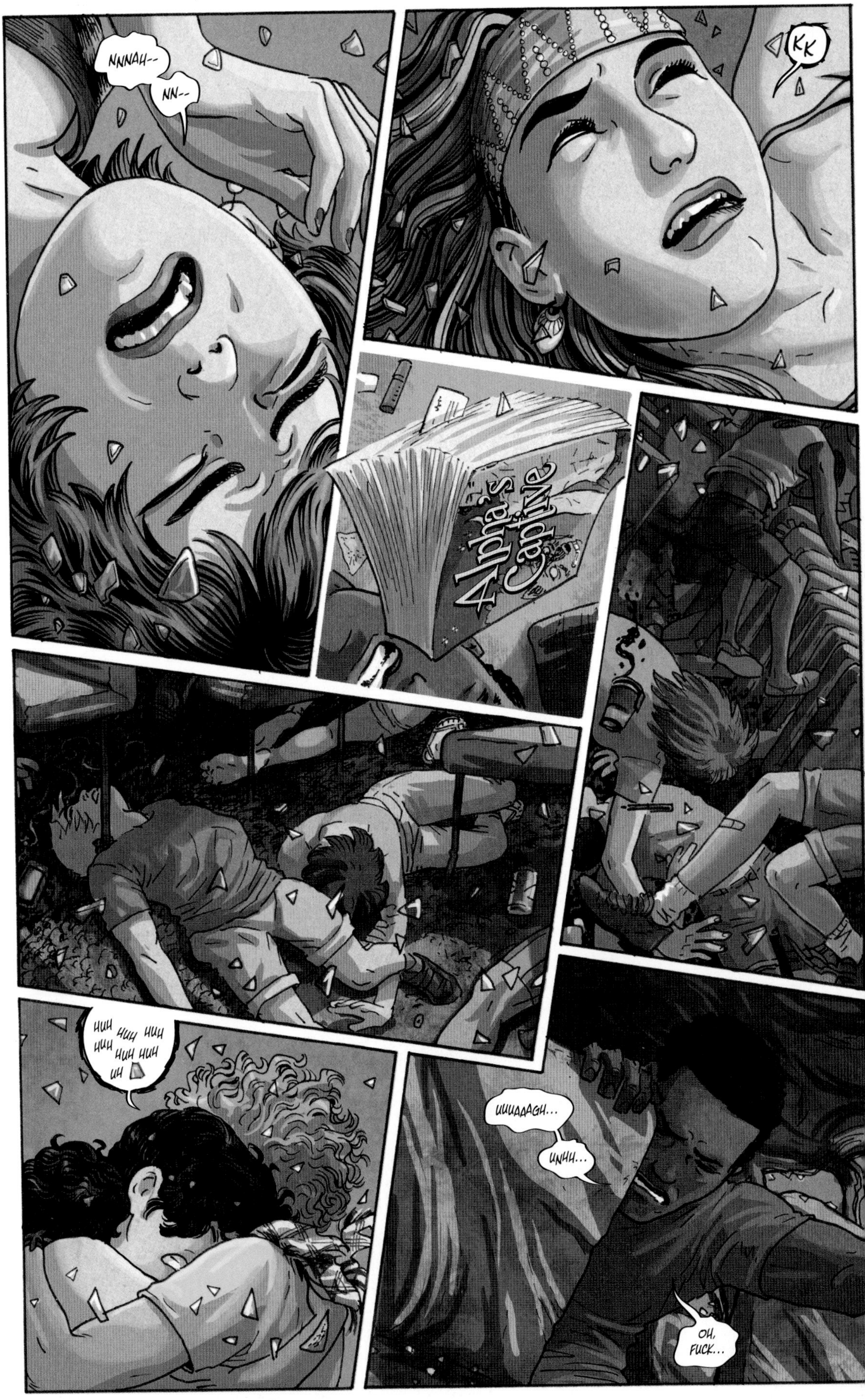
NNNAH--
NN--
KK
Alpha's Captive
HUH HUH HUH HUH HUH HUH UH
UUUAAAGH...
UNHH...
OH, FUCK...

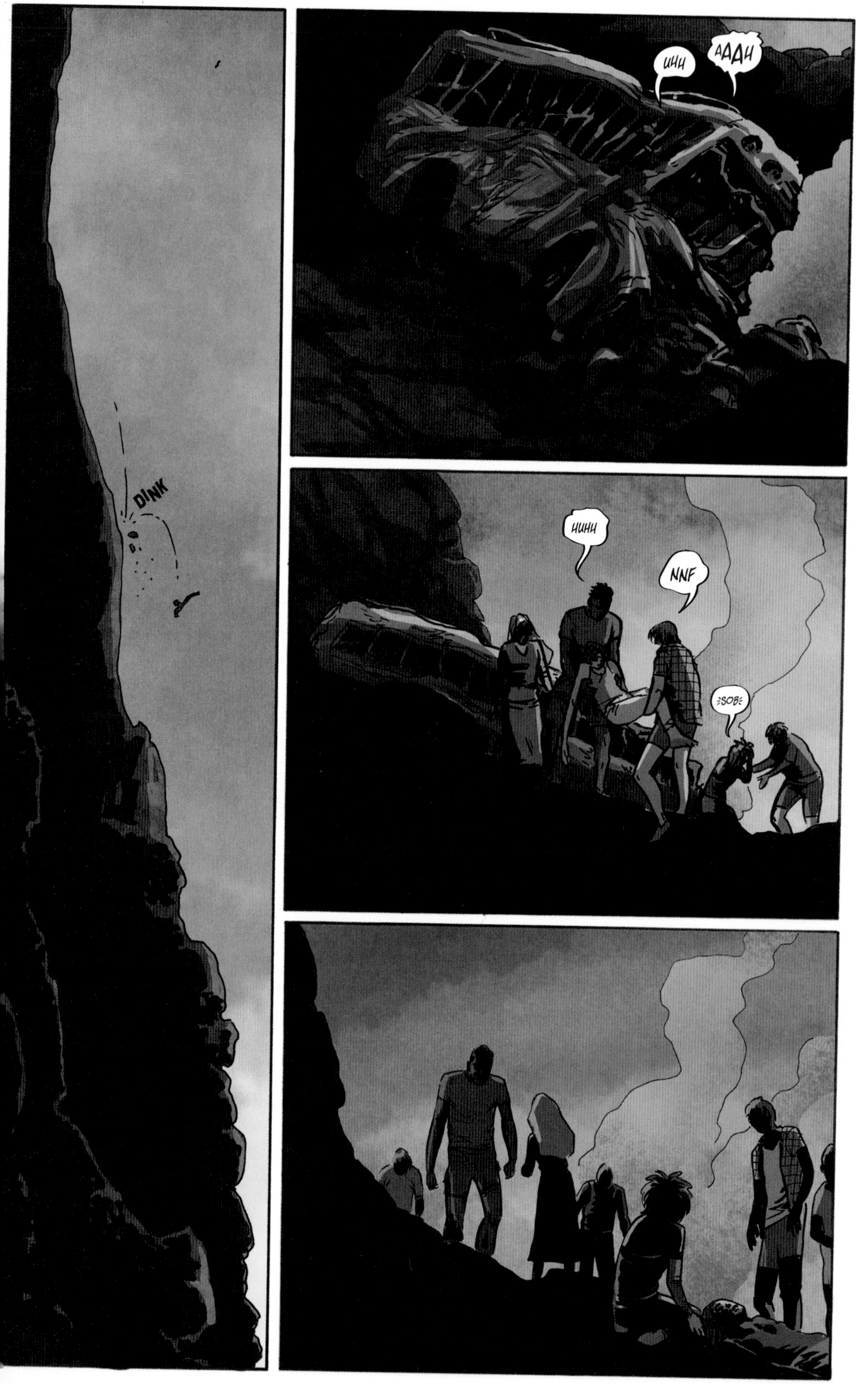

DINK
UHH
AAAH
UHHH
NNF
SOB

THIS IS --

THIS IS -- **NOT** GOOD TERRITORY.

WE HAVE, WE HAVE TO LEAVE HERE **AT ONCE.**

≡HURK≡

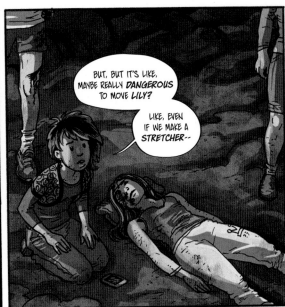

BUT, BUT IT'S LIKE, MAYBE REALLY **DANGEROUS** TO MOVE **LILY?**

LIKE, EVEN IF WE MAKE A **STRETCHER--**

WE CAN NOT STAY. PLEASE, TRUST ME WHEN I SAY THIS.

UM, DOES... DOES ANYBODY MAYBE HAVE A **FLASHLIGHT?**

YIRP
YIRP

WHA--

WHAT THE **HECK** IS THAT?!

YIRPOOOOOO

COYOTES.

THEY SMELL THE **BLOOD.**

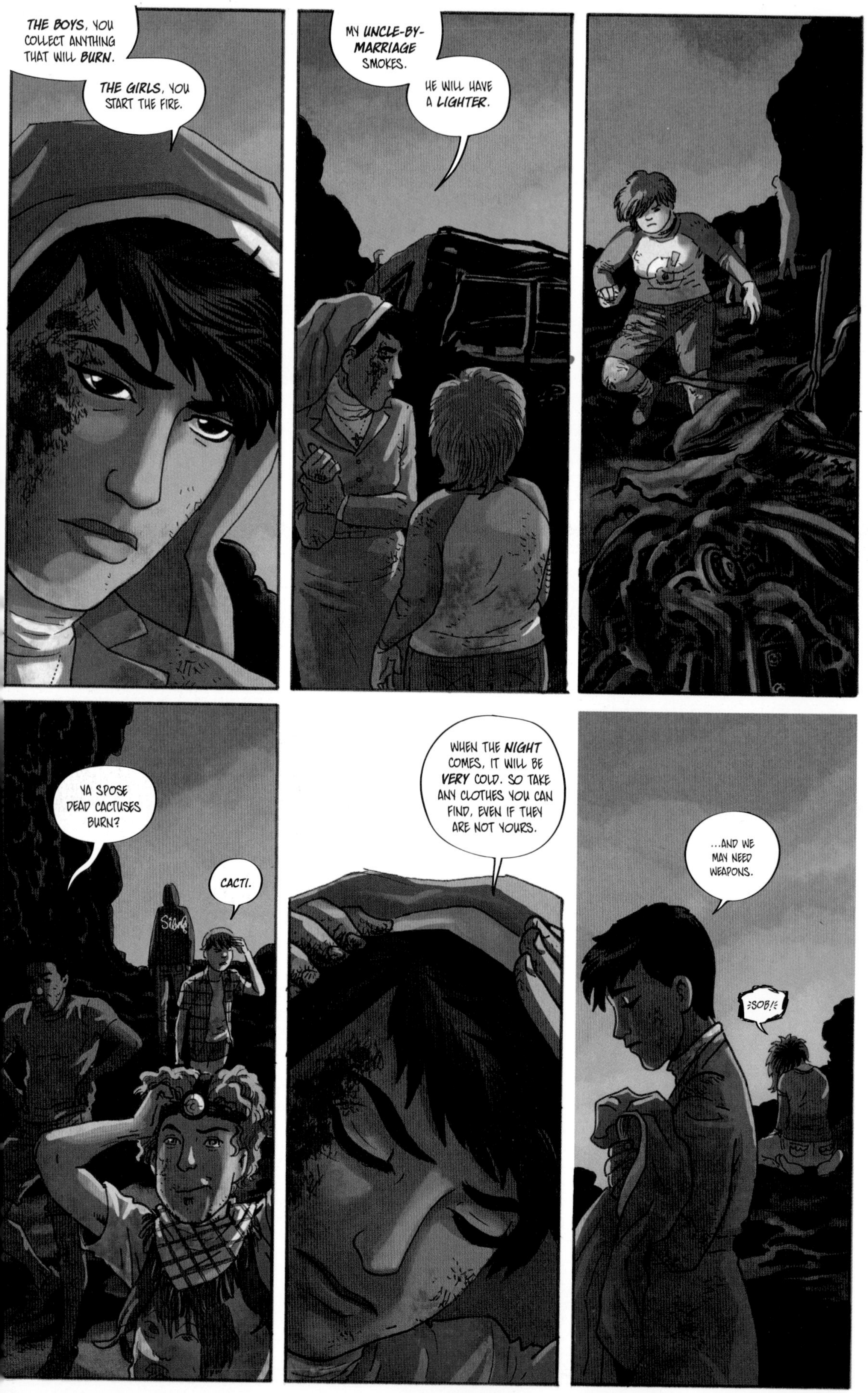
THE BOYS, YOU COLLECT ANYTHING THAT WILL BURN.
THE GIRLS, YOU START THE FIRE.
MY UNCLE-BY-MARRIAGE SMOKES.
HE WILL HAVE A LIGHTER.
YA SPOSE DEAD CACTUSES BURN?
CACTI.
WHEN THE NIGHT COMES, IT WILL BE VERY COLD. SO TAKE ANY CLOTHES YOU CAN FIND, EVEN IF THEY ARE NOT YOURS.
...AND WE MAY NEED WEAPONS.
SOB!

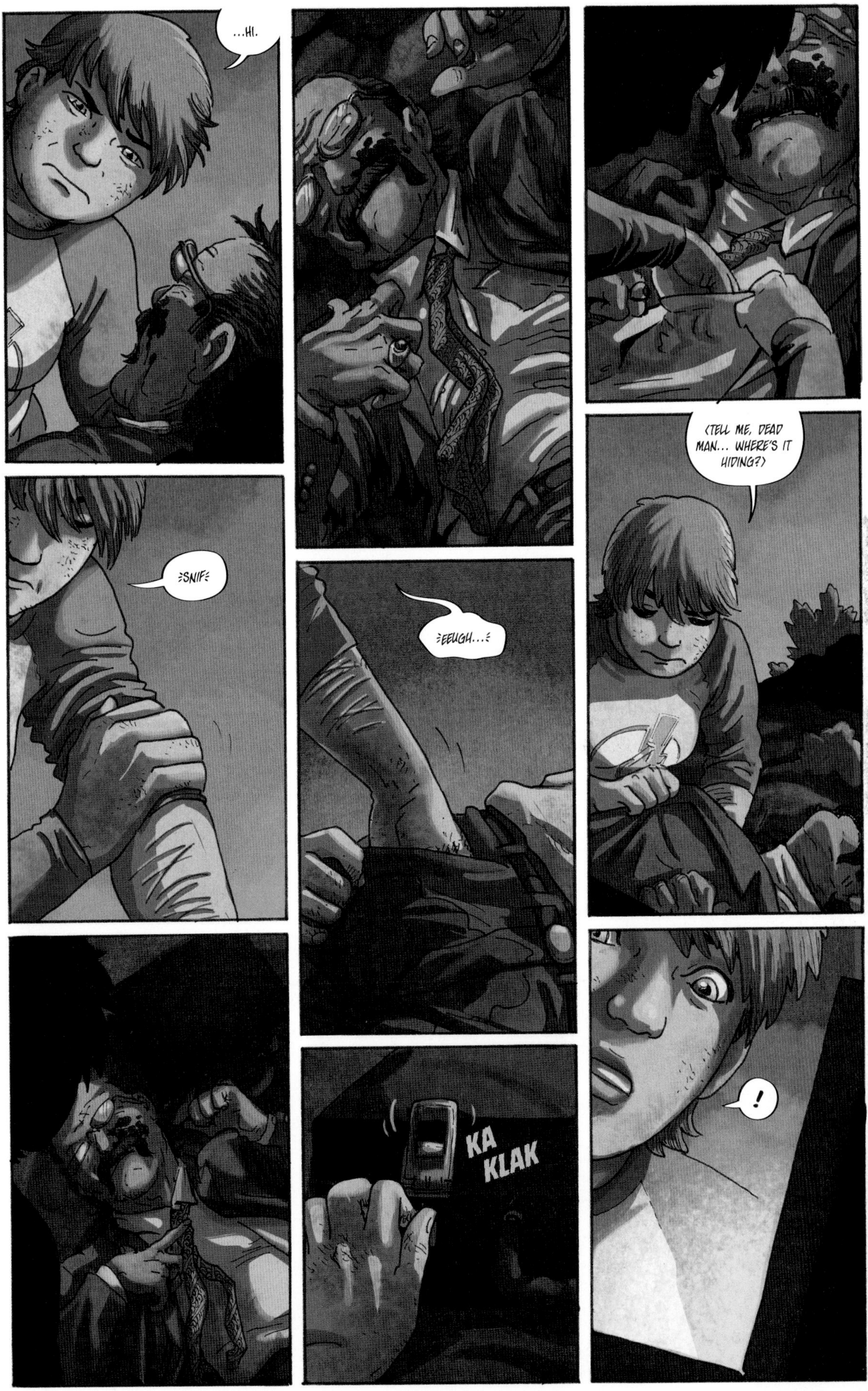
...HI.
⁝SNIF⁝
⁝EEUGH...⁝
<TELL ME, DEAD MAN... WHERE'S IT HIDING?>
KA KLAK
!

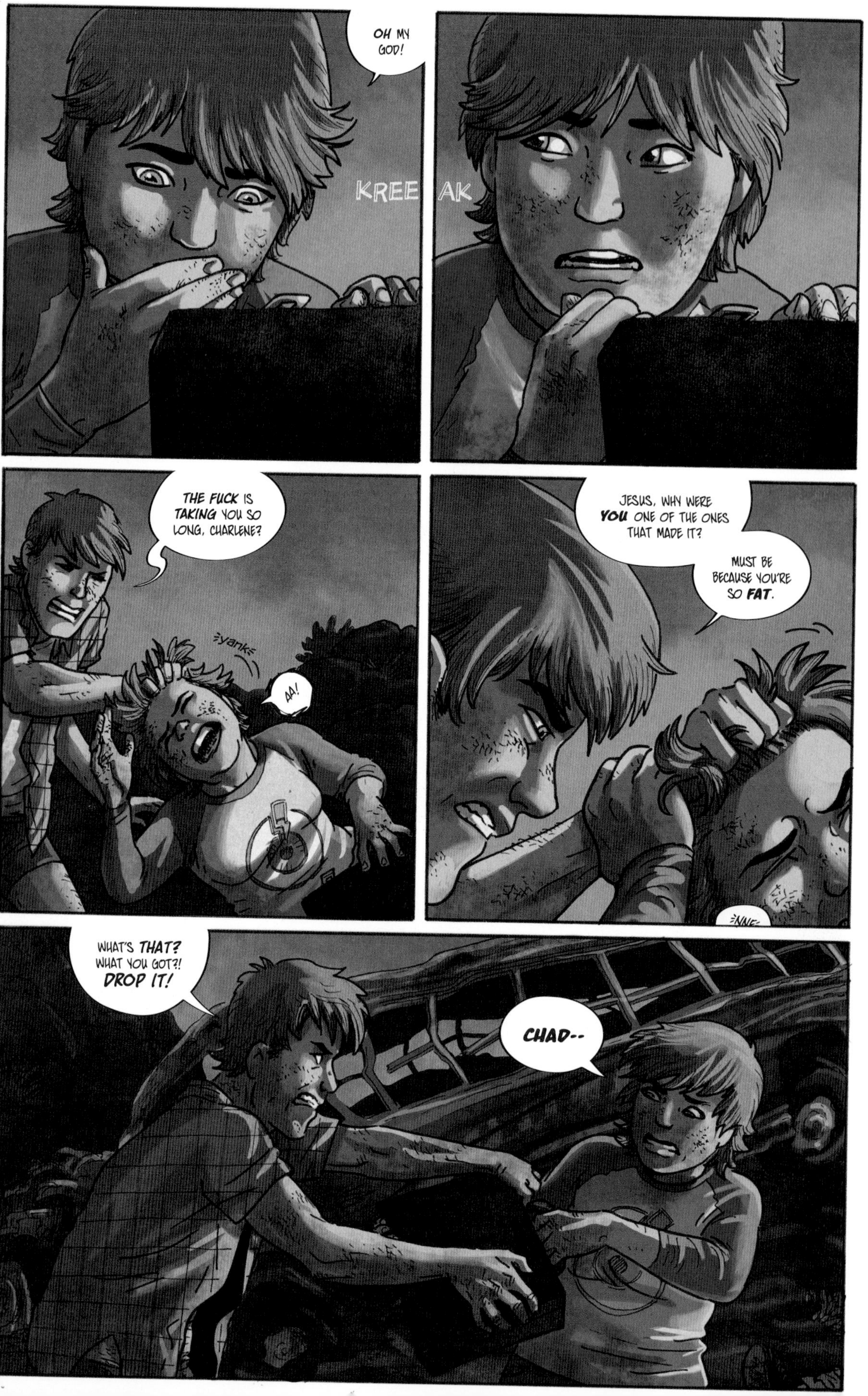
OH MY GOD!
KREEAK
THE FUCK IS TAKING YOU SO LONG, CHARLENE?
=yank=
AA!
JESUS, WHY WERE YOU ONE OF THE ONES THAT MADE IT?
MUST BE BECAUSE YOU'RE SO FAT.
=NNE=
WHAT'S THAT? WHAT YOU GOT?! DROP IT!
CHAD--

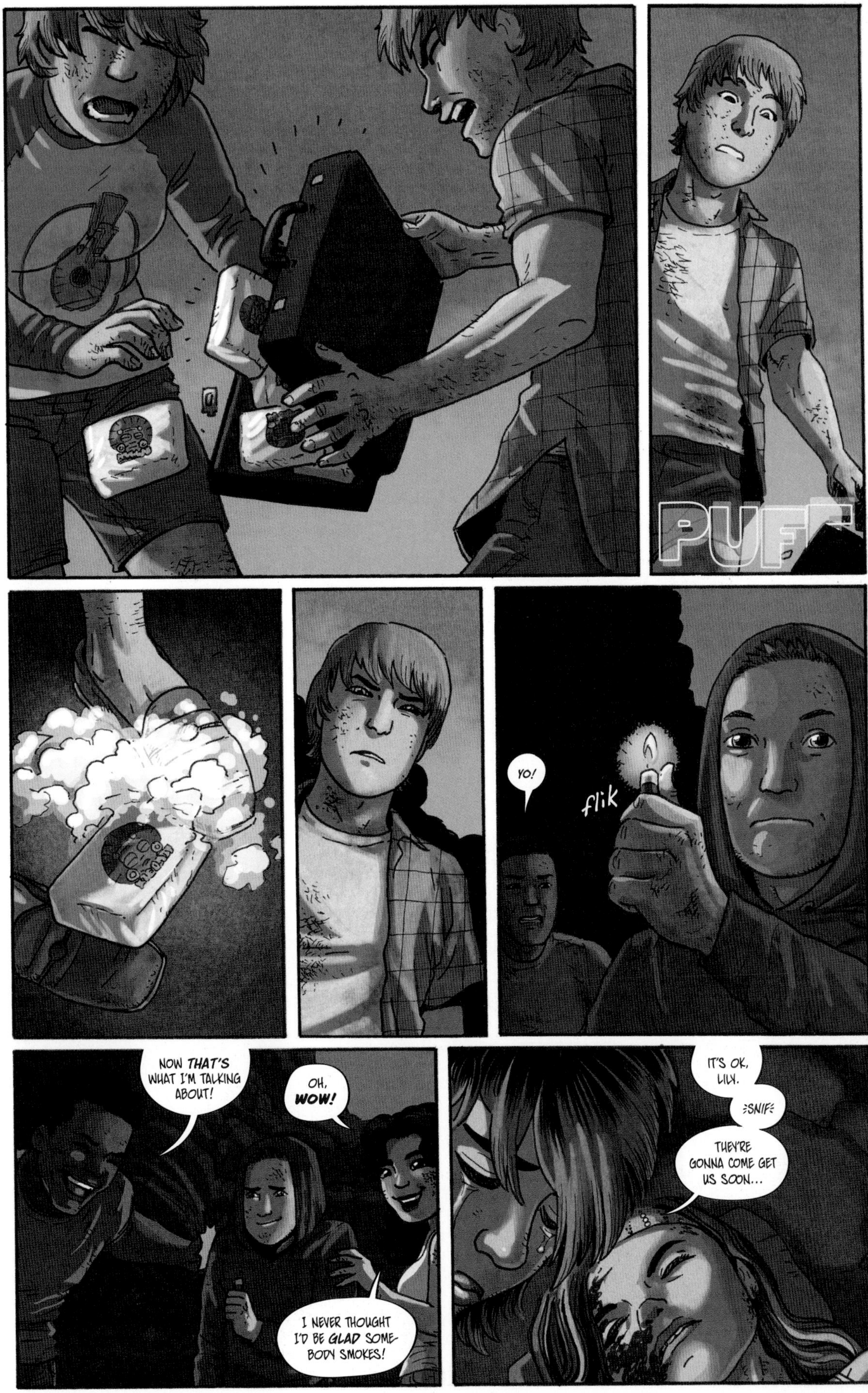
PUFF
YO!
flik
NOW THAT'S WHAT I'M TALKING ABOUT!
OH, WOW!
I NEVER THOUGHT I'D BE GLAD SOMEBODY SMOKES!
IT'S OK, LILY.
SNIF
THEY'RE GONNA COME GET US SOON...

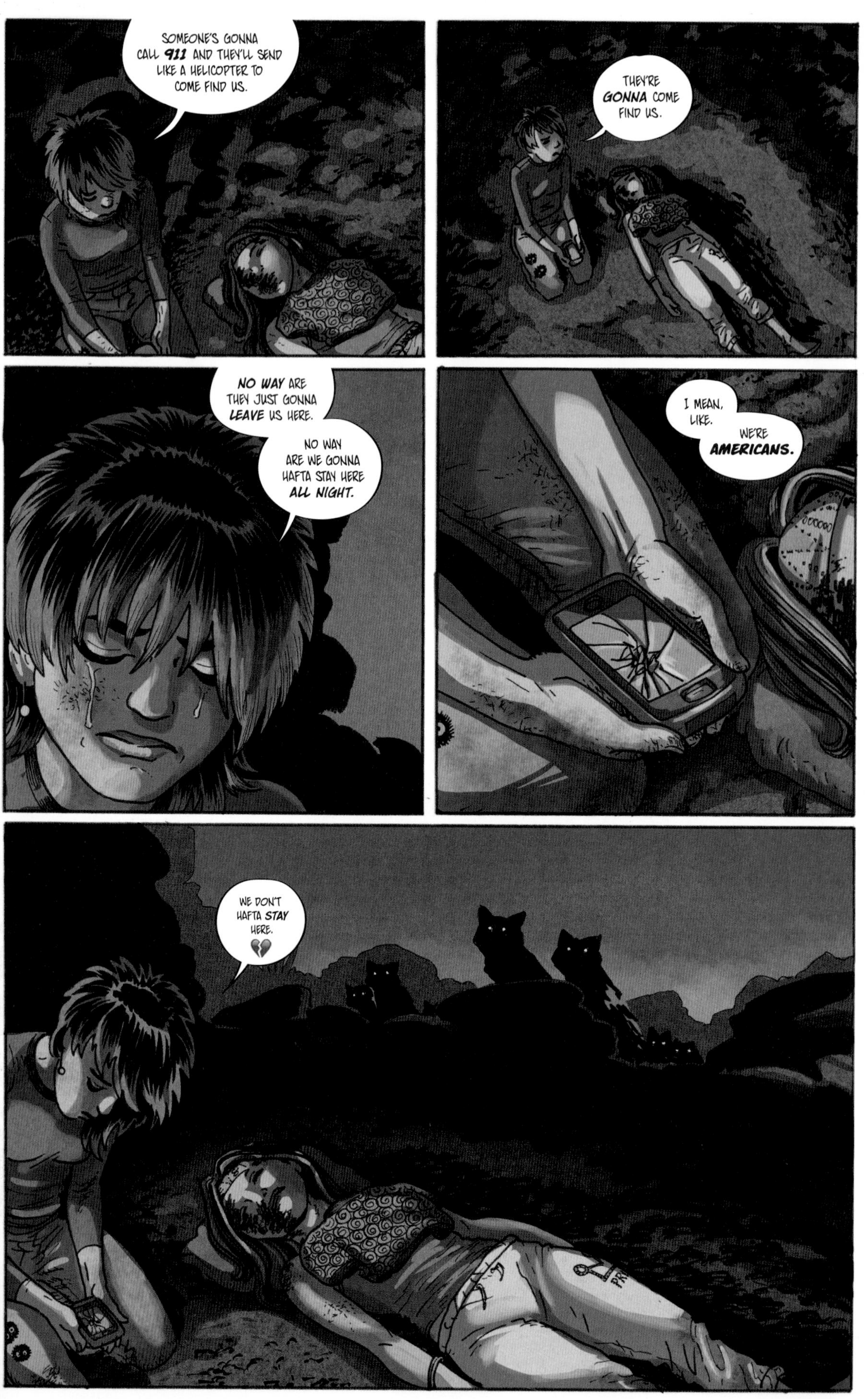
SOMEONE'S GONNA CALL 911 AND THEY'LL SEND LIKE A HELICOPTER TO COME FIND US.
THEY'RE GONNA COME FIND US.
NO WAY ARE THEY JUST GONNA LEAVE US HERE.
NO WAY ARE WE GONNA HAFTA STAY HERE ALL NIGHT.
I MEAN, LIKE.
WE'RE AMERICANS.
WE DON'T HAFTA STAY HERE.

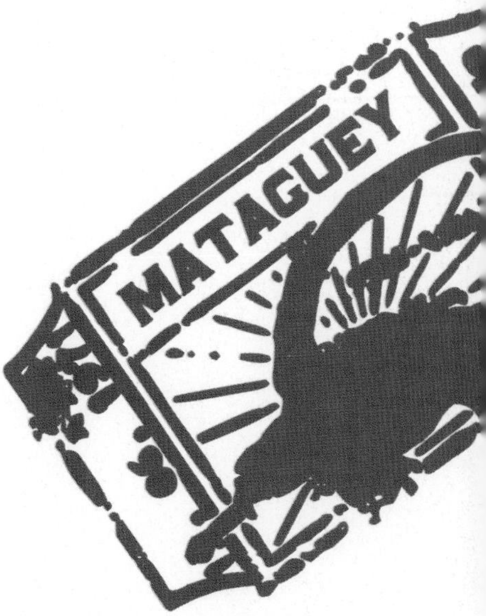
MATAGUEY

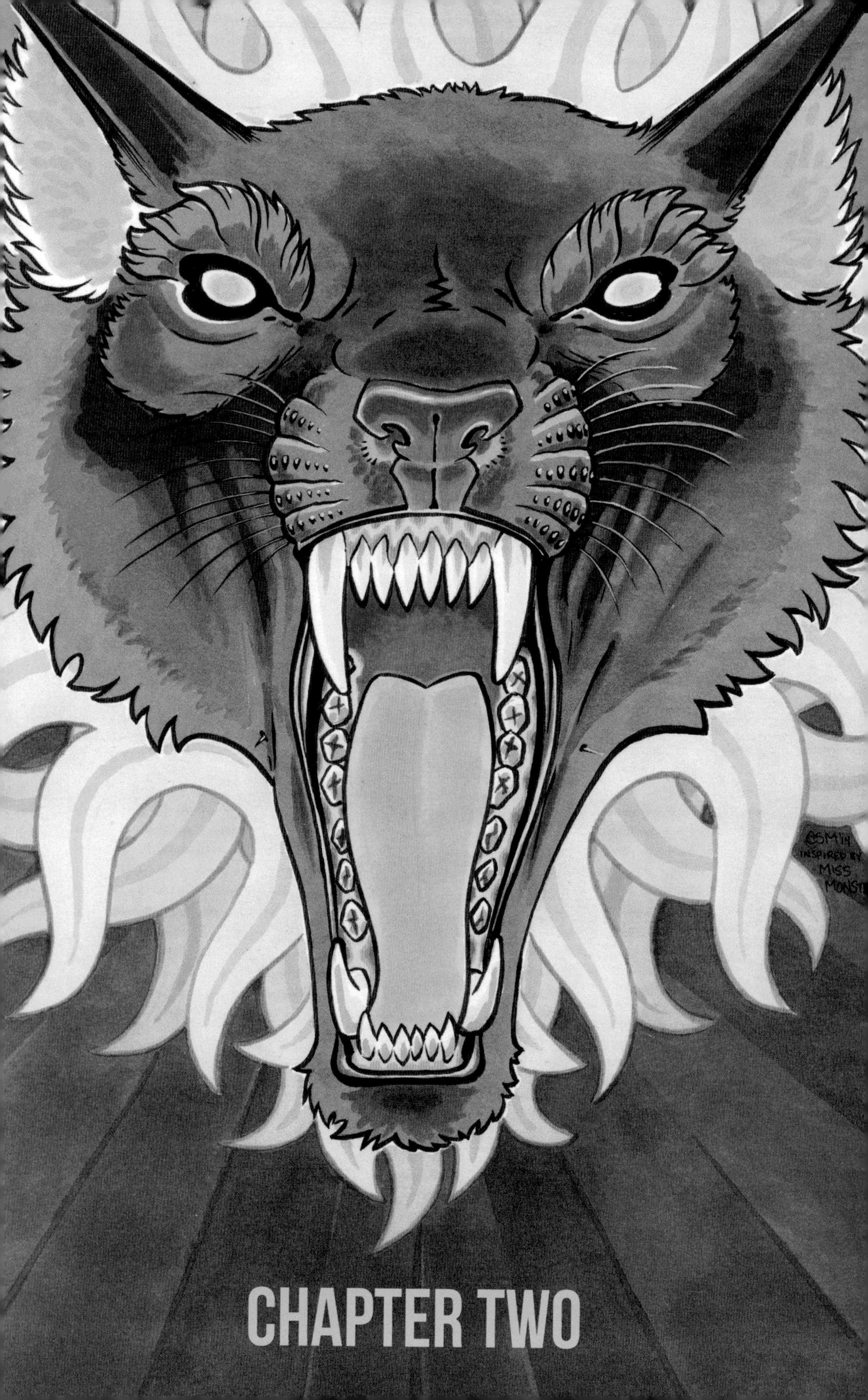
©SM'14
INSPIRED BY
MISS

CHAPTER TWO

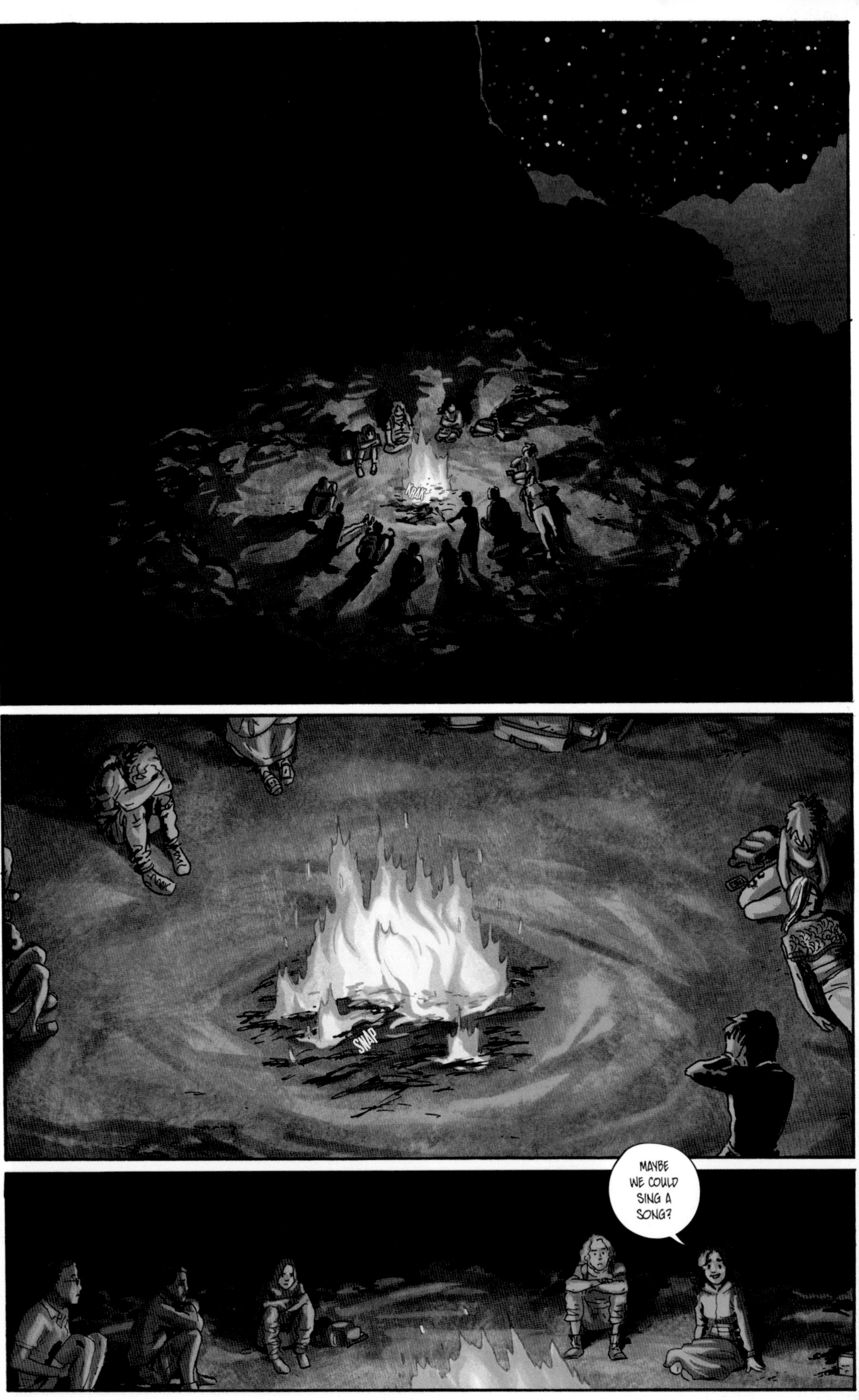
KRAK
SNAP
MAYBE WE COULD SING A SONG?

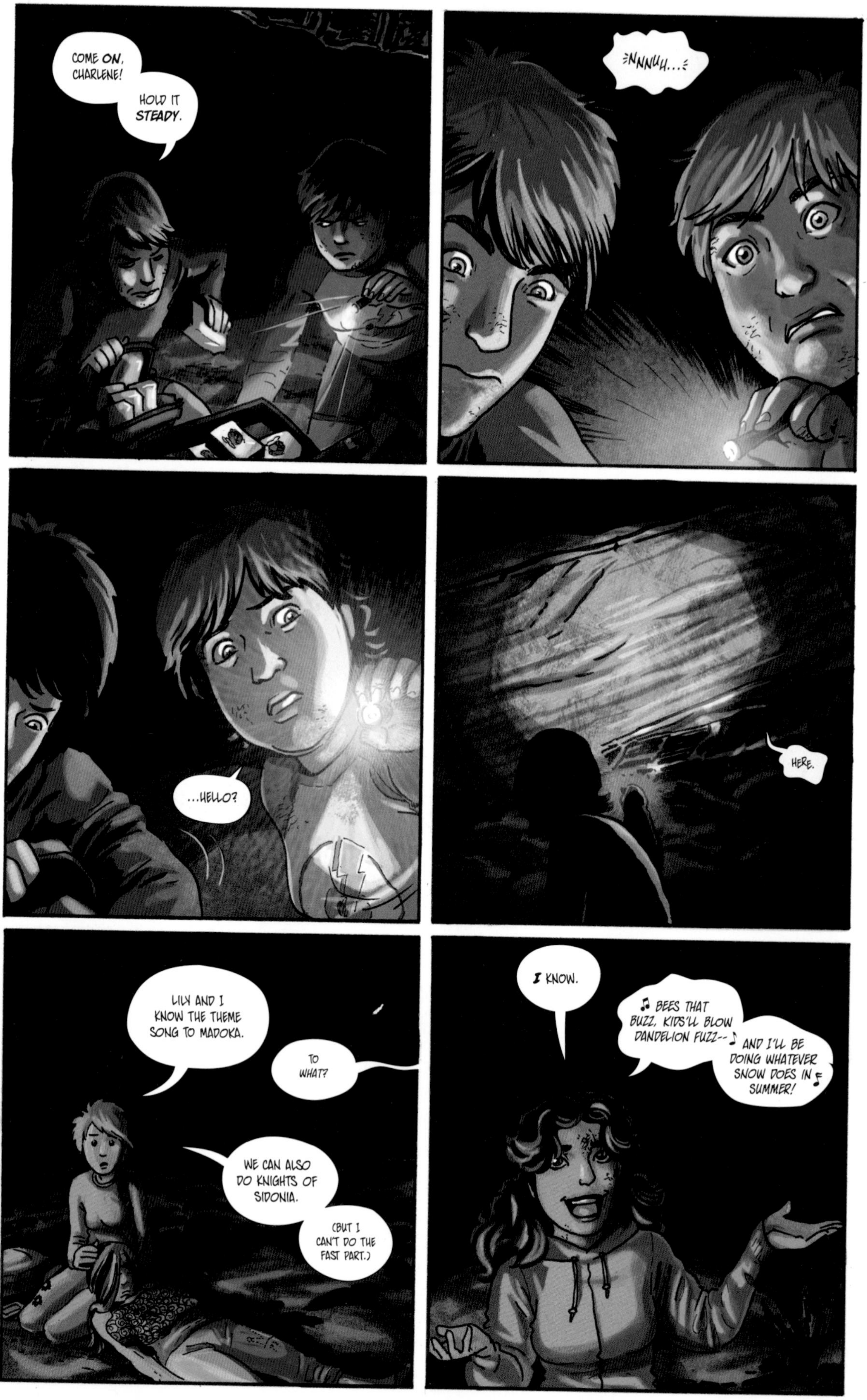
COME ON, CHARLENE!
HOLD IT STEADY.
NNNUH...
...HELLO?
HERE.
LILY AND I KNOW THE THEME SONG TO MADOKA.
TO WHAT?
WE CAN ALSO DO KNIGHTS OF SIDONIA.
(BUT I CAN'T DO THE FAST PART.)
I KNOW.
♪ BEES THAT BUZZ, KIDS'LL BLOW DANDELION FUZZ--
♪ AND I'LL BE DOING WHATEVER SNOW DOES IN SUMMER! ♪

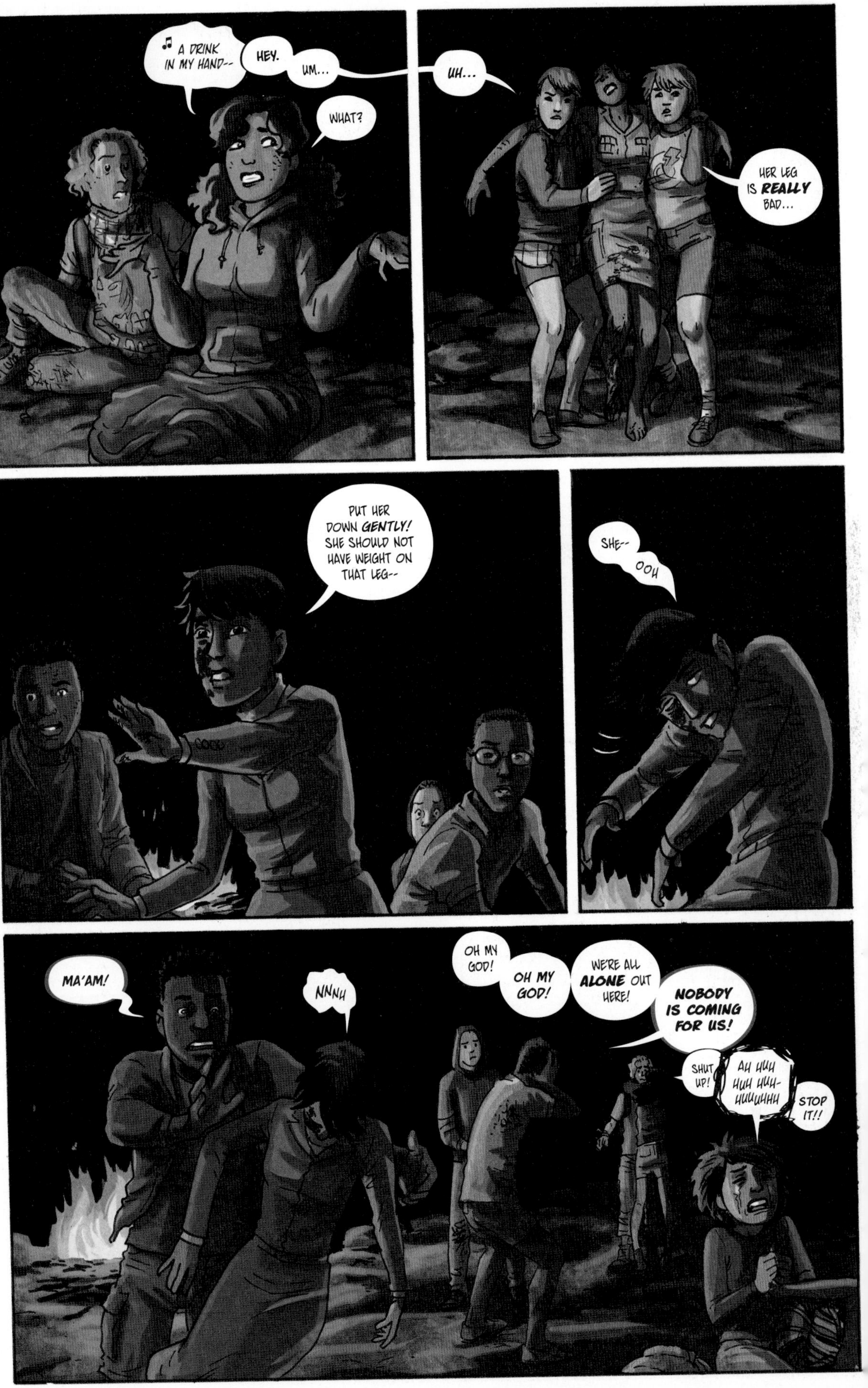

♫ A DRINK IN MY HAND--
HEY.
UM...
WHAT?
UH...
HER LEG IS **REALLY** BAD...
PUT HER DOWN **GENTLY!** SHE SHOULD NOT HAVE WEIGHT ON THAT LEG--
SHE--
OOH
MA'AM!
NNNH
OH MY GOD!
OH MY GOD!
WE'RE ALL **ALONE** OUT HERE!
NOBODY IS COMING FOR US!
SHUT UP!
AH HUH HUH HUH-HUUUHHH
STOP IT!!

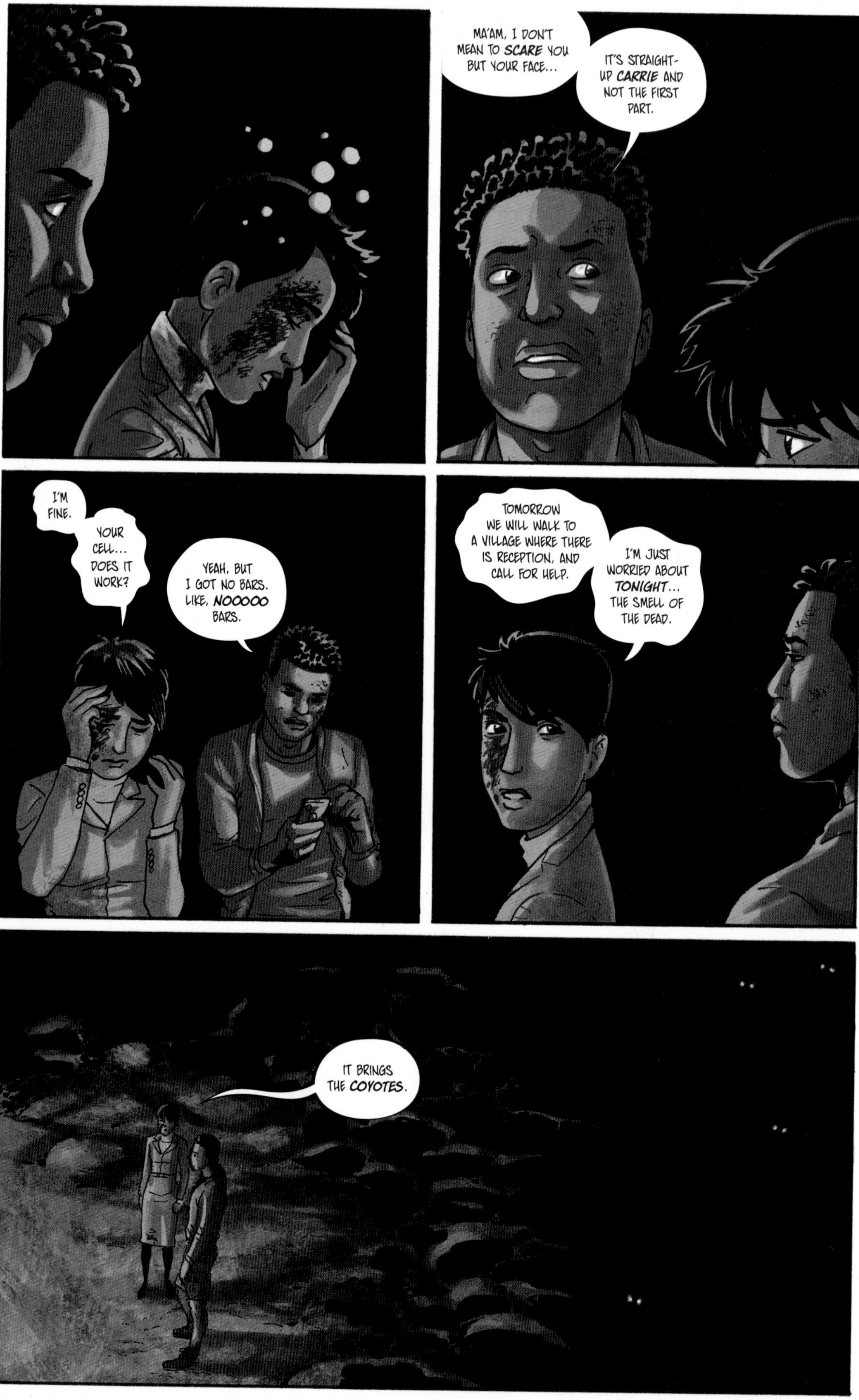
MA'AM, I DON'T MEAN TO SCARE YOU BUT YOUR FACE...
IT'S STRAIGHT-UP CARRIE AND NOT THE FIRST PART.
I'M FINE.
YOUR CELL... DOES IT WORK?
YEAH, BUT I GOT NO BARS. LIKE, NOOOOO BARS.
TOMORROW WE WILL WALK TO A VILLAGE WHERE THERE IS RECEPTION, AND CALL FOR HELP.
I'M JUST WORRIED ABOUT TONIGHT... THE SMELL OF THE DEAD.
IT BRINGS THE COYOTES.

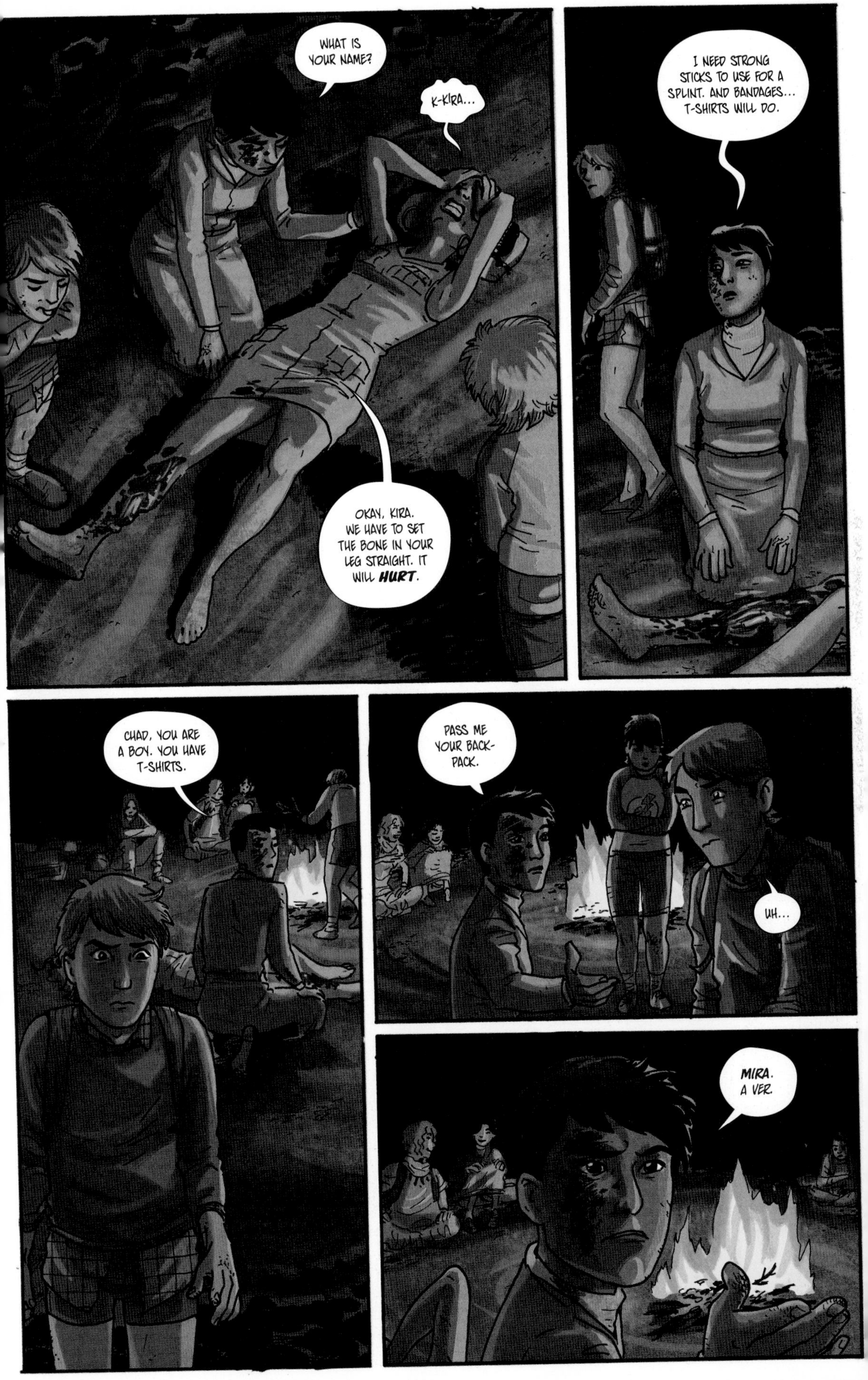
WHAT IS YOUR NAME?
K-KIRA...
OKAY, KIRA. WE HAVE TO SET THE BONE IN YOUR LEG STRAIGHT. IT WILL **HURT**.
I NEED STRONG STICKS TO USE FOR A SPLINT. AND BANDAGES... T-SHIRTS WILL DO.
CHAD, YOU ARE A BOY. YOU HAVE T-SHIRTS.
PASS ME YOUR BACK-PACK.
UH...
MIRA. A VER.

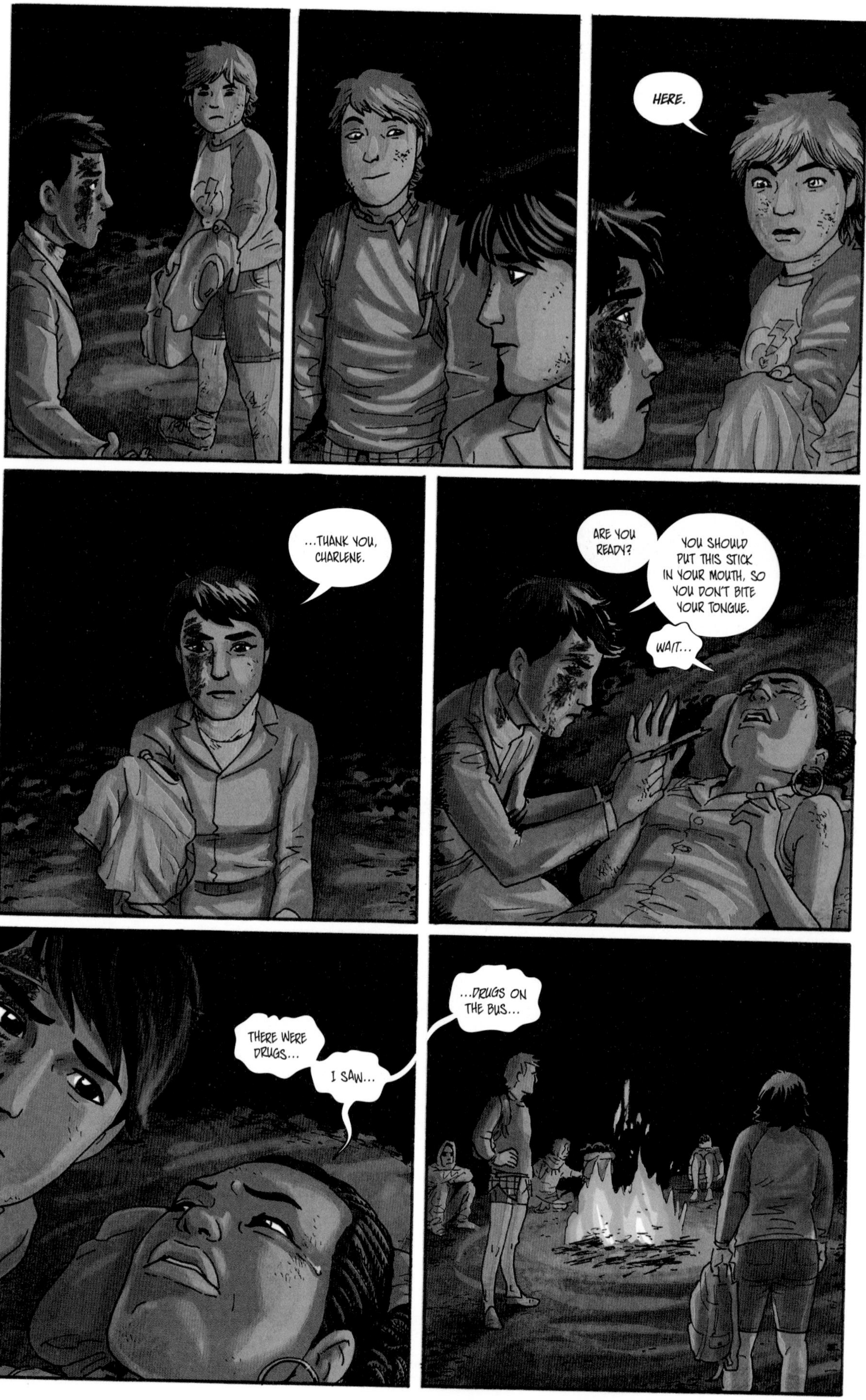
HERE.
...THANK YOU, CHARLENE.
ARE YOU READY?
YOU SHOULD PUT THIS STICK IN YOUR MOUTH, SO YOU DON'T BITE YOUR TONGUE.
WAIT...
THERE WERE DRUGS...
I SAW...
...DRUGS ON THE BUS...

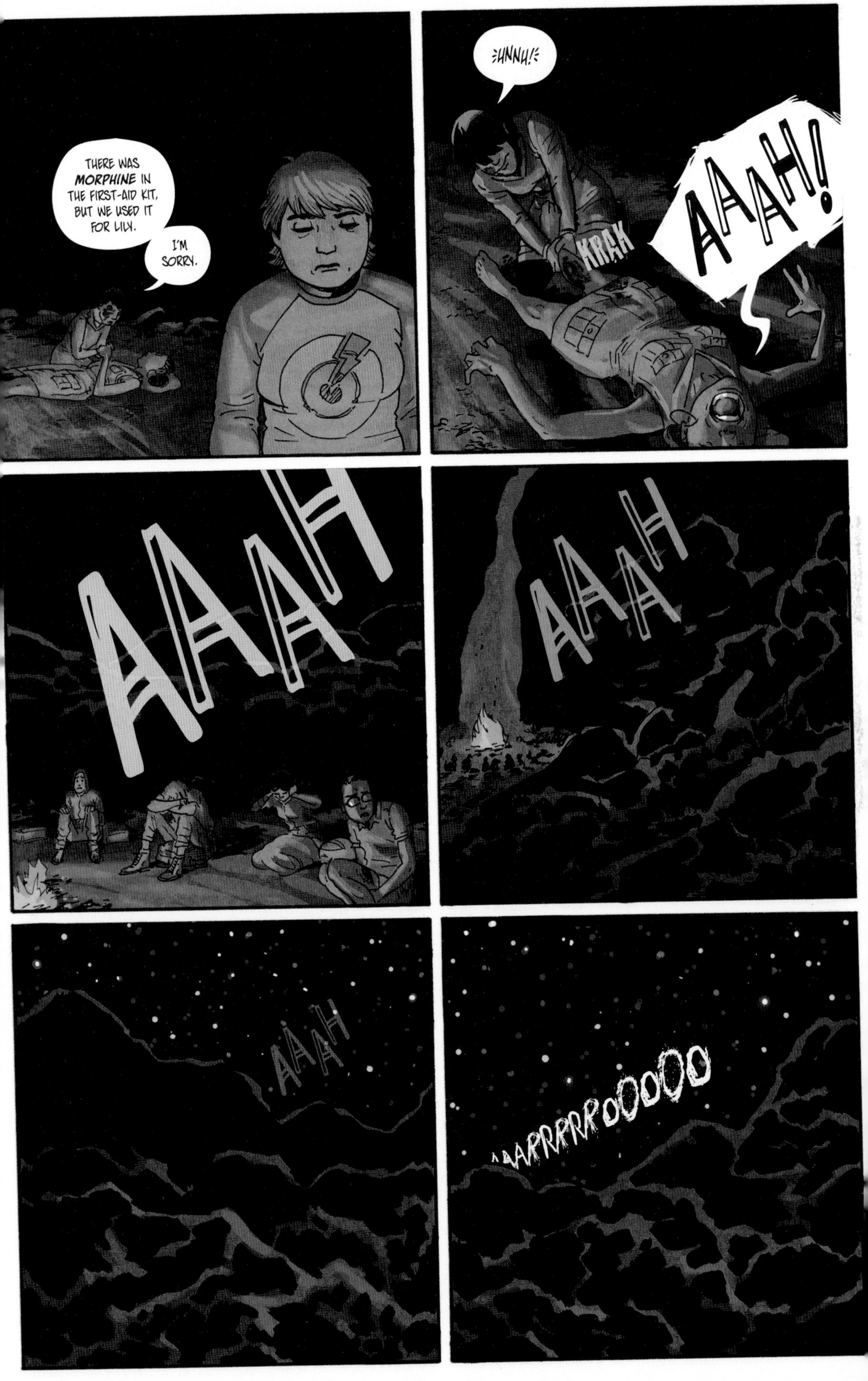
THERE WAS **MORPHINE** IN THE FIRST-AID KIT, BUT WE USED IT FOR LILY.
I'M SORRY.
HNNH!
KRAK
AAAH!
AAAH
AAAH
AAAH
AARRRRROOOOO

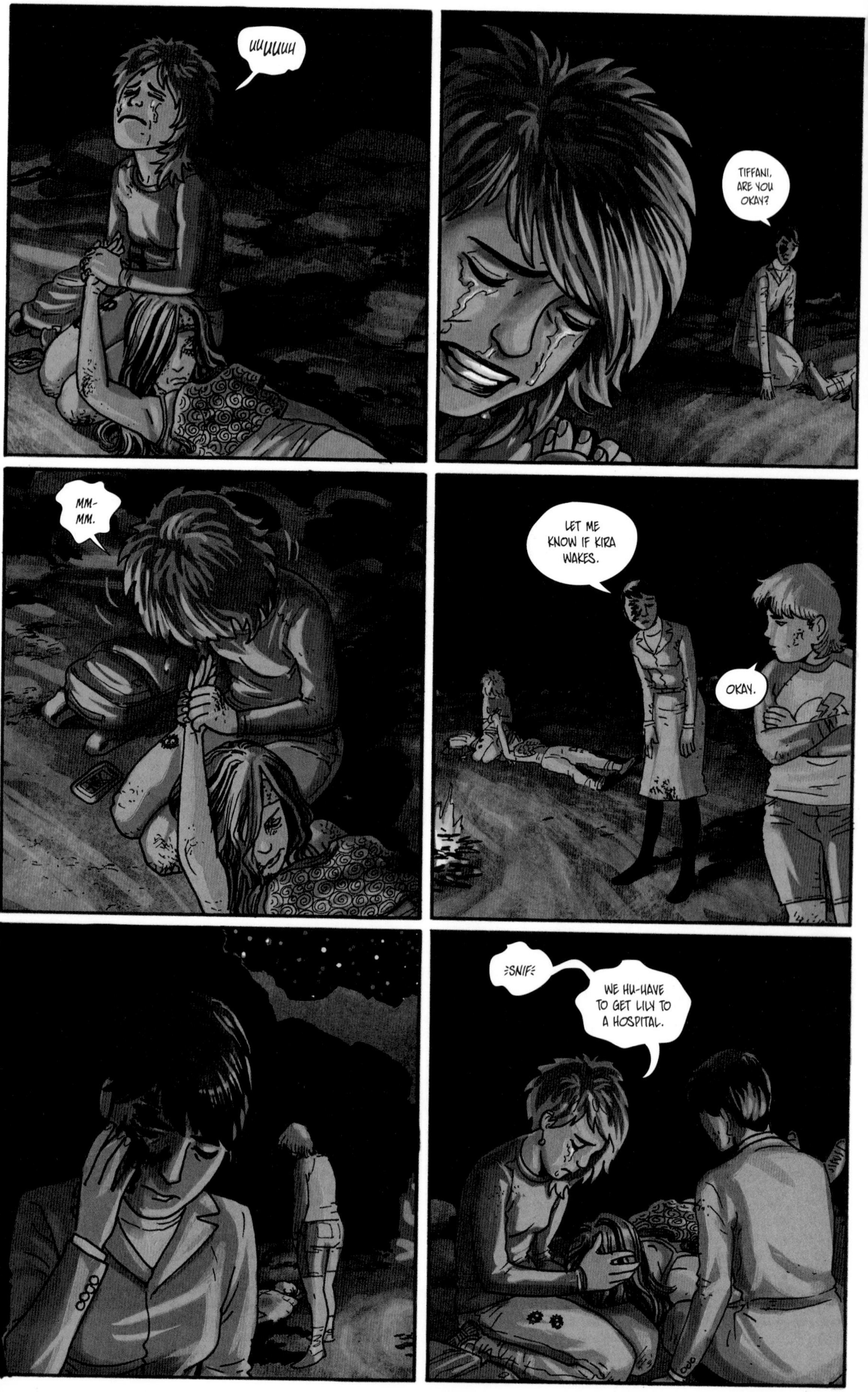
UUUUUH
TIFFANI, ARE YOU OKAY?
MM-MM.
LET ME KNOW IF KIRA WAKES.
OKAY.
SNIF
WE HU-HAVE TO GET LILY TO A HOSPITAL.

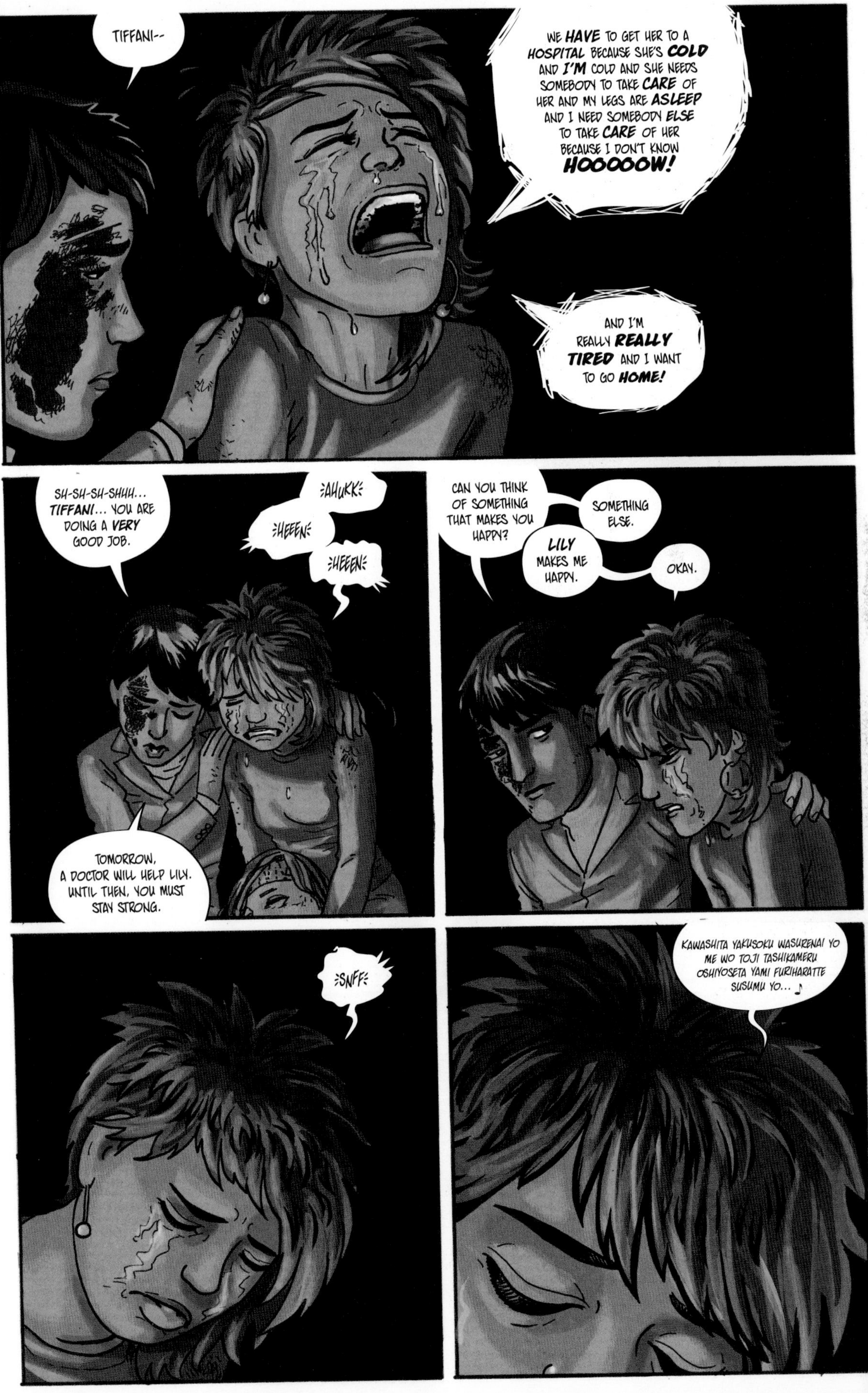
TIFFANI--
WE HAVE TO GET HER TO A HOSPITAL BECAUSE SHE'S COLD AND I'M COLD AND SHE NEEDS SOMEBODY TO TAKE CARE OF HER AND MY LEGS ARE ASLEEP AND I NEED SOMEBODY ELSE TO TAKE CARE OF HER BECAUSE I DON'T KNOW HOOOOOW!
AND I'M REALLY REALLY TIRED AND I WANT TO GO HOME!
SH-SH-SH-SHHH... TIFFANI... YOU ARE DOING A VERY GOOD JOB.
AHUKK
HEEEN
HEEEN
TOMORROW, A DOCTOR WILL HELP LILY. UNTIL THEN, YOU MUST STAY STRONG.
CAN YOU THINK OF SOMETHING THAT MAKES YOU HAPPY?
SOMETHING ELSE.
LILY MAKES ME HAPPY.
OKAY.
SNFF
KAWASHITA YAKUSOKU WASURENAI YO
ME WO TOJI TASHIKAMERU
OSHIYOSETA YAMI FURIHARATTE
SUSUMU YO...♪

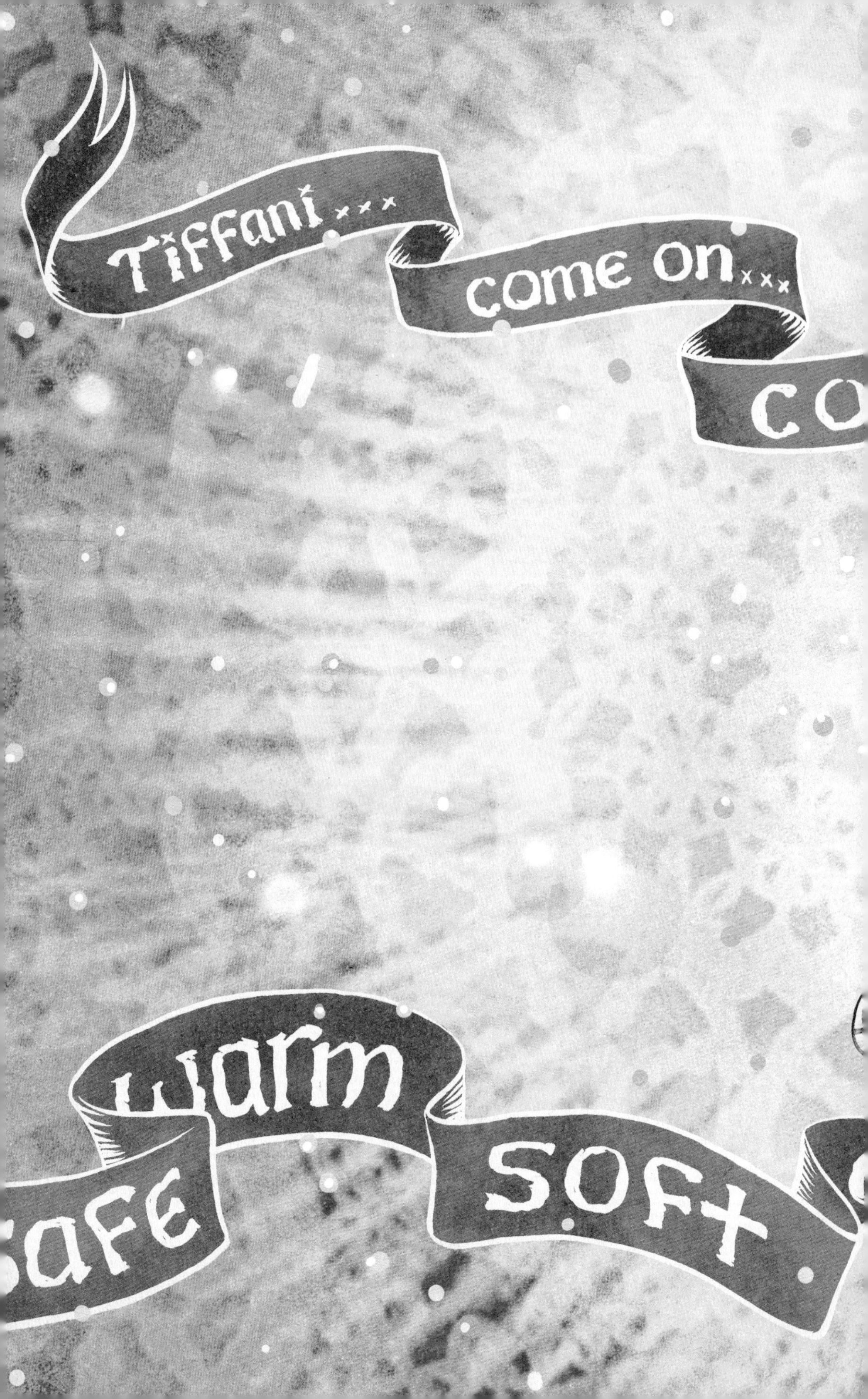
Tiffani...
come on...
CO
warm
afe
soft

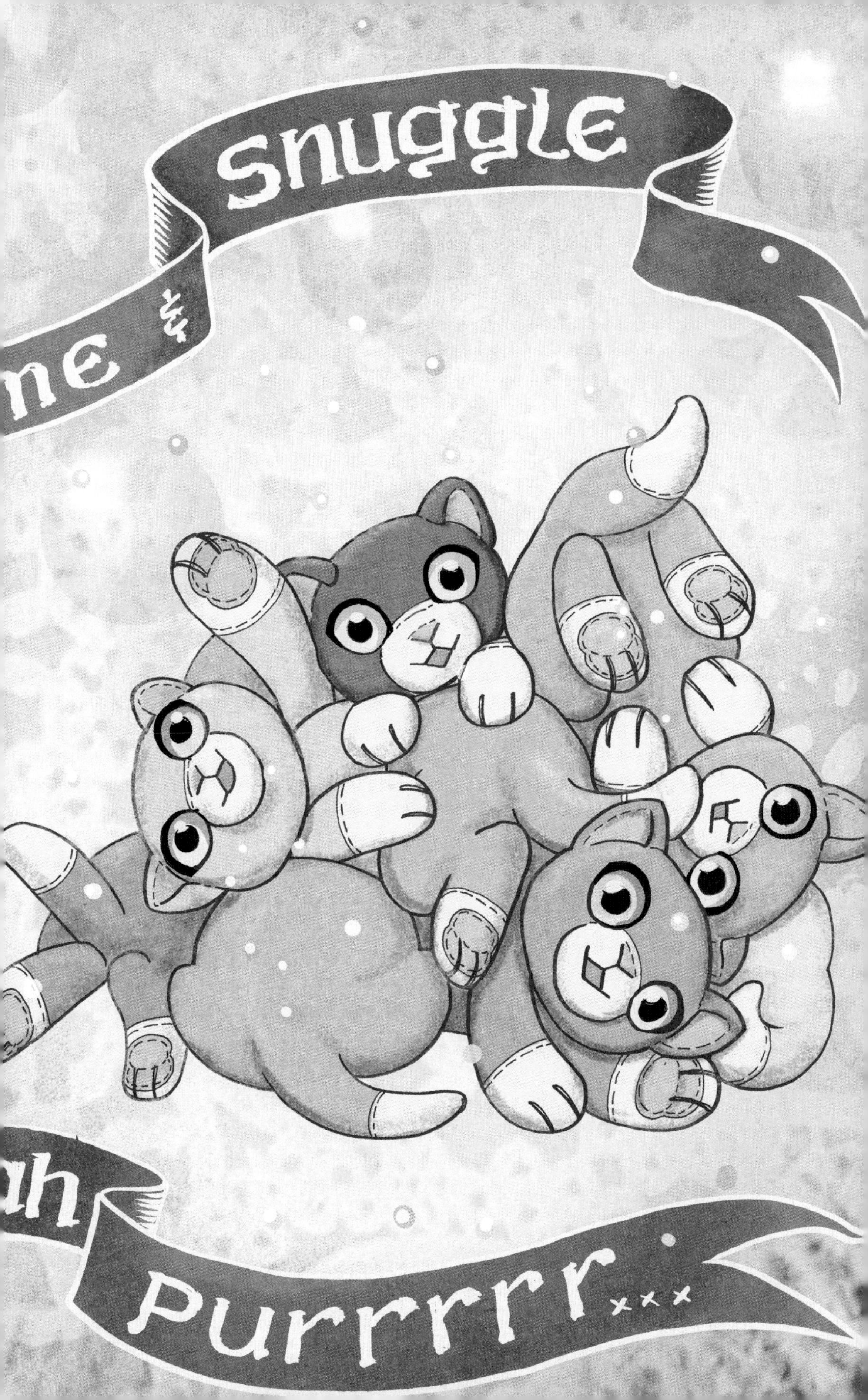
ne &
snuggle
ah
purrrrr...

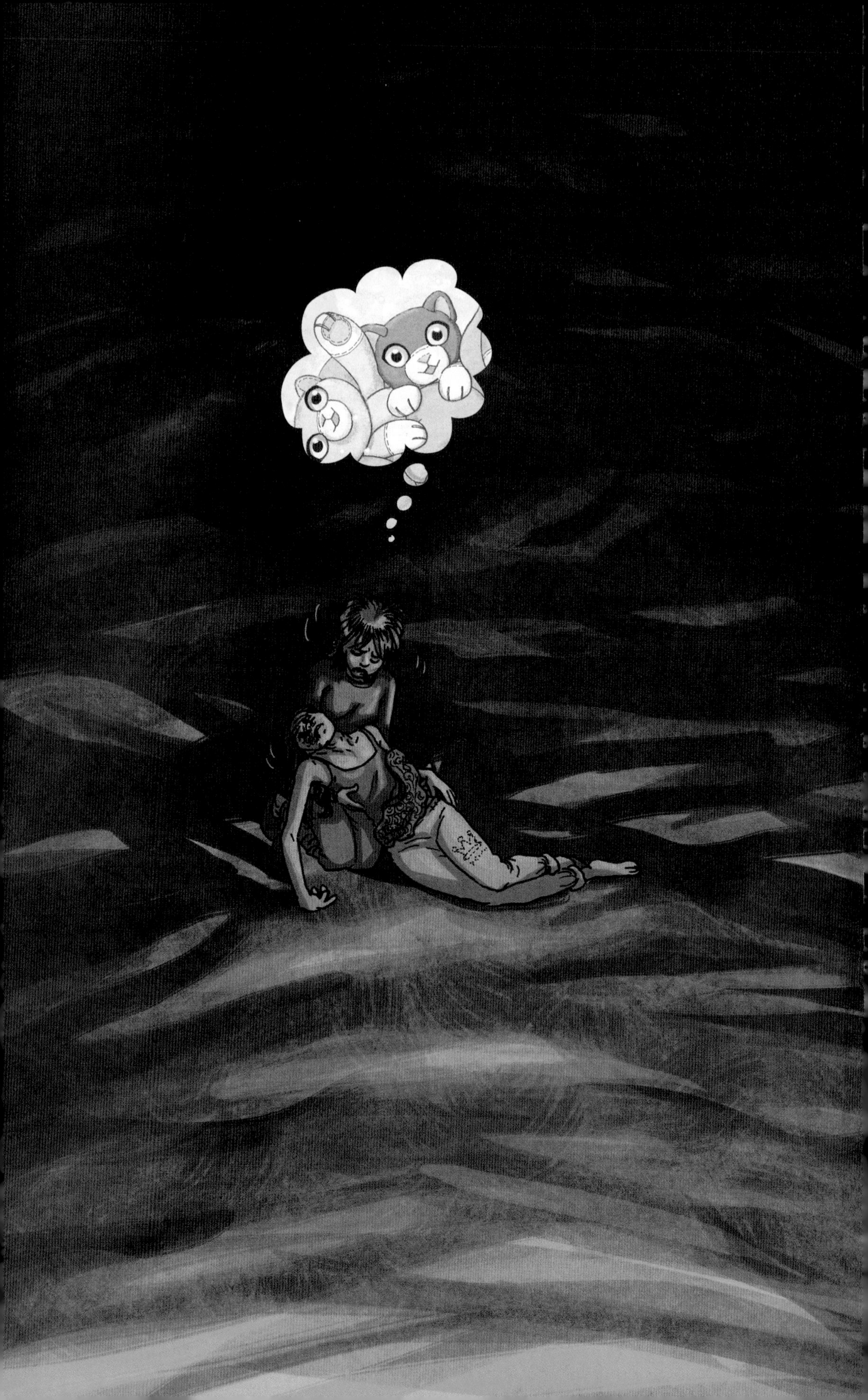

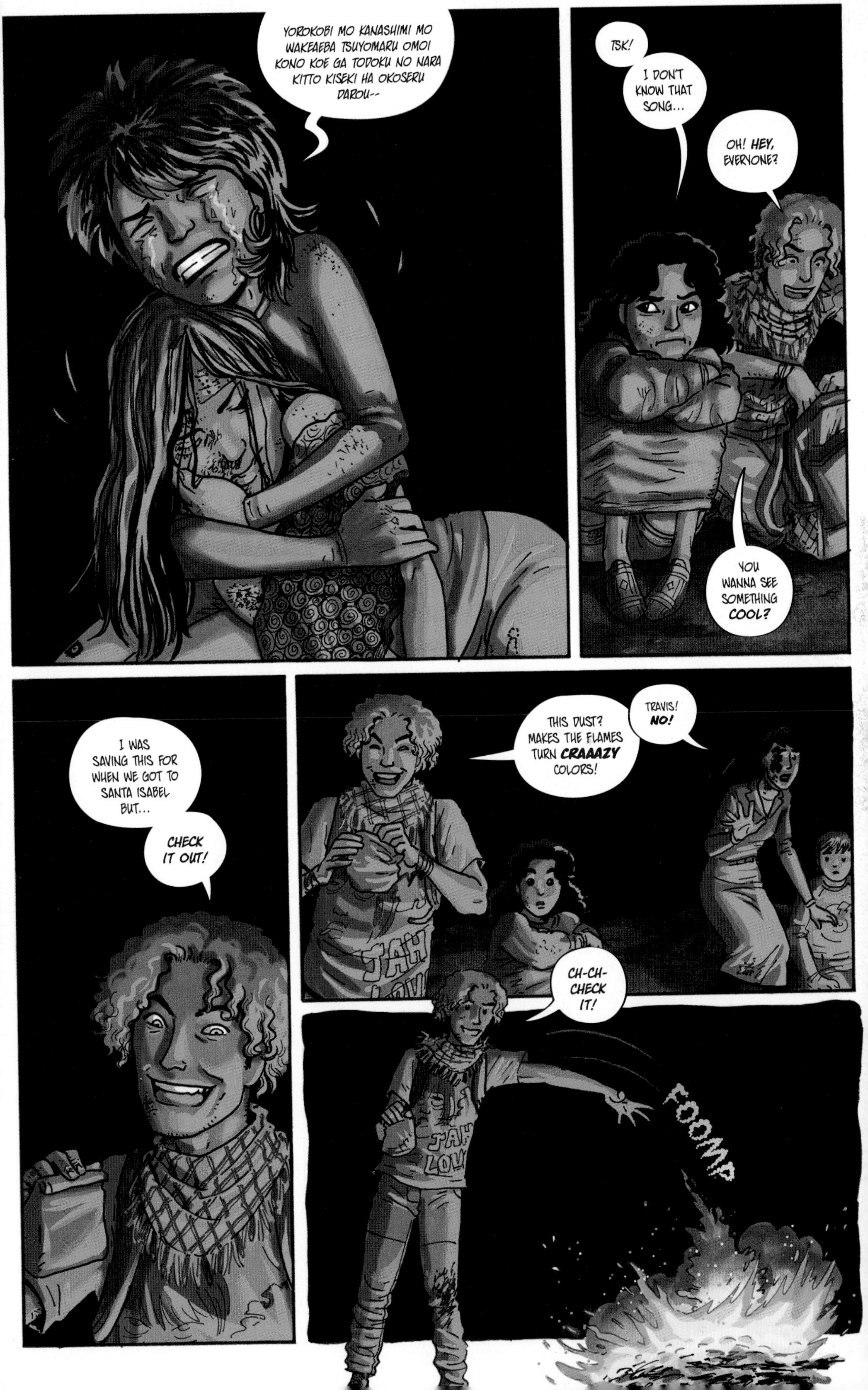
YOROKOBI MO KANASHIMI MO WAKEAEBA TSUYOMARU OMOI KONO KOE GA TODOKU NO NARA KITTO KISEKI HA OKOSERU DAROU--
TSK!
I DON'T KNOW THAT SONG...
OH! HEY, EVERYONE?
YOU WANNA SEE SOMETHING COOL?
I WAS SAVING THIS FOR WHEN WE GOT TO SANTA ISABEL BUT...
CHECK IT OUT!
THIS DUST? MAKES THE FLAMES TURN CRAAAZY COLORS!
TRAVIS! NO!
CH-CH-CHECK IT!
FOOMP

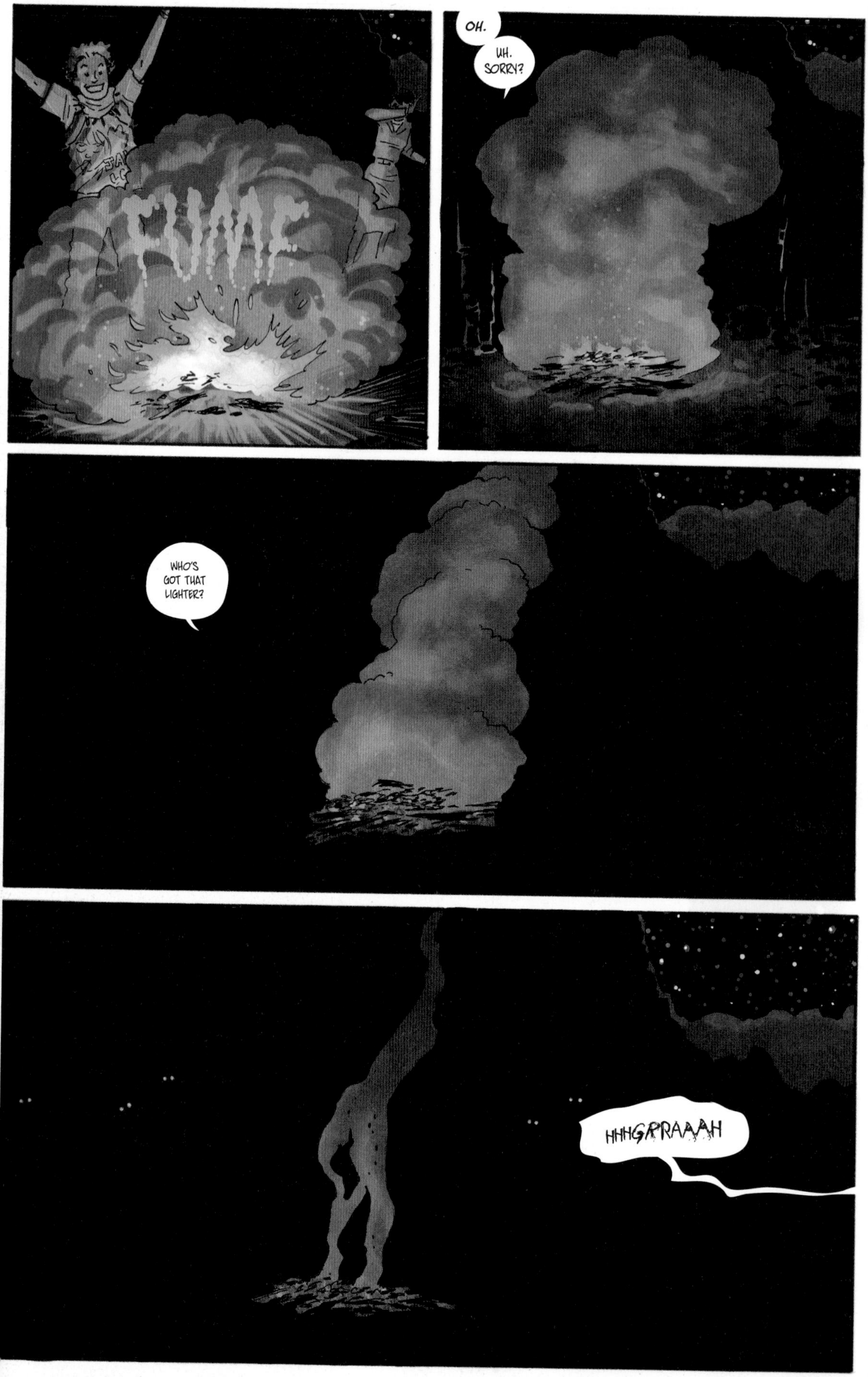
FUMF
OH.
UH. SORRY?
WHO'S GOT THAT LIGHTER?
HHHGRRAAAH

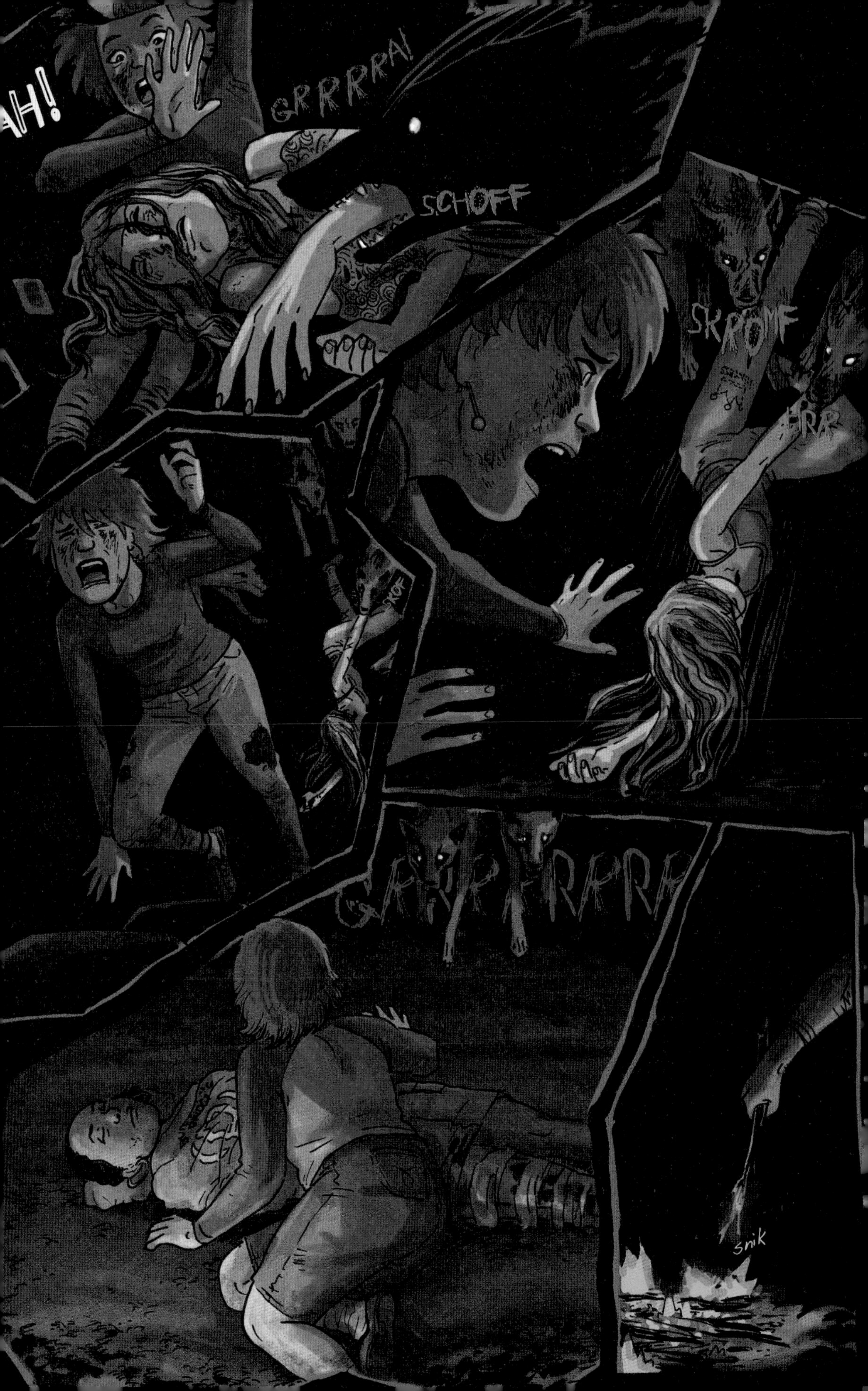
AH!
GRRRRA!
SCHOFF
SKROMF
HRR
SKOF
GRRRRRRRA
snik

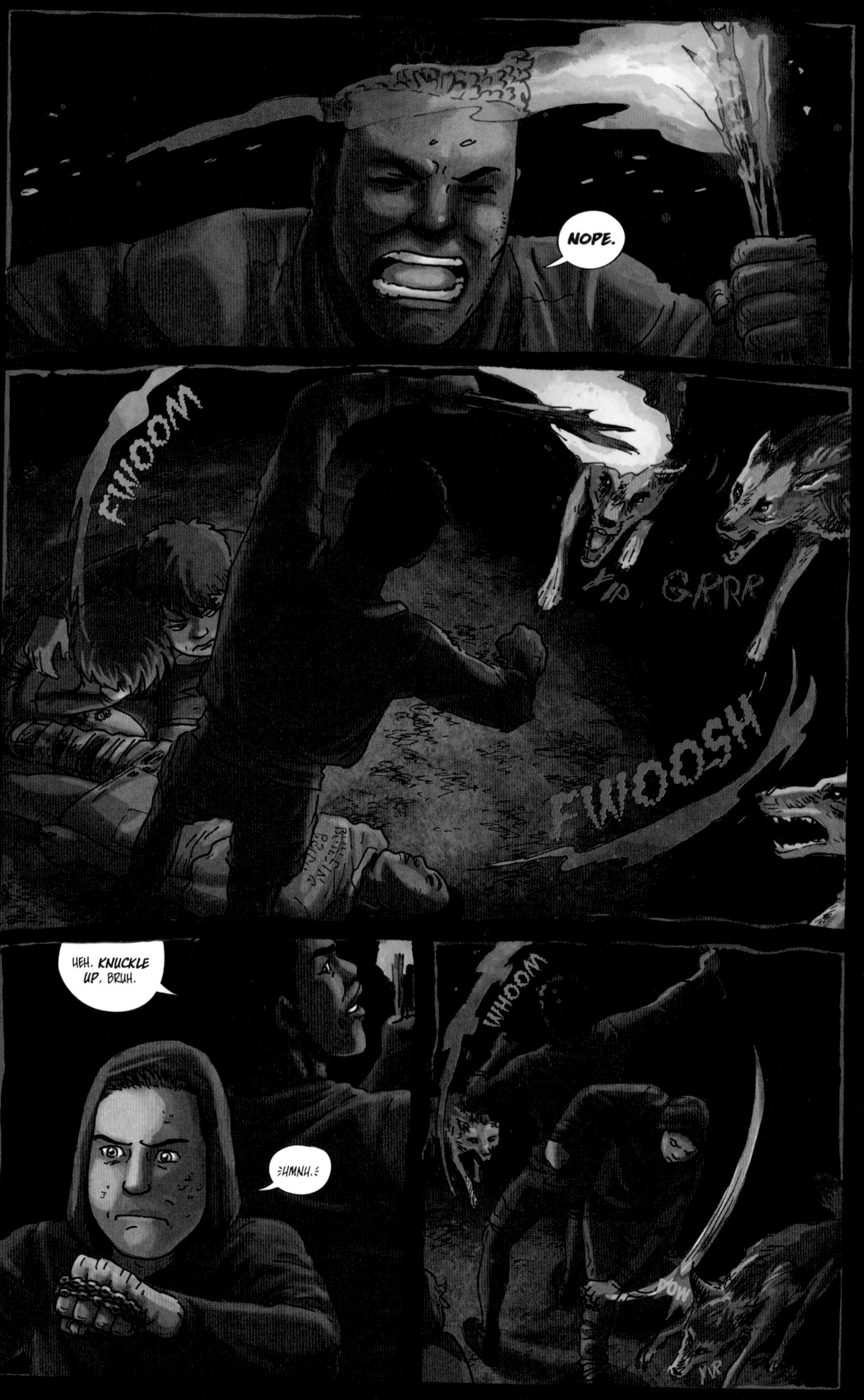
NOPE.
FWOOM
YIP
GRRR
FWOOSH
HEH. KNUCKLE UP, BRUH.
HMNH.
WHOOM
POW
YIP

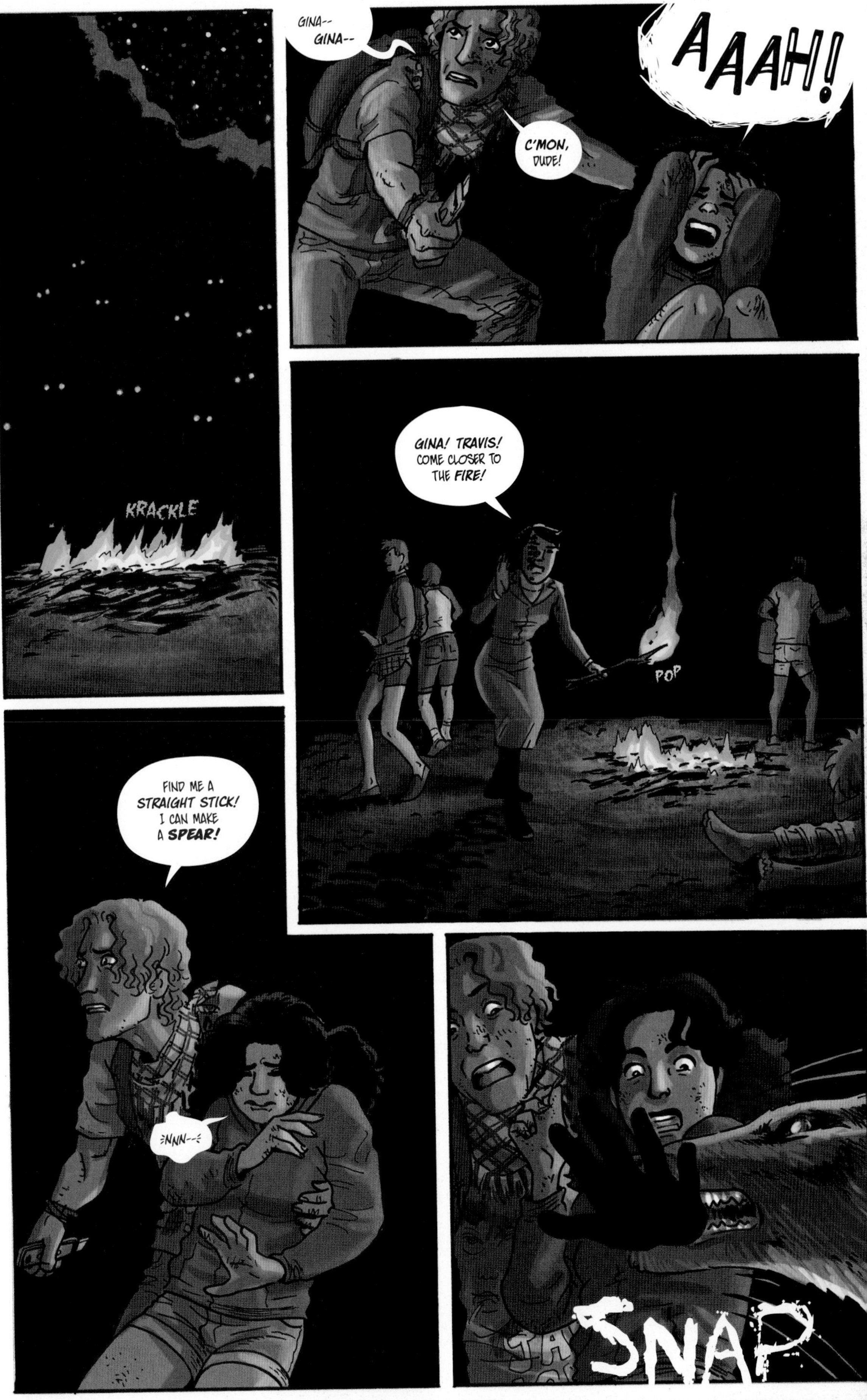
KRACKLE
GINA-- GINA--
C'MON, DUDE!
AAAH!
GINA! TRAVIS! COME CLOSER TO THE FIRE!
POP
FIND ME A STRAIGHT STICK! I CAN MAKE A SPEAR!
NNN--
SNAP

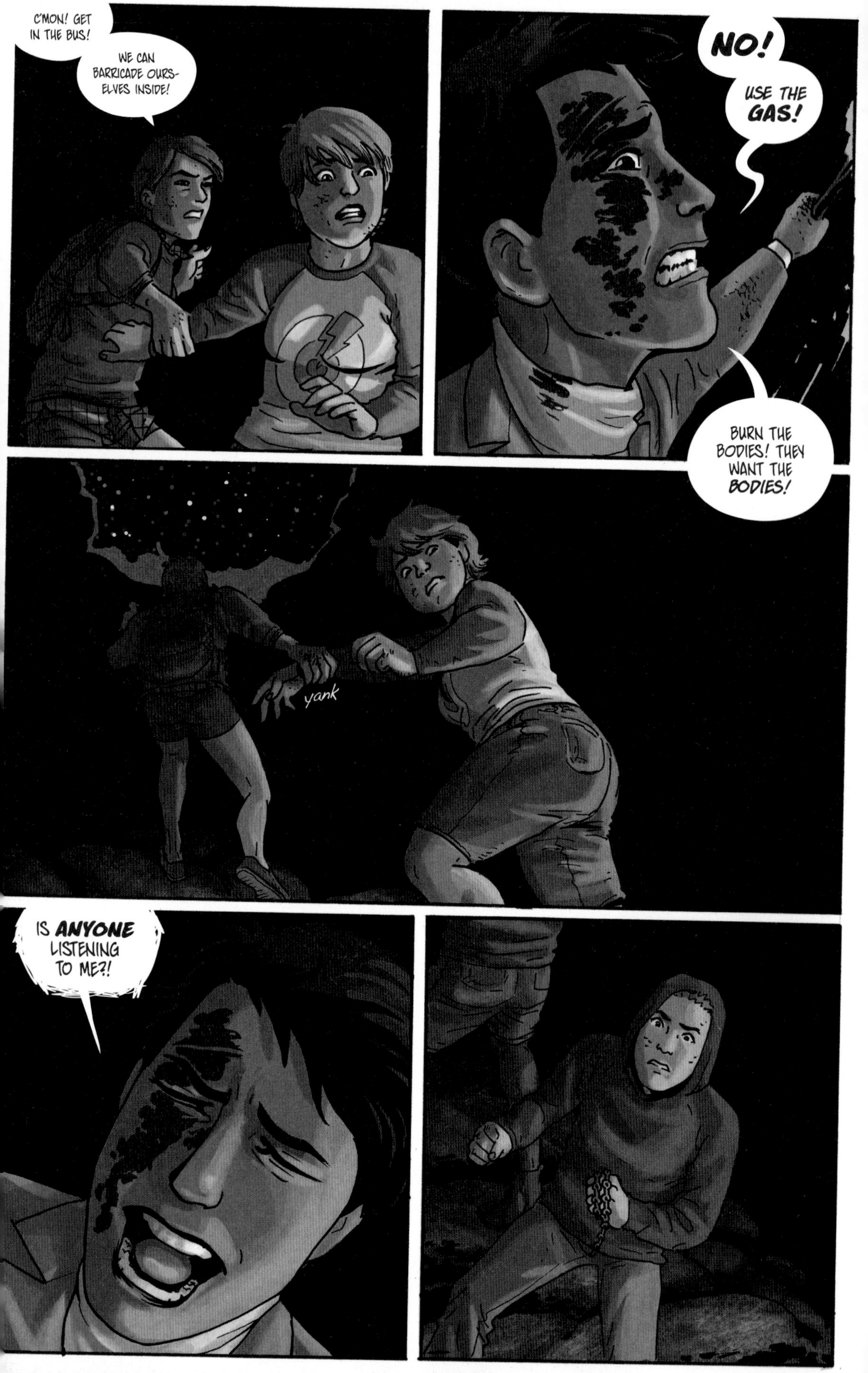
C'MON! GET IN THE BUS!
WE CAN BARRICADE OURS-ELVES INSIDE!
NO!
USE THE GAS!
BURN THE BODIES! THEY WANT THE BODIES!
yank
IS ANYONE LISTENING TO ME?!

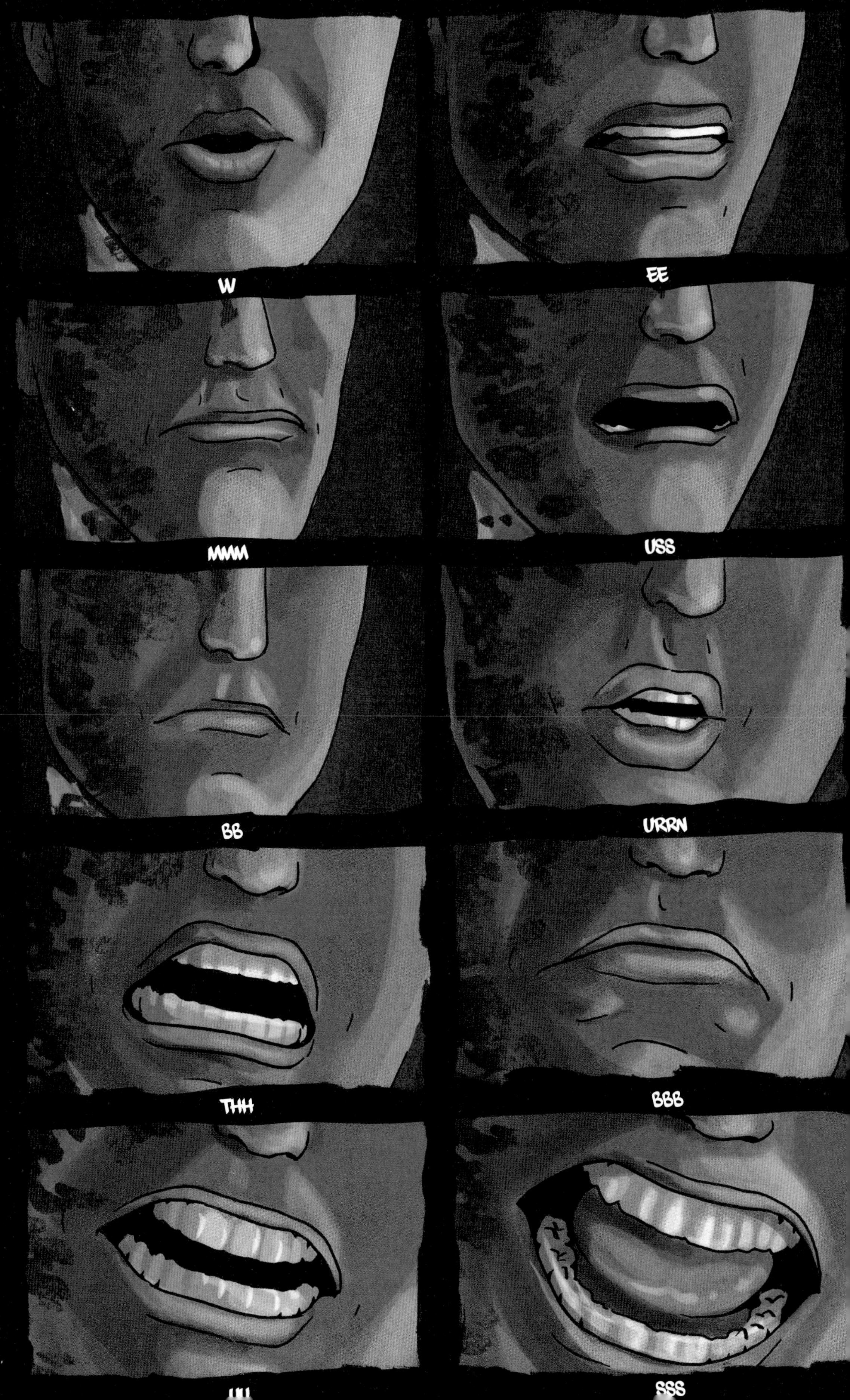
W
EE
MMM
USS
BB
URRN
THH
BBB
SSS

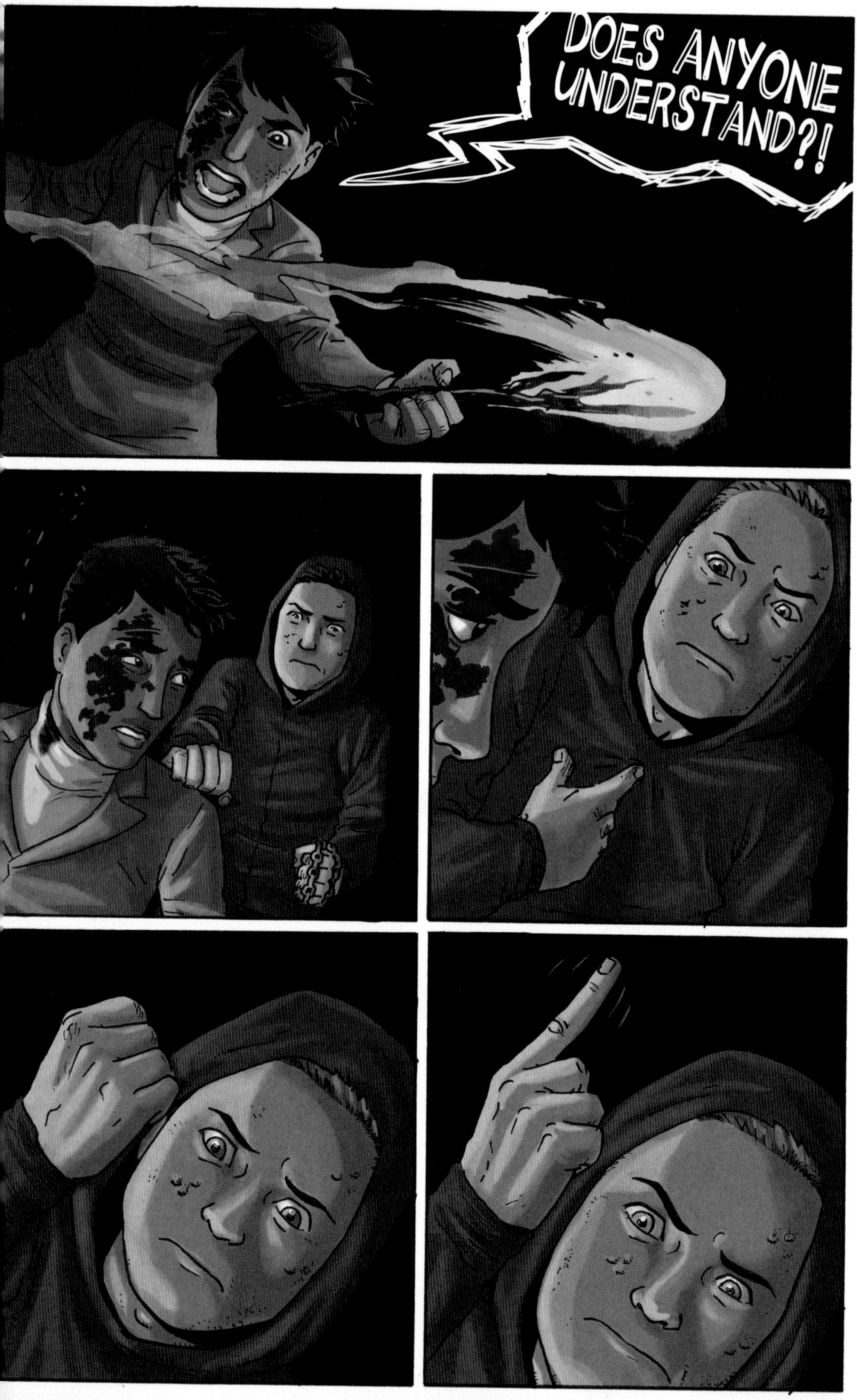
DOES ANYONE UNDERSTAND?!

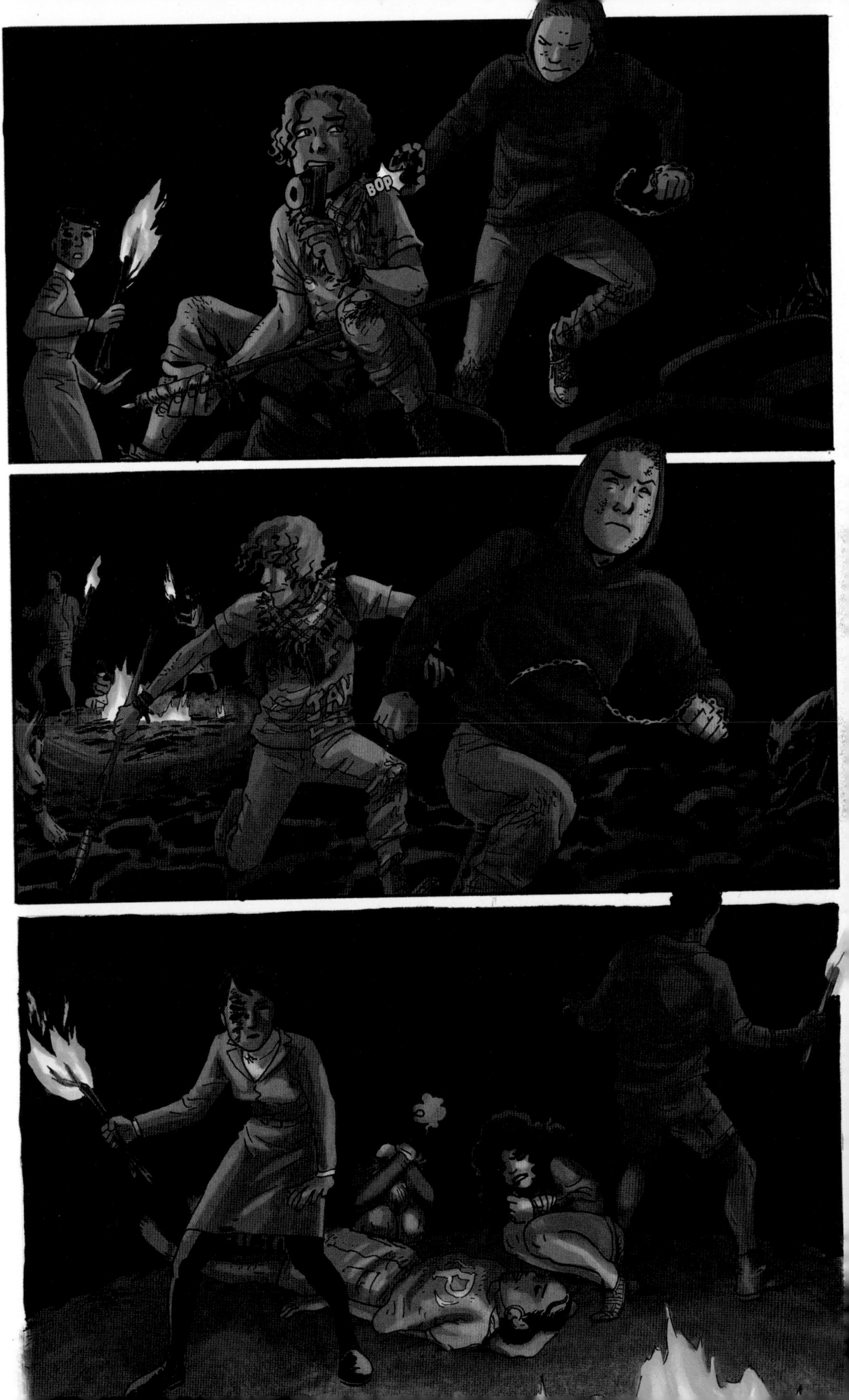
BOP

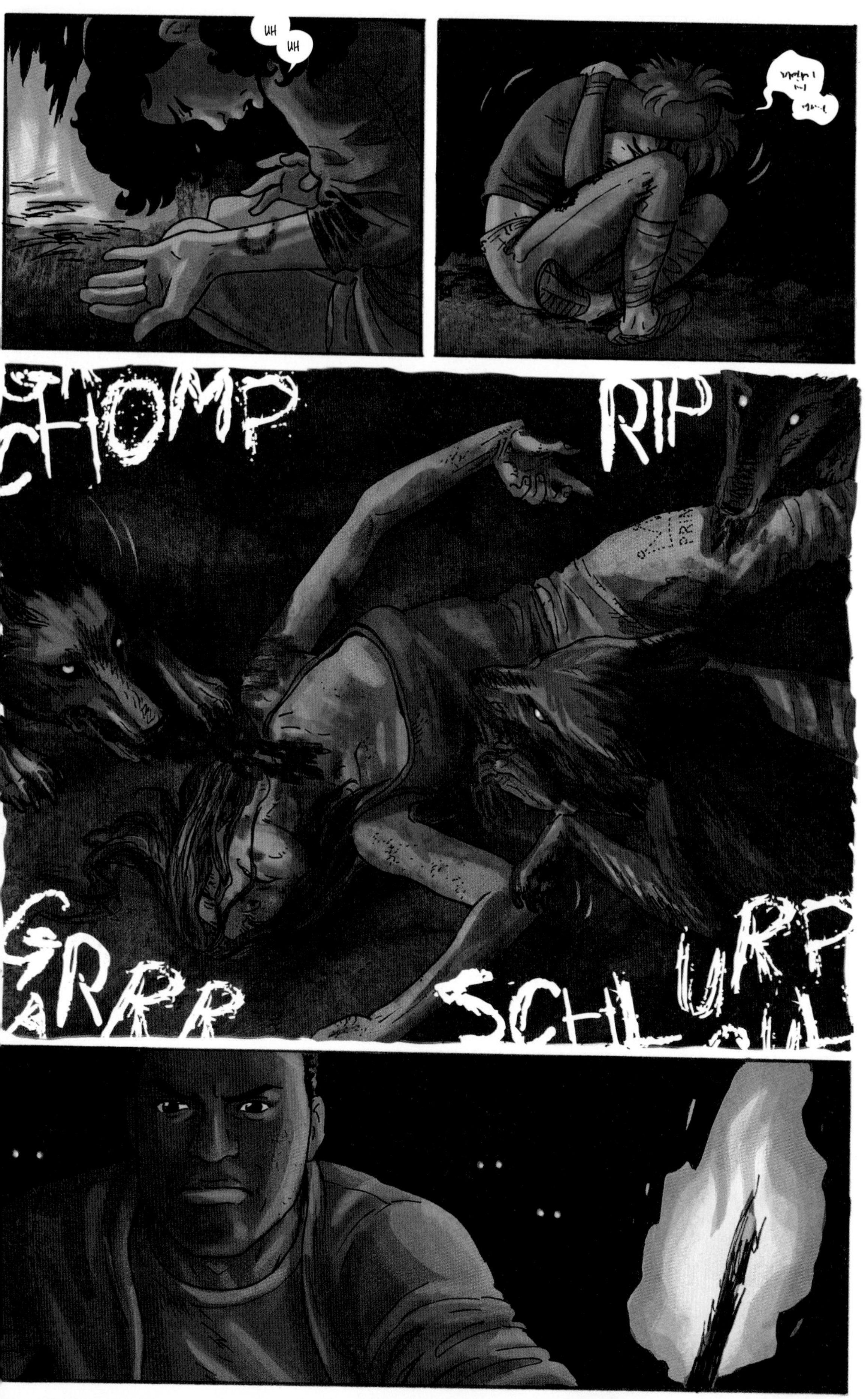
UH
UH
CHOMP
RIP
GRRR
SCHLURP

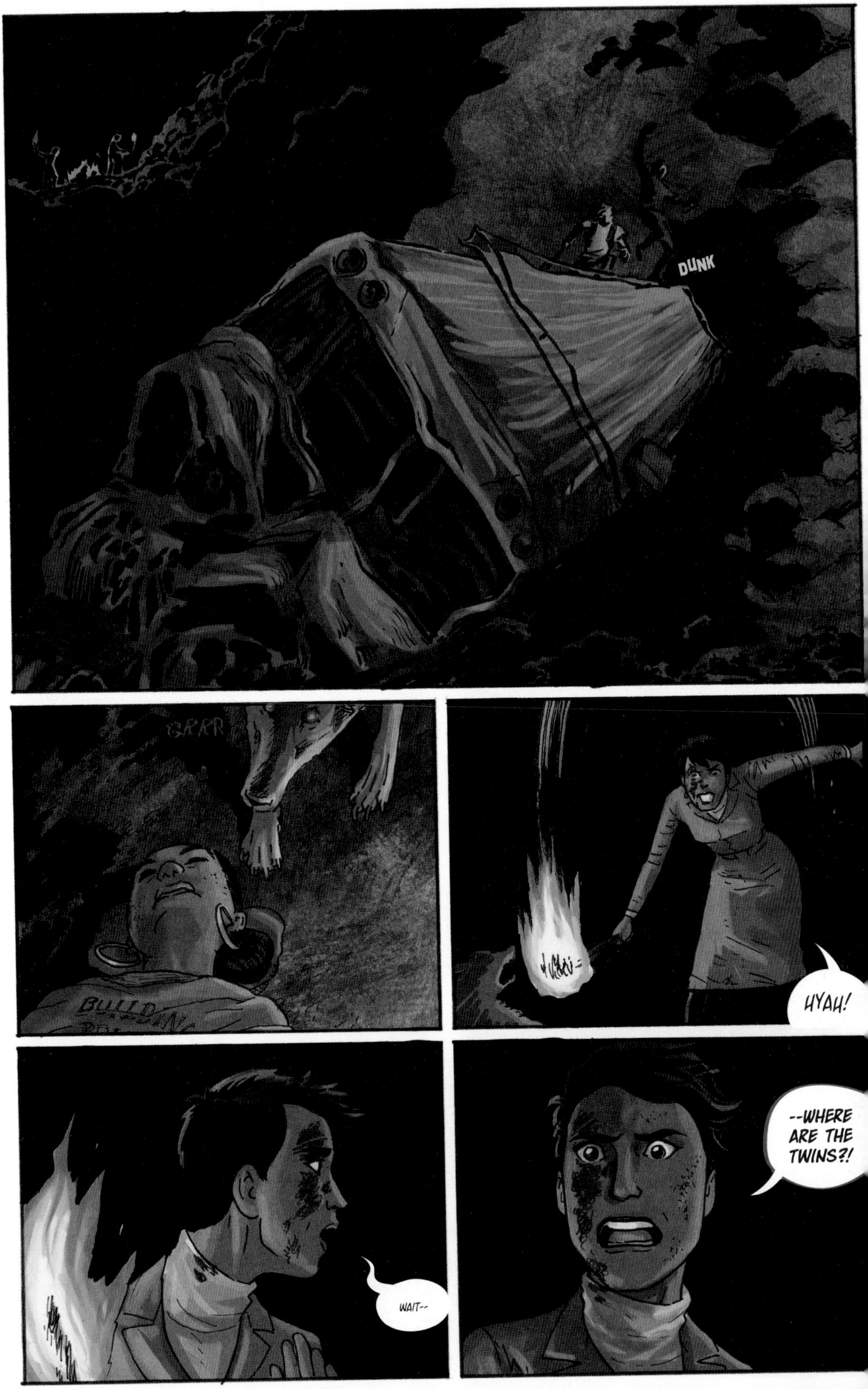
DUNK
GRRR
HYAH!
WAIT--
--WHERE ARE THE TWINS?!

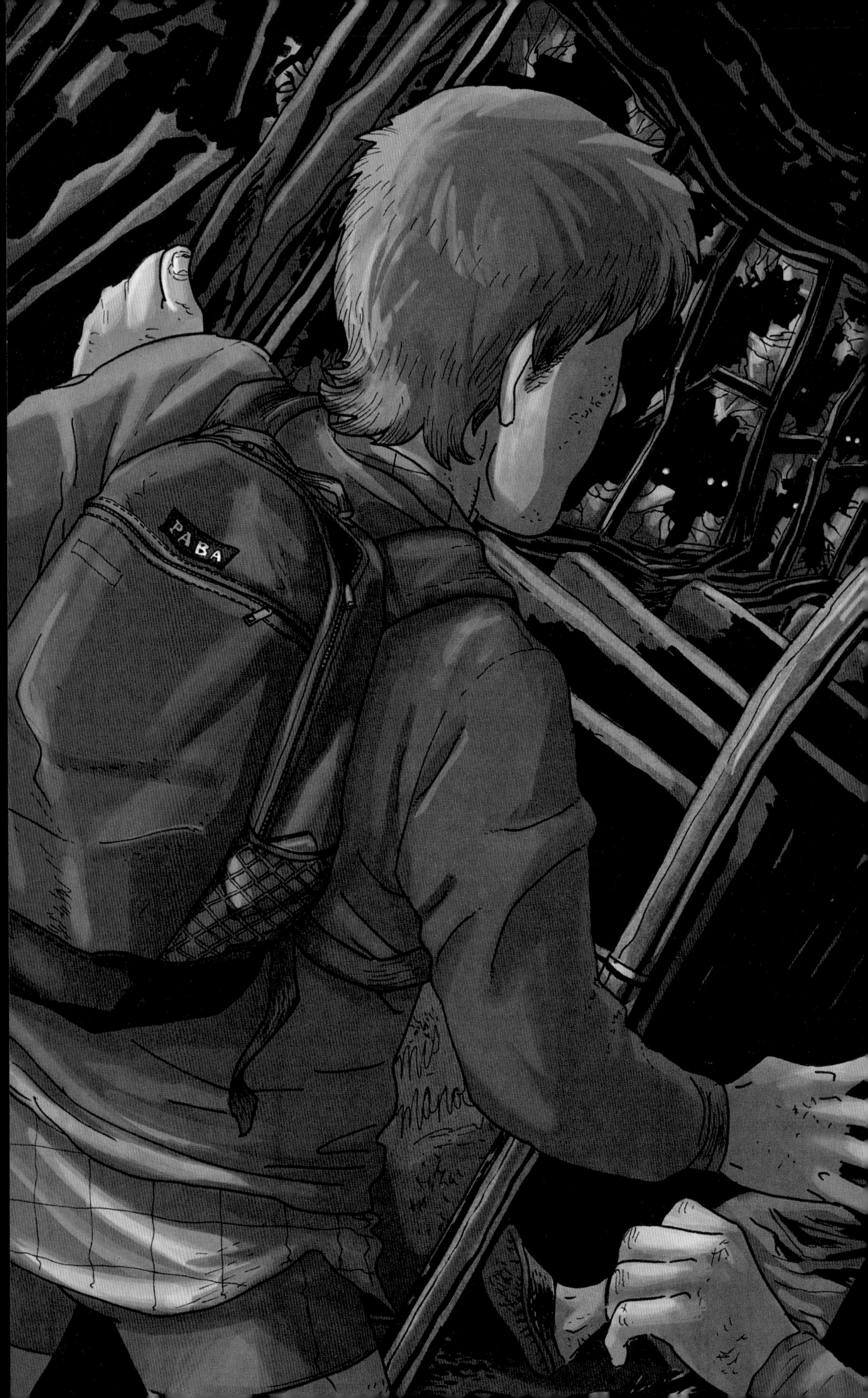
PABA

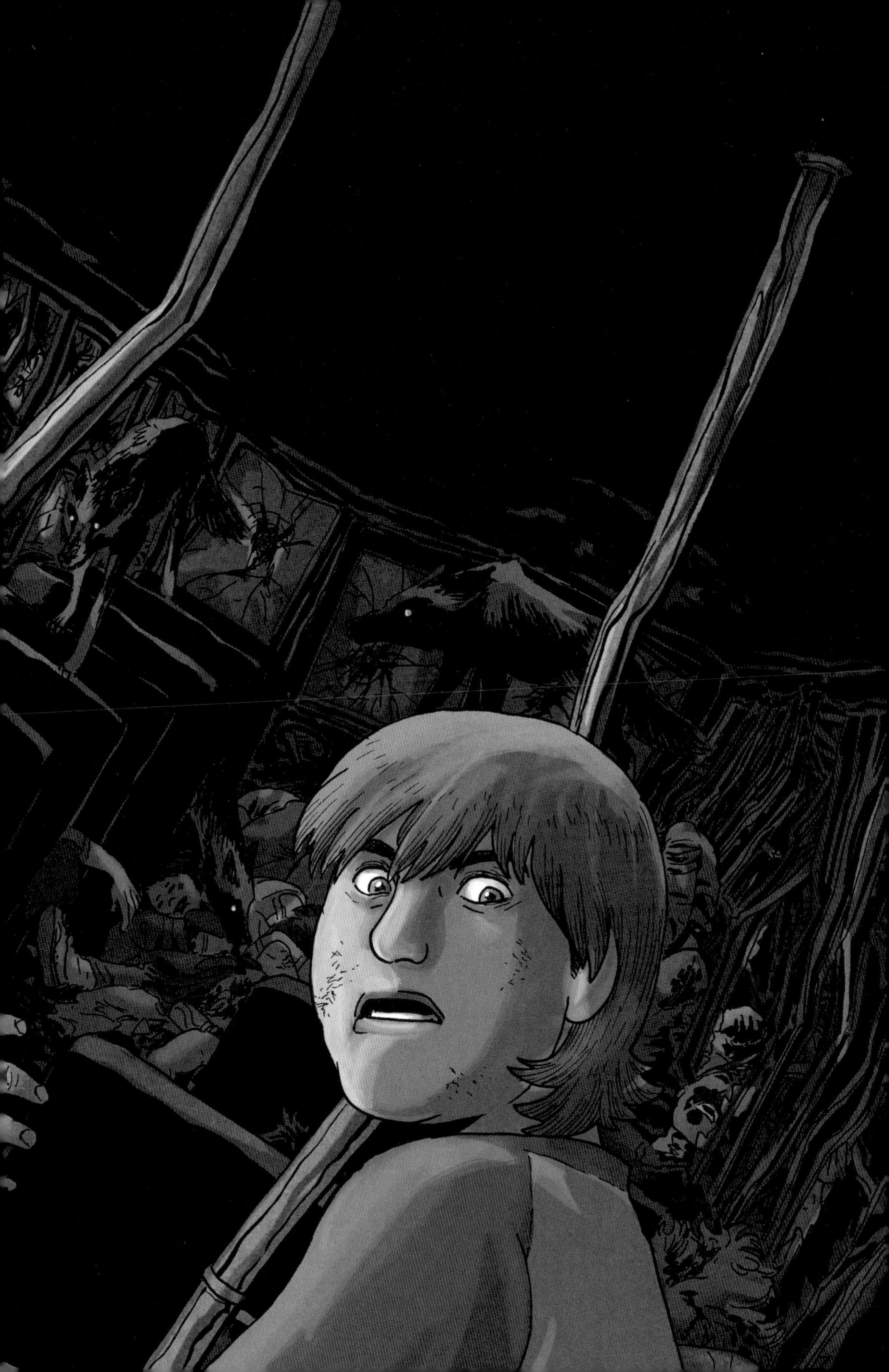

CHAPTER THREE

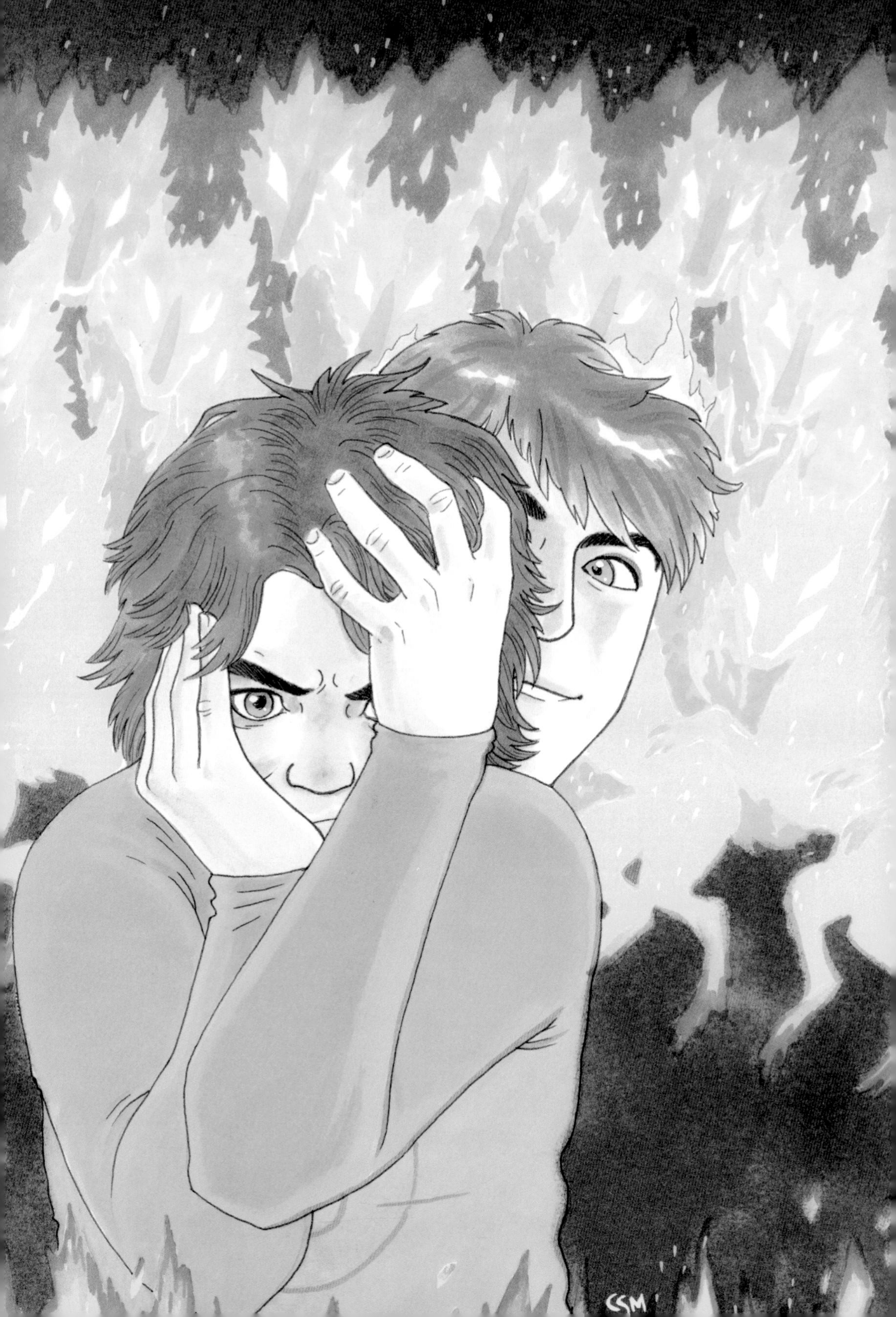
CSM

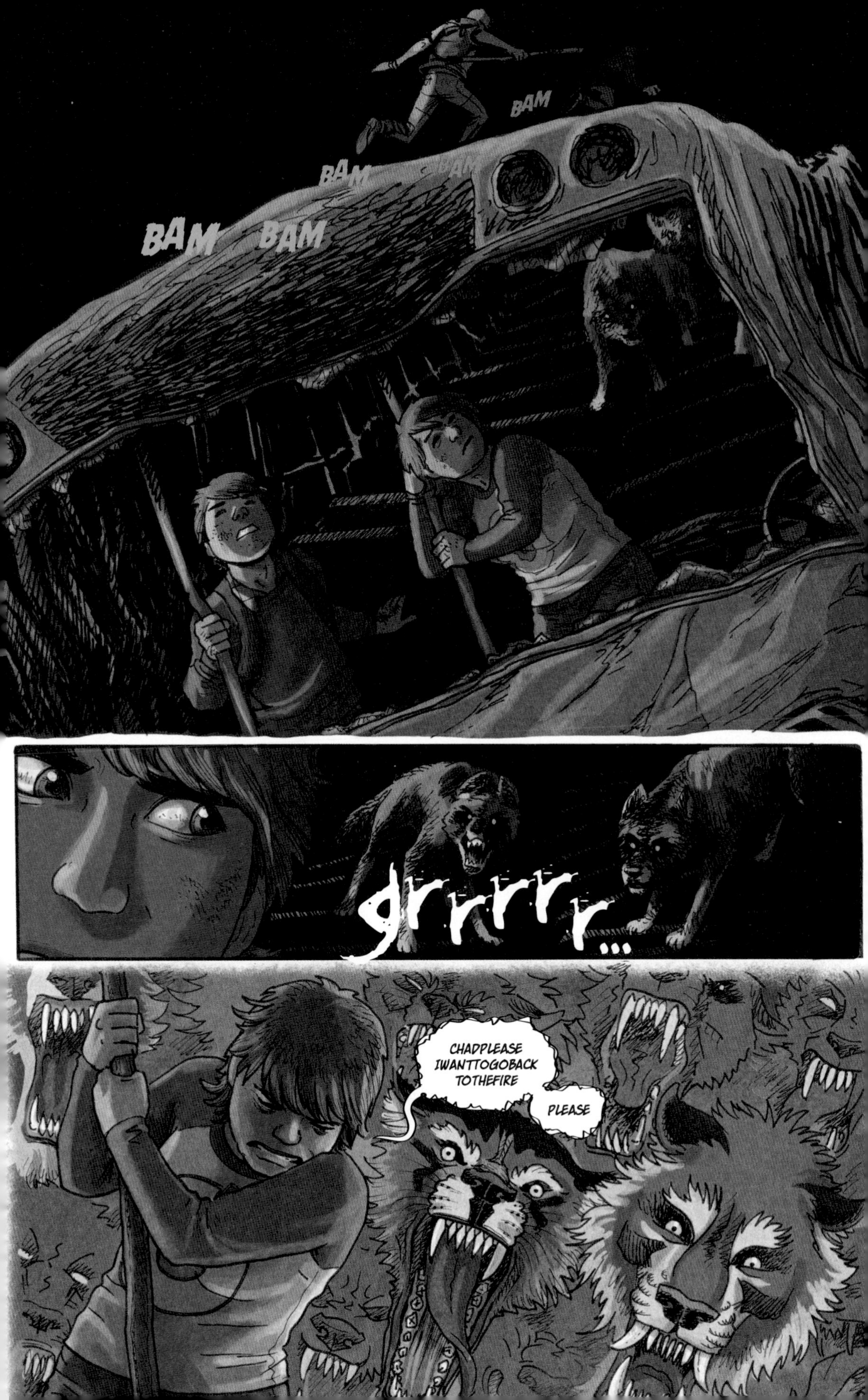
BAM
BAM
BAM
BAM
BAM
grrrrr...
CHADPLEASE IWANTTOGOBACK TOTHEFIRE
PLEASE

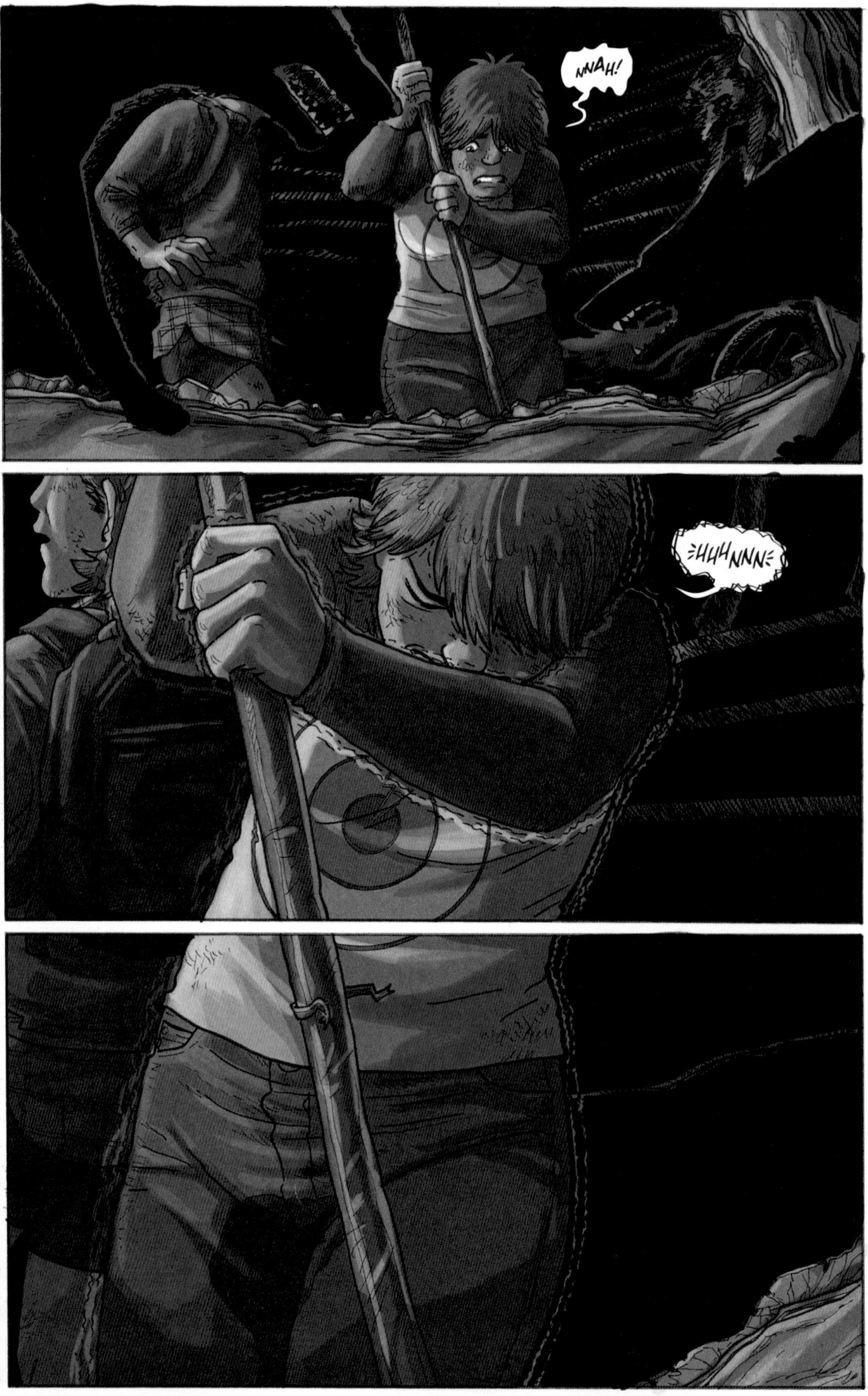
NNAH!
HUHNNN

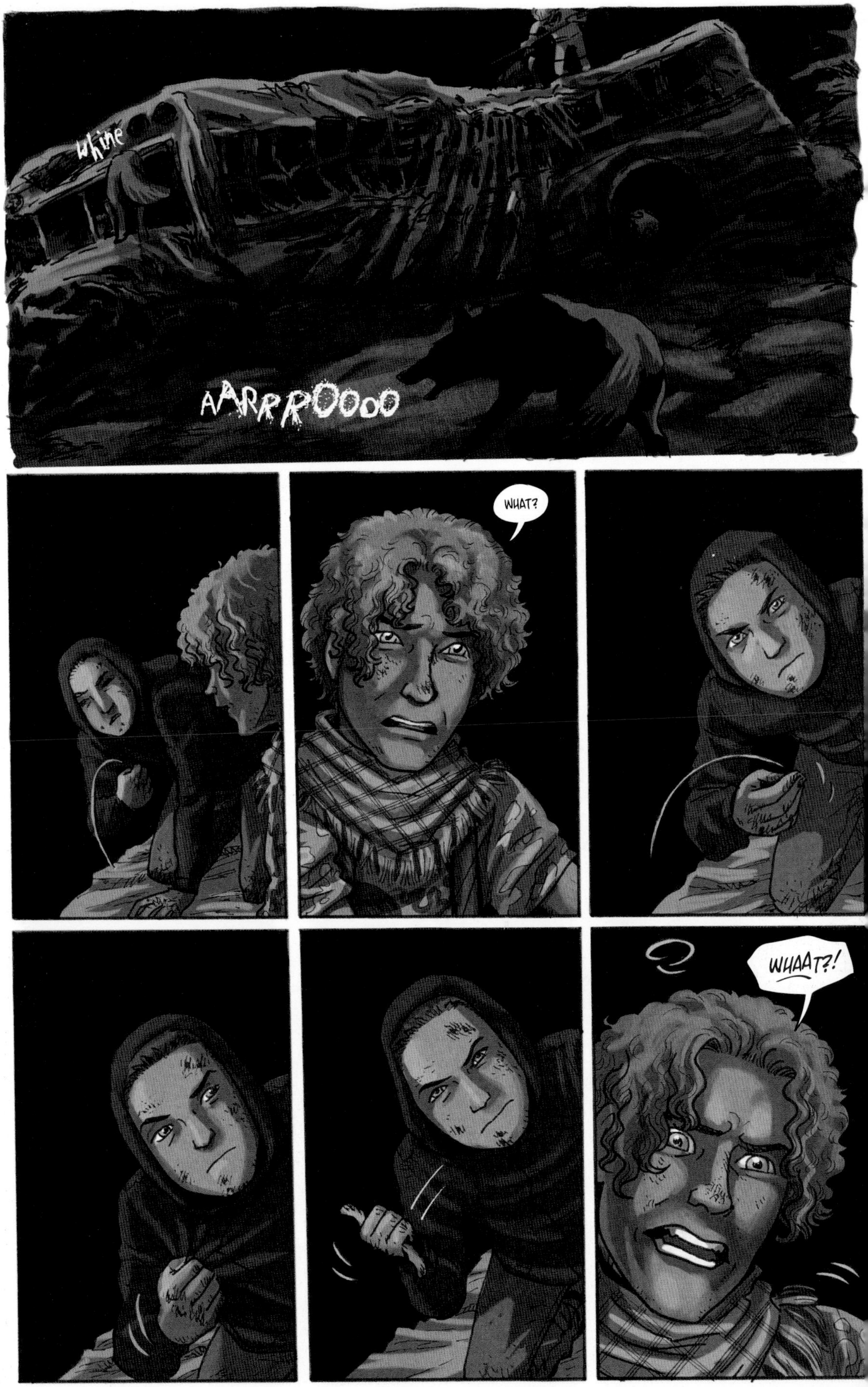
whine
AARRROOOO
WHAT?
WHAAT?!

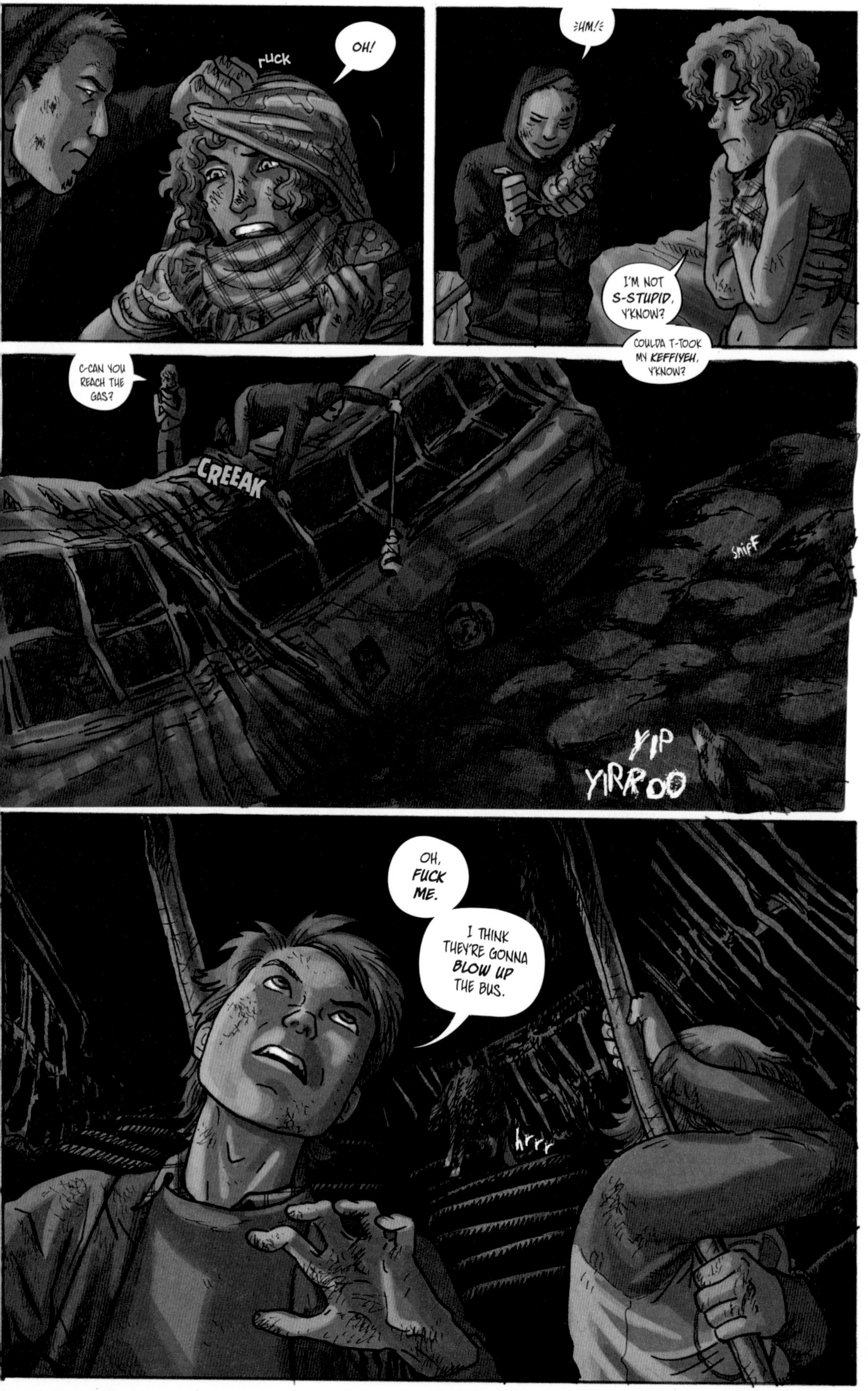

ruck
OH!
HM!
I'M NOT S-STUPID, Y'KNOW?
COULDA T-TOOK MY KEFFIYEH, Y'KNOW?
C-CAN YOU REACH THE GAS?
CREEAK
sniff
YIP YIRROO
OH, FUCK ME.
I THINK THEY'RE GONNA BLOW UP THE BUS.
hrrr

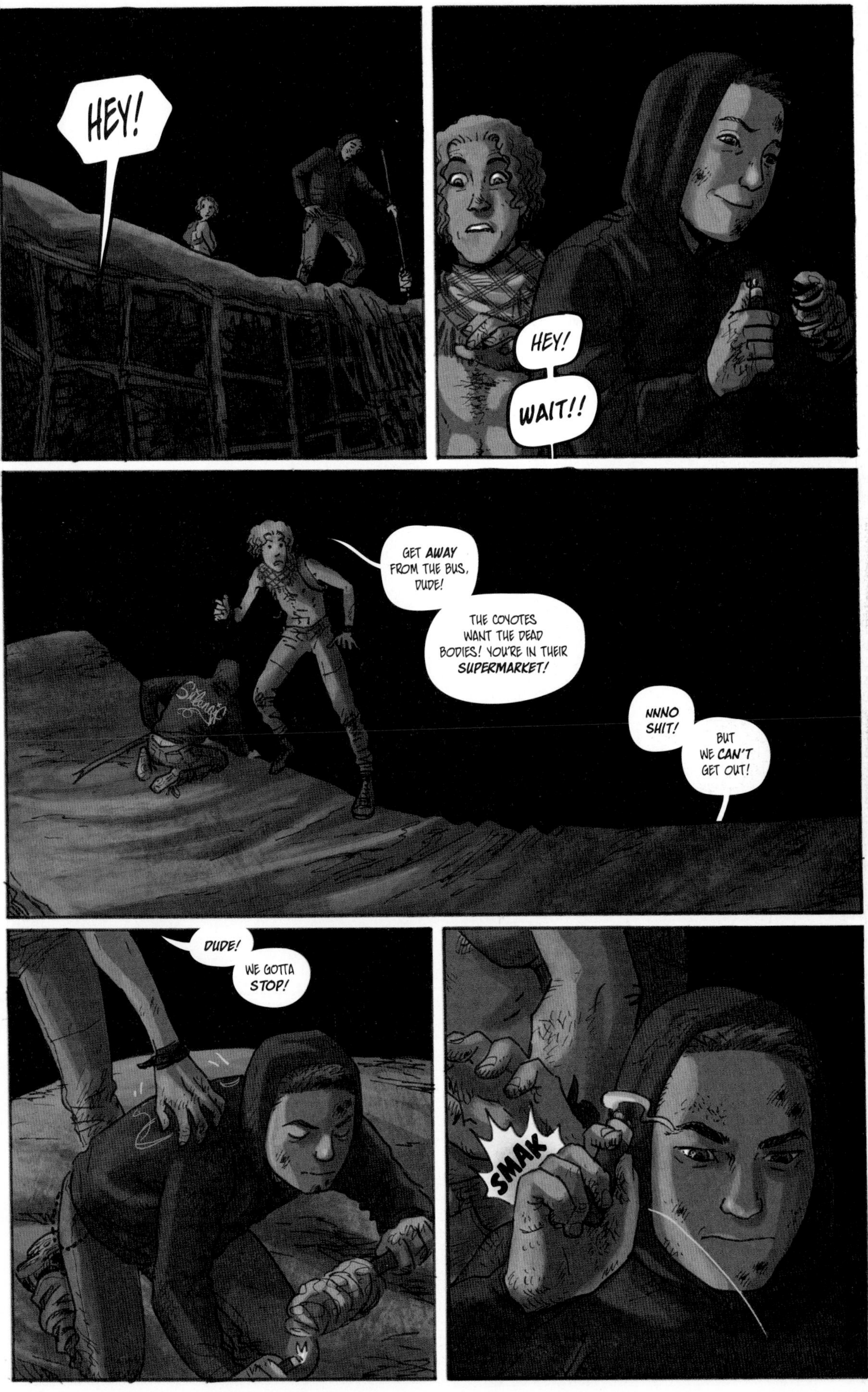
HEY!
HEY!
WAIT!!
GET AWAY FROM THE BUS, DUDE!
THE COYOTES WANT THE DEAD BODIES! YOU'RE IN THEIR SUPERMARKET!
NNNO SHIT!
BUT WE CAN'T GET OUT!
DUDE!
WE GOTTA STOP!
SMAK

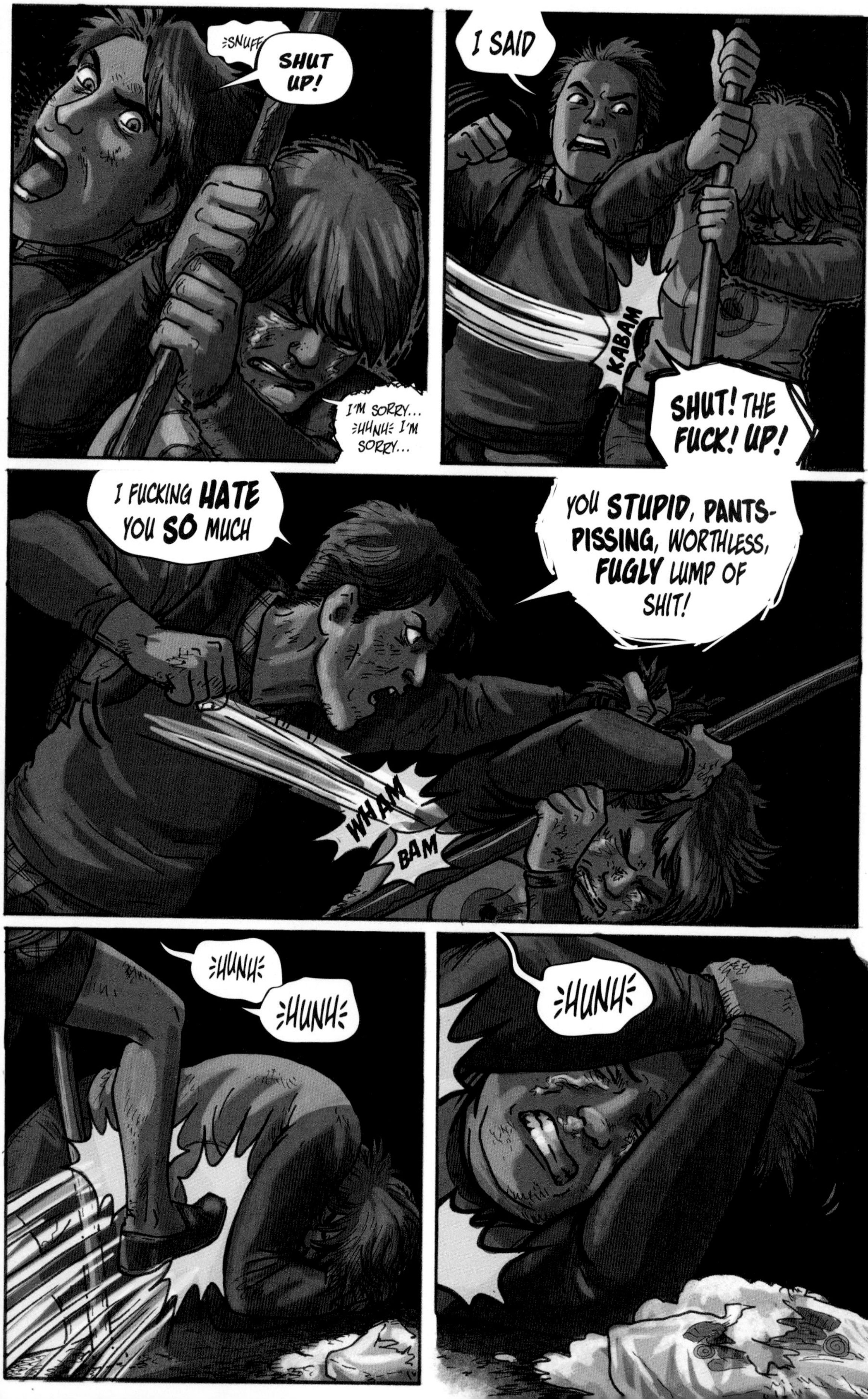

SNUFF
SHUT UP!
I'M SORRY... HUNH I'M SORRY...
I SAID
KABAM
SHUT! THE FUCK! UP!
I FUCKING HATE YOU SO MUCH
YOU STUPID, PANTS-PISSING, WORTHLESS, FUGLY LUMP OF SHIT!
WHAM
BAM
HUNH
HUNH
HUNH

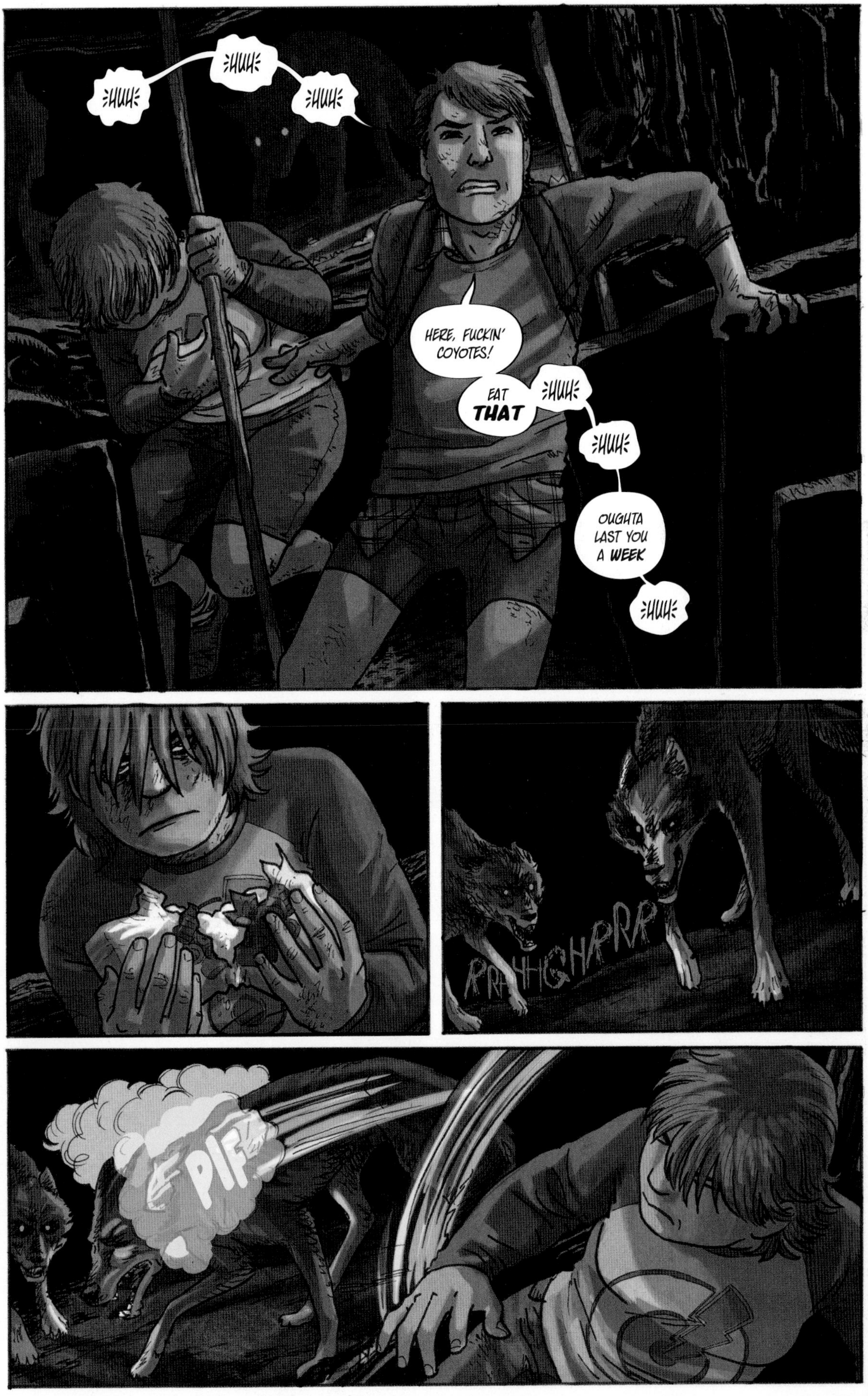
HUH
HUH
HUH
HERE, FUCKIN' COYOTES!
EAT THAT
HUH
HUH
OUGHTA LAST YOU A WEEK
HUH
RRAHHGHRRR
PIF

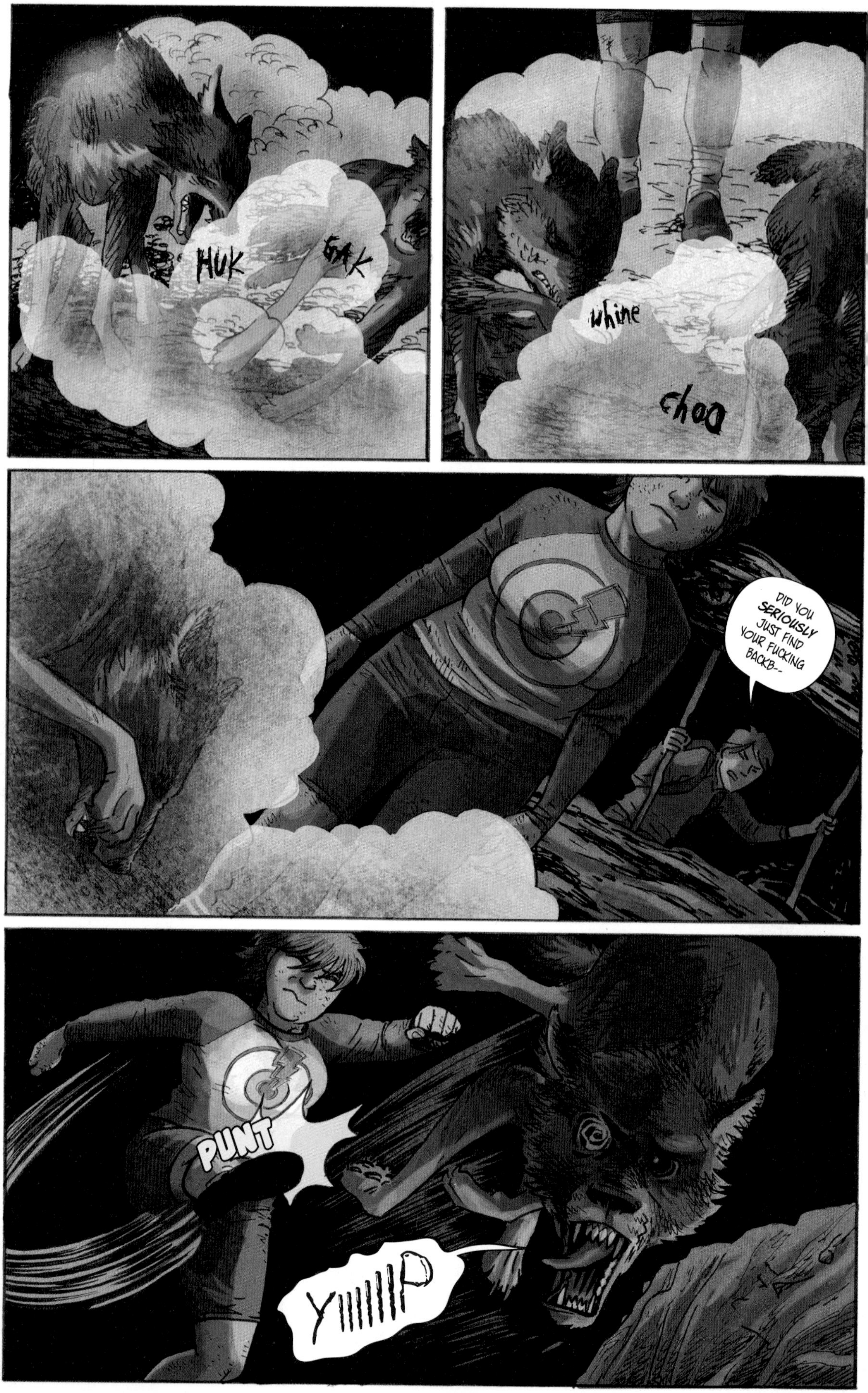
HUK
GAK
whine
choo
DID YOU SERIOUSLY JUST FIND YOUR FUCKING BACKB--
PUNT
YIIIIIIP

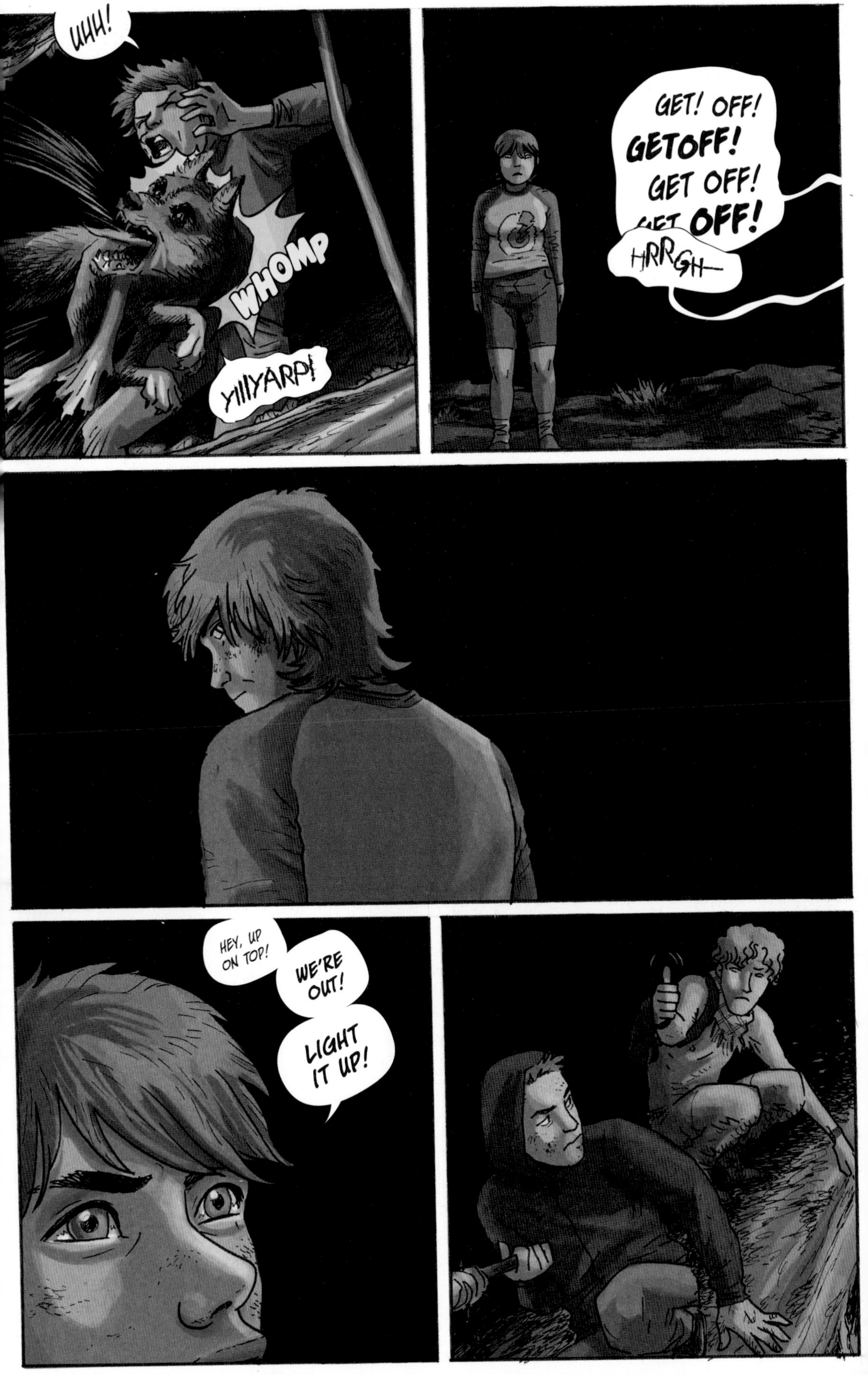
UHH!
WHOMP
YIIIYARP!
GET! OFF!
GETOFF!
GET OFF!
OFF!
HRRGH—
HEY, UP ON TOP!
WE'RE OUT!
LIGHT IT UP!

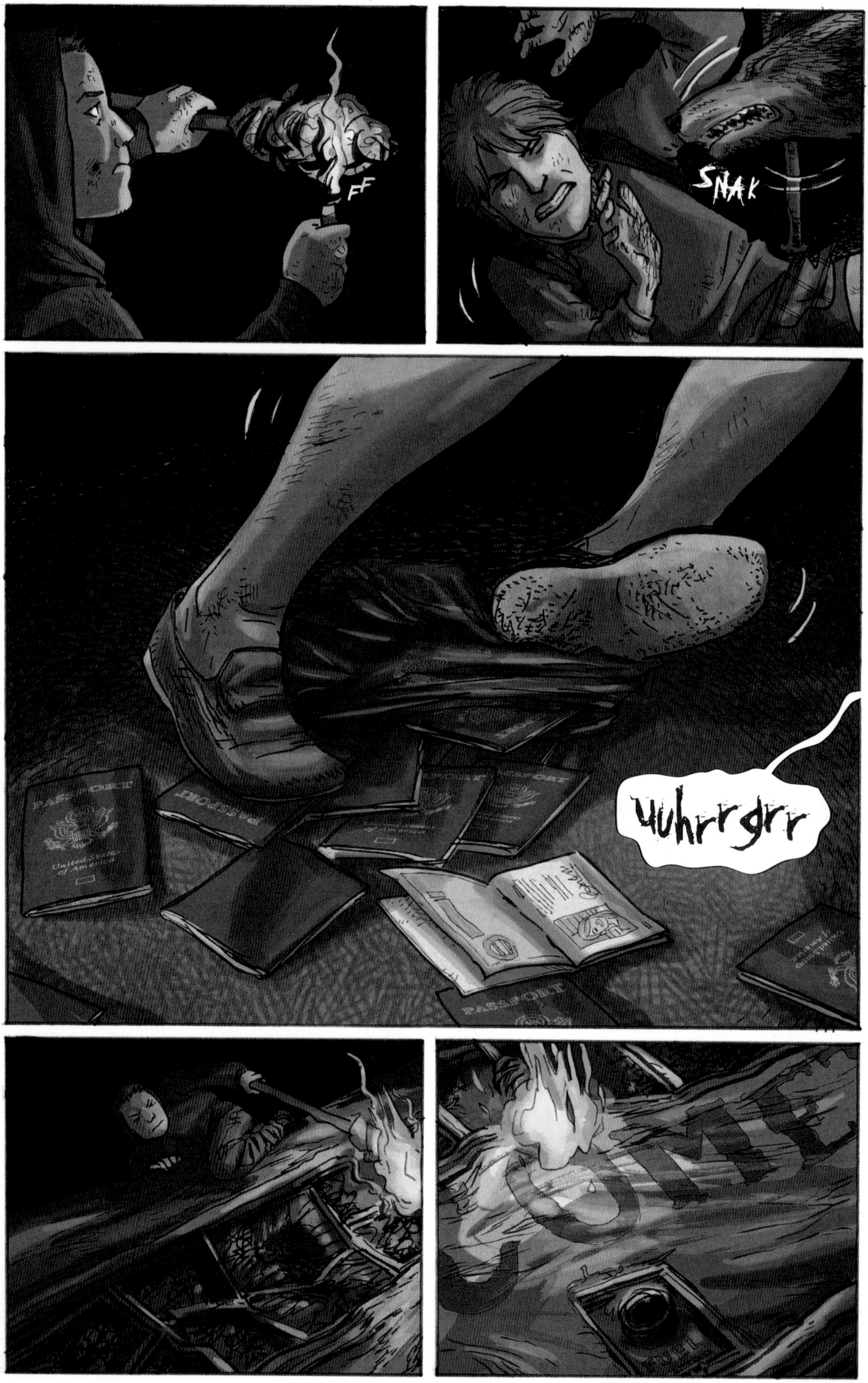
FF
SNAK
uuhrrgrr
PASSPORT
United States of America

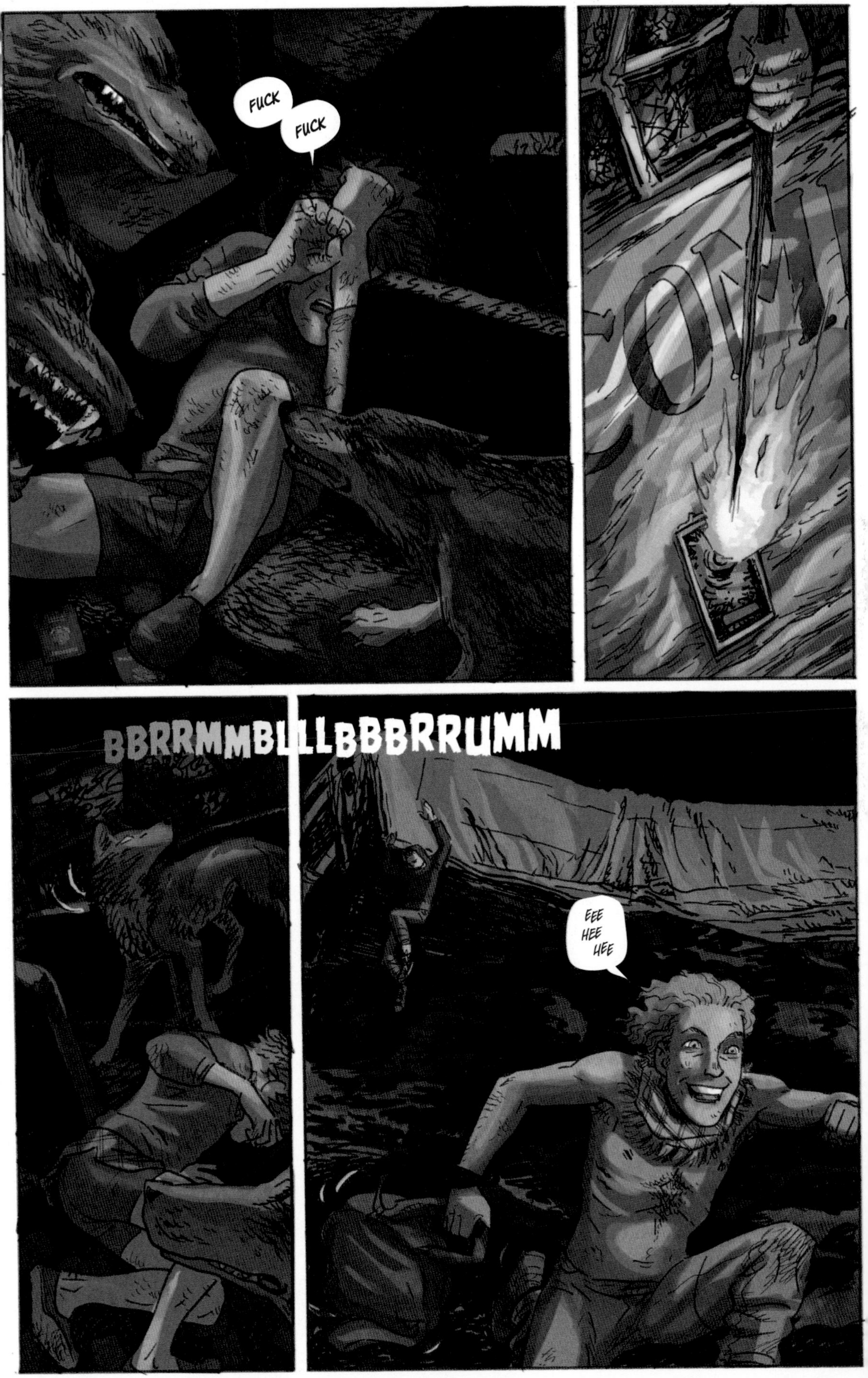
FUCK
FUCK
BBRRMMBLLLBBBRRUMM
EEE HEE HEE

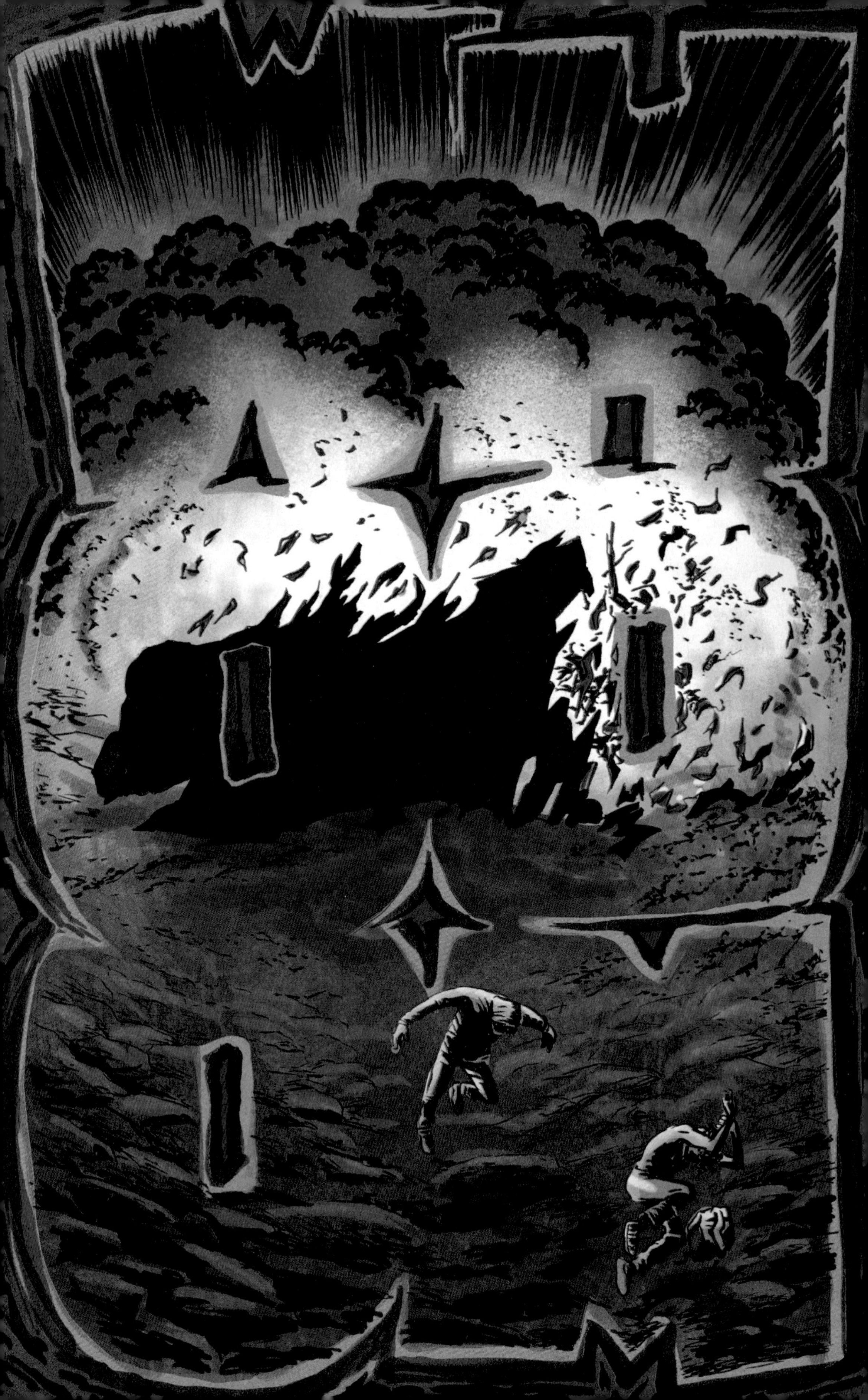

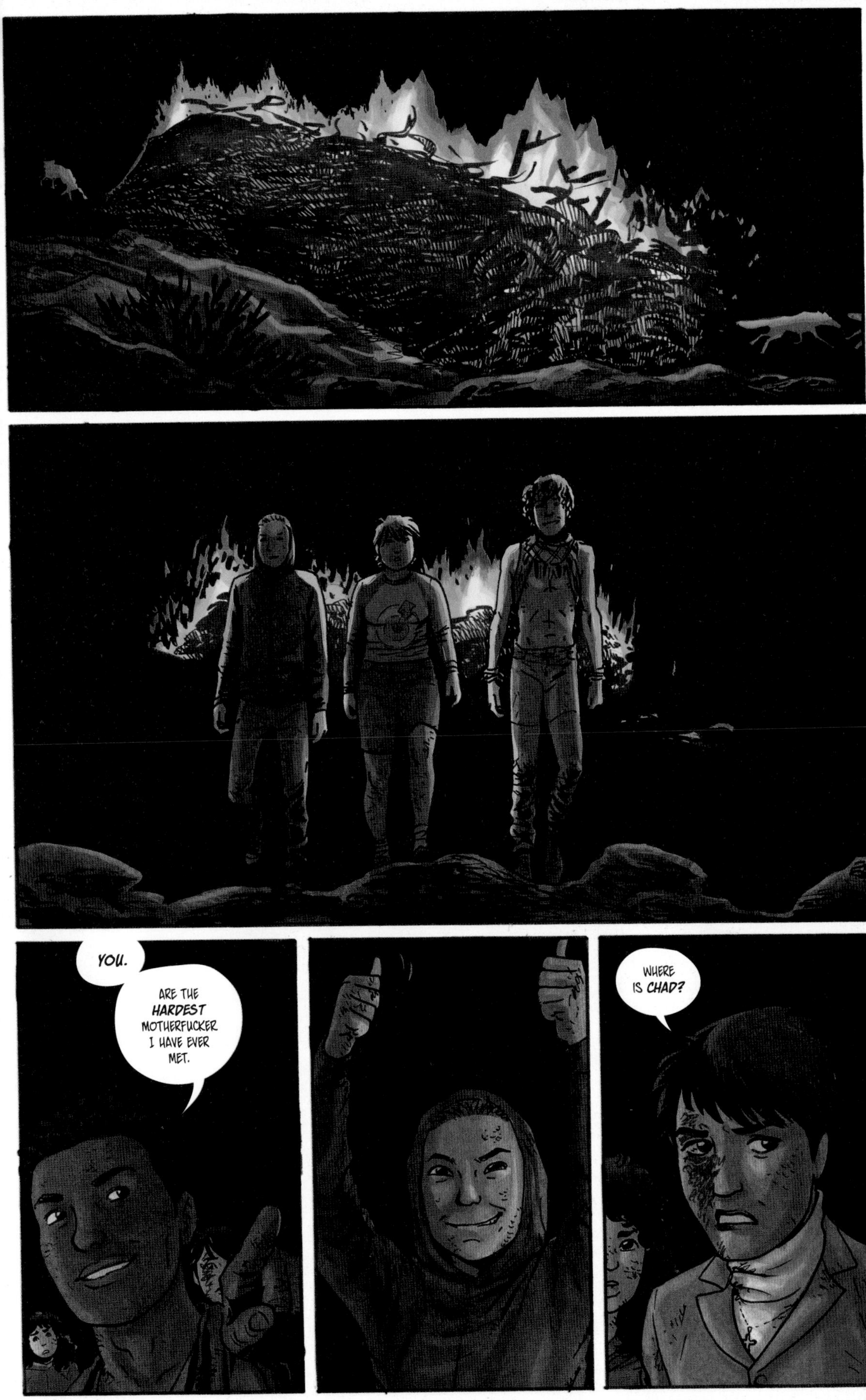
YOU.
ARE THE HARDEST MOTHERFUCKER I HAVE EVER MET.
WHERE IS CHAD?

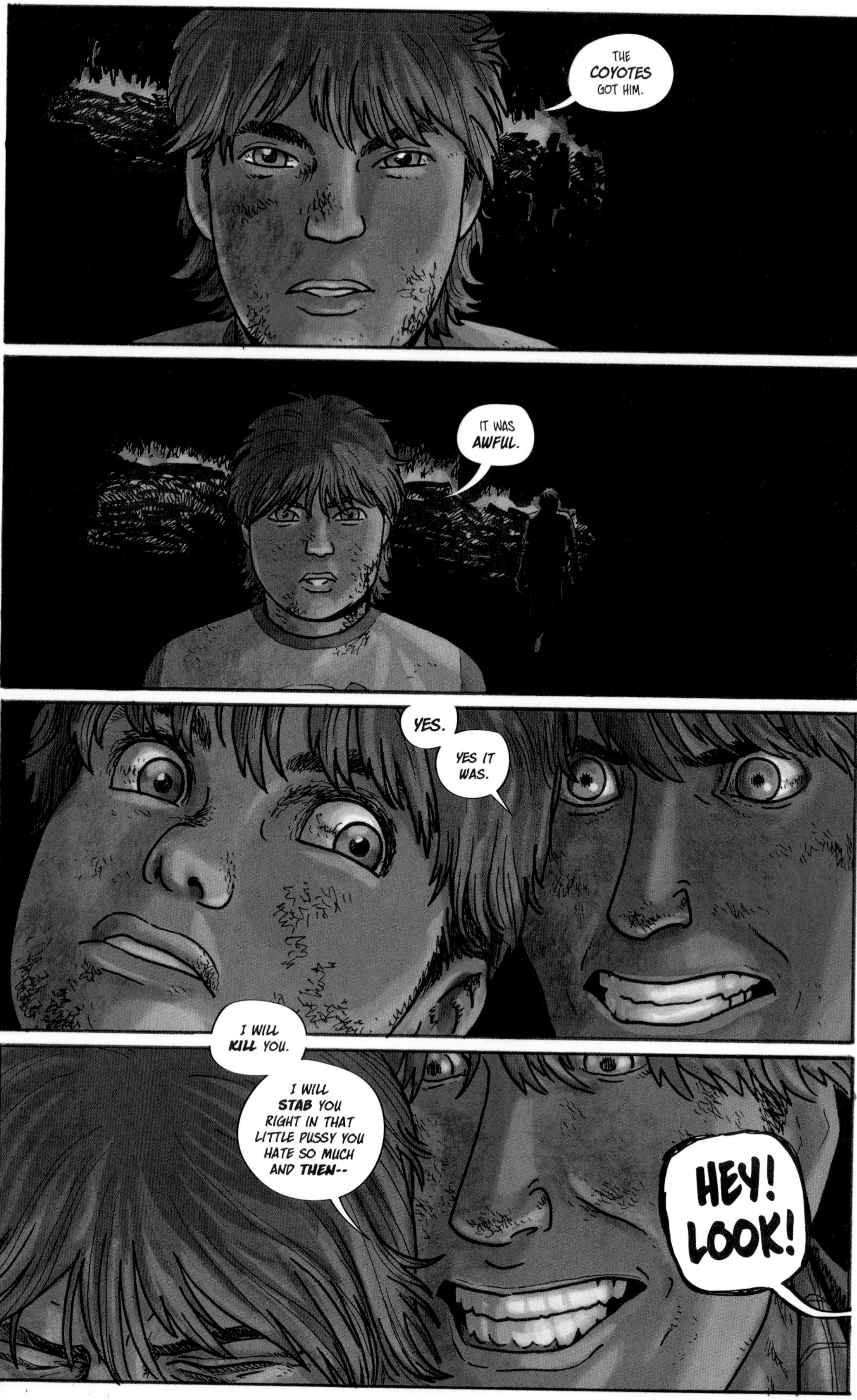
THE COYOTES GOT HIM.
IT WAS AWFUL.
YES.
YES IT WAS.
I WILL KILL YOU.
I WILL STAB YOU RIGHT IN THAT LITTLE PUSSY YOU HATE SO MUCH AND THEN--
HEY! LOOK!

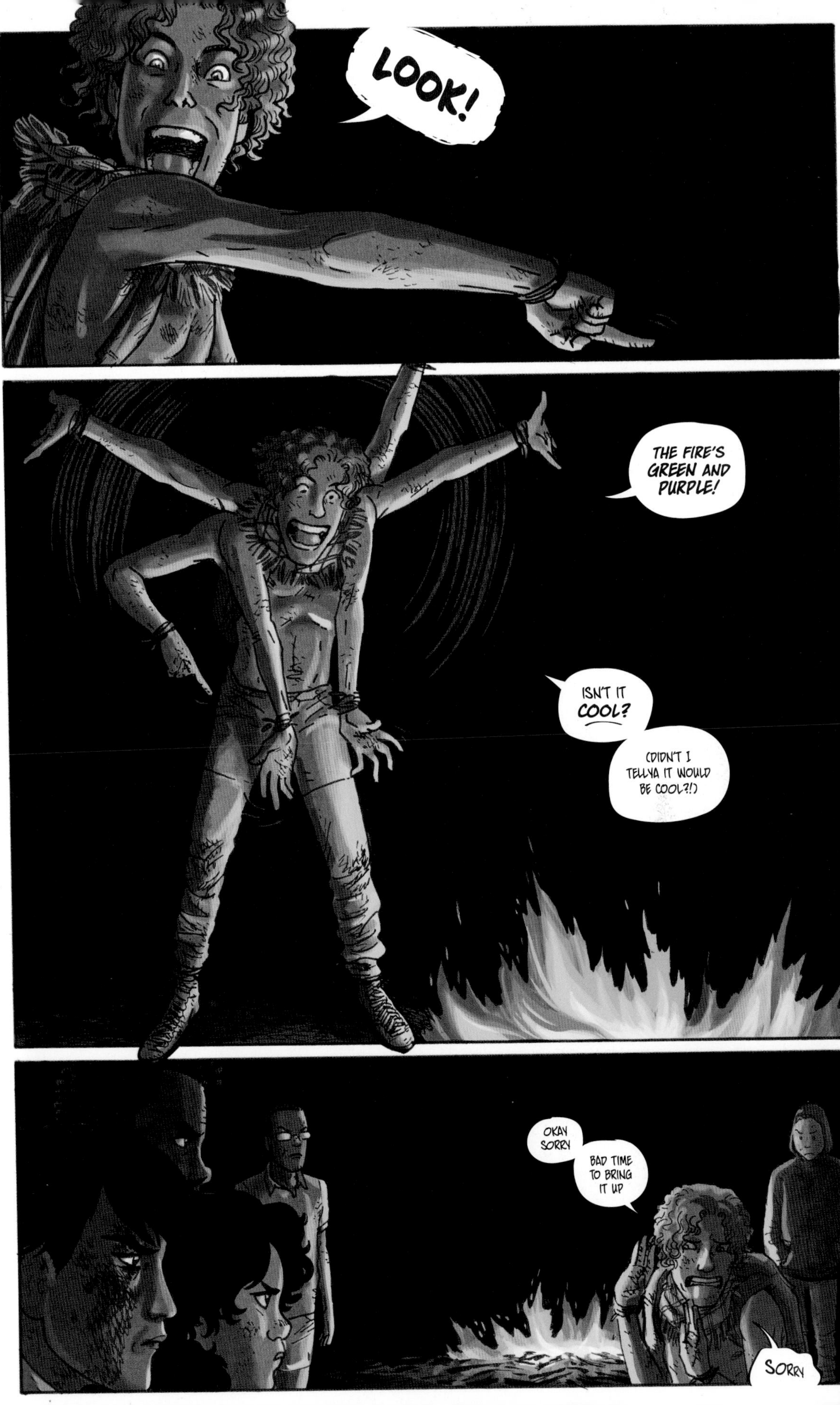
LOOK!
THE FIRE'S GREEN AND PURPLE!
ISN'T IT COOL?
(DIDN'T I TELLYA IT WOULD BE COOL?!)
OKAY SORRY
BAD TIME TO BRING IT UP
SORRY

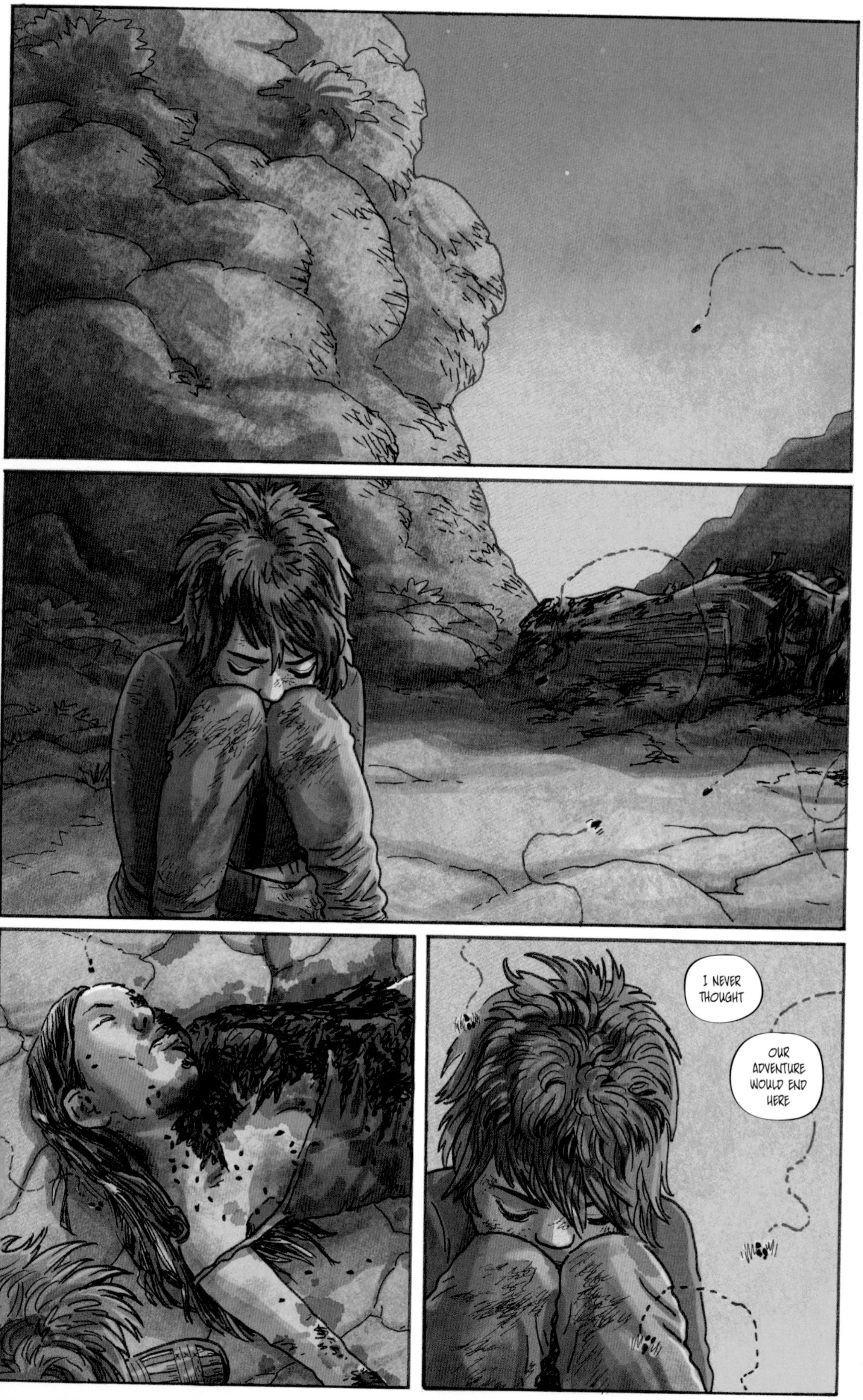
I NEVER THOUGHT
OUR ADVENTURE WOULD END HERE

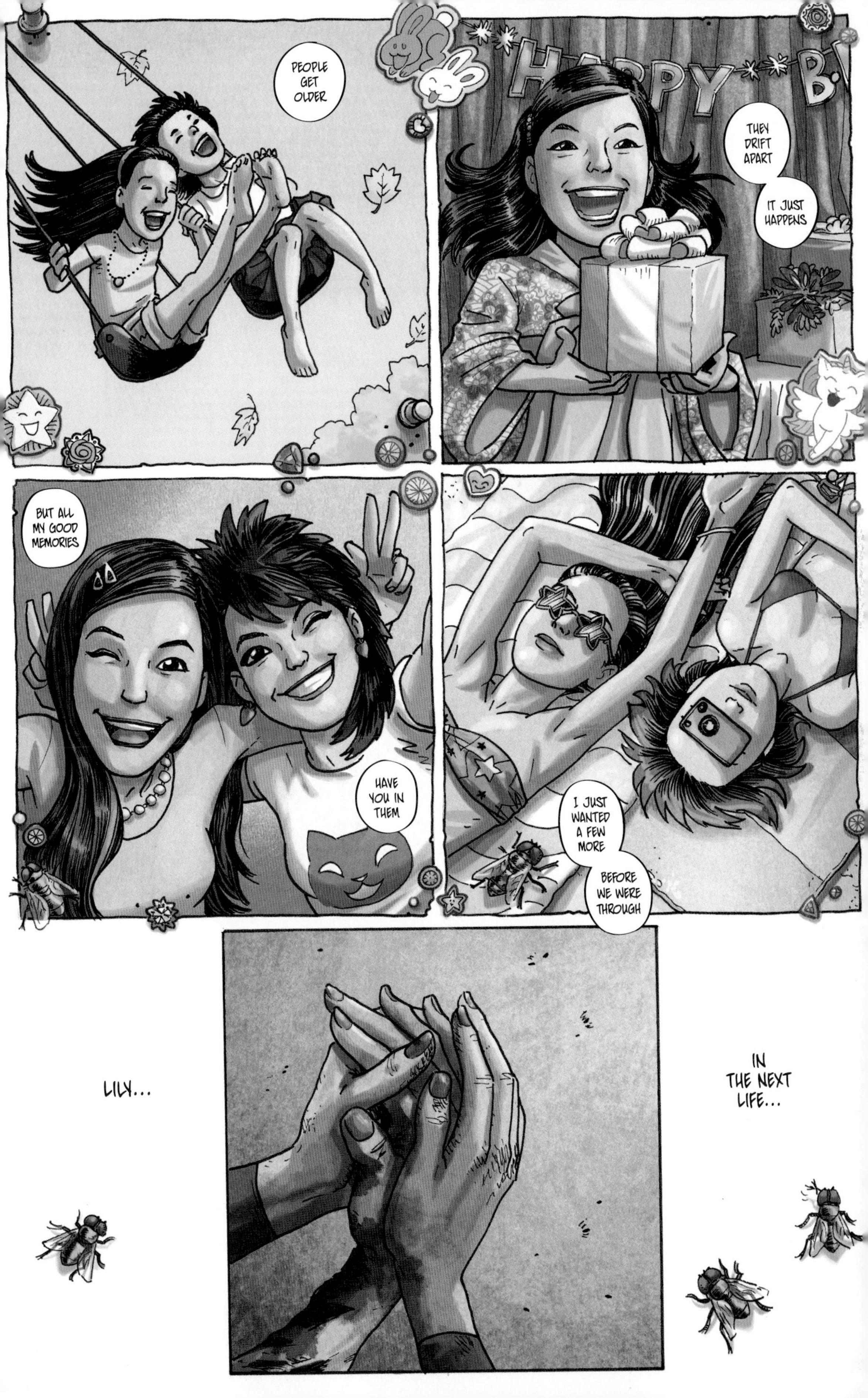
PEOPLE GET OLDER
THEY DRIFT APART
IT JUST HAPPENS
BUT ALL MY GOOD MEMORIES
HAVE YOU IN THEM
I JUST WANTED A FEW MORE
BEFORE WE WERE THROUGH
LILY...
IN THE NEXT LIFE...

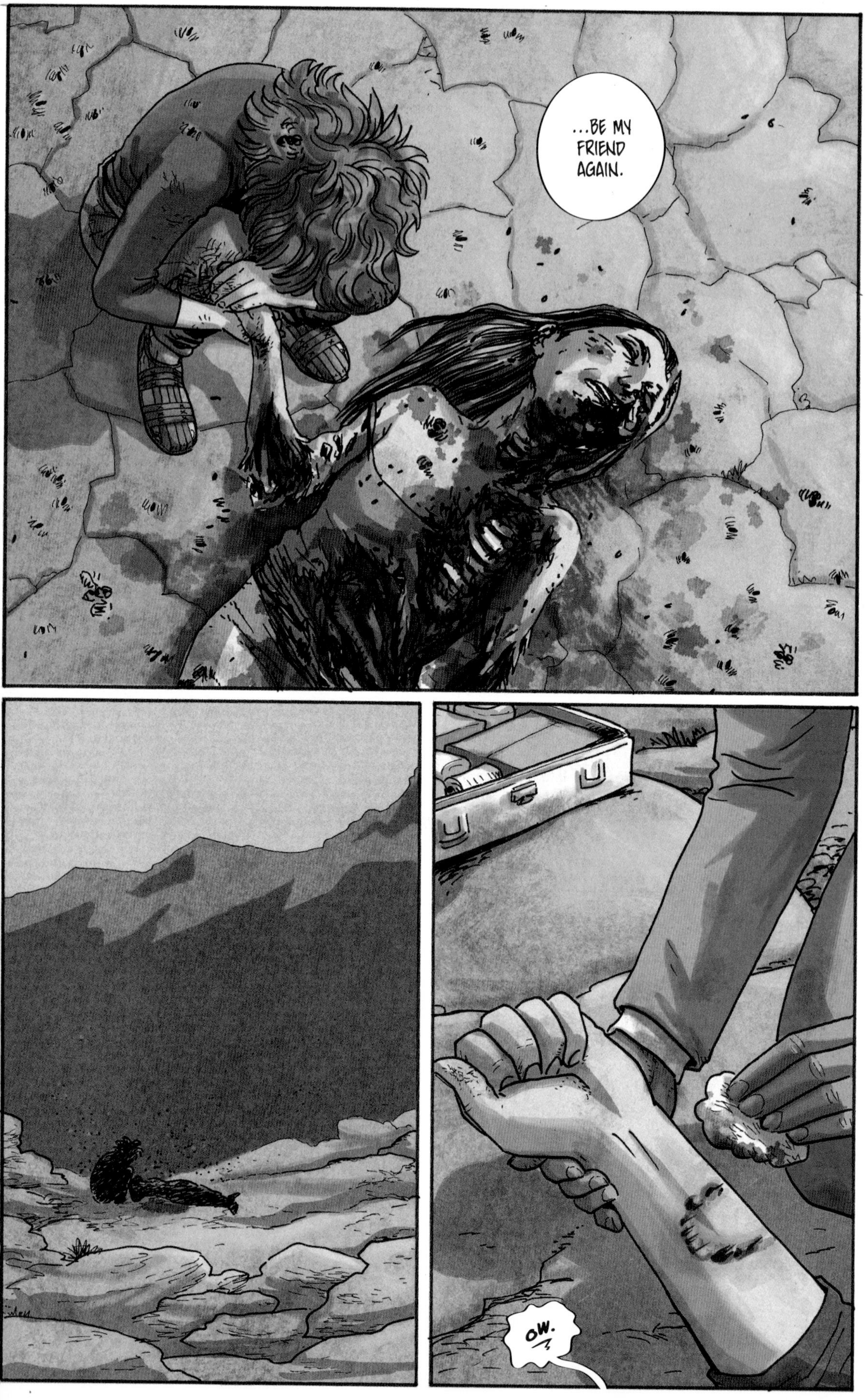
...BE MY FRIEND AGAIN.
OW.

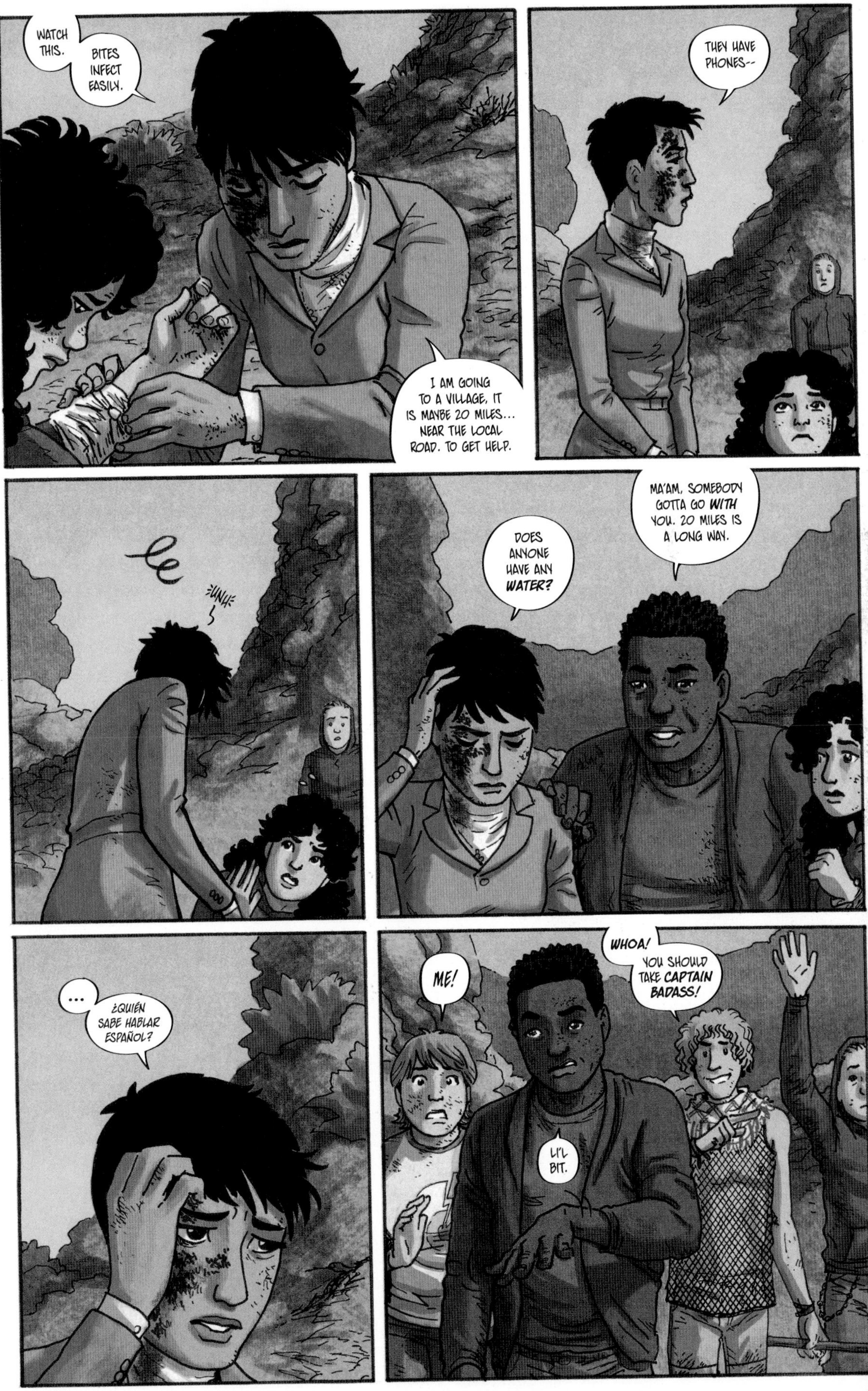
WATCH THIS.
BITES INFECT EASILY.
I AM GOING TO A VILLAGE, IT IS MAYBE 20 MILES... NEAR THE LOCAL ROAD. TO GET HELP.
THEY HAVE PHONES--
UNH
DOES ANYONE HAVE ANY WATER?
MA'AM, SOMEBODY GOTTA GO WITH YOU. 20 MILES IS A LONG WAY.
...
¿QUIÉN SABE HABLAR ESPAÑOL?
ME!
WHOA!
YOU SHOULD TAKE CAPTAIN BADASS!
LI'L BIT.

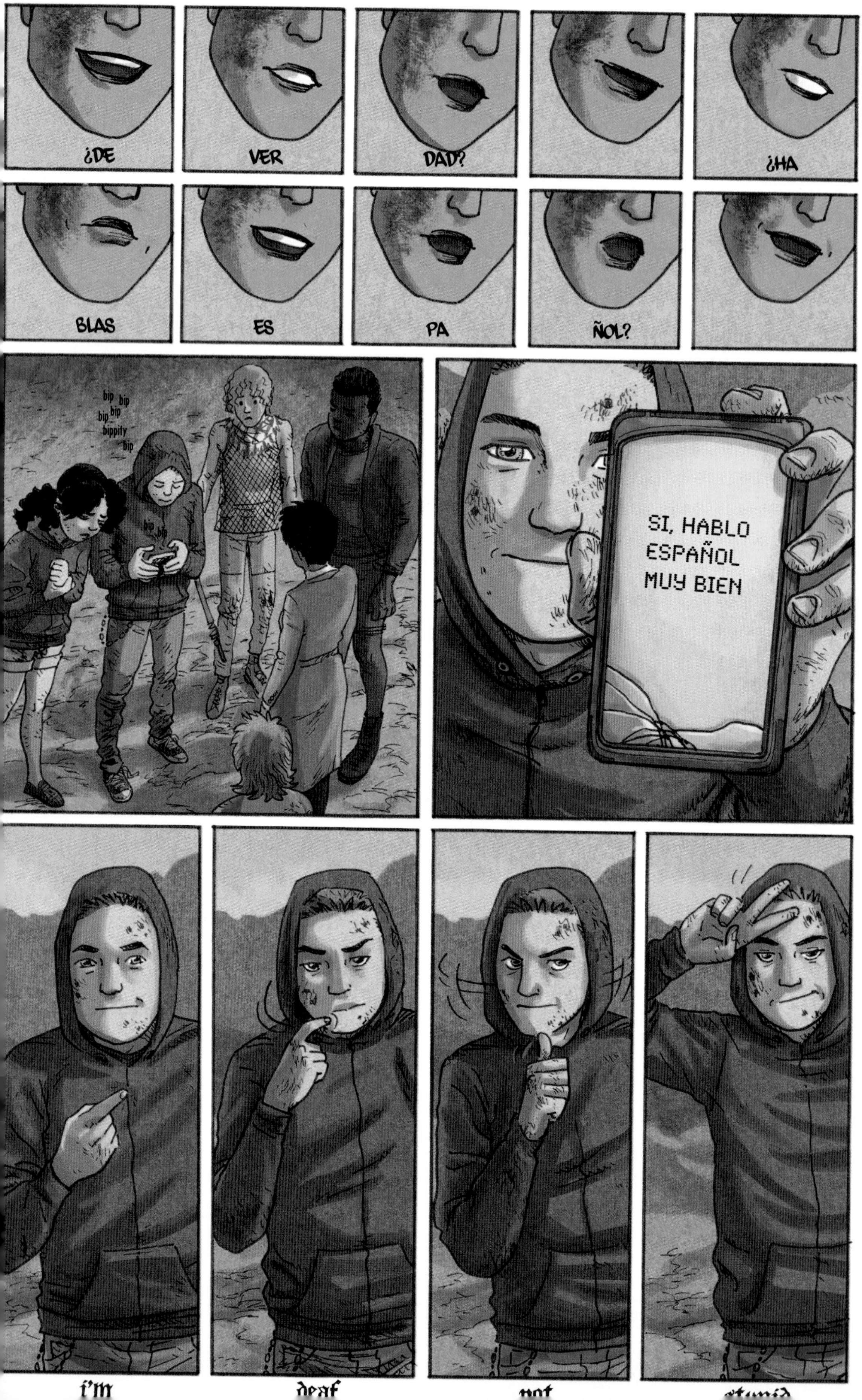

¿DE
VER
DAD?
¿HA
BLAS
ES
PA
ÑOL?
bip bip bip bip bippity bip
bip bip
SI, HABLO ESPAÑOL MUY BIEN
i'm
deaf
not

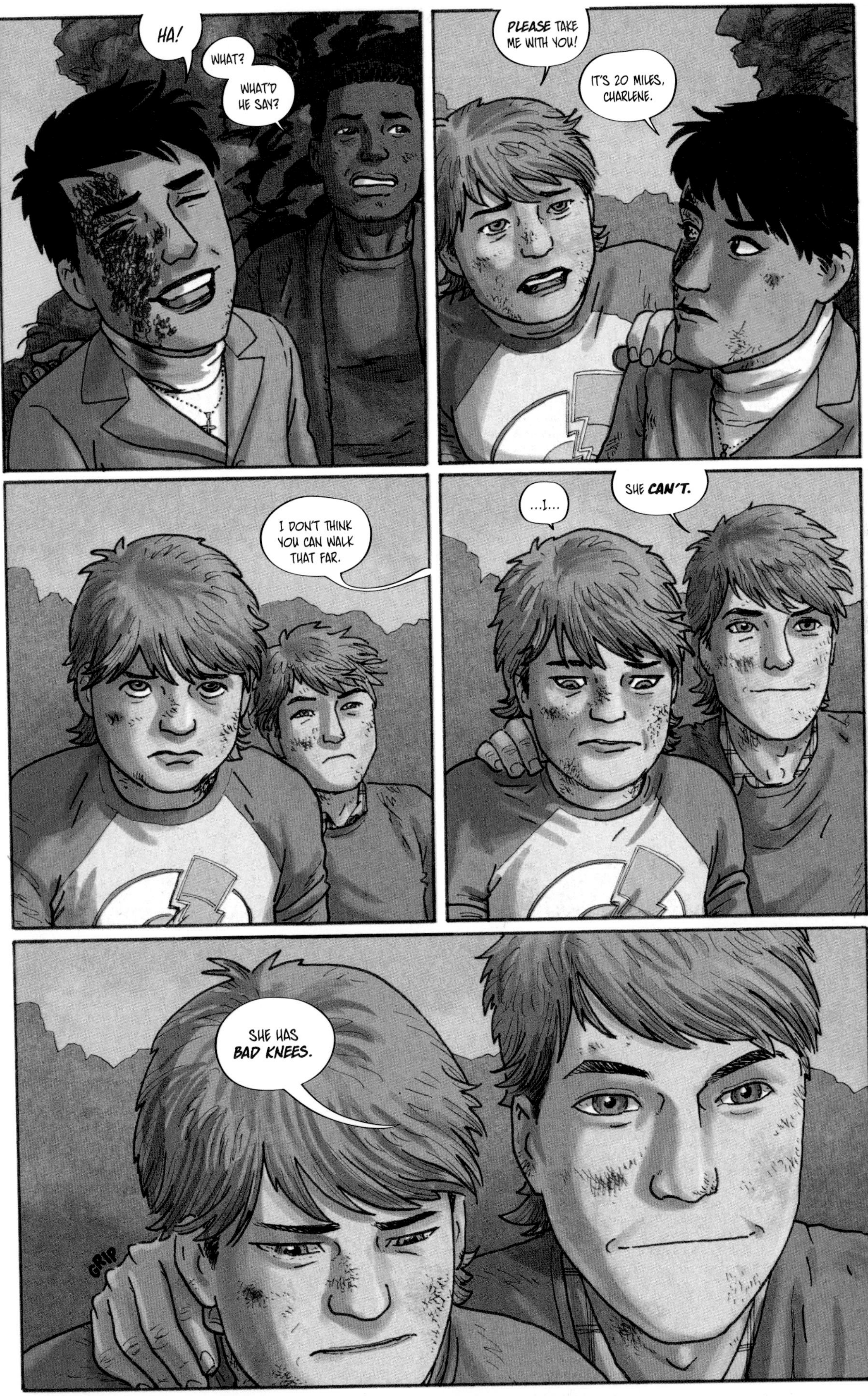
HA!
WHAT?
WHAT'D HE SAY?
PLEASE TAKE ME WITH YOU!
IT'S 20 MILES, CHARLENE.
I DON'T THINK YOU CAN WALK THAT FAR.
...I...
SHE CAN'T.
SHE HAS BAD KNEES.
GRIP

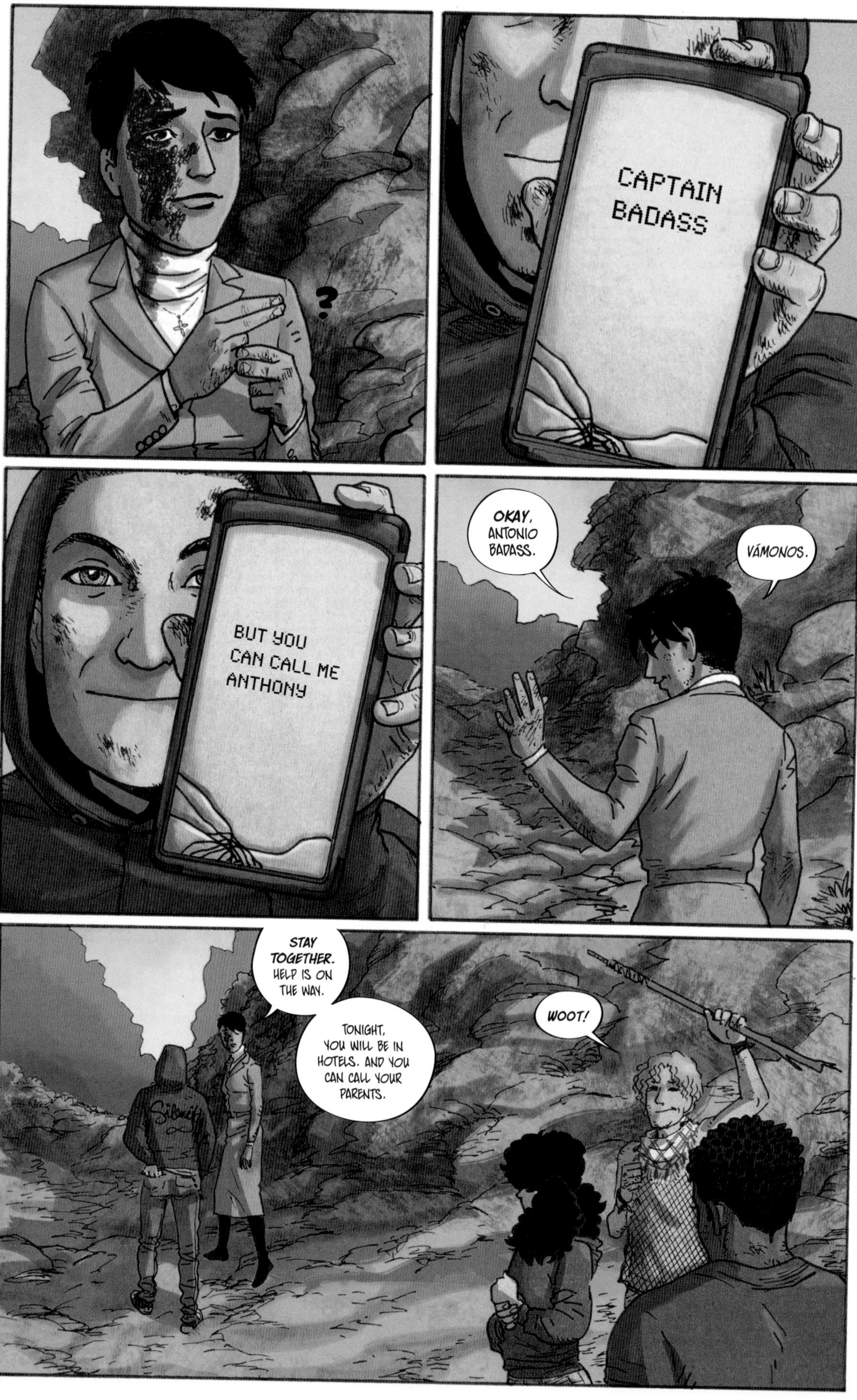
?
CAPTAIN BADASS
BUT YOU CAN CALL ME ANTHONY
OKAY, ANTONIO BADASS.
VÁMONOS.
STAY TOGETHER. HELP IS ON THE WAY.
TONIGHT, YOU WILL BE IN HOTELS. AND YOU CAN CALL YOUR PARENTS.
WOOT!

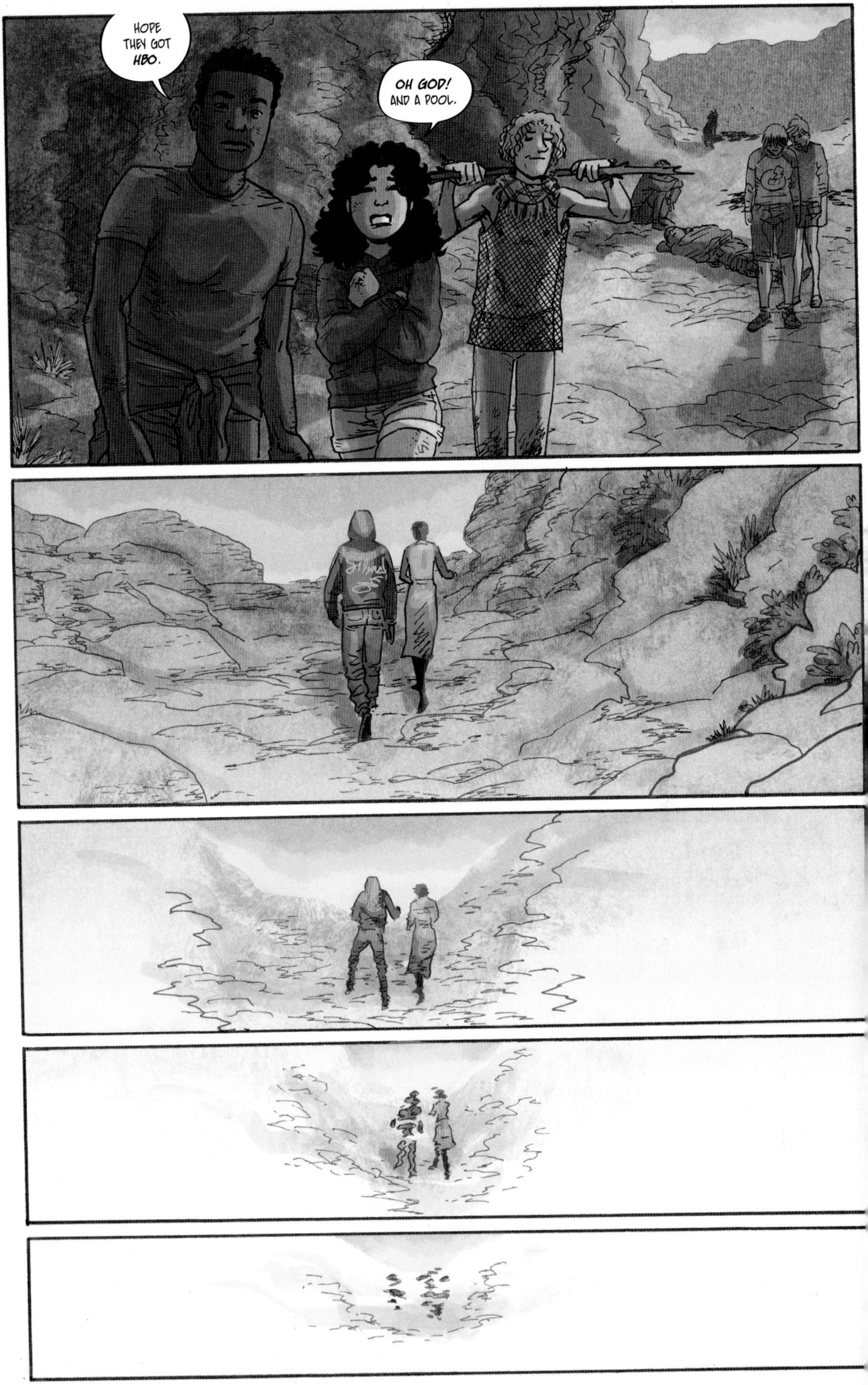
HOPE THEY GOT HBO.
OH GOD! AND A POOL.

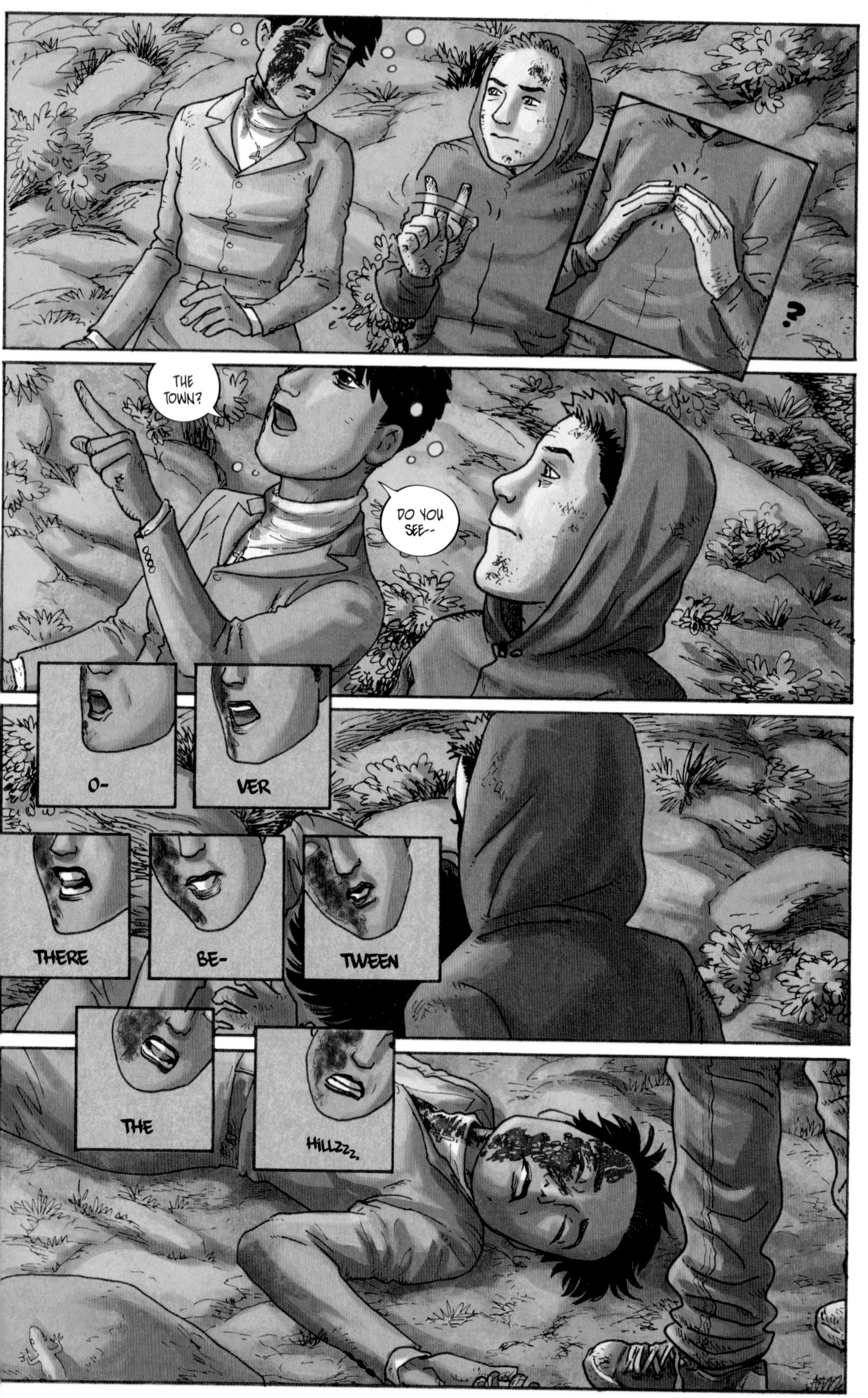
?
THE TOWN?
DO YOU SEE--
O-
VER
THERE
BE-
TWEEN
THE
HILLZZZ

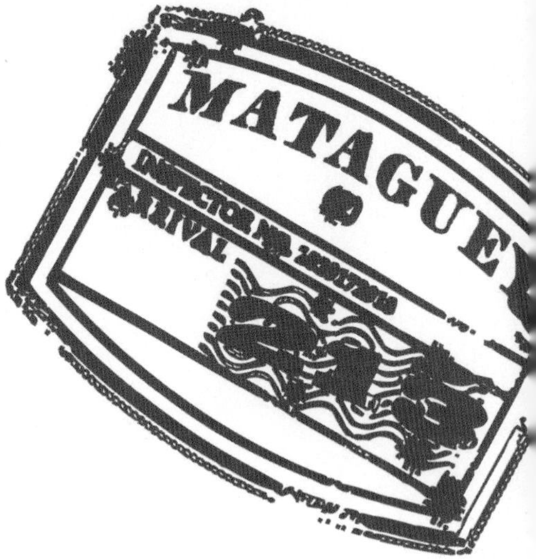
MATAGUE

CHAPTER FOUR

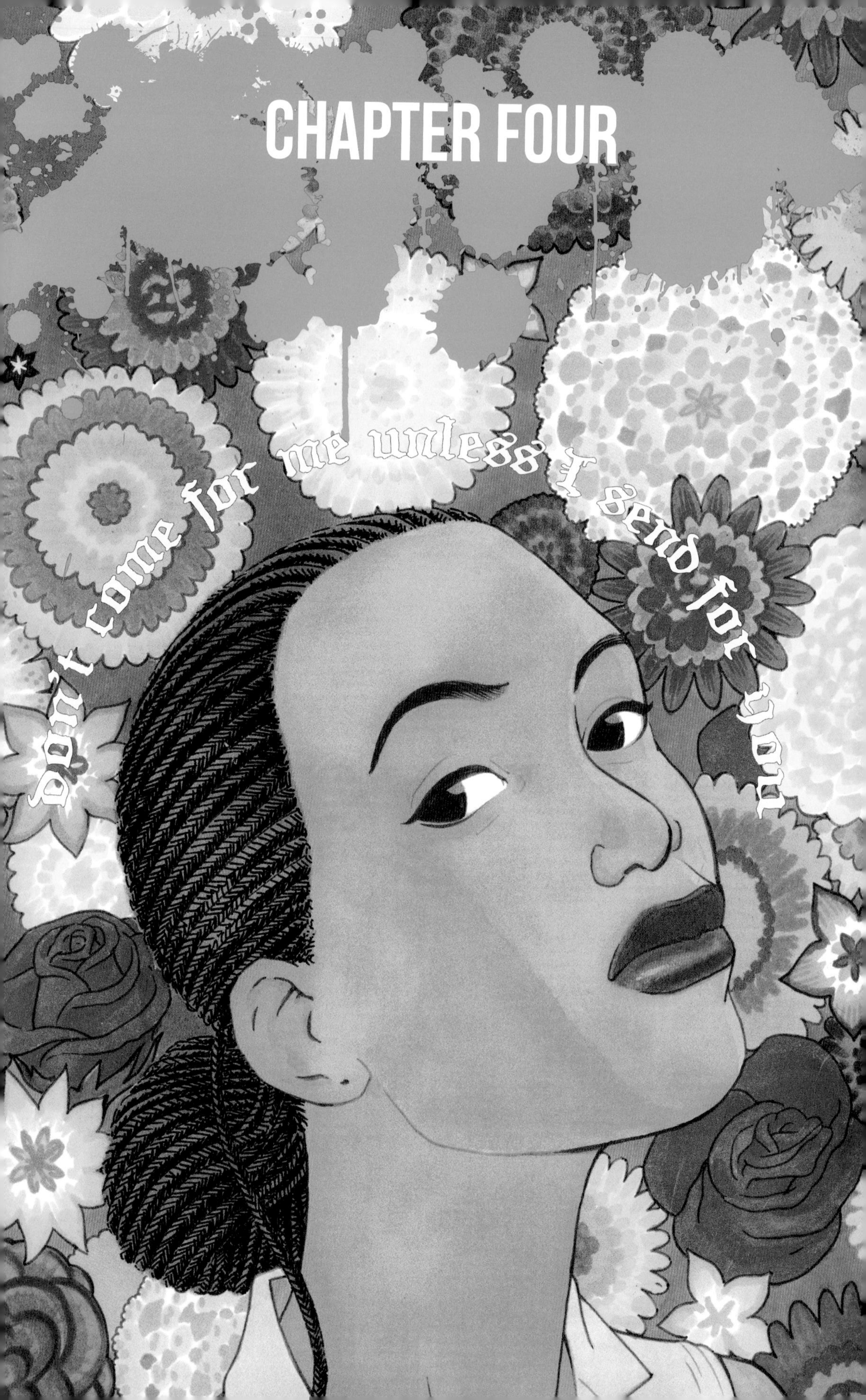
don't come for me unless I send for you

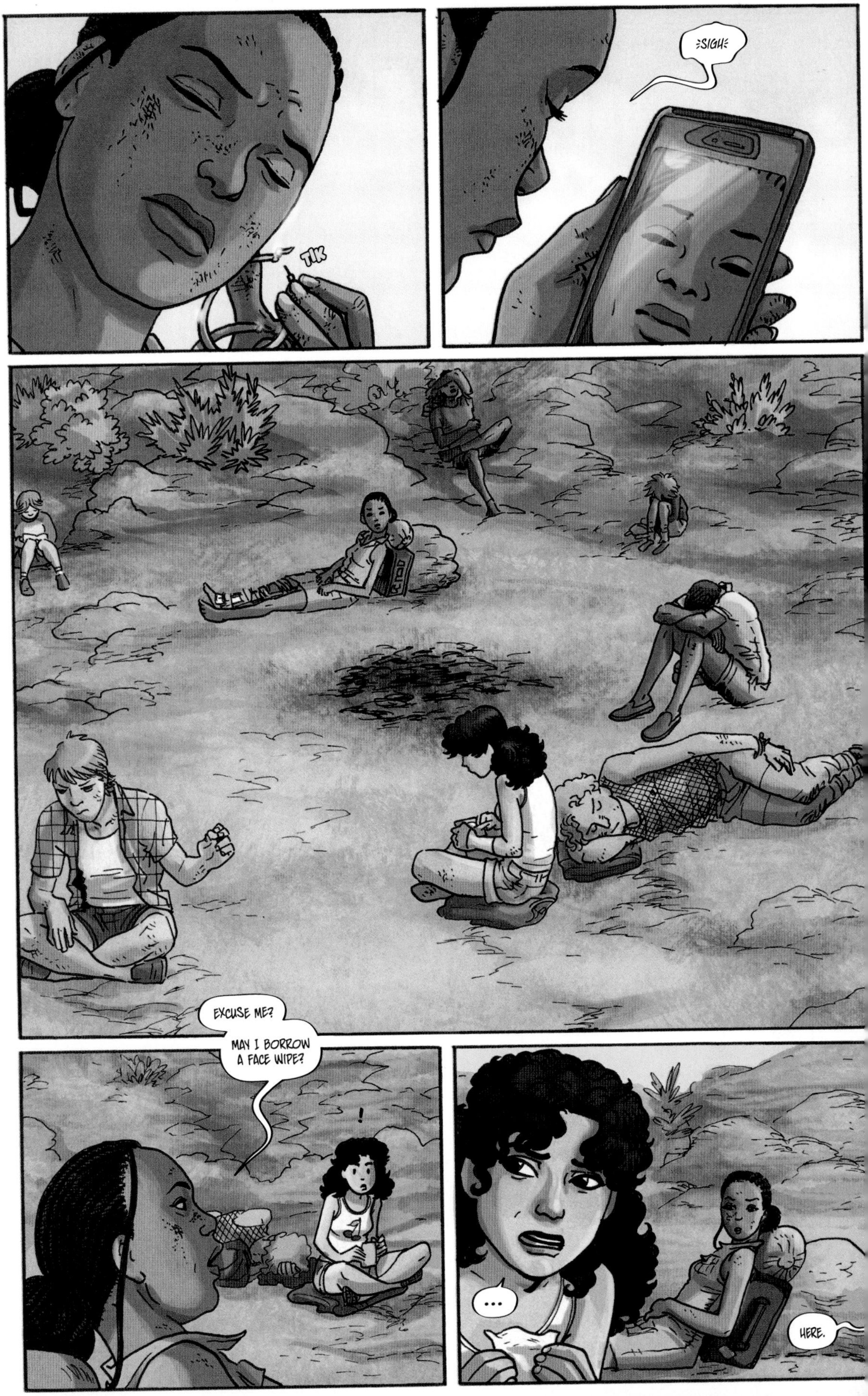
TIK
SIGH
EXCUSE ME?
MAY I BORROW A FACE WIPE?
!
...
HERE.

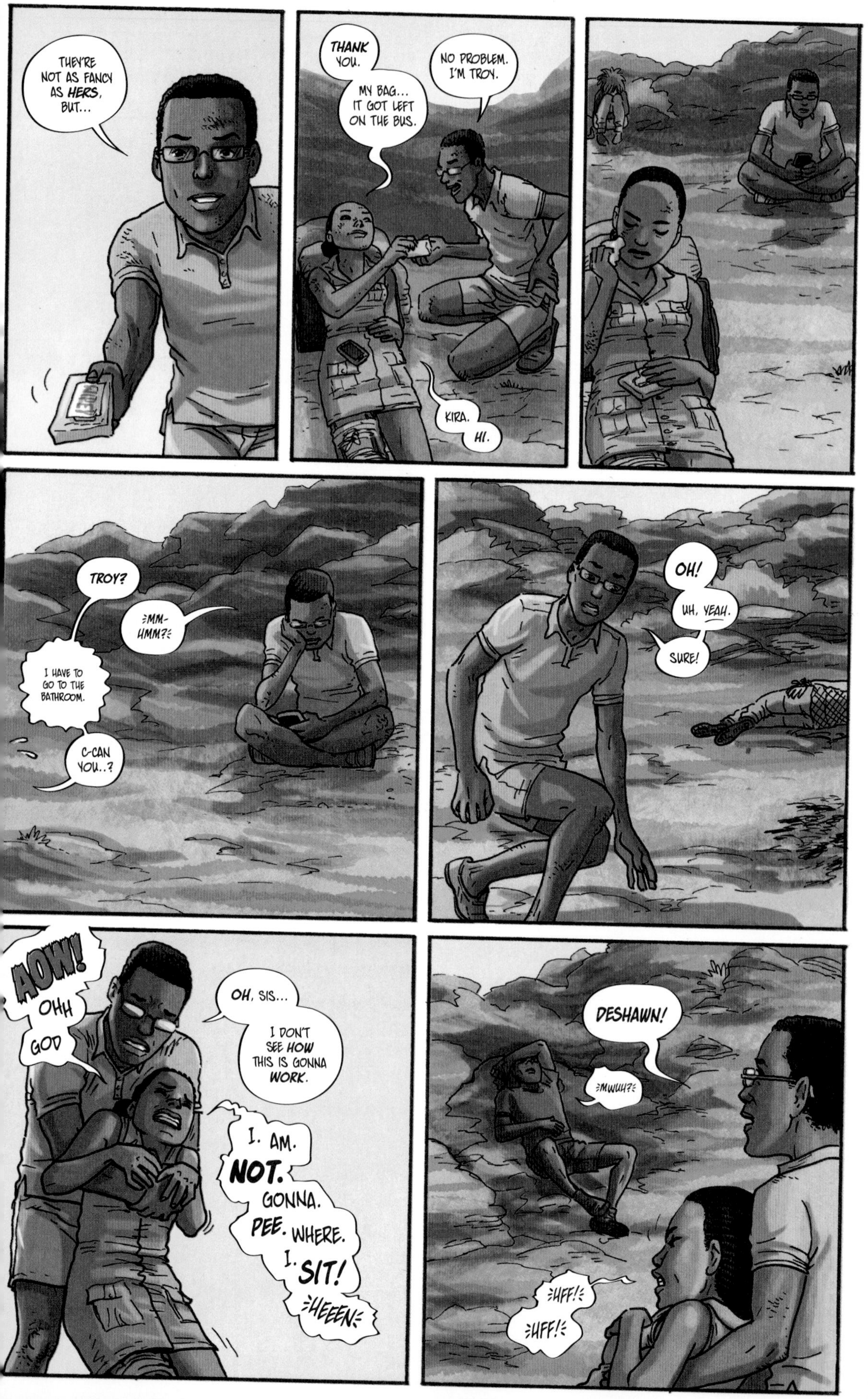
THEY'RE NOT AS FANCY AS HERS, BUT...
THANK YOU.
MY BAG... IT GOT LEFT ON THE BUS.
NO PROBLEM. I'M TROY.
KIRA.
HI.
TROY?
MM-HMM?
I HAVE TO GO TO THE BATHROOM.
C-CAN YOU..?
OH!
UH, YEAH.
SURE!
AOW!
OHH GOD
OH, SIS...
I DON'T SEE HOW THIS IS GONNA WORK.
I. AM. NOT. GONNA. PEE. WHERE. I. SIT!
HEEEN
DESHAWN!
MWUH?
HFF!
HFF!

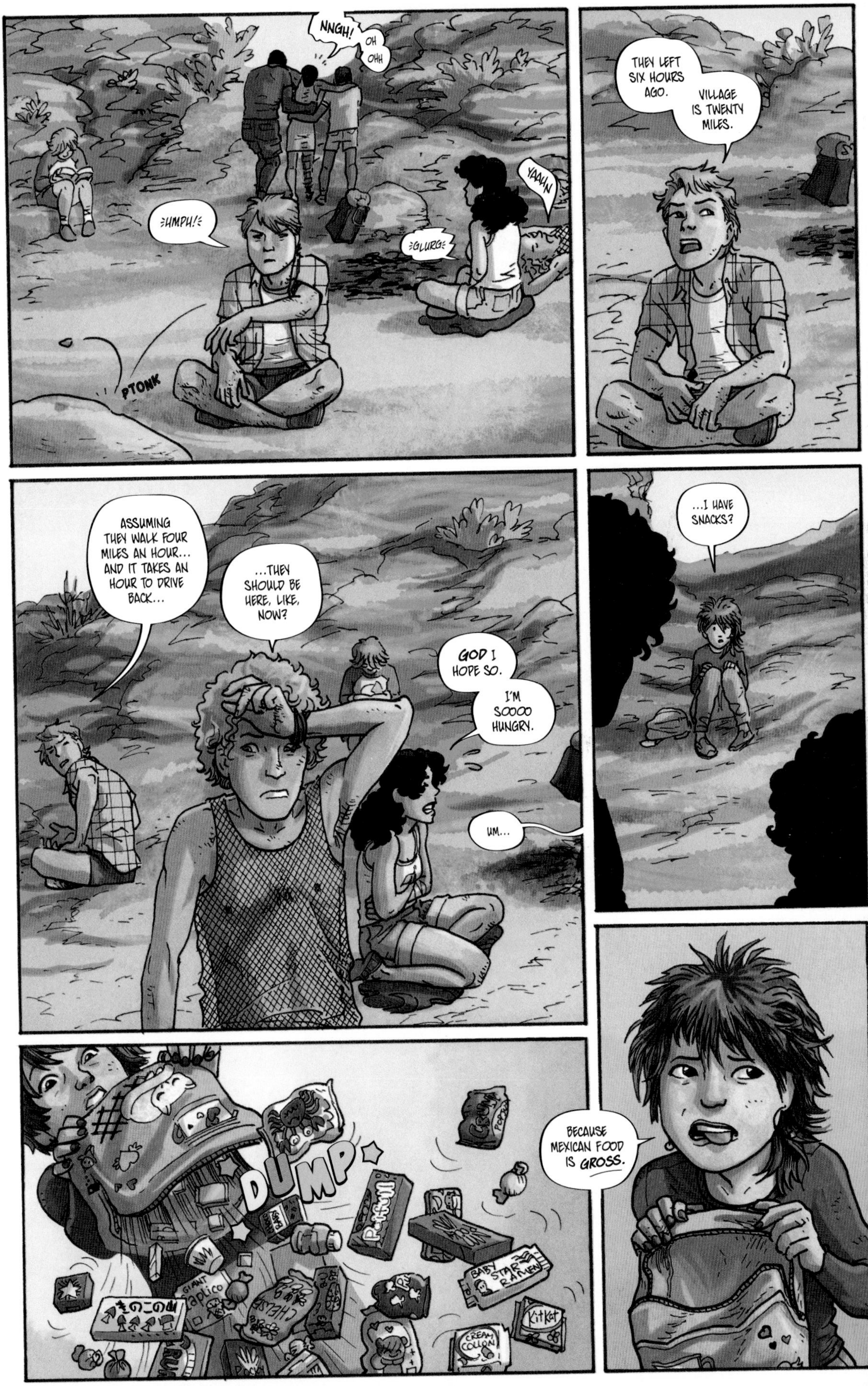
NNGH!
OH OHH
HMPH!
YAAWN
GLURG
PTONK
THEY LEFT SIX HOURS AGO.
VILLAGE IS TWENTY MILES.
ASSUMING THEY WALK FOUR MILES AN HOUR... AND IT TAKES AN HOUR TO DRIVE BACK...
...THEY SHOULD BE HERE, LIKE, NOW?
GOD I HOPE SO.
I'M SOOOO HUNGRY.
UM...
...I HAVE SNACKS?
BECAUSE MEXICAN FOOD IS GROSS.
DUMP
BABY STAR RAMEN
KitKat
CREAM COLLON
GIANT Caplico
きのこの山

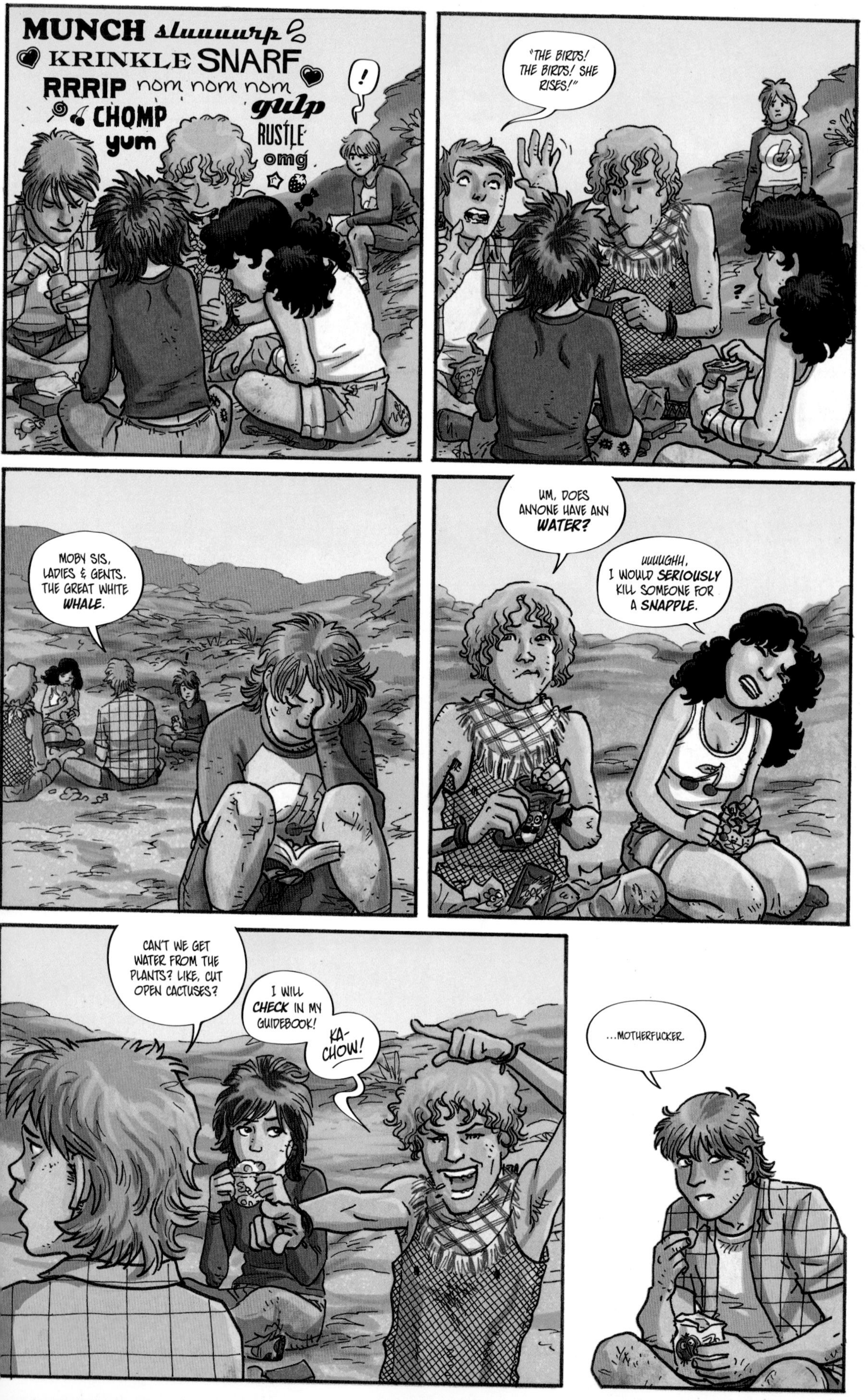

MUNCH sluuuurp
KRINKLE SNARF
RRRIP nom nom nom
CHOMP gulp
yum
RUSTLE
omg
!
"THE BIRDS! THE BIRDS! SHE RISES!"
?
MOBY SIS, LADIES & GENTS. THE GREAT WHITE WHALE.
UM, DOES ANYONE HAVE ANY WATER?
UUUUGHH, I WOULD SERIOUSLY KILL SOMEONE FOR A SNAPPLE.
CAN'T WE GET WATER FROM THE PLANTS? LIKE, CUT OPEN CACTUSES?
I WILL CHECK IN MY GUIDEBOOK! KA-CHOW!
...MOTHERFUCKER.

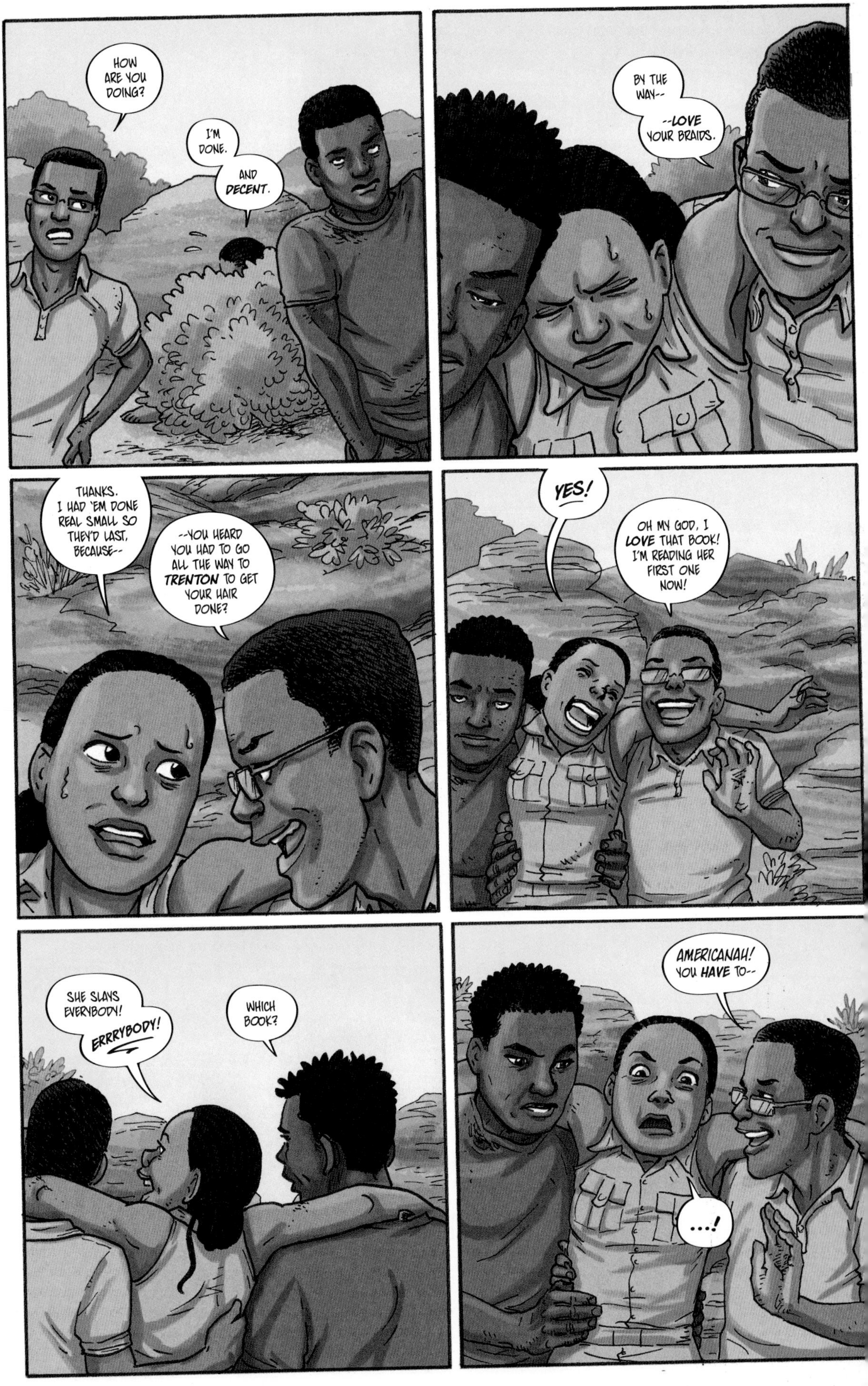

HOW ARE YOU DOING?
I'M DONE.
AND DECENT.
BY THE WAY--
--LOVE YOUR BRAIDS.
THANKS. I HAD 'EM DONE REAL SMALL SO THEY'D LAST, BECAUSE--
--YOU HEARD YOU HAD TO GO ALL THE WAY TO TRENTON TO GET YOUR HAIR DONE?
YES!
OH MY GOD, I LOVE THAT BOOK! I'M READING HER FIRST ONE NOW!
SHE SLAYS EVERYBODY!
ERRRYBODY!
WHICH BOOK?
AMERICANAH! YOU HAVE TO--
...!

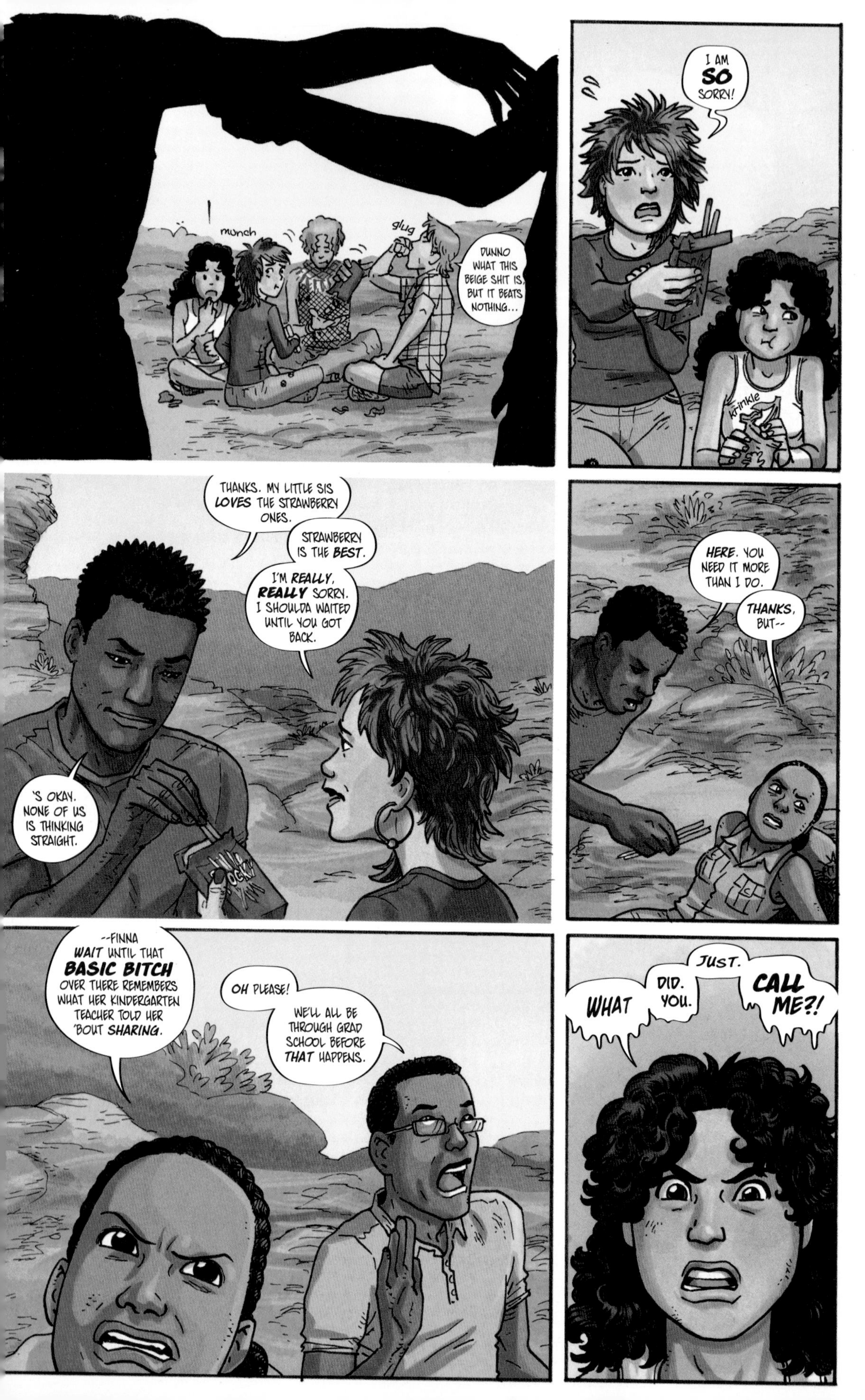

munch
glug
DUNNO WHAT THIS BEIGE SHIT IS, BUT IT BEATS NOTHING...
I AM SO SORRY!
krinkle
THANKS. MY LITTLE SIS LOVES THE STRAWBERRY ONES.
STRAWBERRY IS THE BEST.
I'M REALLY, REALLY SORRY. I SHOULDA WAITED UNTIL YOU GOT BACK.
'S OKAY. NONE OF US IS THINKING STRAIGHT.
HERE. YOU NEED IT MORE THAN I DO.
THANKS, BUT--
--FINNA WAIT UNTIL THAT BASIC BITCH OVER THERE REMEMBERS WHAT HER KINDERGARTEN TEACHER TOLD HER 'BOUT SHARING.
OH PLEASE!
WE'LL ALL BE THROUGH GRAD SCHOOL BEFORE THAT HAPPENS.
WHAT
DID. YOU.
JUST.
CALL ME?!

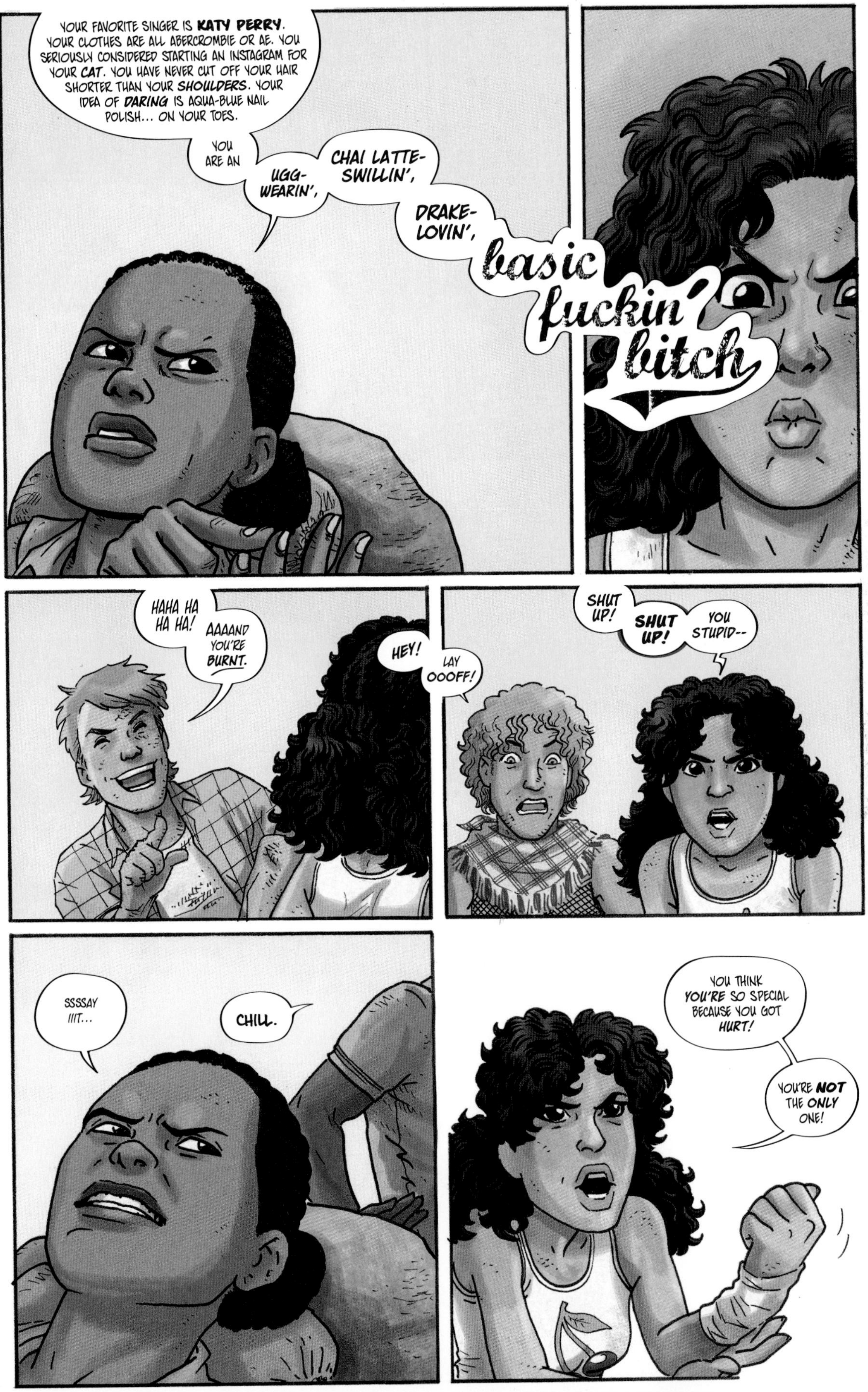
YOUR FAVORITE SINGER IS KATY PERRY. YOUR CLOTHES ARE ALL ABERCROMBIE OR AE. YOU SERIOUSLY CONSIDERED STARTING AN INSTAGRAM FOR YOUR CAT. YOU HAVE NEVER CUT OFF YOUR HAIR SHORTER THAN YOUR SHOULDERS. YOUR IDEA OF DARING IS AQUA-BLUE NAIL POLISH... ON YOUR TOES.
YOU ARE AN
UGG-WEARIN',
CHAI LATTE-SWILLIN',
DRAKE-LOVIN',
basic fuckin' bitch
HAHA HA HA HA!
AAAAND YOU'RE BURNT.
HEY!
LAY OOOFF!
SHUT UP!
SHUT UP!
YOU STUPID--
SSSSAY IIIT...
CHILL.
YOU THINK YOU'RE SO SPECIAL BECAUSE YOU GOT HURT!
YOU'RE NOT THE ONLY ONE!

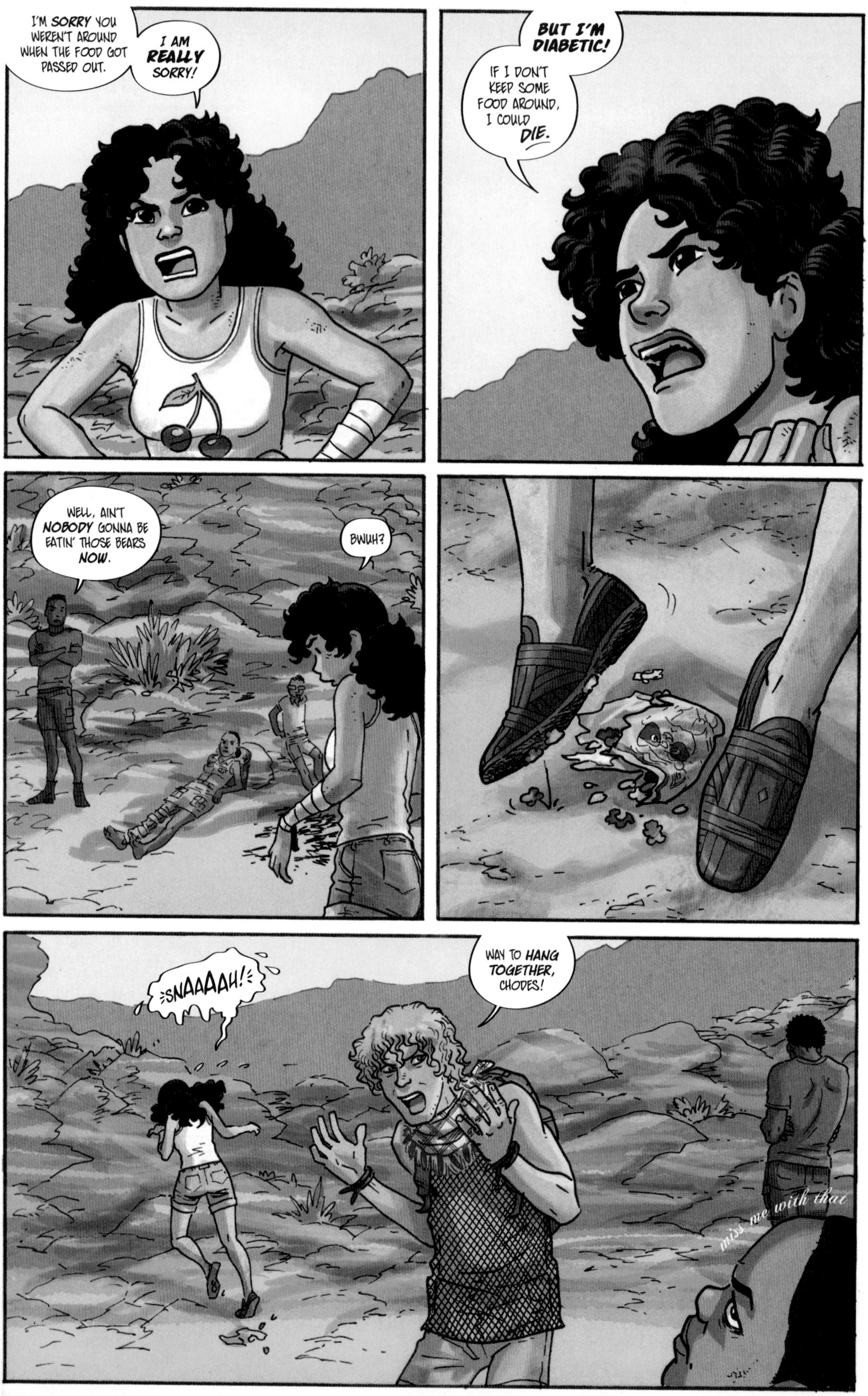
I'M SORRY YOU WEREN'T AROUND WHEN THE FOOD GOT PASSED OUT.
I AM REALLY SORRY!
BUT I'M DIABETIC!
IF I DON'T KEEP SOME FOOD AROUND, I COULD DIE.
WELL, AIN'T NOBODY GONNA BE EATIN' THOSE BEARS NOW.
BWUH?
SNAAAAH!
WAY TO HANG TOGETHER, CHODES!
miss me with that

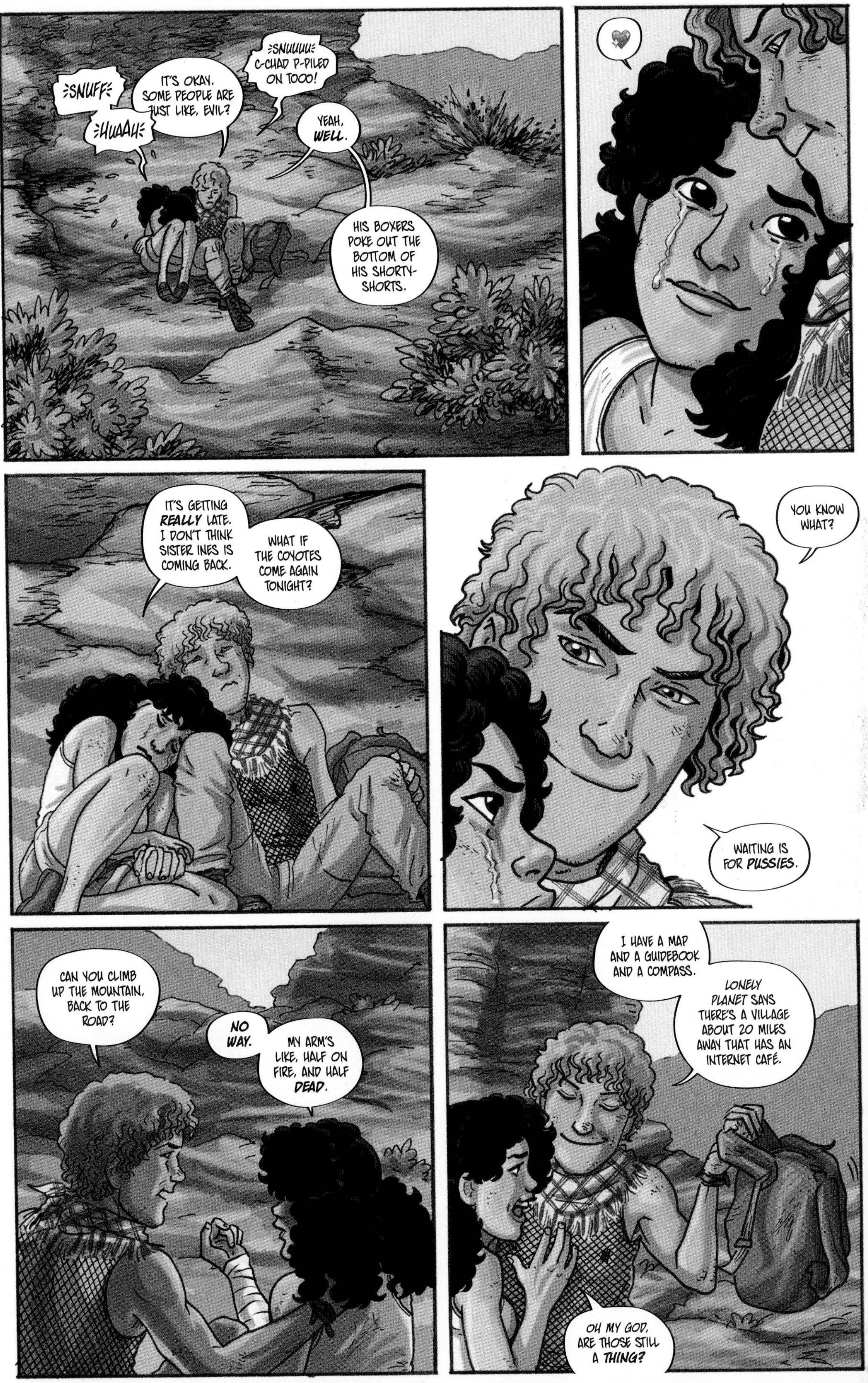

SNUFF
HUAAH
IT'S OKAY. SOME PEOPLE ARE JUST LIKE, EVIL?
SNUUUU C-CHAD P-PILED ON TOOO!
YEAH, **WELL**.
HIS BOXERS POKE OUT THE BOTTOM OF HIS SHORTY-SHORTS.
IT'S GETTING **REALLY** LATE. I DON'T THINK SISTER INES IS COMING BACK.
WHAT IF THE COYOTES COME AGAIN TONIGHT?
YOU KNOW WHAT?
WAITING IS FOR **PUSSIES**.
CAN YOU CLIMB UP THE MOUNTAIN, BACK TO THE ROAD?
NO WAY.
MY ARM'S LIKE, HALF ON FIRE, AND HALF **DEAD**.
I HAVE A MAP AND A GUIDEBOOK AND A COMPASS.
LONELY PLANET SAYS THERE'S A VILLAGE ABOUT 20 MILES AWAY THAT HAS AN INTERNET CAFÉ.
OH MY GOD, ARE THOSE STILL A **THING?**

C'MON, BABE. LET'S GET THE HELL OUT OF DODGE.

YEAH!

"FUCK THOSE CHODES FOR COYOTE SNACKS."

≶NHUH!≶

¿DONDE...?

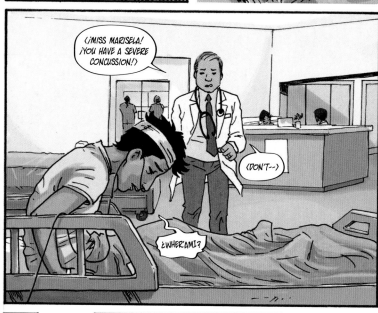

⟨¡MISS MARISELA! ¡YOU HAVE A SEVERE CONCUSSION!⟩

⟨DON'T--⟩

¿WHER'AMI?

⟨¿WHERE IS ANTONIO?⟩

⟨¿ANTONIO? I DON'T--⟩

⟨YANKEE BOY. WEARS A HOODIE.⟩

⟨¿LUZ, DID THIS PATIENT COME IN WITH ANYONE?⟩

⟨YES, THE SILENT BOY WHO SAVED HER.⟩

⟨¡HE CARRIED HER ALMOST TEN KILOMETERS TO QUILALWI!⟩

⟨BUT HE LEFT A WHILE AGO.⟩

〈¿WHERE DID HE GO?〉

〈OH, HE LEFT WITH YOUR BROTHER.〉

¡HEE! TAN GUAPO, EL SEÑOR LUGO.

〈¿BRAULIO?〉

〈¿HE IS WITH **BRAULIO?!**〉

〈I NEED TO GO, **NOW!**〉

〈¡PLEASE! AT LEAST GET ME TO A--〉

〈TELE--

--PHONE...〉

〈I AM AFRAID THAT IS NOT POSSIBLE, MISS MARISELA.〉

〈¡TSK!〉

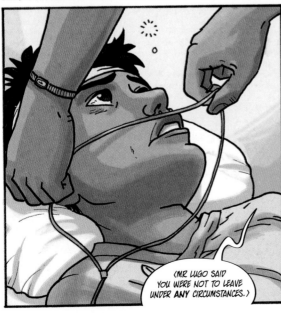

〈MR LUGO SAID YOU WERE NOT TO LEAVE UNDER **ANY** CIRCUMSTANCES.〉

〈YOU MUST GET YOUR HEALTH BACK FIRST. YOU ARE WELL LOOKED AFTER.〉

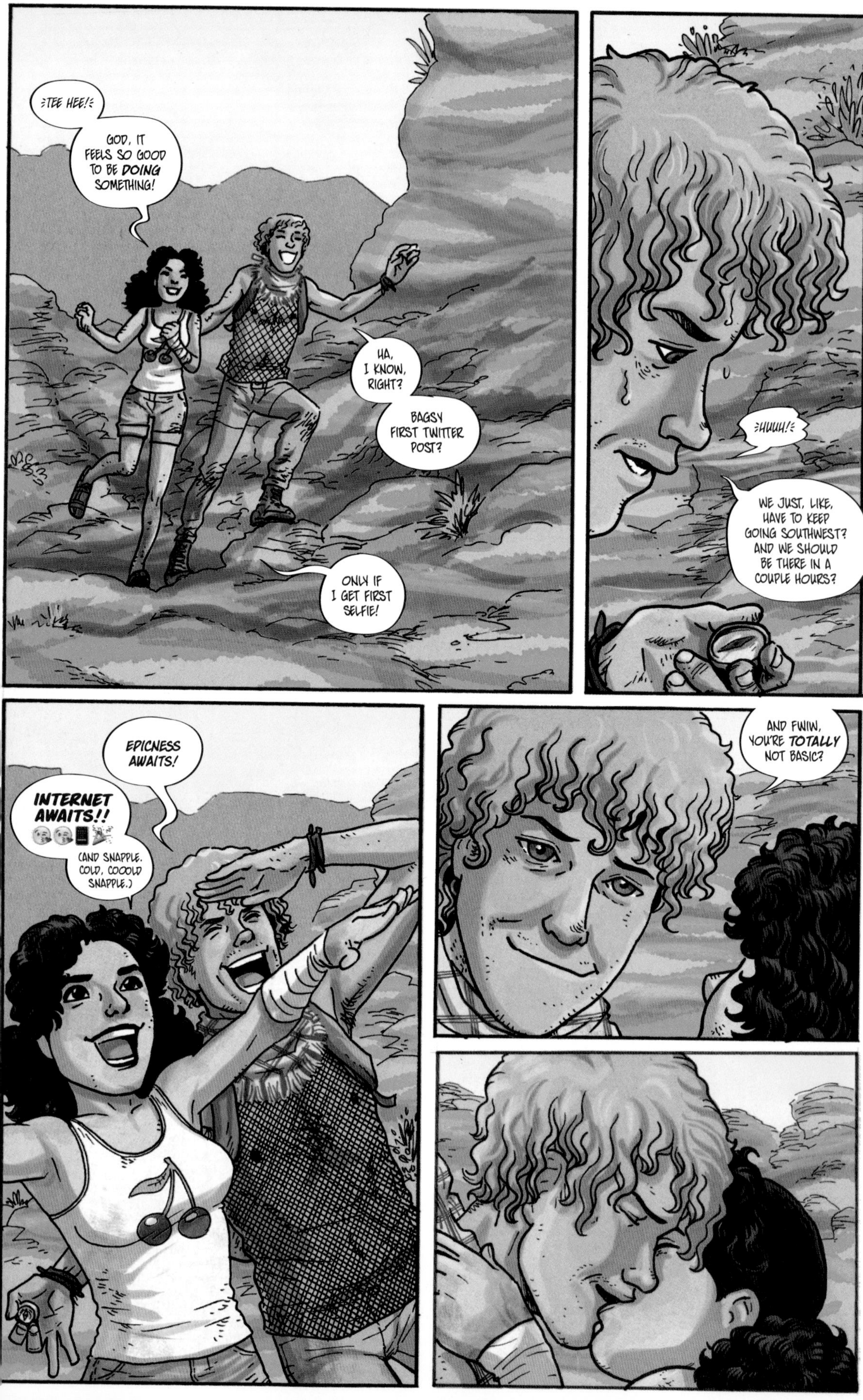

TEE HEE!
GOD, IT FEELS SO GOOD TO BE **DOING** SOMETHING!
HA, I KNOW, RIGHT?
BAGSY FIRST TWITTER POST?
ONLY IF I GET FIRST SELFIE!
HUUH!
WE JUST, LIKE, HAVE TO KEEP GOING SOUTHWEST? AND WE SHOULD BE THERE IN A COUPLE HOURS?
EPICNESS AWAITS!
INTERNET AWAITS!!
(AND SNAPPLE. COLD, COOOLD SNAPPLE.)
AND FWIW, YOU'RE **TOTALLY** NOT BASIC?

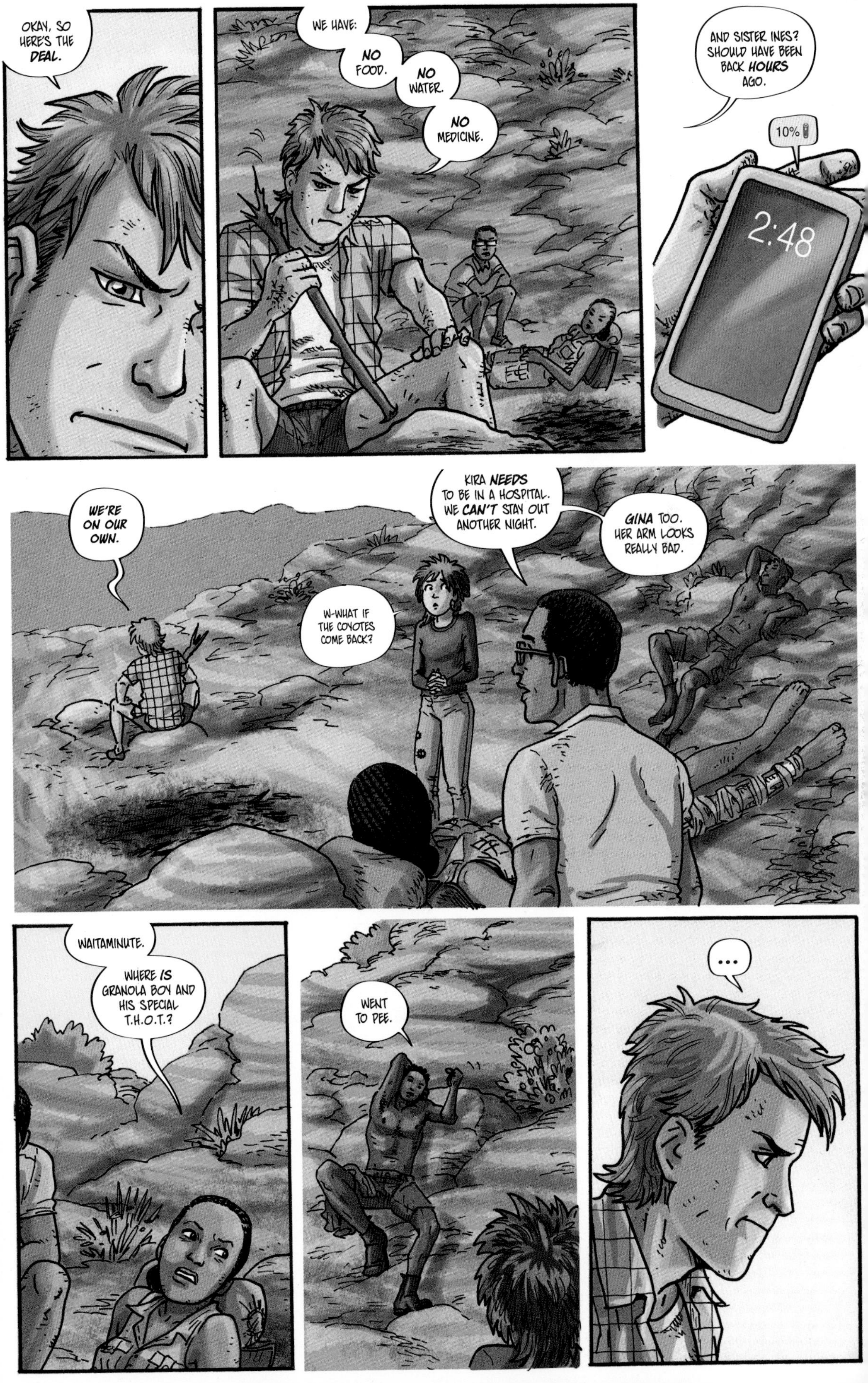
OKAY, SO HERE'S THE **DEAL.**
WE HAVE:
NO FOOD.
NO WATER.
NO MEDICINE.
AND SISTER INES? SHOULD HAVE BEEN BACK **HOURS** AGO.
10%
2:48
WE'RE ON OUR OWN.
KIRA **NEEDS** TO BE IN A HOSPITAL. WE **CAN'T** STAY OUT ANOTHER NIGHT.
GINA TOO. HER ARM LOOKS REALLY BAD.
W-WHAT IF THE COYOTES COME BACK?
WAITAMINUTE.
WHERE ***IS*** GRANOLA BOY AND HIS SPECIAL T.H.O.T.?
WENT TO PEE.
...

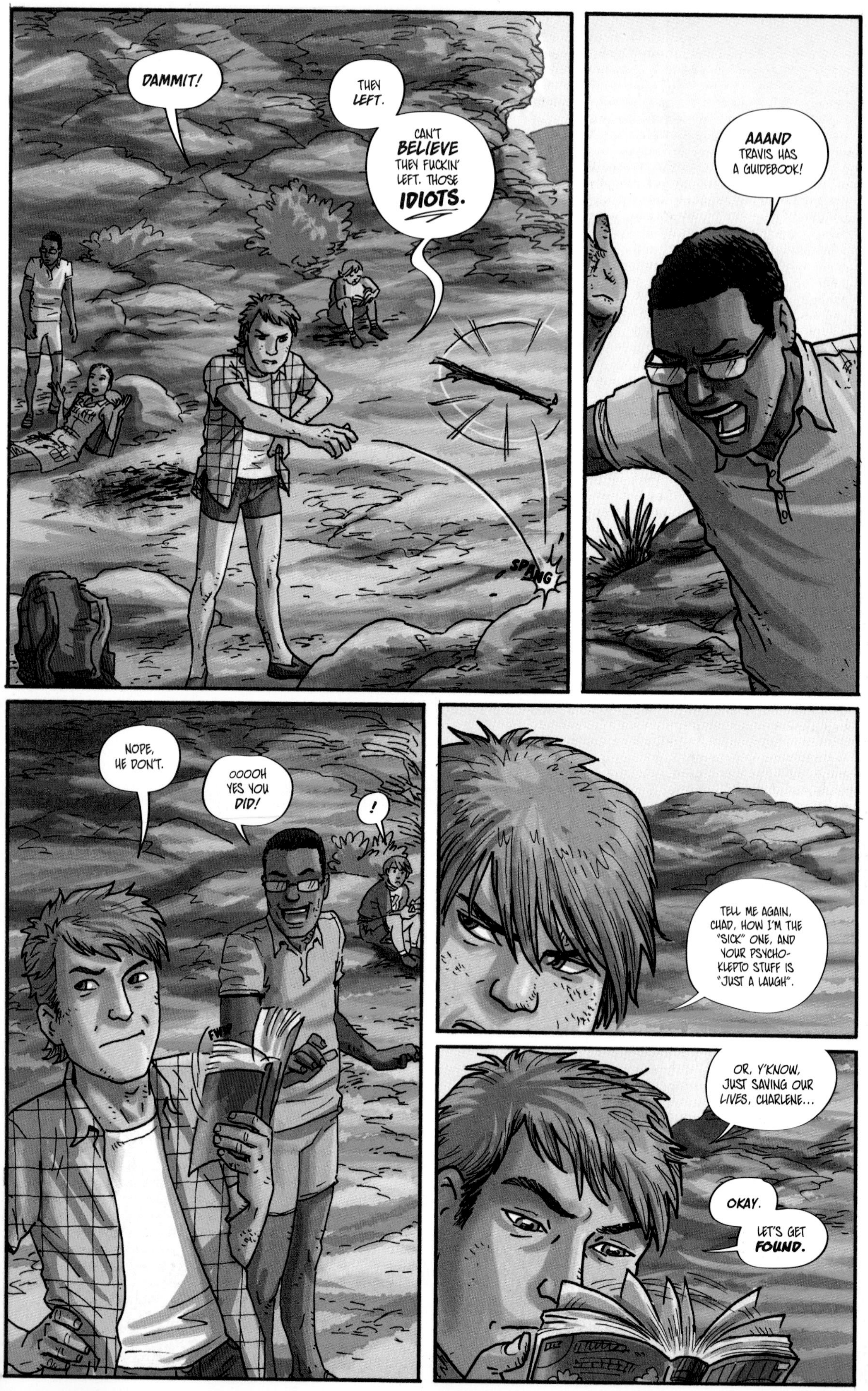
DAMMIT!
THEY LEFT.
CAN'T BELIEVE THEY FUCKIN' LEFT. THOSE IDIOTS.
SPANG
AAAND TRAVIS HAS A GUIDEBOOK!
NOPE, HE DON'T.
OOOOH YES YOU DID!
!
TELL ME AGAIN, CHAD, HOW I'M THE "SICK" ONE, AND YOUR PSYCHO-KLEPTO STUFF IS "JUST A LAUGH".
OR, Y'KNOW, JUST SAVING OUR LIVES, CHARLENE...
OKAY.
LET'S GET FOUND.

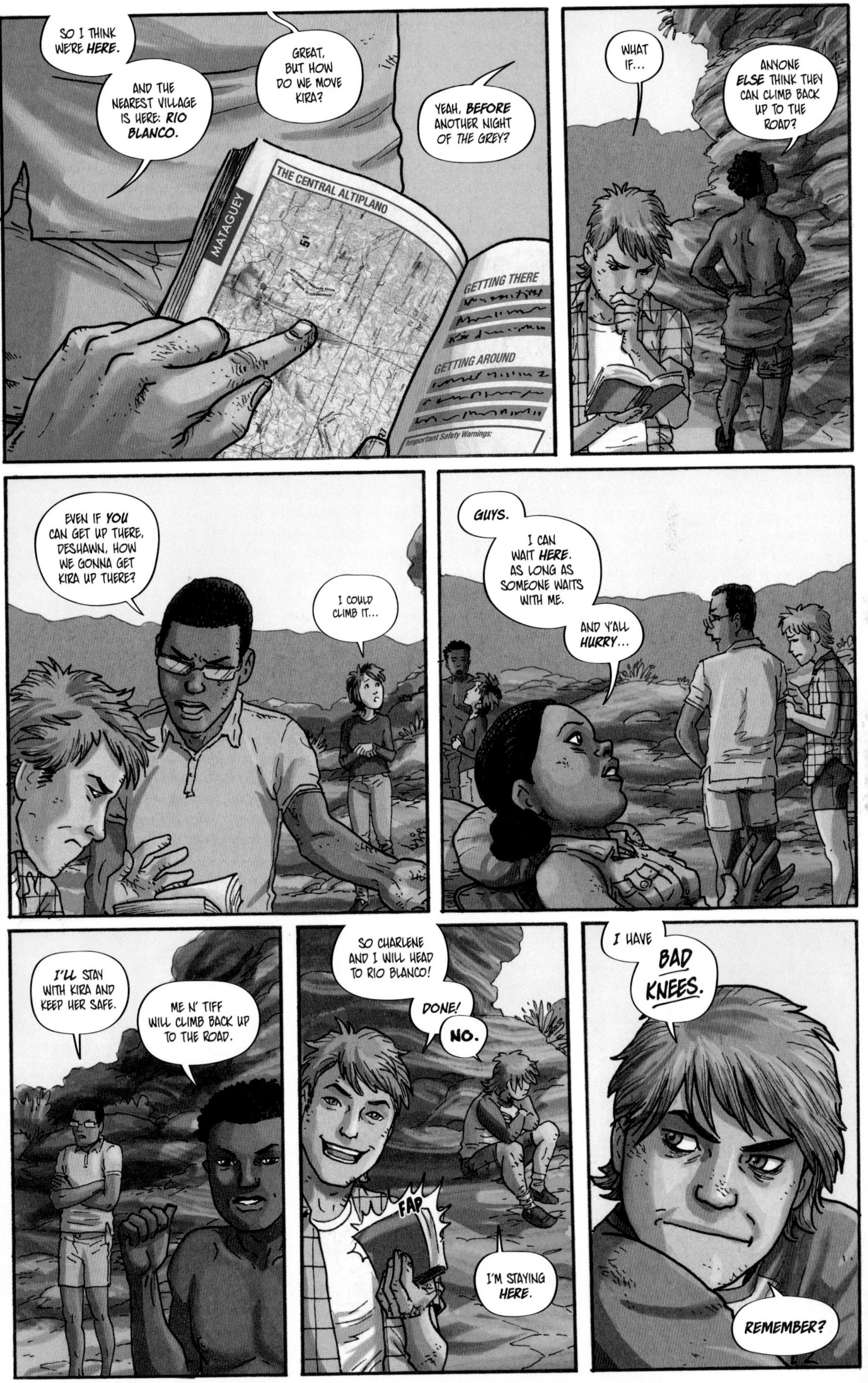
SO I THINK WE'RE **HERE**.
AND THE NEAREST VILLAGE IS HERE: **RIO BLANCO**.
GREAT, BUT HOW DO WE MOVE KIRA?
YEAH, **BEFORE** ANOTHER NIGHT OF THE GREY?
MATAGUEY
THE CENTRAL ALTIPLANO
GETTING THERE
GETTING AROUND
Important Safety Warnings:
WHAT IF...
ANYONE **ELSE** THINK THEY CAN CLIMB BACK UP TO THE ROAD?
EVEN IF **YOU** CAN GET UP THERE, DESHAWN, HOW WE GONNA GET KIRA UP THERE?
I COULD CLIMB IT...
GUYS.
I CAN WAIT **HERE**. AS LONG AS SOMEONE WAITS WITH ME.
AND Y'ALL **HURRY**...
I'LL STAY WITH KIRA AND KEEP HER SAFE.
ME N' TIFF WILL CLIMB BACK UP TO THE ROAD.
SO CHARLENE AND I WILL HEAD TO RIO BLANCO!
DONE!
NO.
FAP
I'M STAYING **HERE**.
I HAVE **BAD KNEES.**
REMEMBER?

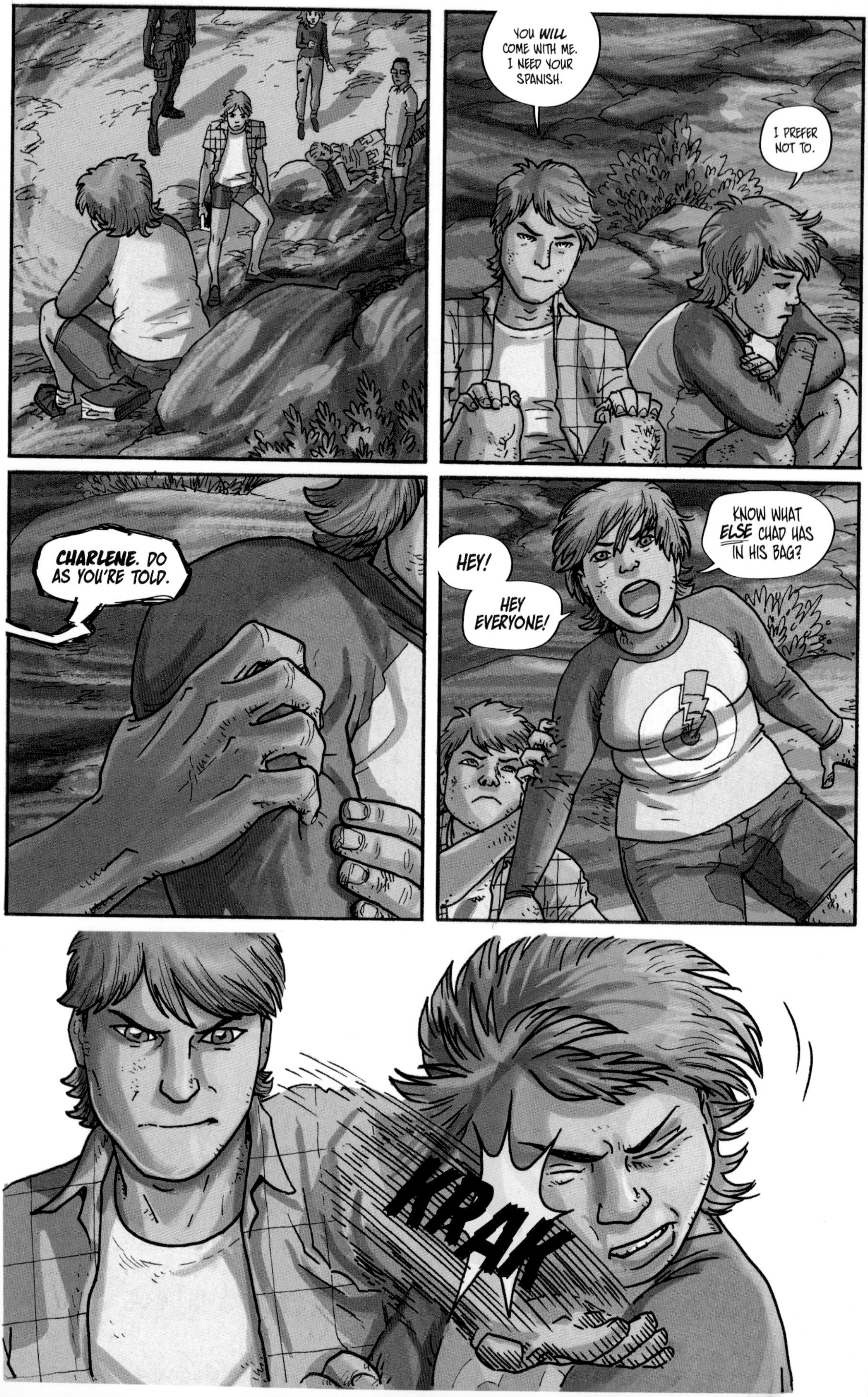
YOU WILL COME WITH ME. I NEED YOUR SPANISH.
I PREFER NOT TO.
CHARLENE. DO AS YOU'RE TOLD.
HEY!
HEY EVERYONE!
KNOW WHAT ELSE CHAD HAS IN HIS BAG?
KRAK

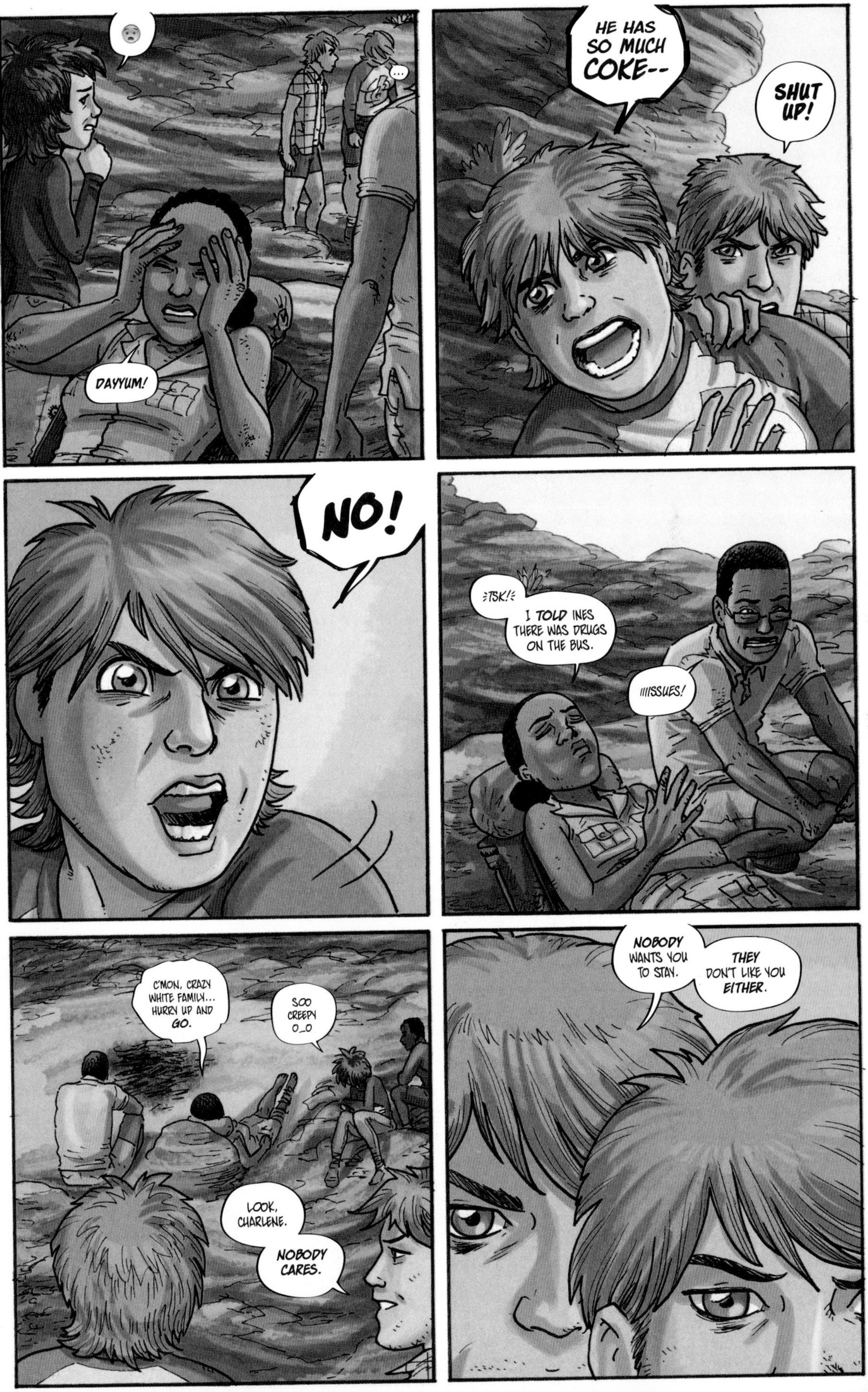
...
DAYYUM!
HE HAS SO MUCH COKE--
SHUT UP!
NO!
TSK!
I TOLD INES THERE WAS DRUGS ON THE BUS.
IIIISSUES!
C'MON, CRAZY WHITE FAMILY... HURRY UP AND GO.
SOO CREEPY O_O
LOOK, CHARLENE.
NOBODY CARES.
NOBODY WANTS YOU TO STAY.
THEY DON'T LIKE YOU EITHER.

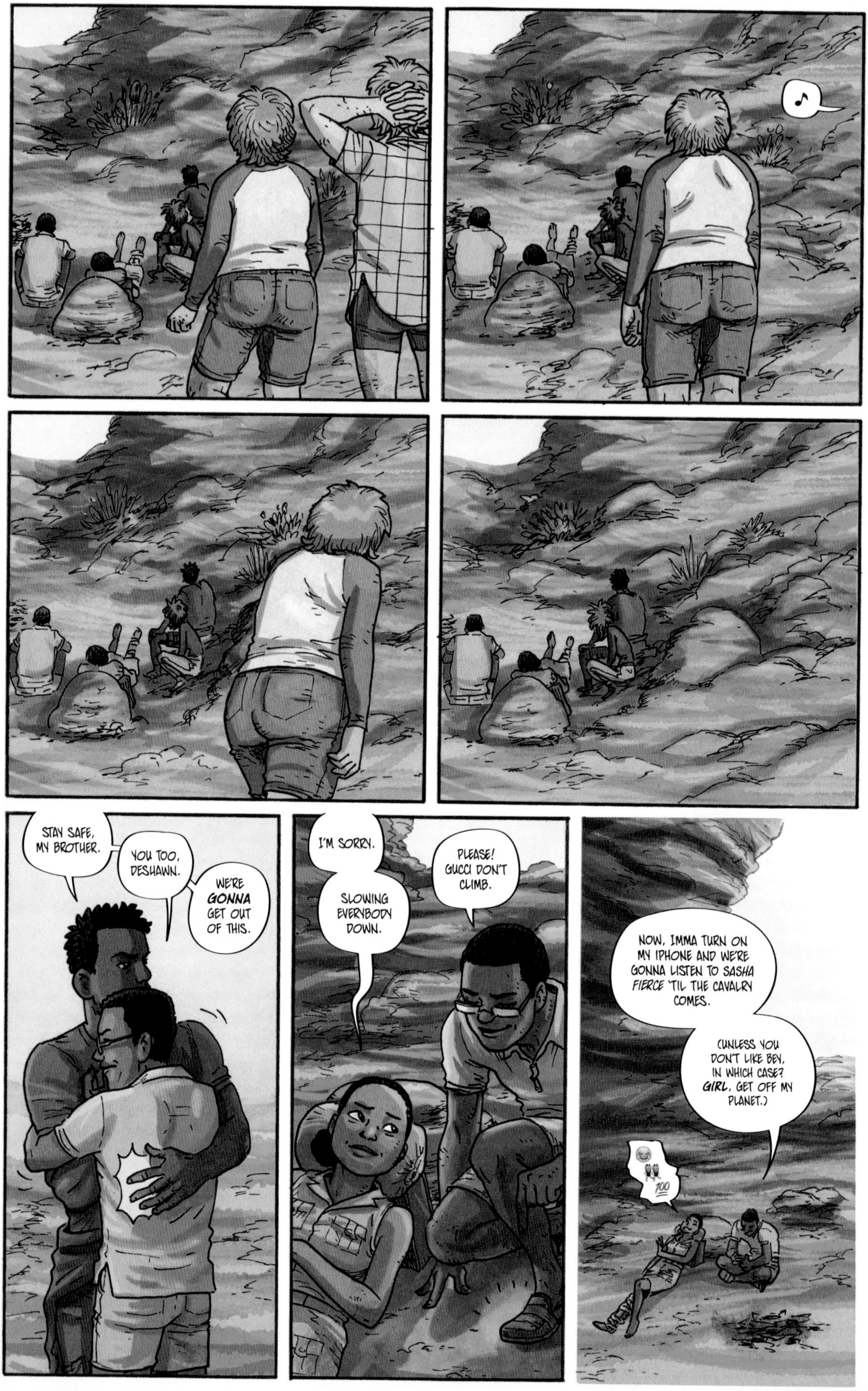
♪
STAY SAFE, MY BROTHER.
YOU TOO, DESHAWN.
WE'RE **GONNA** GET OUT OF THIS.
I'M SORRY.
SLOWING EVERYBODY DOWN.
PLEASE! GUCCI DON'T CLIMB.
NOW, IMMA TURN ON MY IPHONE AND WE'RE GONNA LISTEN TO SASHA *FIERCE* 'TIL THE CAVALRY COMES.
(UNLESS YOU DON'T LIKE BEY, IN WHICH CASE? **GIRL**, GET OFF MY PLANET.)
100

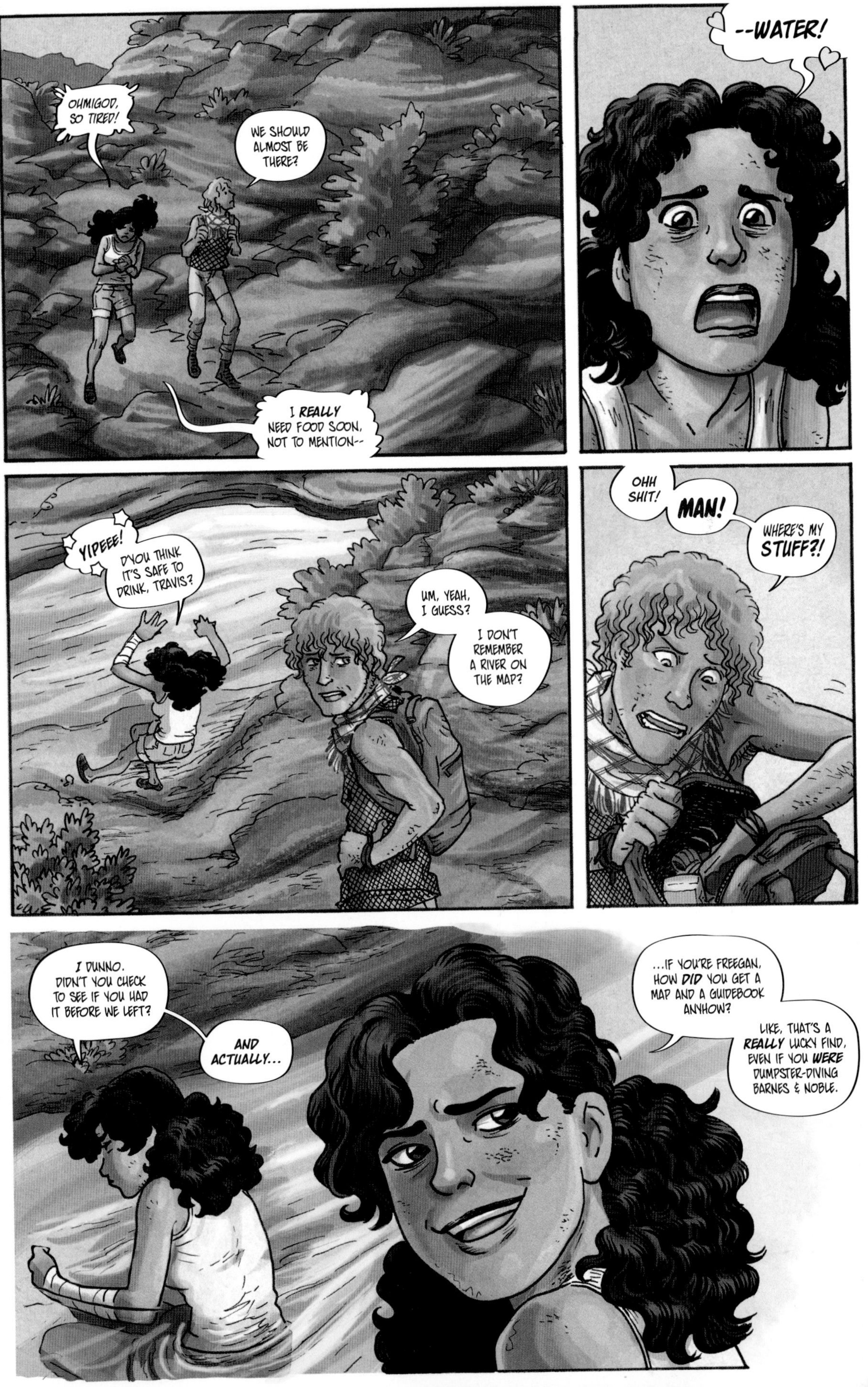
OHMIGOD, SO TIRED!
WE SHOULD ALMOST BE THERE?
I REALLY NEED FOOD SOON, NOT TO MENTION--
--WATER!
YIPEEE!
D'YOU THINK IT'S SAFE TO DRINK, TRAVIS?
UM, YEAH, I GUESS?
I DON'T REMEMBER A RIVER ON THE MAP?
OHH SHIT!
MAN!
WHERE'S MY STUFF?!
I DUNNO. DIDN'T YOU CHECK TO SEE IF YOU HAD IT BEFORE WE LEFT?
AND ACTUALLY...
...IF YOU'RE FREEGAN, HOW DID YOU GET A MAP AND A GUIDEBOOK ANYHOW?
LIKE, THAT'S A REALLY LUCKY FIND, EVEN IF YOU WERE DUMPSTER-DIVING BARNES & NOBLE.

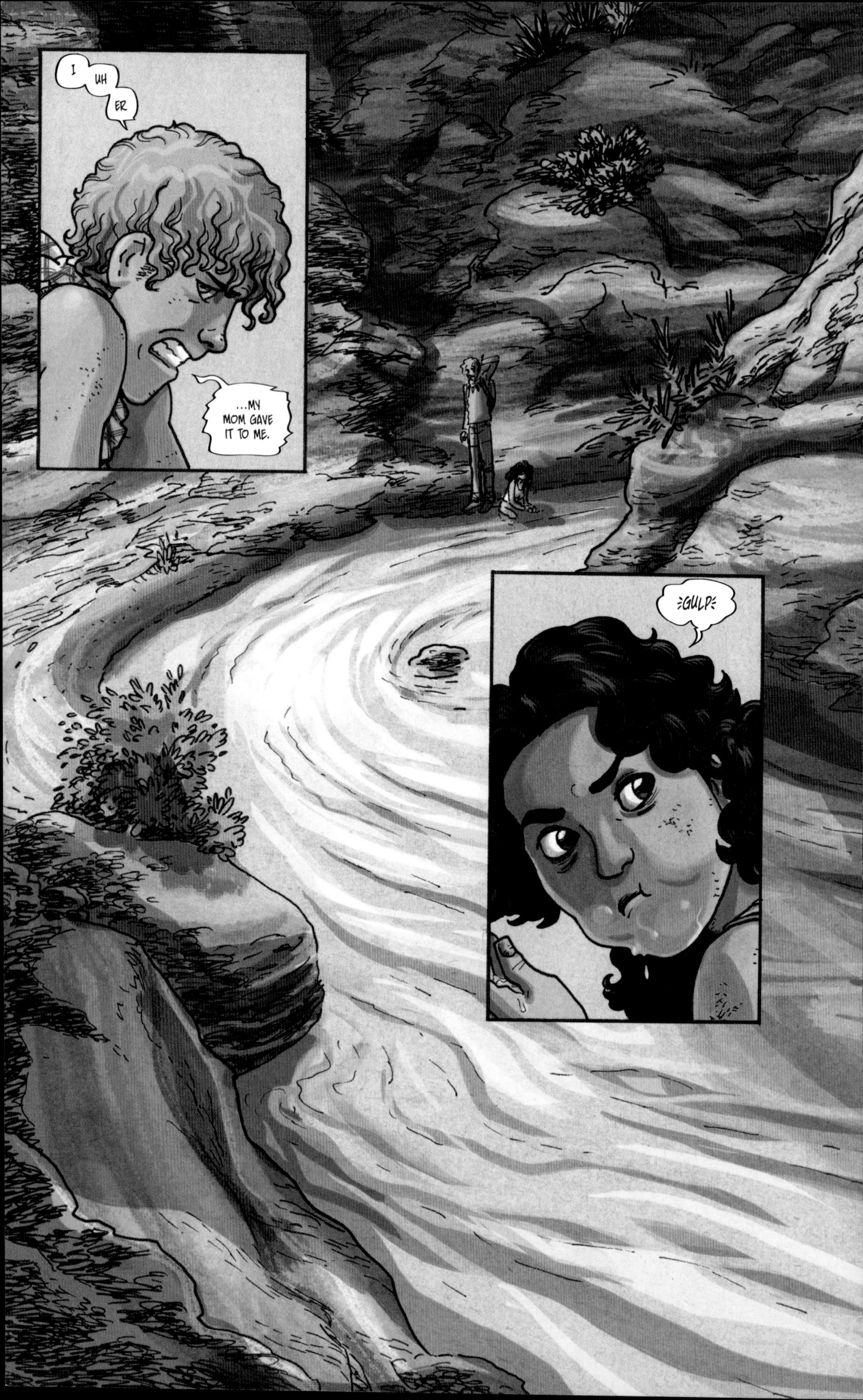
I
UH
ER
...MY MOM GAVE IT TO ME.
GULP

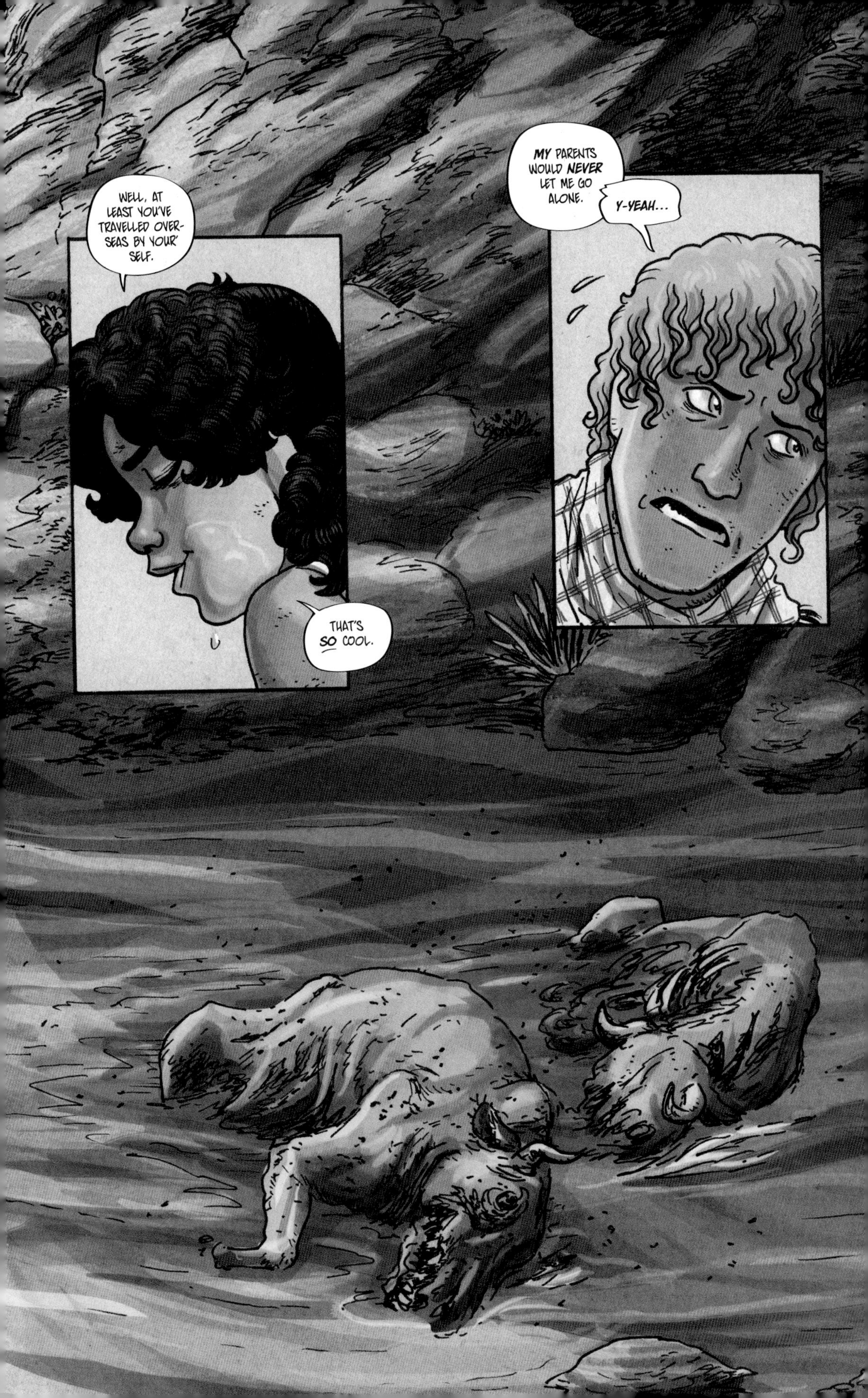
WELL, AT LEAST YOU'VE TRAVELLED OVER-SEAS BY YOUR' SELF.
THAT'S SO COOL.
MY PARENTS WOULD NEVER LET ME GO ALONE.
Y-YEAH...

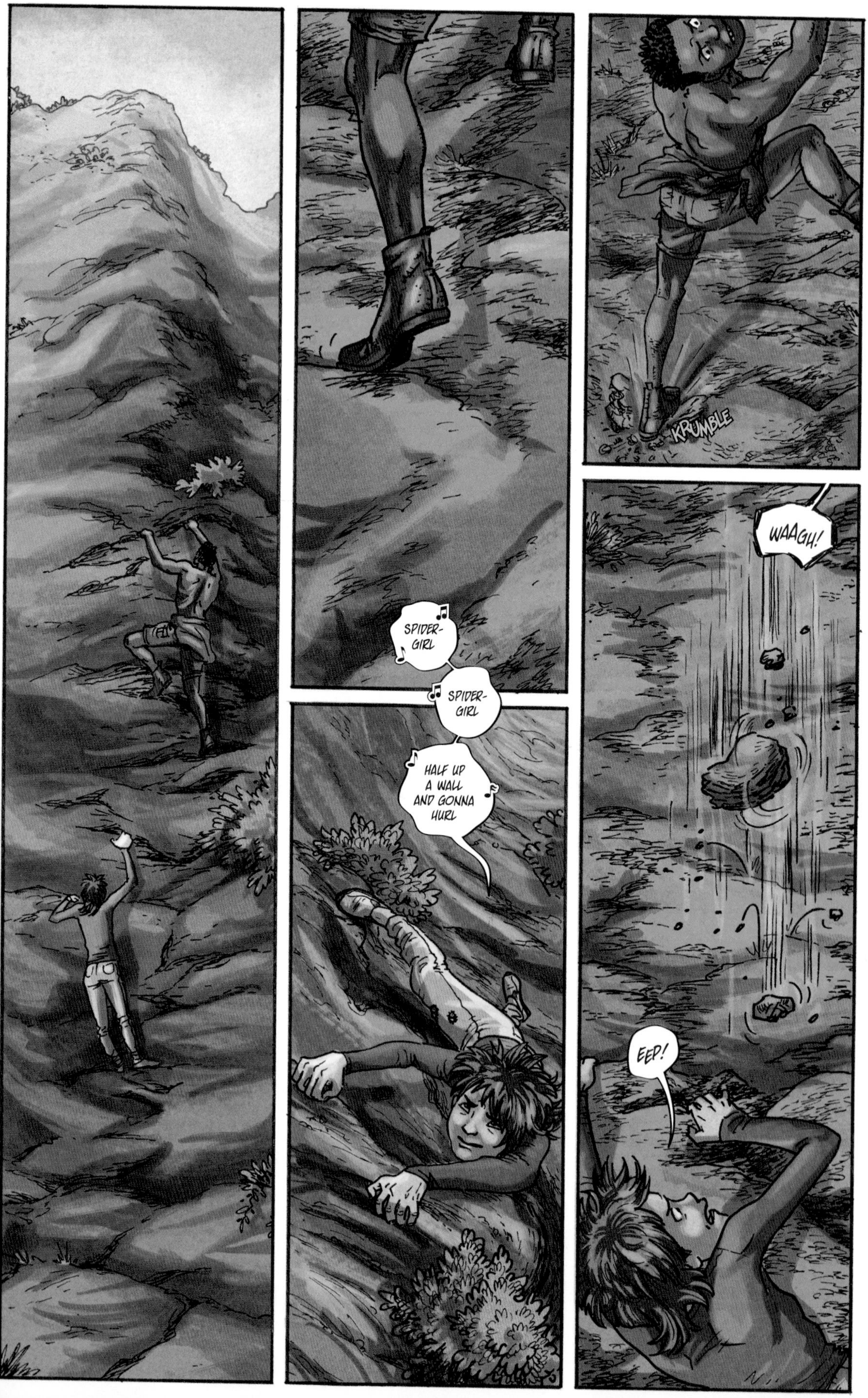
KRUMBLE
SPIDER-GIRL
SPIDER-GIRL
HALF UP A WALL AND GONNA HURL
WAAGH!
EEP!

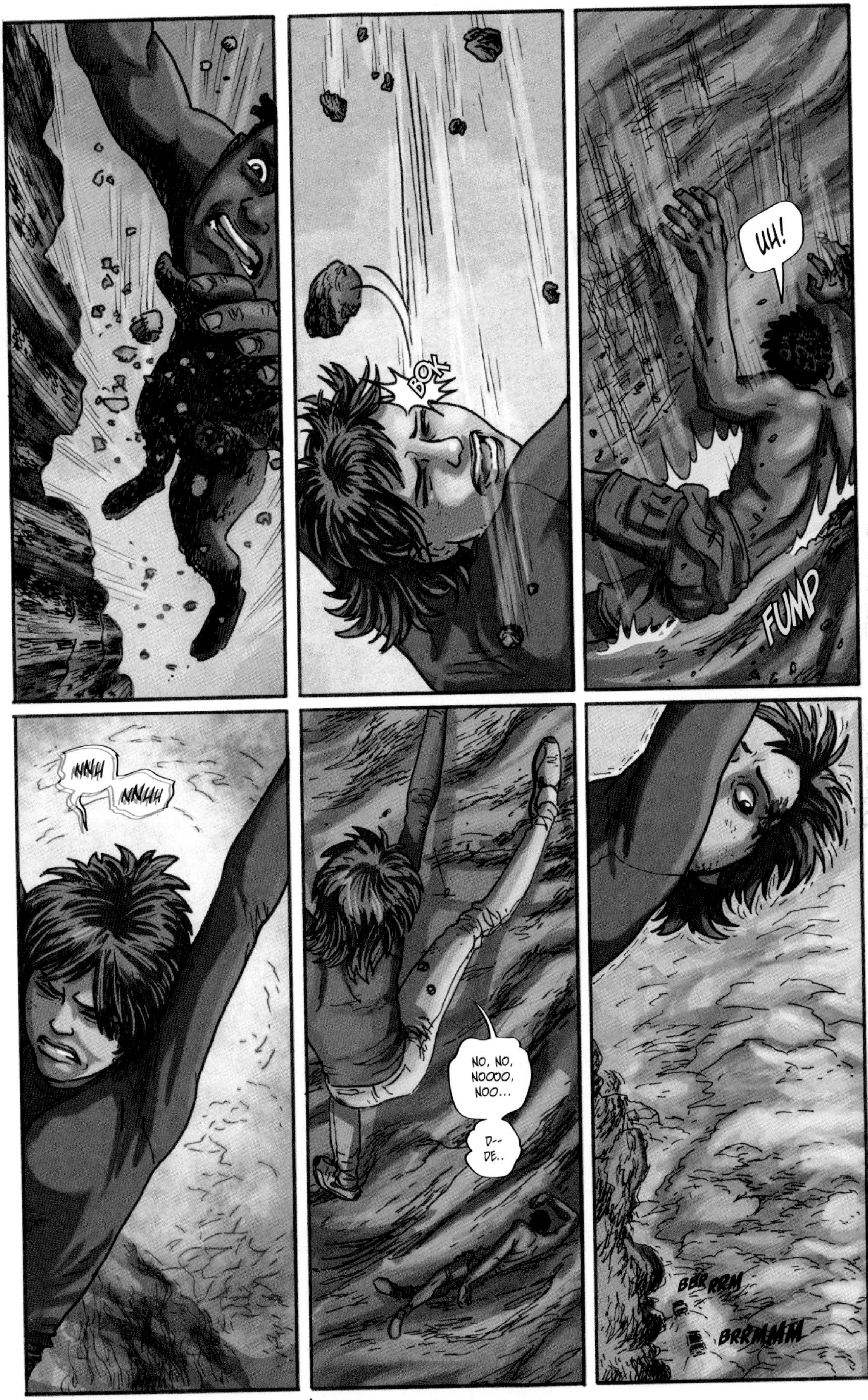
BOX
UH!
FUMP
NNH
NNH
NO, NO, NOOOO, NOO...
D-- DE..
BBRRRM
BRRMMM

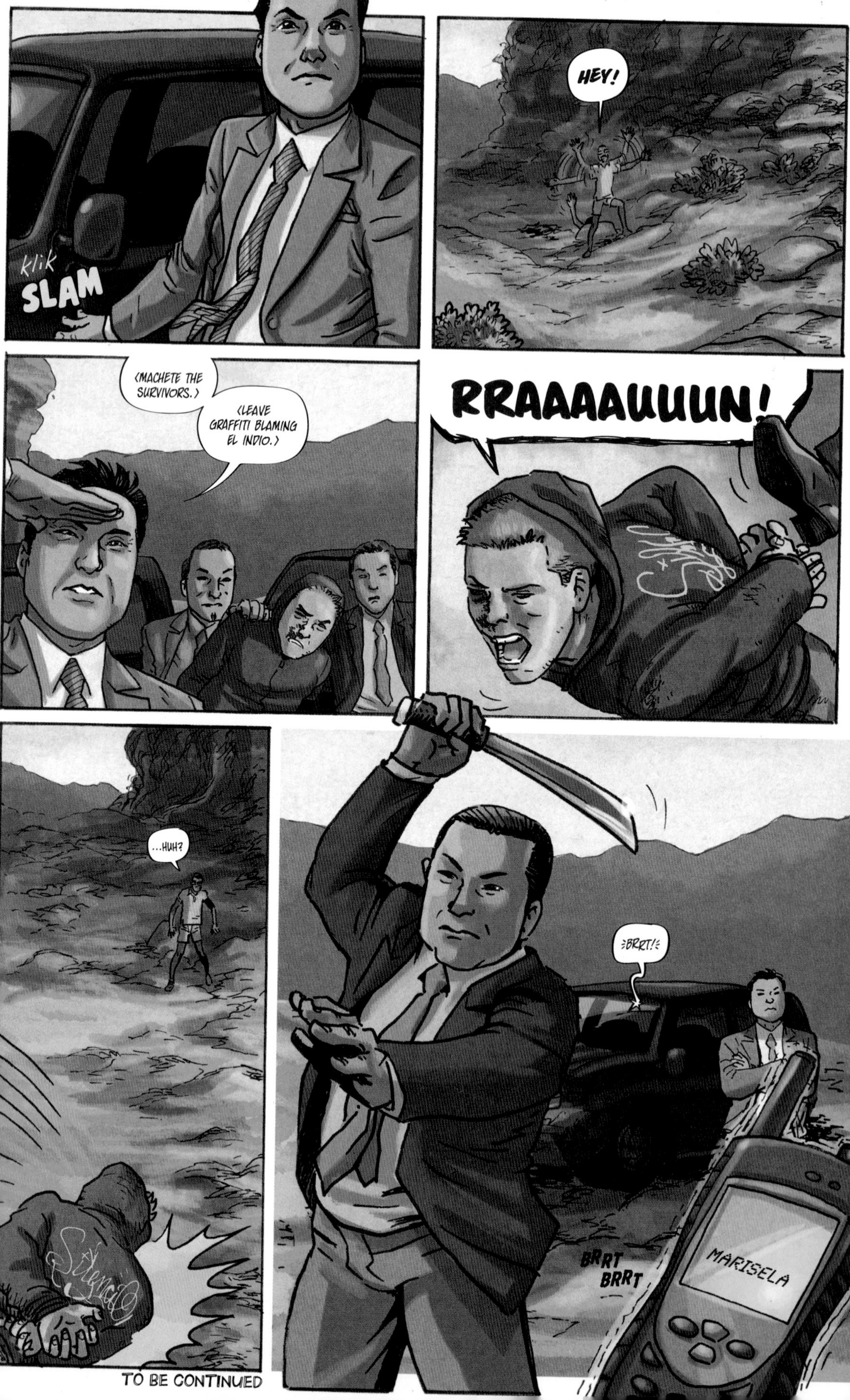
klik
SLAM
HEY!
<MACHETE THE SURVIVORS.>
<LEAVE GRAFFITI BLAMING EL INDIO.>
RRAAAAUUUN!
...HUH?
BRRT!
BRRT BRRT
MARISELA

TO BE CONTINUED

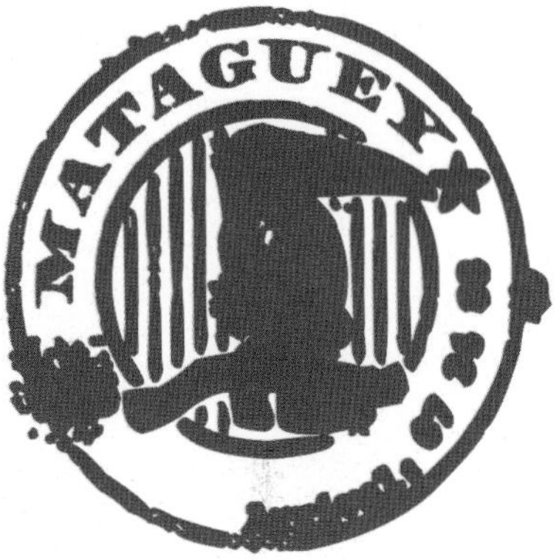
MATAGUEY

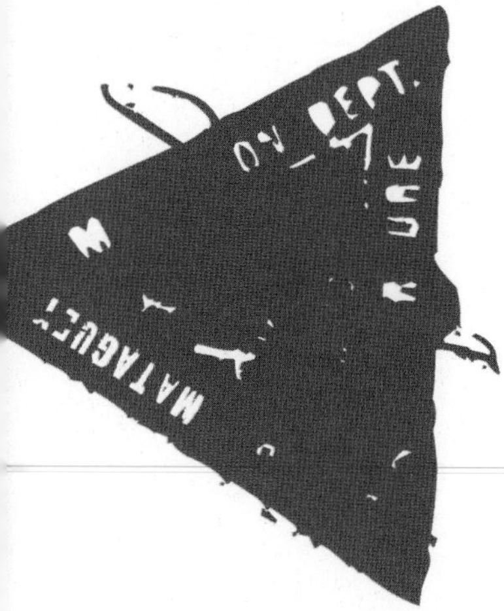
DEPT.
MATAGUEY

CHARACTER DEVELOPMENT

GINA

Michigan beauty queen.

Curvier Judy Garland.

Old-fashioned glamour girl.

Sweet but sheltered.

Not a coathanger but quite slim.

Round face, pointy chin, huge brown eyes and "worried" brow line, rather heavy.

No freckles.

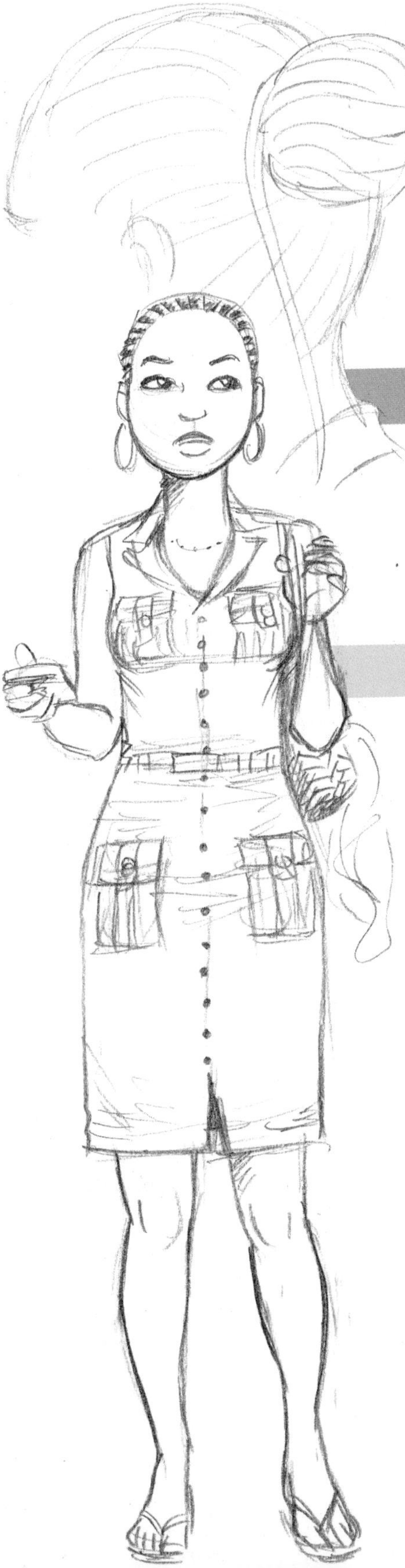

KIRA

Kira's hair is a mass of tiny braids tied into a bun high on the back of her head.

MURRAY & ALICE

They're in charge.

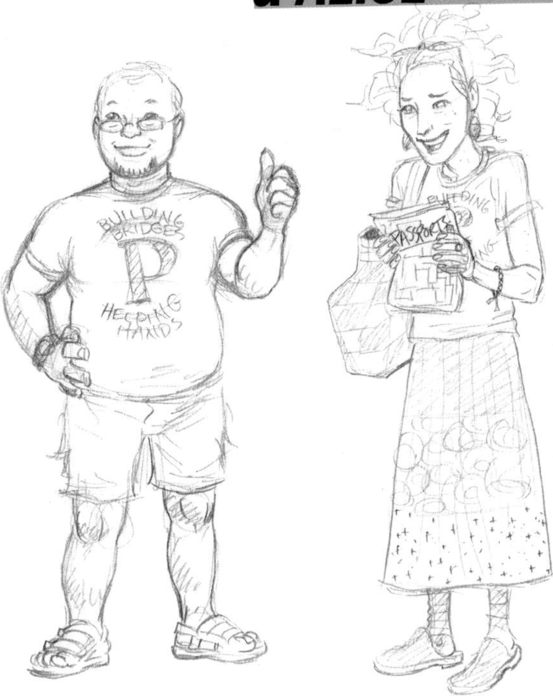
BUILDING BRIDGES
P
PASSPORTS

SILENCIO

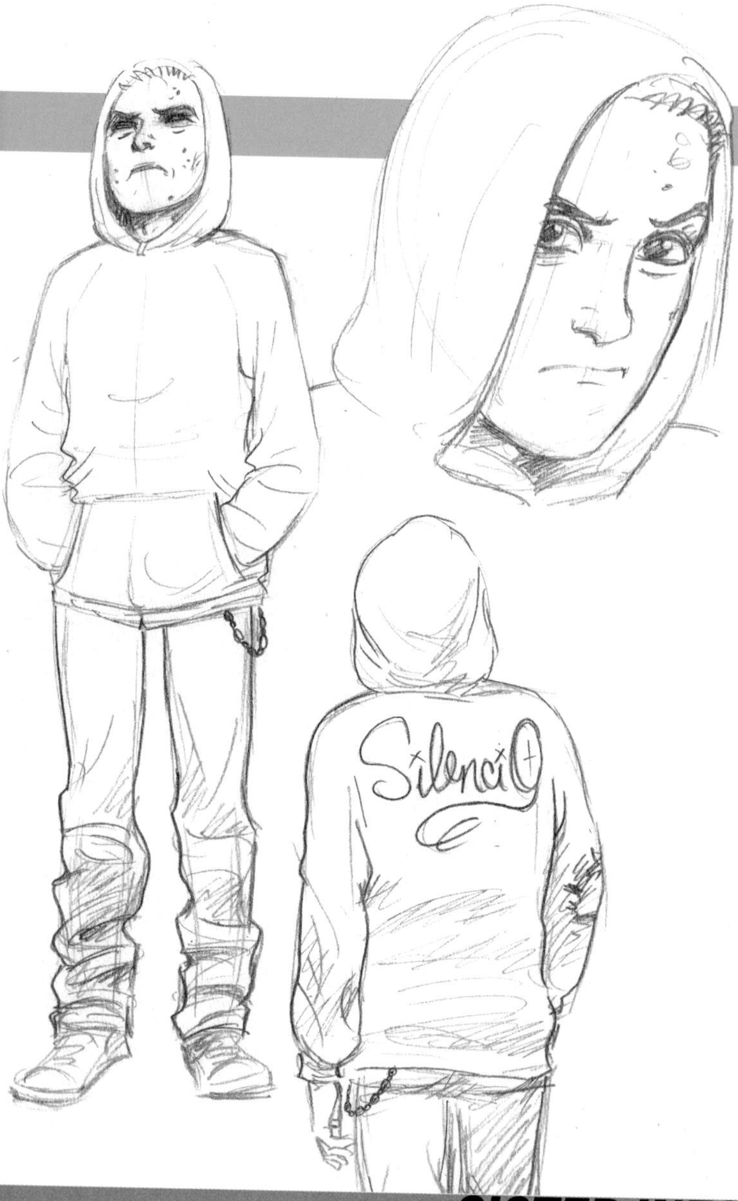
Silencio

SISTER INES

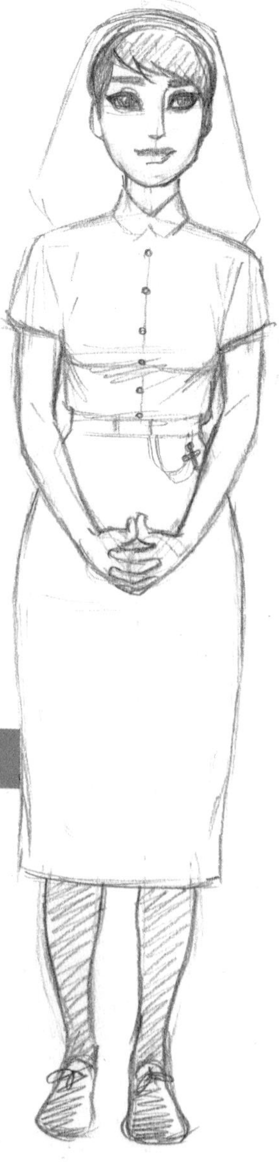

Doe eyes, long nose, full lips, very Audrey Hepburn.

Hard to find an order that still wears the wimple but isn't cloistered. Dunno how the kids would know immediately that she's a nun if she isn't wearing a wimple.

TRAVIS

Most punchable character of the lot, at least initially.

He's a FREEGAN.

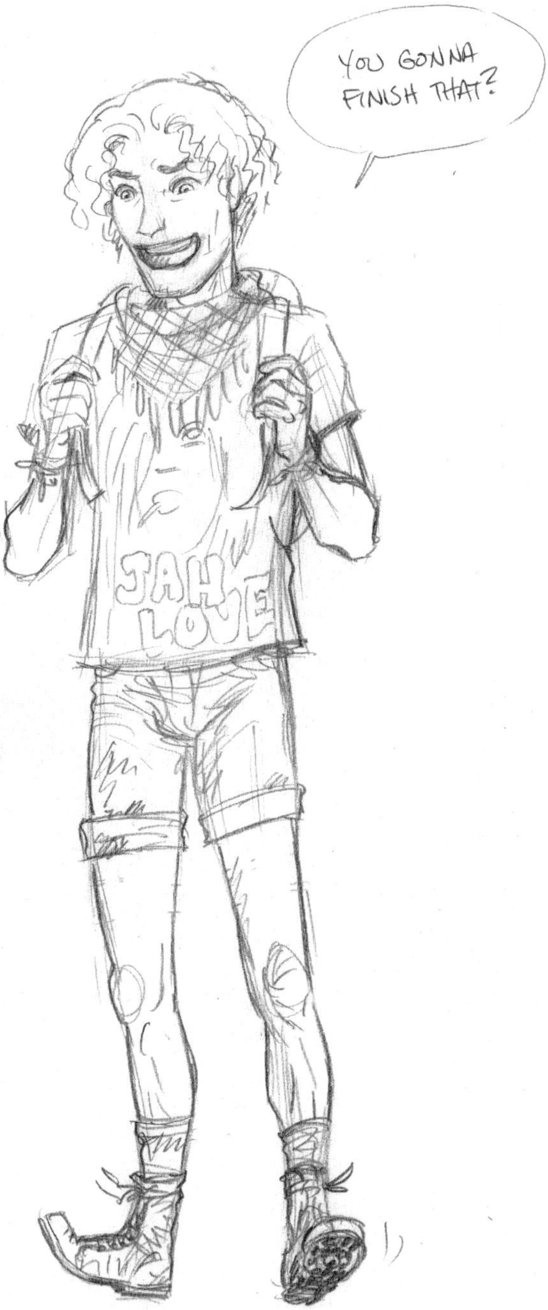
YOU GONNA FINISH THAT?
JAH LOVE

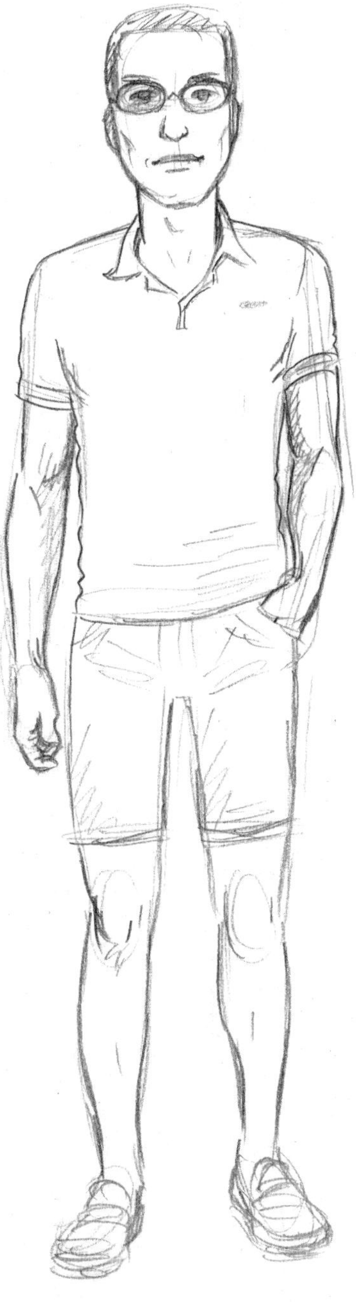

TROY

Fairly tall?

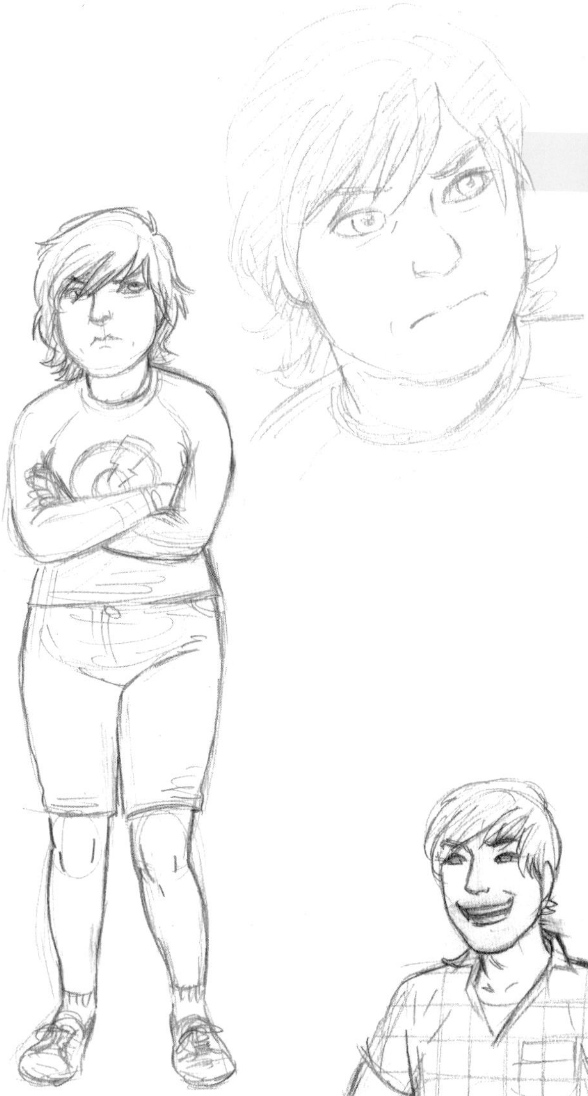

CHARLENE

Brownette/dirty blondelight eyes-- blue, gray, or green. Though hazel could do.

Ears pierced but no earrings.

Overweight but quite strong.

Far more endurance than her female peers.

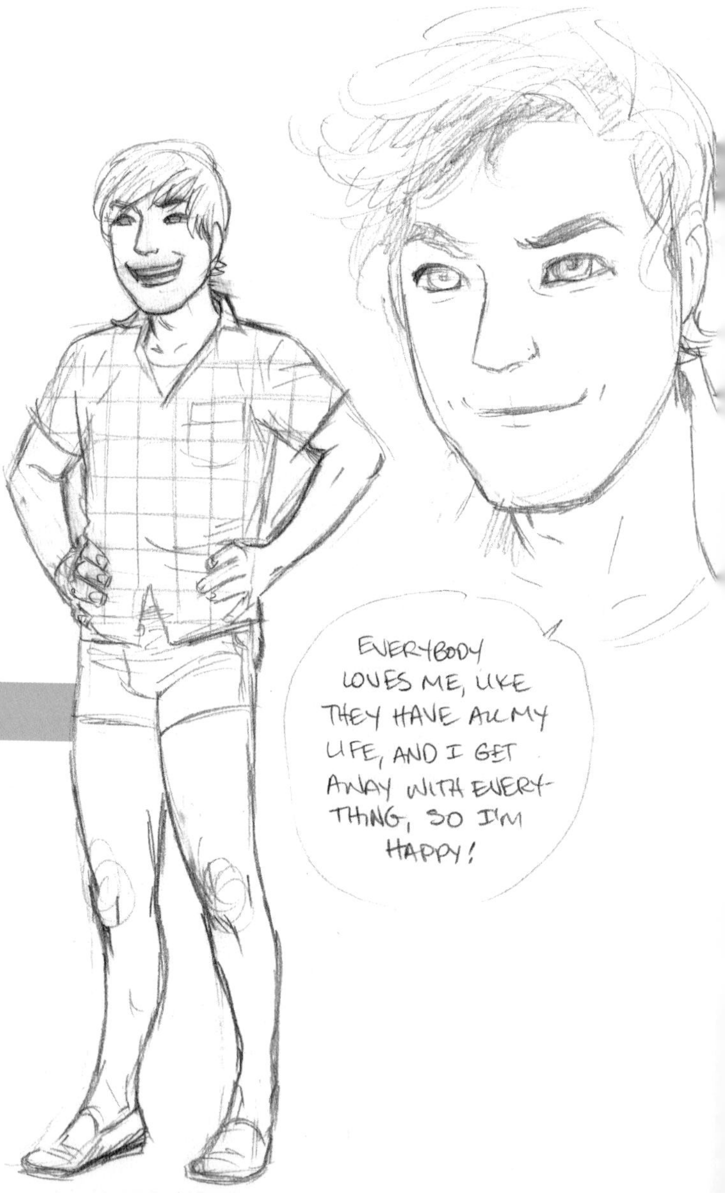
EVERYBODY LOVES ME, LIKE THEY HAVE ALL MY LIFE, AND I GET AWAY WITH EVERYTHING, SO I'M HAPPY!

CHAD

Charlene's twin.

Roughly the same coloring as his twin, hair maybe a bit more sun-bleached, skin more tan.

Not all that tall. Maybe 5'9".

Really competitive-- but won't try anything he can't win quickly.

NO MERCY #4: SCRIPT

PAGE 7. SIX PANELS

PANEL 1. Kira counts off on her fingers. No bg, lots of head-space, bg will be mostly/all words.

> KIRA: Your favorite singer is Katie Perry. Your clothes are all Abercrombie or AE. You are seriously considering starting an instagram account for your cat. You have never cut your hair shorter than your shoulders, and your idea of daring is aqua-blue nail polish. You are an ugg-wearing, chai latte swilling, Drake-loving

PANEL 2. Kira balloon continued over to Gina's furious face. Truth hurts, bitch.

> KIRA: Basic. Fucking. Bitch.

PANEL 3. Chad laughing.

> CHAD: Hahaha! *Aaaand* you're burnt!

PANEL 4. Travis and Gina respond. Tears starting.

> TRAVIS: Hey! Lay off!
>
> GINA: Shut up! Shut up, you stupid--

PANEL 5. Kira real quiet, real mad. DeShawn puts a hand on her shoulder. DeShawn can be off panel, and we just see the hand.

> KIRA (whispers): ssssaay iiiiit....
>
> DESHAWN: Chill.

PANEL 6. Gina holds out her arm. The bite is getting swollen/pus-dripping/nasty (and I think it needs to be seen close up). I think there are tears.

> GINA: You think you're so special because you got hurt!
>
> GINA (linked): You're not the only one!

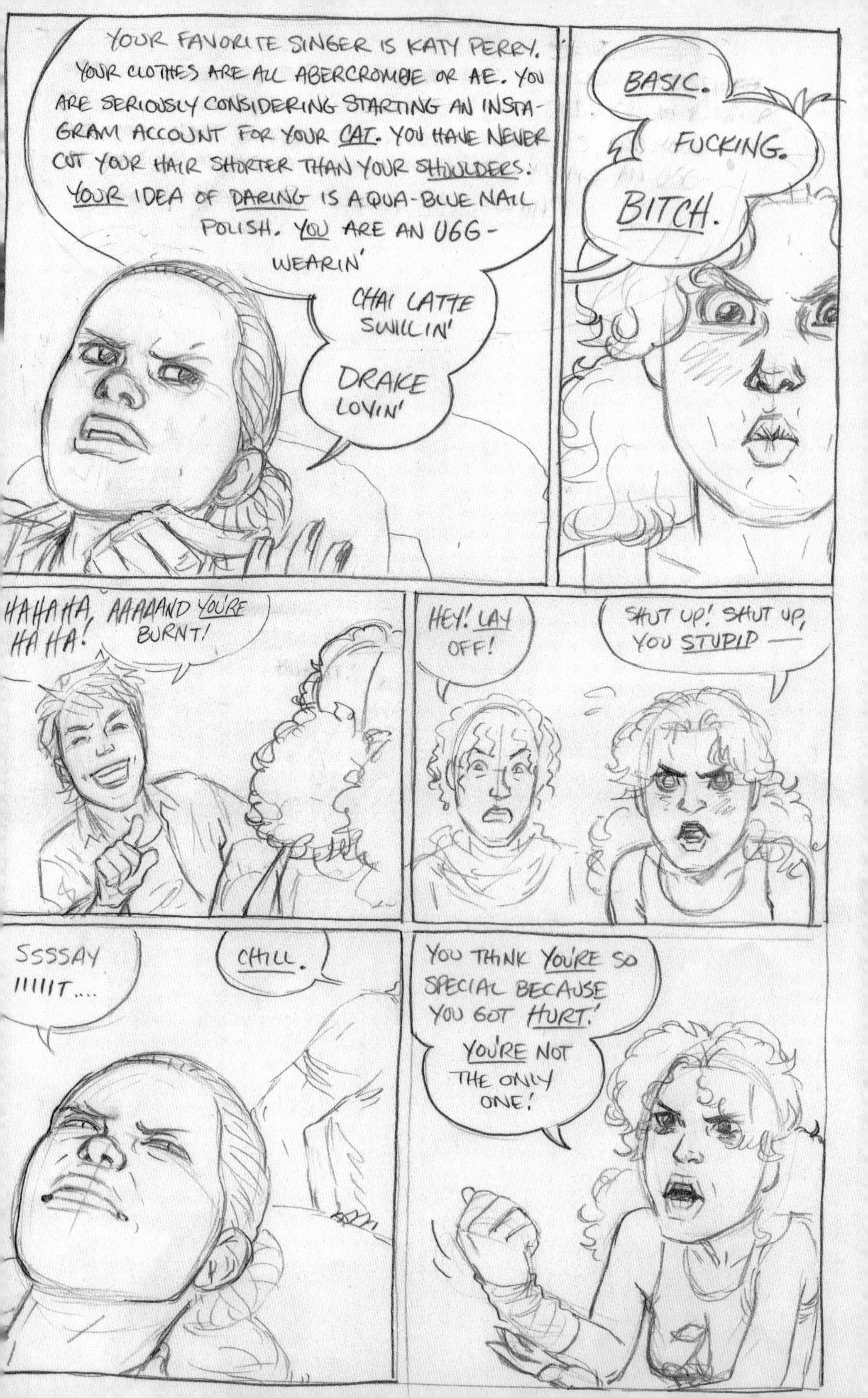
YOUR FAVORITE SINGER IS KATY PERRY. YOUR CLOTHES ARE ALL ABERCROMBIE OR AE. YOU ARE SERIOUSLY CONSIDERING STARTING AN INSTA-GRAM ACCOUNT FOR YOUR CAT. YOU HAVE NEVER CUT YOUR HAIR SHORTER THAN YOUR SHOULDERS. YOUR IDEA OF DARING IS AQUA-BLUE NAIL POLISH. YOU ARE AN UGG-WEARIN'
CHAI LATTE SWILLIN'
DRAKE LOVIN'
BASIC. FUCKING. BITCH.
HAHAHA, HAHA!
AAAAAND YOU'RE BURNT!
HEY! LAY OFF!
SHUT UP! SHUT UP, YOU STUPID —
SSSSAY IIIIIT....
CHILL.
YOU THINK YOU'RE SO SPECIAL BECAUSE YOU GOT HURT! YOU'RE NOT THE ONLY ONE!

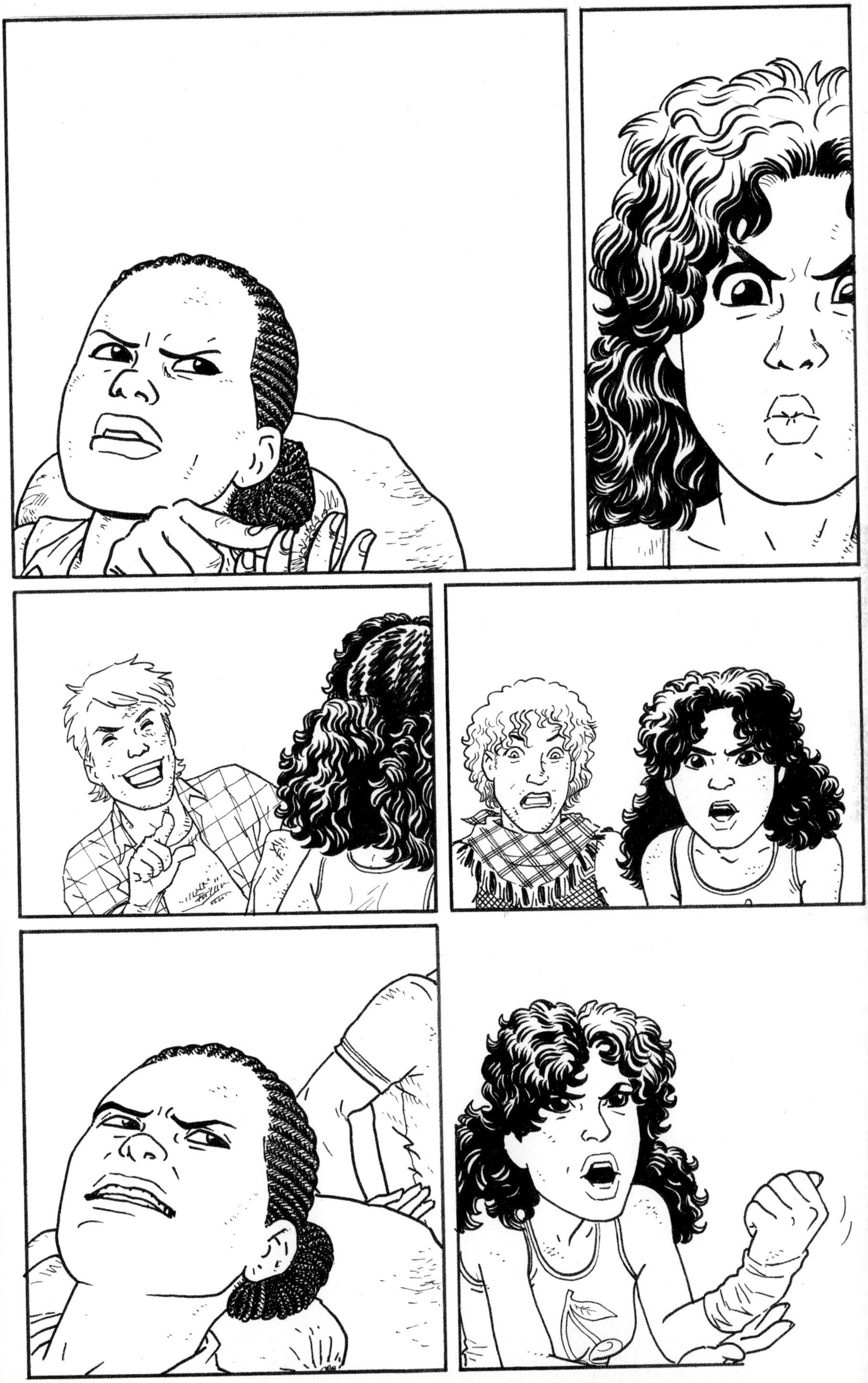

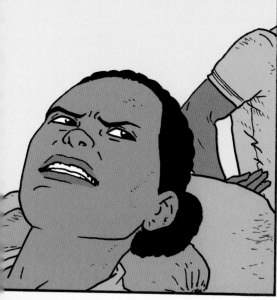

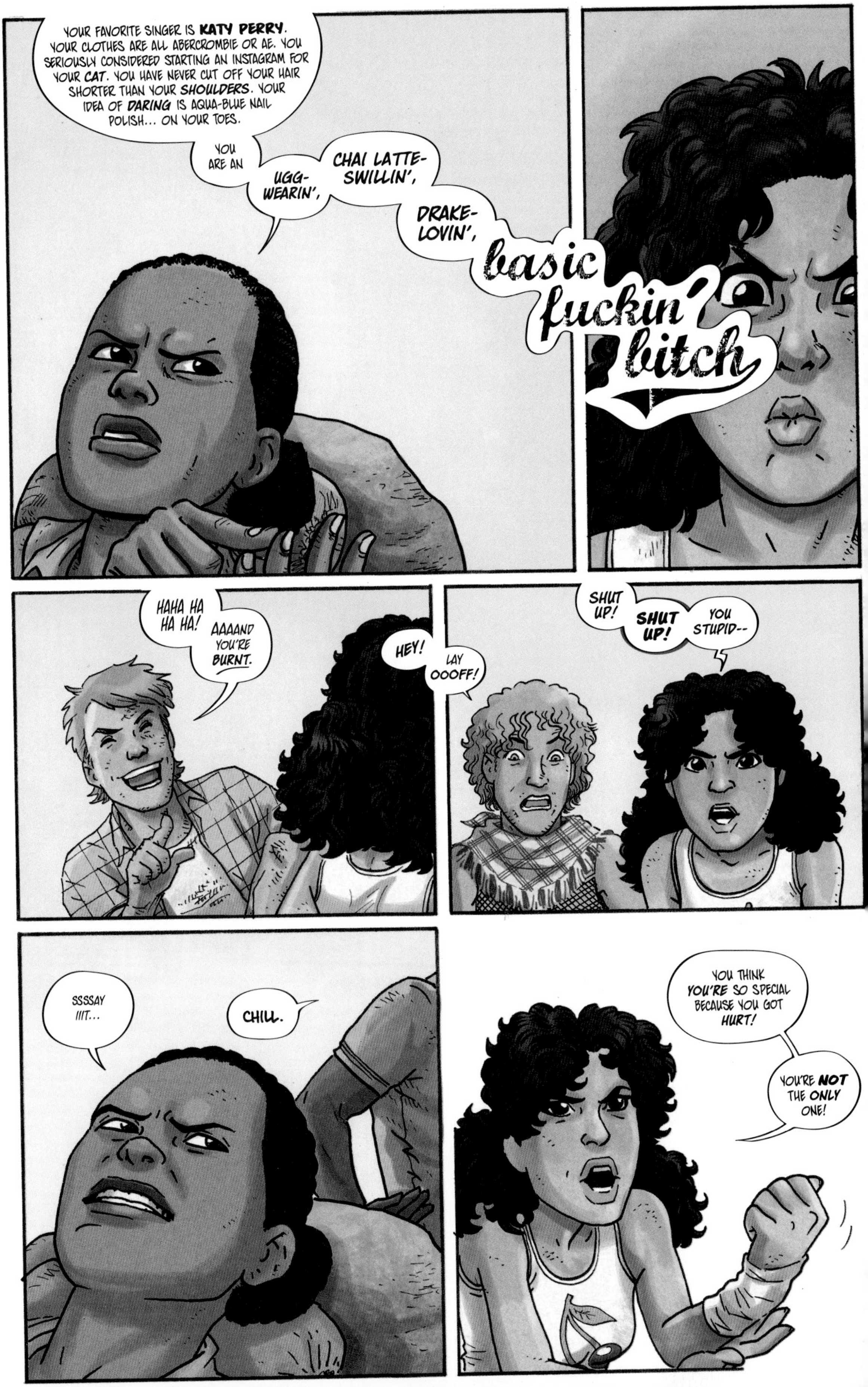

YOUR FAVORITE SINGER IS **KATY PERRY**. YOUR CLOTHES ARE ALL ABERCROMBIE OR AE. YOU SERIOUSLY CONSIDERED STARTING AN INSTAGRAM FOR YOUR **CAT**. YOU HAVE NEVER CUT OFF YOUR HAIR SHORTER THAN YOUR **SHOULDERS**. YOUR IDEA OF **DARING** IS AQUA-BLUE NAIL POLISH... ON YOUR TOES.
YOU ARE AN
UGG-WEARIN',
CHAI LATTE-SWILLIN',
DRAKE-LOVIN',
basic fuckin' bitch
HAHA HA HA HA!
AAAAND YOU'RE BURNT.
HEY!
LAY OOOFF!
SHUT UP!
SHUT UP!
YOU STUPID--
SSSSAY IIIT...
CHILL.
YOU THINK **YOU'RE** SO SPECIAL BECAUSE YOU GOT **HURT**!
YOU'RE **NOT** THE **ONLY** ONE!

COVER COLOR STAGES

Here are what I think of as my basic stages of coloring a page, from the pure line art, to the final rendering. There are dozens of moves and decisions to make at each of them, and in between; these represent the milestones. And as I was sharing the progress of this cover with Alex and Carla as it went along, I have some decent, real-time documentation of how the color continues to shift and change throughout the collaborative process. *– Jenn*

1

First, of course, is getting the *line art from Carla.* I clean it up a bit, then place it in a PSD template I've prepared.

2

The basic flat-color stage. I've set up three basic layers I'll work with: background, figures, and foreground objects.

Fleshing out and composing. I begin to add design elements, like the free-form painting of a Wile E. Coyote canyon seen through the bus windows, as requested by Carla. I also start blocking out the shading, figuring out the lighting, and giving focus to the art.

3

Detailing and rendering. First I make the final color shifts, such as Alex's suggestion to make the seats teal, to help them pop and break up the space, and add textures and other effects. Then I go in and add to and refine the rough shading, as well as add accents and highlights, until we can call it done.

4

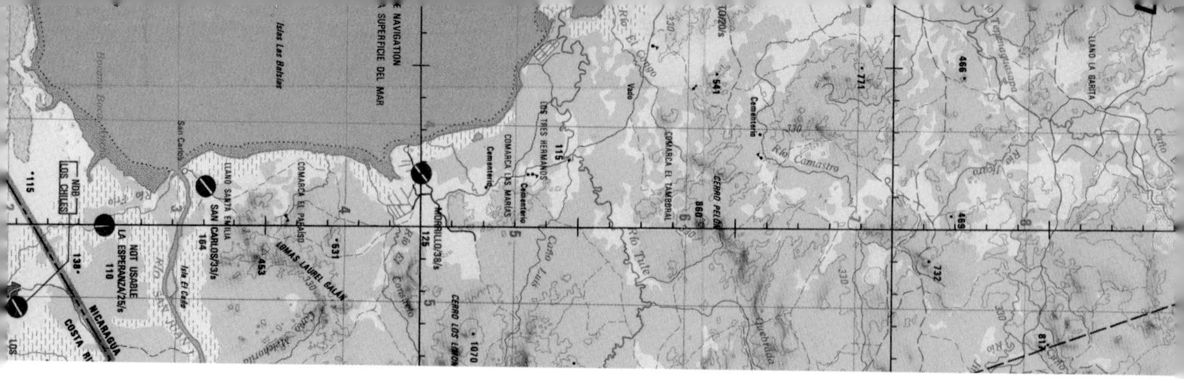
SUPERFICIE DEL MAR
LOS CHILES
NDB
NOT USABLE
LA ESPERANZA/25/s
SAN CARLOS/33/s
NICARAGUA
COSTA
LLANO SANTA EMILIA
COMARCA EL PARAISO
LOMAS LAUREL GALAN
LOS TRES HERMANOS
COMARCA LAS MARIAS
COMARCA EL TAMBORAL
CERRO PELON
Río Camastro
Río Tule
LLANO LA GARITA
Cementerio

Some Stories

I lived outside the US from 1992 until the end of 2007. You could say I was a bad person then. I'm still a bad person now, but in different ways. In 2005, I wrote up some of the things I saw and did from those rebel years. I've recently disinterred those essays from the elderly hard drive in which they lay, and (with mixed emotions) now display their corpses for your entertainment. – Alex

THE REBEL YEARS:

ISSUE 1

THE ONGOING SAFETY ISSUES OF JUNIOR A

Any way you cut it, Junior A was a player. The second son of an impossibly wealthy Philippine entrepreneur, he was above most of the rules that apply to the rest of us. But he had his problems too. For example: his brother was trying to kill him. This, and the endless legal battles surrounding his family's assets, defined his life more than the polo playing and the blondes. There were apparently five siblings, two illegitimate, but it was the older brother – who had been fobbed off with prawn farms in East Luzon while Junior got the family bank – who was the difficulty.

In consideration of Junior's situation, the management of Venezia nightclub in Manila excused him from their "no guns or bodyguards" rule. So Junior walks into the nightclub and waves hi to me as he passes to his usual table. Close behind lumber two large men carrying heavy black leather gym bags. The bags make a >chink!< sound when the bodyguards put them down. Junior orders champagne and asks if I want some. Junior is in his forties, with pock-marked cheeks and a flat expression in his black eyes as he looks at me, the ennui of the vivisectionist. I decline.

I knew Junior from around. Manila's a small town. Well, it is if you're rich, or an expat. You walk down the streets of Makati and if you see another white person you automatically raise your hand to wave hello, because chances are it's someone you know. Junior was all right, really, if a disastrous businessman. He didn't run the family bank so much as treat it with benign neglect.

One of the last times I saw Junior was down in Calatagan, a three hour drive south of Manila, on the estate of one of the oldest Spanish families in the country. It was a polo weekend; I was along because I could ride, but mainly because they wanted a few more girls around.

The journey from Manila to Calatagan is exhausting. The main North-South freeway in Luzon is still only two lanes in most places. But now, in the centre of the X family's vast estate, I stand in dappled shade by the pony lines trading with friends the inconsequential chismis which is the life or death of Manila's gilded set, and waiting for the last arrivals to appear. The X family are acknowledged as the straightest, most honest family in the Philippines (Lord only knows how they've survived), and their estate is a haven of peace and order.

I was just running out of things to say to the person next to me when the staccato roar of a chopper, bound for the helipad in the next field over, neatly clipped the thread of conversation. Three drowsy-looking men, someone's retainers, look up to identify the helicopter. It's black, with gold stripes. The three snap into a dog-trot towards a nearby Mercedes sedan with tinted windows. The sedan hangs lower than it should; I wonder if it has been bullet-proofed. They reverse the car at speed, kicking up brown dust as they spin it around. The ponies shift uncomfortably; one screams. The sedan shoots pell-mell out the gates of the polo field, around the corner, and towards the helipad. The helipad is not 150 yards from where we stand, separated from the polo field by a wooden post-and-beam fence.

The retainers pick up the helicopter's occupant and then drive back down along the fence, out the helipad field gates, around the corner, through the polo field gate and up the other side of the fence to the pony lines. Junior steps out of the car. The logic of recent activity reveals itself: Junior had organised his bullet-proof Merc to be driven down the three hours from Manila so it could ferry him the 150 yards from the helipad to the polo fields. I think how if I were his host, I would be insulted by this pantomime. But it's not really my business, so I turn back to my friend and ask about news of H's affair.

A pony is led over and Junior mounts up. As his groom hands him up a mallet, I notice something weighing down the pocket of the groom's black sweatpants. It's a white-handled 45 magnum, shiny and silver in the early afternoon sunlight.

Midway through the first chukka, Junior's horse rears unexpectedly, stung by a fly. Junior falls off and breaks his arm.

[October 1997, Manila, Philippines]

DOORBELL DITCH, POLISH STYLE

The summer between my junior and senior year of university I went to Poland to teach English in a little seaside Scout camp in the village of Puck, up the coast from Gdansk in the northeastern corner of the country. That was 1991, the year of the attempted coup in Moscow against Gorbachev, the year that the trendy backpacker destination switched from recently-unified Berlin to recently-opened Prague. It was a magic summer, full of promise. The kind of summer where, sitting on an empty station platform late one night, I was serenaded with folk songs from a train window by a lovely blonde Polish teacher and her equally blond charges, simply because I was the first American they had ever met.

The kids I taught in Puck came from Przemysl (if you say "puh-SHEH-mish" you'll be pretty close), all the way in the southeastern corner. They were in Puck ("PUT-sku") to learn to sail – a passion for Poles, it appears, and to learn English. At this point the Warsaw Pact had only recently shaken off communism, and schools in Poland mainly taught Russian (the language of a country the Poles have hated for most of the 20th century) or German (the language of a country the Poles have hated for even longer). This, not Hong Kong, is where I first learned to sail – and in Polish. I think one of the reasons I now sail better than most (but not as good as some) is that when I learned, I had to figure out why I had to do things, because I sure as hell couldn't understand what people were telling me to do.

But I digress. Having some time at the end of my teaching stint, I travelled south to the Polish Ukraine to meet my students back in their home city of Przemysl. The day before I was to meet them I went by train and bus to Ustrzyki Gorne, as far as you could go into the Bieszczady range of hills. I arrived mid-morning. From there I set out on foot towards the hills of Rawka and Krzemieniec. They were the highest in the area, just over the treeline at 1307 and 1221 metres respectively, and they were bang on the border where Poland, Slovakia and the (still at that point) Russian Ukraine met. On my back I carried the pack I had lived out of for the past three months.

I don't know what I expected when I go to the top of Rawka, but it certainly wasn't to look down at utterly silent, tree-covered hills, with the national borders cut in swathes along the ridge-lines. Those grass strips, a regular 10 feet wide and branching off in three directions, were the only human signs for as far as I could see. I knew that half a day's walk down the thin dirt trail east of me was the town of Ustrzyke Gorne, but there was not a house, a road, anything visible from where I stood, atop the highest hill in the Bieszczady.

The shadows were already long as I stared at the hills with their clearly-marked borders. It was like standing on a map. I knew that unless I hurried back to Ustrzyki Gorne, I risked being caught out here after dark, and would have difficulty finding the hostel that my guidebook told me lay somewhere in the town. But what's one little risk, when you can take a much bigger one? I legged it for Krzemieniec, right on the border. Down into a high valley then up again. The trail petered out and I pushed on through trees and, finally, as the sky was already fading to orange, I could see the clear-cut strip ahead of me that separated Poland from the Russian Ukraine.

I slid my grubby blue pack off my shoulder and walked across the strip. It was just some grass, seven steps, eight steps, and then some trees. In Russia, by a matter of inches, I bounced up and down on the balls of my feet and felt absurdly pleased with myself. The Bieszczady remained deafeningly silent. Then I hightailed it back across the border, grabbed my pack, and beat it for Ustrzyki Gorne.

By the time I got back to the village, it was dark. Small villages in the Polish Ukraine don't exactly come equipped with extensive streetlighting systems. My legs were a mass of cuts from crashing through branches and thorns. Even worse, my guidebook was being extremely coy about the exact location of the hostel where, hopefully, I would spend the night. I was exhausted to the point where I was starting to cast evaluatory looks at various bushes and hedgerows to determine which would be the softest to kip in for the night. This, I know, is not a good idea, but I wasn't looking like I have any other choices.

A middle-aged man walks quickly past me, head down and determined for home. I run after him, and in my grammatically mangled Polish I ask him where the hostel is. He looks at me, squinting a bit. "What hostel? There is no hostel," he responds.

"Oh. Crap," I say, deflating.

"Where are you from?"

"I'm an American student. I was walking in the Bieszczady…"

"Why don't you have a tent?" he asks. "Polish people, when they go walking, they bring tents."

My lack of language lets me down at this point, so instead of launching into an explanation of how I was only going to be walking for a couple of hours, but en route I thought it would be rather fun to break a few international laws and this kept me out longer than intended, I just look at him and shrug. "Because I'm stupid, OK?"

The guy laughs. He's not very tall, and has the tan, thin, leathery face of someone who has spent most of his life in manual labour, outdoors. His shoulders are bent.

"Is there anywhere I can stay?" I ask.

"You should have brought a tent," the man comments.

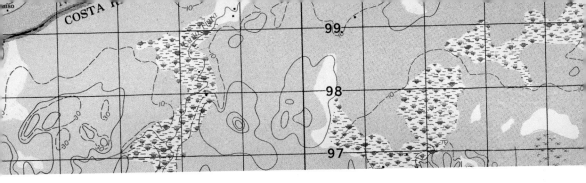

"Yes, I should have brought a tent," I agree, exasperated.

This seemed to galvanise something in the man. He nodded, pleased I had finally admitted my deep wrongness in camping preparation, and said, "You can stay with us. This way." He turned and took off quickly down a side road.

This could go very badly wrong, I think, as I follow him. He ducks into a tiny house, not more than three rooms, and motions me to follow. Inside is a small sitting room and attached kitchen, a bedroom off to one side, and a bathroom off to the other. And a stout wife in a floral dress, who is not happy to see me. Mine host explains that he met this stupid American on the road, who tried to go camping without a tent, and he offered for her to stay here.

The woman explodes. A rapid fire exchange follows, too complex for my limited Polish, but the upshot of the problem seems to be that if I stay, I get the daybed in the sitting room, and the husband and wife have to sleep in the same room. This seems to be an event which has not occurred in recent history. I look around the room as they argue. On one wall is a framed marriage photograph of the couple, two head shots, hand tinted. He leans forward, eyes wide open, startled and innocent. She gazes towards him, coquettish, radiant. Blue eyes, sandy blonde hair, flushed cheeks against a pale red background. You can smell the hope shining from the picture.

My host, having re-established marital superiority, grabs a brown bottle of Tatry beer out of the refrigerator, opens it, and upends it into his mouth. I have never seen someone drink a beer so fast. It was like the bottle was being emptied down a drain. I curl up on the daybed and attempt to sleep, wary but grateful.

I board a bus for Przemysl at 5.30am the following morning. The stop is on a lonely, backcountry road. The man sees me off and I thank him profusely. I offer him some zlotys, to pay for the trouble I've caused, but he refuses. Polish hospitality is Polish hospitality, and it wouldn't be right for him to accept money for it. He smiles and waggles his finger at me. "Next time…" "Yes! Tent! Tent! I know!" He laughs. Thirteen years later, one of the few words of Polish I still remember is namiot – tent.

As the bus honks impatiently, I shake his hand and slip some cash into it. He looks startled, and before he can give it back I dive onto the bus. The driver muscles the doors shut and the heavy old bus lumbers into a turn. The man smiles and waves. I wondered idly, resting my throbbing head against the cold glass window, how much of that cash his wife would see, if any. I wondered how far it was from a photograph's young hope to a cold and sour bed, and bottles drained in anger. Not far, I know now. Not far at all.

When I get to Przemysl that afternoon, I tell my kids the story of my little adventure across the Russian border. Ben, one of the more practical boys, rolls his eyes and thumps his forehead in the international gesture for, You are such an idiot!.

"You know why those grass strips are there? They have motion detectors all along them, and they send jeeps down those paths to pick up people who try to sneak across the border!".

Oh, I said. I didn't hear any jeeps…

"Well. The Russians were probably too amazed that anyone wanted to cross into Russia to do anything," said one of the girls, pale and whip-smart.

"Shut UP, Edyta."

"It's true! Tell Alex about the old lady."

Ben sighs and folds his arms. He explains how the city of Lvov in the Ukraine used to be part of Poland, and plenty of people in Przemysl (which was the border town on the main road to Lvov) still have family there. But under the Communist government you weren't even allowed to mention the city. The Russians set up a huge, gated checkpoint at the border, a mile or two from Przemysl, with high walls, towers, barbed wire, and alarm-triggering motion detectors; Lvov no longer existed for the Poles, and that was that.

Or it would have been, except for a very irascible old lady who lived in Przemysl. She hated the Russians, and hated their huge, ugly border. So once a fortnight or so, she would walk out to the border at night, with her tricornered, old-lady shuffle. Once she got to the gate, she would march straight up to the areas where the motion detectors were, and jump up and down on them, and thump the ground with her stick. Alarms would screech, lights would come on, and detachments of Russian border guards, clumsy with sleep, would stumble to the walls. And be faced with the rump view of a gnarled, heavyset old baba, stomping slowly homewards to Przemysl in a state of righteous indignation.

The old lady died soon after they opened the border. There was nothing large enough left to take her anger.

[August 1991, Przemysl, Poland]

THE CULT
OF THE BROKEN OBJECT

IN 1994, the Khmers Rouge in North Cambodia put down their weapons for long enough that my stupid socialite friends and I could travel to Angkor Wat, break into a boarded-up luxury hotel, and drink all the champagne in Siem Reap.

We started off in the Foreign Correspondents' Club in Phnom Penh, with pink gins, leaning against the club's bright yellow walls, and watching the brown, brown Mekhong slide by. Little green lizards watched us, scuttling along the walls if we moved too quickly. The only thing greener than the lizards was the baize of the pool table, which was placed so close to one wall that there was a special short cue, only three feet long, for playing that side. Cambodia is one of those places where the Brightness and Contrast levels are set a bit higher than Westerners are accustomed.

The roads were, by general agreement, still too dangerous to travel, so we flew a Royal Air Cambodiana flight to Siem Reap airport. The plane was ancient, and the information on the back of the tray-tables was in Romanian, which made me have a sudden yearning to be anywhere else than airborne. But we got there, and I resolved to pray more often. I may be an existentialist, but it never hurts to hedge your bets.

And Angkor… To understand my reaction to Angkor, you first have to understand the depths of my tourism ennui. I was a lucky kid, even for an American. My dad had a job where he travelled to a lot of interesting places. He tried to take the family with him as much as possible, and he went out of his way to convince his only child that the world outside America was a fascinating and worthwhile place.

Dad engineered my first trip overseas with military precision. Mother and I would be accompanying him on a business trip to Cairo, which was nirvana for an Ancient Egypt-obsessed eight year old like me. But Dad didn't want me to think the rest of the world was like Cairo, or indeed like the Athens International Airport, which in the 1970s was the flop-house for the entire Arab world, and the place where you had to change planes if you were flying from the US to anywhere with a desert. So first we spent four or five days in Zurich, at a lovely hotel called the Dolder Grand. It was OK, apparently, if I thought the rest of the world was like Zurich.

And, because the Dolder Grand had a mini-golf course, I decided the world outside America was, in fact, an excellent place. So excellent that I haven't lived in America for the past fourteen years. My mother's voice now has an edge of desperation to it whenever she asks when I'm going to move back to the USA. I think in her heart she blames Dad, but she should really blame it on the Dolder's mini-golf course.

The point is that by the time I was in my early 20s, I had seen every great church, cathedral, museum, and architectural wonder the world had to offer, with the exception of Petra and Angkor Wat. I was a prime sufferer of Church Fatigue. The only thing I enjoyed anymore about touring churches was checking out how gory the figure of Jesus was on the crucifix, and using it as a gauge to the socio-economic status of the place I was visiting. In rich areas, he's just kind of hanging out up there on the cross, wondering if his highlights need re-touching. But the poorer the area, the more gruesome and bloody the Jesus, because He always has to suffer more than you.

Yes, I know this is a cruel and heartless way to view the House of God. It's almost as bad as betting on the obituary columns as to whether more people died "suddenly" or

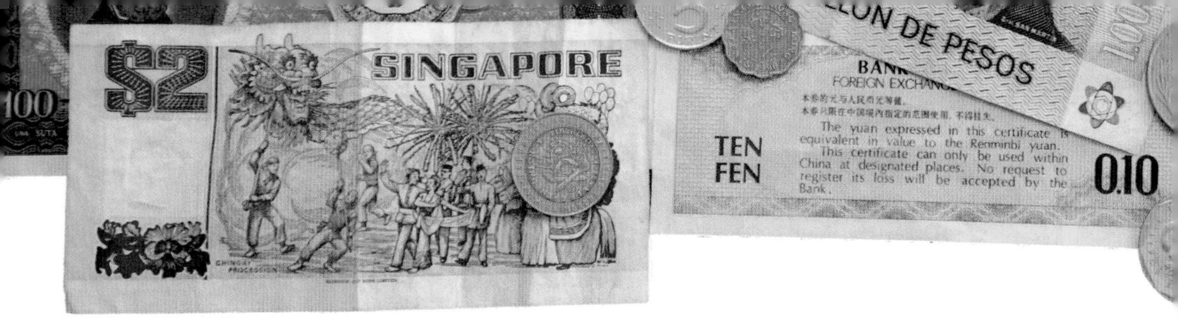
$2
SINGAPORE
100
TEN
FEN
0.10
The yuan expressed in this certificate
equivalent in value to the Renminbi yuan.
This certificate can only be used within
China at designated places. No request to
register its loss will be accepted by the
Bank.

"peacefully" that week. I've done that, too. But I've seen a lot of churches. My four socialite friends from Hong Kong were equally jaded.

And Angkor completely knocked us for six. It was majestic, elemental, beautiful. Even more affecting was the temple of Ta Prohm, which had been left as it had been discovered, with vines crumbling its walls and trees growing through its floors. One felt like an 18th-century explorer, finding the remains of an ancient civilisation. No one had prettied up Ta Prohm for visitors, and it was all the more impressive for that.

Of course we do love ruins, we Westerners. In art, it's called the Cult of the Broken Object. How much less would we love Ta Prohm without its intruding, destroying vines? How much less our pristine white Greek statues, with their arms and their noses intact, and painted in the gaudy polychromes which originally covered them?

We went back to our little hostel in silence, none of us willing to admit how much we had been affected by the vast, empty stone city. The boys then started acting up, perhaps to make light of their earlier rapt silences. It was now dusk, and they convinced us we should break into the nearby pale-yellow, neo-Palladian extravaganza that was the Grand Hotel d'Angkor. At the time, "Grand" seemed like gross overstatement. The hotel had been boarded up for years. It had recently been bought by one of the big Asian luxury hotel chains, the same people that had Disneyfied Singapore's Raffles Hotel. The new owners were still a bit concerned about the Khmers Rouge, so the hotel rested in the dust and waited for its fairy godmother. The diamond-shaped fountain out front was broken, and knee-deep in green slime.

The main door had a sheet of plywood loosely nailed over it. One quick pull from the larger of the boys, and it came loose enough that we could duck under it. One of the girls tsked in annoyance as a loose nail caught at her short skirt. She was the kind of girl that had gone to see Angkor Wat in a miniskirt and high-heeled sneakers, and that never broke up with one boyfriend until she was sure she could move seamlessly to another.

We crept through the main hallway to the bar, a colonial affair with a brass bar-rail and dark red leather Chesterfield sofas. Although the hotel seemed completely empty, there were hurricane lamps lit in the bar, and as we stood there plotting Grand Theft Alcohol, two small, thin waiters in dinner jackets emerged soundlessly from the back. Their dinner jackets were as dusty as the bottles behind the bar.

We all goggled at each other for a moment, our brains silently screaming questions that would never be answered. Why were they here? If they were just squatting, why the dinner jackets? Dinner jackets in an un-airconditioned building in the warm season didn't bear thinking about. Were they still getting paid, by someone? Had there been some long-forgotten slip-up, and their payroll was never cancelled when the war began? Justin spoke for all of us when he finally looked at them and asked, "Do you have any champagne?"

They nodded and smiled, and hurried into the back to fetch glasses and other accessories. Champagne was duly brought out. It was warm, and French. I can't remember the brand. It was very sweet, and we drank all they had, caught up in the magic of the day and the surreal feeling of having stumbled into a place which had been mis-laid by time. The waiters didn't know much English, so we were never able to satisfy our curiosity about why they were there, waiting, presumably every night.

The Grand Hotel d'Angkor has since been done up into a five-star luxury hotel, and no doubt Siem Reap is now overrun by tourists and souvenir-sellers. You should have seen it then, in 1994. You're too late, now. If you go to Bali now, they'll tell you that you're ten years too late. But I was ten years too late for Bali in 1994, too. Everyone is always ten years too late for everywhere.

And on quiet, humid nights at dusk, my thoughts return to those two silent, elderly waiters, precise in their dusty black dinner jackets. Every day they showed up at their empty bar, waiting for the women in their short skirts and lipstick, they'd want gin-tonics, and their red-faced and faintly patronising men, they liked whisky or lager; waiting for life to start up in the Grand Hotel again. And since I went to Siem Reap, I've lived in six different cities in three continents, always moving on sooner or later. Some people spend their lives waiting for their ship to come in; others spend it waiting for a harbour.

THE REBEL YEARS:

ISSUE 4

THE EASTERN END

Scott Simpson was the best dancer on the island or the island next to it and besides that, he only had one arm. He was also a drunk. These were the only obvious things about Scott Simpson. He was a retired lobsterman who lived with his brother Ernest on the Eastern side of the island, twenty minutes by foot from the main group of houses next to the harbour and from the clubhouse where the dances were held.

Many a dark night had Scott and Ernest formed an odd and noisy procession on the path to the Eastern End, Scott shouting at his demons and waving his flashlight, frightening the small creatures of the spruce forest, Ernest adding his low, stuttering laugh, "Uh-uh-uh-uh", when Scott stumbled and (more often than not) crashed his white head on a low-hanging branch.

Scott wasn't tall, but forty years of working the sea had made him wide. From salt spray and sun, his face was graven with deep wrinkles. Once you had rested your gaze on the deepest lines – the parentheses around his mouth, and the three parallel lines on his forehead – you were led to the more delicate web of lines around his eyes, then finally to his eyes themselves, small and well-hidden. They were as clear blue as the Maine sky in summer, and they had an intensity to them, of tightly bound strength, of anger at some great, past injustice that had left him deeply distrustful of the intentions of this world.

Ernest's eyes held an entirely different kind of intensity. His great, wet eyes, illuminating his angular face and its afterthought of skin, were the blue of a newborn, keen but unable to understand. Ernest was, in the old sense of the word, simple. Things which others of his years had long since forgotten to look at, like the movements and shapes of clouds, held him spellbound. Ernest was several inches taller than his brother, and much thinner, as if nature had not seen fit to give much mass to a man who could not comprehend the gravity of life. He stood like a question mark, shoulders deeply hunched, hands in pockets, as he waited for his brother at the clubhouse, or on the porch of Buzzy's house to be let in to watch TV, or on the State Wharf for the mailboat to arrive.

Ernest had a sixth sense about the mailboat. The island was twenty-five miles off the shore of Maine: two hunched shoulders of granite and spruce perched on the edge of the continental shelf, North America's last huzzah. There used to be a school here, but as better engines cut the lobsterboats' journey time to the mainland, it closed. Then the store closed, and the post office too, and soon all the mailboat brought was summer people or someone's wife for the weekend. But Ernest would still stand with his feet on the first few planks of the State Wharf twenty minutes before anyone could see the mailboat, or hear it, his jaw quivering like pudding in excitement and announcing to any passerby in his oatmeal stutter: "M-m-m-mailboat's comin'. Mm-hmm, M-m-m-mailboat," rocking a little as he spoke.

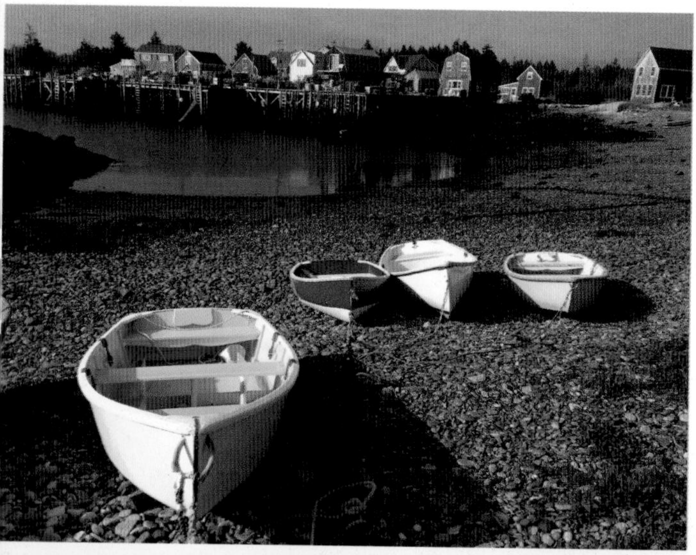

He said it like it was fifty or seventy years ago, when the mailboat was regular, and brought supplies for the store and timber for houses and children and sheep and mail and the Outer Islands preacher, seasick in black.

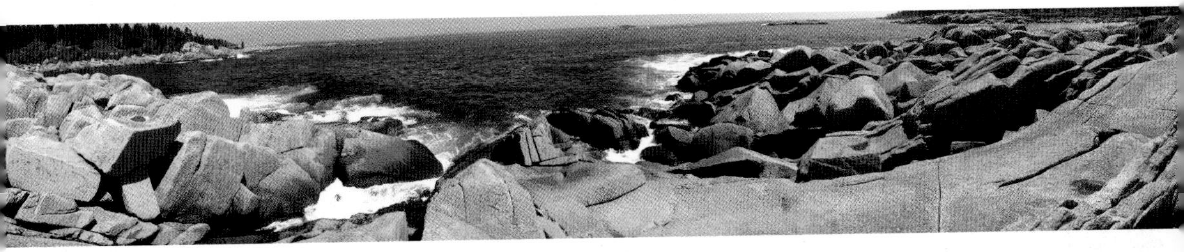

And then one day Scott and Ernest just disappeared, like smoke, or like old photographs left in sunlight. When no one had seen them for a while, some folks wandered down to the Eastern End to see if everything was OK. It looked for all intents and purposes as if Scott and Ernest had just stepped out: the table was set for a meal, with food on the plates, and Santillana's Age of Adventure lay open at Scott's place.

Many years later I was sitting on John Tripp's wharf idly watching a lovely blue-hulled sailboat moor in the harbour, and trying to imagine what in that book, a history of Renaissance philosophy, might have caused such feeling in the drunk one-armed lobsterman and his simple brother to drive them to leave at that very moment, their dinners barely touched. What page was the book opened to? Had they drowned, or had they just left, never to return?

A little rowboat detached itself from the yacht and lumbered toward the wharf. Soon enough, a head appeared at the top of the wharf's ladder. It was sandy, with blonde streaks, and had gold hoop earrings in its ears. The rest of the woman appeared. She was wearing white shorts and sandals, and from where I sat Indian-style, my back against a lobster trap, I could see the perfect coral-coloured polish on the toenails of her tan feet. I was not wearing shoes, and my feet were dirty. She smoothed her immaculate shirt and looked down at me. "Is this your little village?" she said, gesturing towards the harbour and its houses. She sounded disappointed. Behind, her husband, balding, in a bright polo shirt, chinos, and docksiders, waited for her next command. I smiled at her, baring my teeth. "Yes, lady, this is our little village."

[2001, Ragged Island, Maine]

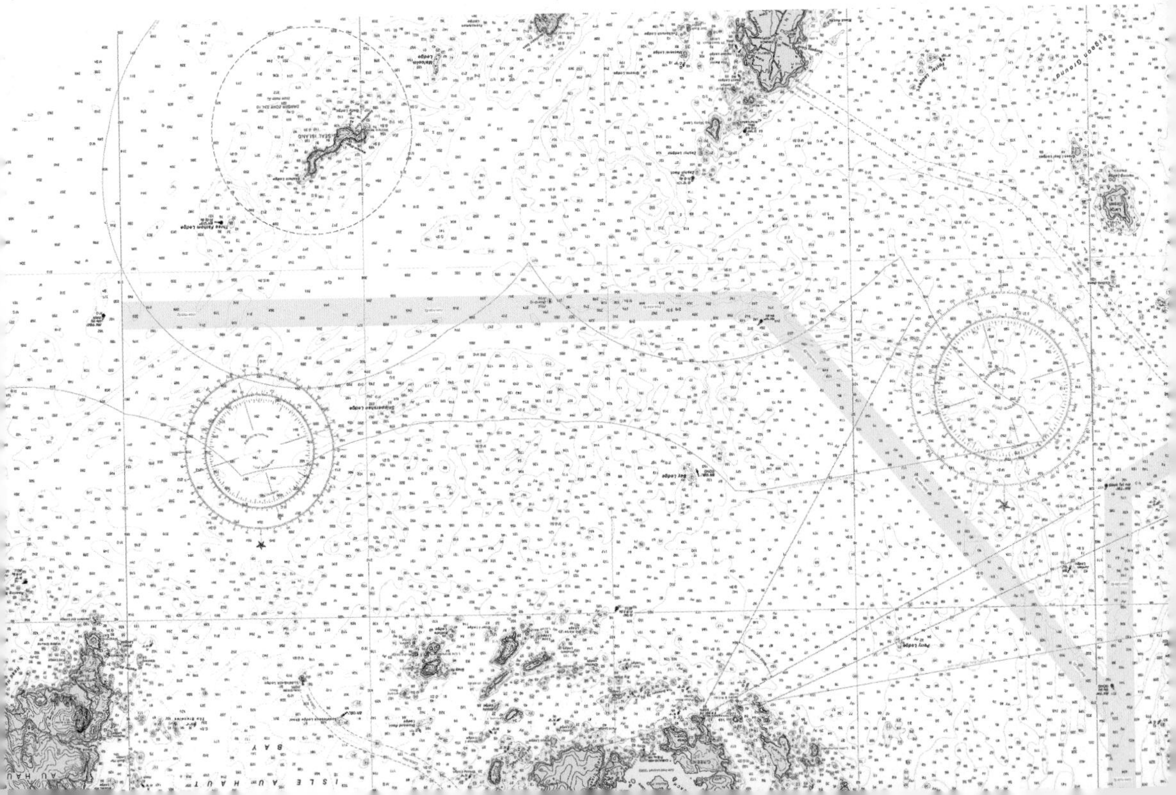

PRINCETON UNIVERSITY

Office of Admission
P.O. Box 430
Princeton, New Jersey 08542-0430

December 15, 2015

Lily J. Park
~~Address~~
Anaheim, CA 92804

Dear Lily:

Congratulations! I am delighted to offer you admission to Princeton's Class of 2020. Your academic accomplishments, extracurricular achievements and personal qualities stood out in an early action pool of more than 3,000 applications. We know from reading your file that you are the kind of student who will take advantage of all Princeton has to offer, and the University will benefit from your many talents.

If you applied for financial aid, a letter from the Financial Aid Office is enclosed with this mailing. For those students who qualify for aid, the financial aid package contains a scholarship grant and a job. Our policy does not require students to take loans to finance a Princeton education. As a result, all Princeton students have the opportunity to graduate debt free. Members of the financial aid staff are available to respond to any questions you may have.

I invite you and your parents or guardians to join us on April 13 or April 28 for one of our Princeton Preview programs. You may attend classes with our outstanding faculty, eat in our dining halls, and meet current Princeton students. You may reply to the enclosed invitation and participate in the admitted students website at https://admitted.princeton.edu.

Included in this packet is the response card you may use to let us know your final decision. You may return it as soon as you wish, but it must be postmarked no later than May 1. Alternatively, you may submit an online response through our website on the same timetable. A deposit is not required. If you choose to enroll. we will send you more materials in May and June about preparing for your freshman year.

Let me remind you that your admission to Princeton is contingent upon the successful completion of your senior year. We expect that you will keep up the high academic standards and good conduct you have maintained throughout high school. We also expect you to carry the same course load you started at the beginning of this academic year. Please have your counselor send us the Mid-Year School Report as soon as your mid-year grades are available.

Once again, congratulations. We are thrilled to be sending you this splendid news.

Sincerely,

Lucy Pevensie

Lucy Amelia Pevensie
Dean of Admission

Congratulations!